About the Authors

Rebecca Winters lives in Salt Lake City, Utah, USA. With canyons and high alpine meadows full of wild-flowers, she never runs out of places to explore. They, plus her favourite vacation spots in Europe, often end up as backgrounds for her romance novels, because writing is her passion, along with her family and church. Rebecca loves to hear from readers. If you wish to e-mail her, please visit her website at: www.cleanromances.com

When **Robin Gianna** decided she wanted to write romance novels, she embarked on that quest by joining RWA, Central Ohio Fiction Writers, and working hard at learning the craft. She loves sharing the journey with her characters, helping them through obstacles and problems to find their own happily-ever-afters. When not writing, Robin likes to create in her kitchen, dig in the dirt, and enjoy life with her tolerant husband, three great kids, drooling bulldog and grouchy Siamese cat.

To learn more about her work visit her website: www.RobinGianna.com

D1149964

Dreaming of...
COLLECTION

April 2018

May 2018

June 2018

July 2018

August 2018

September 2018

Dreaming of...
Greece

REBECCA WINTERS

ROBIN GIANNA

MILLS & BOON

Published in Great Britain 2018
by Mills & Boon, an imprint of HarperCollins*Publishers*
1 London Bridge Street, London, SE1 9GF

Dreaming of… Greece © 2018 Harlequin Books S.A.

The Millionaire's True Worth © 2015 Rebecca Winters
A Wedding for the Greek Tycoon © 2015 Rebecca Winters
Her Greek Doctor's Proposal © 2015 Robin Gianakopoulos

ISBN: 978-0-263-26666-5

09-0818

MIX
Paper from
responsible sources
FSC **FSC™ C007454**
www.fsc.org

This book is produced from independently certified FSC™ paper to ensure responsible forest management.

For more information visit: www.harpercollins.co.uk/green

Printed and bound in Spain
by CPI, Barcelona

THE MILLIONAIRE'S TRUE WORTH

REBECCA WINTERS

CHAPTER ONE

"CHLOE? I'M SORRY I can't be your maid of honor, but you know why."

Following that statement there was a long silence on Chloe's part. But Raina had her job plus the many responsibilities thrown onto her shoulders since the death of her grandfather. She was now heiress to the Maywood billion-dollar fortune and was constantly in the news. When she went out in public, the paparazzi were right on her heels.

Chloe's family were high-profile Greek industrial-ists, a favorite target of the European paparazzi. Her marriage would be the top story in Athens. "If I were your maid of honor, the media would make a circus out of your special day." Raina feared it would take the spotlight off her dear friend. For Chloe's sake, she couldn't risk it.

Too much had happened in the intervening years. It had been eight years, in fact, since Chloe had lived with Raina and her grandparents during her senior year of high school. But they'd stayed in touch by phone and the internet.

Three years ago Raina's grandmother had died and Chloe had come to California with her parents for the funeral. Just nine months ago Raina's grandfather had died and once again Chloe and her family had flown over to be with her for his funeral. Their close friendship had helped her get through her grief, and Chloe's family had begged Raina to come back to Greece with them.

"Please tell me you understand, Chloe. I have no desire to intrude on your joy."

"I don't care about me."

"But I *do*."

After a resigned sigh Chloe said, "Then at least stay at the house with me and my family. After all you did for me when I lived with you, my parents are anxious to do everything they can for you."

"Tell you what. After you've left on your honeymoon I'll be thrilled to spend time with them before I fly back to California."

"They'll want you to stay for several months. Think about it. We could have such a wonderful time together."

"I will think about it. As for right now I can't wait to be at your reception. The photos you sent me in your wedding dress are fabulous!"

"But you won't get to see me married at the church."

"Much as I'm sorry about that, it's better this way. I've already booked a room at the Diethnes Hotel. You can reach me on the phone there or on my cell phone. Chloe? You promise you haven't told your fiancé my plans?"

"I swear it. Of course he knows all about you, but he doesn't have any idea that you are coming to Greece."

"Good. That's how I want things to stay. This is going to be *your* day! If the press finds out I'm there, I'm afraid it will ruin things for you. Later this year I'll fly over to meet him, or you can fly to California."

"I promise. He's so wonderful, I can't eat or sleep."

"That doesn't surprise me. *Ta le-me*, Chloe," she said, using one of the few Greek expressions she still remembered, before hanging up.

Six years ago Raina had been in the same excited condition as her friend. Halfway through college she'd met Byron Wallace, a writer. After a whirlwind romance they were married. But it didn't take long to see his selfish nature and suspect her new husband of being unfaithful. Armed with proof of his infidelity even before their two-year marriage anniversary, she'd divorced him, only to lose her grandmother to heart failure.

In her pain she vowed never to marry again. She'd told as much to her beloved, ailing grandfather who'd passed away from stomach cancer.

Chloe's phone call a month ago about her impending marriage had come as a wonderful surprise. Since the death of Raina's grandfather, it was the one piece of news that put some excitement back into her life.

The head of her team at the lab was aware she hadn't taken a vacation in several years. He urged her to take the time off for as long as she wanted. "Go to Greece and be with your friend," he'd said. "We'll still be here when you get back."

Raina thought about it. A change of scene to enjoy Chloe's nuptials might be exactly what she needed.

* * *

Maybe it was the stress of everything she'd had to do before her flight to Athens, Greece. All Raina knew was that she had developed a splitting headache. She needed a strong painkiller. After filing out of the coach section to clear customs wearing jeans and a T-shirt, she retrieved her medium-sized suitcase and left the terminal late morning to find a taxi.

"The Diethnes Hotel, please," she told the driver. The man at the travel agency in Carmel-by-the-Sea, California, had booked the budget hotel for her. From there she could walk to Syntagma Square and the city center without problem.

Chloe had phoned her from Athens yesterday to exclaim over the gorgeous seventy-eight-degree temperature, perfect for her June wedding that would take place tomorrow. Considering the prominence of the Milonis and Chiotis families, it promised to be one of the country's major society events of the summer.

Raina, a strawberry blonde with wavy hair cut neck length, looked at the clear blue Greek sky, a good omen for the impending festivities. Chloe was the sweetest girl in the world. Raina hoped she was marrying an honorable man who'd be true to her.

Raina hadn't been so lucky in that department, but four years had passed since the divorce and she refused to let any remaining clouds dampen the excitement for her friend. Every woman went into marriage praying it would last forever. *A woman had that right, didn't she?*

Once she'd been shown to her room and had unpacked, Raina went back downstairs for directions to the nearest pharmacy for headache medicine. The concierge told her there was a convenience store in the next block many of the American tourists frequented.

Raina thanked him and made her way down the street.

Akis Giannopoulos smiled at his best friend. "Are you ready to take the big plunge?"

Theo grinned. "You already know the answer to that question. If I'd had my way, I would have kidnapped Chloe and married her in private several months ago. But her mother and mine have had an agenda since the engagement. Wouldn't you know the guest list includes a cast of thousands?"

"You're a lucky man." Akis was happy for him. Theo and Chloe seemed to be a perfect match. "Can I do any last-minute service for you before you become a married man?"

"You did more than enough helping me make all the hotel arrangements for our out-of-town guests. I suggest you go back to the penthouse. I need my best man relaxed before the big day tomorrow. Will your brother be there?"

"Vasso phoned me earlier. He'll make it to the wedding, but then he has to get back to the grand opening so he'll miss the reception."

"Understood. So, I'll see you at the church in the morning?"

Akis hugged him. "Try to keep me away."

The two men had been friends for a long time. Naturally Akis was thrilled for Theo, but he was surprised to discover just how much he would miss the camaraderie they'd shared as bachelors. Having done so many things together, Akis was feeling a real sense of loss.

Theo's life would now be swept up with Chloe's. Falling in love with her had changed his friend. He was excited for this marriage. Akis marveled that Theo wanted it so much.

How could he feel so certain that marrying Chloe was the right thing for him?

Marriage meant a lifelong commitment. The woman would have to be so sensational. Akis couldn't fathom finding such a woman.

Aware he was in a despondent mood that wasn't like him, he left the bank Theo's family had owned for several decades and decided to walk to the penthouse in order to shake it off. After the wedding rehearsal that had taken place this morning, exercise was what he needed.

Tourists had flooded into Athens. He saw every kind and description as he made his way to the Giannopoulos complex. After turning a corner, he almost bumped into a beautiful female in a T-shirt and jeans coming in his direction.

"Me seen xo rees, thespinis," he apologized, getting out of her way just in time.

She murmured something he didn't quite hear. For a moment their eyes locked. He felt like he'd suddenly come in contact with an electric current. She must have felt it, too, because he saw little bursts of violet coming from those velvety depths before she walked on. By the way she moved, she had a definite destination in mind. The last thing he saw was her blondish-red hair gleaming in the sun before she rounded the corner behind him.

Raina slowed down, shocked by what had just happened. Maybe it was her bad headache that had caused her to almost walk into the most gorgeous male she'd ever seen in her life. Not in her wildest dreams could she have conjured such a man.

She needed medicine fast!

Luckily the sign for the convenience store was in Greek and English. Alpha/Omega 24. Translation—everything from A to Z. That was a clever name for the store. Its interior looked like "everywhere USA." There was a caution sign saying Wet Floor in both languages as you walked in.

She tiptoed over the newly mopped floor in her sandals to the counter. The male clerk, probably college age, helped her find the over-the-counter medicine section for headaches.

After picking it out plus a bottle of water, she followed him back to the counter to pay for the items with some euros. While she waited, she opened the water and took two pills. On her way out, the clerk asked her where she was staying. Raina told him she was just passing through and started for the exit. But somehow, she didn't know how, she slipped and fell.

"Whoa—" Pain radiated from her ankle. The clerk rushed from behind the counter to help her get up. When she tried to stand, it really hurt. Hopefully the medicine would help tamp down the pain.

He hurried into a back room and brought out a chair so she could sit down. "I'm calling the hospital."

"I don't think there's a need for that."

He ignored her. "This is the store's fault. You stay there."

She felt the fool sitting there while there were customers coming in and out. The other clerk who'd mopped the floor waited on them. In a few minutes an ambulance drove up in front. By then she'd answered a few questions the clerk had asked in order to fill out an incident form.

Because she was incognito, she gave her grandmother's name with her information so no one would pick up on her name. To her dismay there was a small crowd standing around as she was helped outside. Great! Exactly what she didn't want.

"Thank you," she said to the clerk before being helped into the back by one of the attendants. "You've been very kind and I appreciate it."

Two hours later her sprain had been wrapped. She needed to put ice on it and elevate her leg to cut down the swelling. The ER doctor fitted her with crutches and sent them with her in the taxi, letting her know the bill would be taken care of by the store where she'd fallen.

After the wedding reception, Raina would make certain her insurance company would reimburse the store. After all, the accident was her fault.

For the time being, she needed to lie down and call room service for her meals and ice. How crazy was it that she would have to go to the reception tomorrow evening on crutches. No matter what, she refused to miss her dear friend's celebration.

After flying all this way, how even crazier was it that all she could think about was the man she'd come close to colliding with earlier in the day. She'd never experienced anything like that before. The streets of Athens were crowded with hundreds of people. How was it that one man could rob her of breath just looking at him?

With a champagne glass in hand, Akis stood at the head table to toast the bride and groom. "It was a great honor Theo Chiotis bestowed on me when he asked me to be his best man. No man has had a better friend." Except for Vasso, of course. "After meeting and getting to know Chloe, I can say without reservation that no man could have married a sweeter woman. To Theo and Chloe. May you always be as happy as you are today."

After the crowd applauded, other friends of the bridal couple made their toasts. Akis was thankful his part in the long wedding-day festivities was officially over. When he felt a decent interval of time had passed, he would slip out of the luxurious Grand Bretagne Hotel ballroom unnoticed and leave for the penthouse.

To love a woman enough to go through this exhaustive kind of day was anathema to Akis. No man appreciated women more than he did, but his business affairs with thirty-year-old Vasso kept him too busy to enjoy more than a surface relationship that didn't last long.

Though he congratulated himself on reaching the age of twenty-nine without yet succumbing to marriage, Theo's wedding caused Akis to question what was going on with him and his brother.

The two of them had been in business since they were young boys. To this point in time no enduring love interest had interfered with their lives and they'd managed to make their dream to rise out of poverty come true. Besides owning a conglomerate of retail stores throughout Greece, they'd set up a charity Foundation with two centers, one in Greece, the other in New York City.

Their dirt-poor background might be a memory,

but it was the one that drove them so they'd never know what it was like to go hungry again. Unfortunately their ascent from rags to riches didn't come without some drawbacks. For various reasons both he and Vasso found it difficult to trust the women who came into their lives. They enjoyed brief relationships. But they grew leery when they came across women who seemed to love them for themselves, with no interest in their money. He thought about their parents who, though they were painfully poor and scraped for every drachma, had loved and were devoted to one another. They came from the same island with the same expectations of life and the ability to endure the ups and downs of marriage. Both Akis and Vasso wanted a union like their parents', one that would last forever. But finding the right woman seemed to be growing harder.

Akis's thoughts wandered back to the words he'd just spoken to the guests in the ballroom. He'd meant what he'd said about Chloe, who was kind and compatible. She suited Theo, who also had a winning nature. They both came from the same elite, socioeconomic background that helped them to trust that neither had an agenda. If two people could make it through this life together and be happy, he imagined they would.

Every so often he felt the maid of honor's dark eyes willing him to pay attention to her. Althea Loris was one of Chloe's friends, a very glamorous woman as yet unattached. She'd tried to corner him at various parties given before the wedding. Althea came from a good family with a modest income, but Akis sensed how much she wanted all the trappings of a marriage like Chloe's.

Even if Akis had felt an attraction, he would have wondered if she'd set her eyes on him for what he could give her monetarily. It wasn't fair to judge, but he couldn't ignore his basic instinct about her.

There was nothing he wanted more than to be loved for himself. An imperfect self, to be sure. Both he and Vasso had been born into a family where you worked by the sweat of your brow all the days of your life. The idea of a formal education was unheard of, but he hadn't worried about it until the summer right before he had to do his military service.

An Italian tourist named Fabrizia, who was staying on the island that July, had flirted with Akis at the store where he worked. He couldn't speak Italian, nor she Greek, so they managed with passable English. He was attracted and spent time swimming with her when he could get an hour off. By the time she had to go home, he'd fallen for her and wanted to know when she'd be back.

After kissing him passionately she'd said, "I won't be able to come." In the next breath she'd told him she'd be getting married soon to one of the attorneys working for her father in Rome. "But I'll never forget my beautiful grocery boy. Why couldn't you be the attorney my parents have picked out for me?"

Not only had his pride taken a direct hit, her question had made him startlingly aware of his shortcomings, the kind that went soil-deep. The kind that separated the rich from the poor. From that time on, Akis had enjoyed several relationships with women, but they didn't approach the level of his wanting to get married.

Too bad his brother had to leave after the wedding

at the church and couldn't attend the reception. He was away on important business at the moment so he couldn't rescue Akis with a legitimate excuse to leave early. Akis would have to manufacture a good one on his own.

Thankfully the speeches were almost over. Chloe's father was the last person to speak. After getting choked up because he was losing his precious daughter to Theo, he urged everyone to enjoy the rest of the evening and dance.

Akis watched as Theo escorted Chloe to the floor for the first dance. Soon other couples joined them. That meant Akis had to fulfill one last duty. It was expected that he ask Althea, who was more than eager to find herself in his arms.

"I've been waiting for this all day, Akis."

He knew what she was saying, what she was hoping for, but he couldn't force interest that wasn't there. The long, exhausting wedding day was almost over. Akis couldn't wait to leave, but he needed to choose his words carefully. "Unfortunately I still have business to do after the reception is over."

Her head jerked up. "Business? Tonight?"

"My work is never done." As the music was coming to an end, he danced her over to her parents' table and let her go. "Thank you, Althea. Theo asked me to mingle so if you'll excuse me, there's one more person I should dance with before I leave." The lie had just come to him.

While she looked at him with genuine disappointment, he smiled at her parents before he moved through the crowded room toward the rear of the ballroom. In order to prove he hadn't told an untruth, he looked for any woman at one of the tables who didn't have an escort, whom he could ask to dance.

At the round table nearest the rear doors he saw a woman sitting alone. Another couple sat across from her, but it was clear she didn't have a man with her. Knowing Althea was still watching him, he walked toward the stranger. Maybe she was waiting for someone, but he'd take his chances.

Closer now he could make out classic features beneath hair an incredible light gold with a natural hint of red. He'd only seen hair that color on one other woman. His breath caught. She wore a pale blue silk suit jacket with a small enamel locket hanging around her neck. He imagined she was in her mid-twenties. He saw no rings.

Akis approached her. "Excuse me, *thespinis*. I see you're alone for the moment. As best man of this wedding, if you'd permit, I'd like to dance with you."

Her eyes lifted to his.

Those eyes. They were the same eyes he'd looked into yesterday, but tonight he discovered they were a stunning shade of lavender blue and he found himself lost in them.

"I'm sorry, but I don't speak Greek."

Her comment jarred him back to the present. What was this American beauty doing at Theo's wedding reception? Switching to unpolished English he said, "We passed in the street yesterday."

"I remember almost bumping into you," she murmured, averting her eyes. He noticed with satisfaction that a nerve throbbed in her throat above her locket. She was as excited as he was by this unexpected meeting. "I came close to knocking you down because I wasn't watching where I was going."

He smiled. "No problem. Just now I asked you to dance, but perhaps you're waiting for the man who brought you."

A delicate flush filled her cheeks. "No. I came alone. Thank you for the invitation, but I was just getting ready to leave."

He wasn't about to let her go a second time. "Surely you can spare one dance with me? I need rescuing."

"Where's your wife?"

"I've never had a wife. As for a girlfriend, I haven't had one in months." It was the truth.

"Then who was the woman with the long black hair you were dancing with moments ago?"

So she'd noticed. "You're very observant. She was the maid of honor. It would have been unkind not to dance with her."

With a twinkle in her eyes, she leaned to the right and retrieved a pair of crutches from the floor. She stood them on end. "Unless you're prepared for your feet to be impaled by one of these, I'll do you a favor and exit the room."

She'd surprised Akis. This had to be a very recent injury. Her legitimate excuse to turn him down only fed his determination to get to know her better. Yesterday he'd wanted to pursue her, but hadn't dared for fear of alarming her. "Then let me help you."

Without hesitation he took the crutches from her and waited until she got to her feet. She was probably five foot seven, with enticing curves. The matching suit skirt covered womanly hips and slender legs. His gaze fell lower to the left ankle that had been wrapped. She wore a sandal on her foot and a low-heeled shoe on the other.

"Thank you." She reached for the crutches and fit them beneath her arms. The delicate fragrance emanating from her assailed him. "Why don't you ask the other woman at my table to dance? I'm sure her partner won't mind."

"I'd rather help you to your room."

"I'm not staying here."

That was interesting. He'd helped Theo make arrangements for all their out-of-town guests to stay here. "Then I'll walk you outside and take you wherever you'd like to go."

"As long as you're offering, I wouldn't say no if you hailed a taxi for me. I'm craving my hotel room so I can elevate my leg."

"I'll do better than that." Akis accompanied her from the ballroom and down the hall to the foyer. The woman at his side managed her crutches with little trouble. En route he phoned his driver and told him to come to the hotel entrance.

As they walked outside, flashes from the cameras of the paparazzi blinded them. Chloe and Theo's wedding would be the top story making the ten o'clock news on television. Video of prominent guests and the best man attending the reception filmed by TV news crews would be included.

Some of the paparazzi called out questions about the beautiful woman with Akis. He hated the attention though he was used to it, and kept walking her to the smoked-glass limo without answering them. He took her crutches so she could get in, then he fol-

lowed and shut the door before sitting opposite her.
"Are you all right?"

"I am. Are you?"

"I am now. The press is unrelenting. Tell me where
you're staying and I'll let the driver know."

"The Diethnes."

A lot of tourists on a budget frequented two-star
hotels like that one. Until he and Vasso had started
making money, he could never have afforded to stay at
any hotel. Period. Akis gave his driver directions and
they pulled away from the Grand Bretagne. "When
did you have time to injure your ankle?"

She let out a sound of exasperation. "It happened
right after you and I passed on the sidewalk. I had a
headache and was on my way to a store for some medicine. While I was inside, I slipped on the wet floor.
It was such a stupid accident, totally my fault for not
paying attention. The clerk was incredibly kind and
called the ambulance for me."

Akis mulled over her answer. Had she decided it
would be easier to attend the reception rather than the
wedding because of her injury? If she'd been at the
church, he wouldn't have been able to take his eyes
off her during the ceremony.

"Are you in pain?"

"Not really. It's more a dull ache until I rest it."

"I'm sorry you had to fall, especially the day before the wedding."

"Funny about life, isn't it?" she murmured. "You
never know what's going to happen when you get up
in the morning." The almost haunted tone in her voice
intrigued him.

"How true. When I left for the wedding, I didn't

know I was going to meet the lovely stranger who'd passed me on the street yesterday."

"Or be chased by the maid of honor tonight," she said in a wry tone. "Am I mistaken, or were you taking flight?"

"You noticed that."

"It was hard not to." She chuckled without looking at him. "I would imagine a man with your looks and minus a wedding ring needs rescuing from myriads of females."

He blinked. "*My* looks?"

"You know very well you're the embodiment of a Greek god."

Akis frowned. "Which terrifying one are you referring to?"

At this point she laughed. "I didn't have any particular god in mind. It's something American women say when they've met an exceptionally good-looking man."

"Then they haven't seen one of our Greek statues up close or they'd run for their lives in the other direction."

Her laughing continued. He decided she was somewhat of a tease.

"I don't know. Despite your fearsome expression, the female pursuing you tonight didn't seem turned off by you. Quite the opposite, in fact."

That's exactly what Althea had been doing for weeks. Maybe he'd misjudged her, but it didn't matter because he hadn't been attracted. "You saved me from being caught. For that, I'm in your debt."

"I'm in yours for giving me a lift to the hotel," she came right back. "We're even."

Akis had never met a woman like her. "Are you a friend of Theo's or Chloe's? I don't even know your name."

"Let's keep it that way."

Her remark shouldn't have bothered him, but it did...

They continued down the busy street. "Oh— Look—" she cried softly. "See that store on the right? Alpha/Omega 24?" He nodded. "That's the one where I fell. My hotel is in the next block."

Raina couldn't believe that the incredible man she'd seen on the street yesterday was none other than Theo's best man. It was an amazing coincidence. She was actually upset with herself for having any feelings about seeing him again tonight.

Since her divorce, there'd been no man in her life and she'd purposely kept it that way. She didn't want to fall in love again and take the chance of being hurt. For this man to have already made an impact on her without even trying was disturbing. After the pain she'd been through because of Byron, she never wanted to experience it again.

When the driver drove up in front of the hotel, Raina was relieved that the striking Greek male sitting next to her had gone quiet and didn't pressure her for more information. That was good.

She found that when she used a man's tactics of a little false flattery on him, the fun went out of it on his part. Knowing Raina could see through his strategy, his interest had quickly waned. She wanted to leave Greece with no complications. Already she knew this man was unforgettable. The sooner she could get away from him, the better.

"Thanks again for the lift," she said in a cheery voice, needing to escape the potency of his male charisma.

He opened the door and took her crutches to help her from the back of the limo. She put them underneath her arms and started for the entrance. After pushing the hotel door open, he accompanied her as far as the foyer. She kept moving toward the elevator. While she waited, she turned in his direction.

"Like you, I appreciated being rescued." The lift door finally opened. "Good night." She stepped inside without looking back, praying for it to close fast in case he decided to go upstairs with her.

Raina willed her heart to stop thudding. She hadn't been kidding when she'd said he looked like a Greek god. From his black hair and eyes to his tall, powerful build, he was the personification of male perfection. She hadn't been able to take her eyes off him all evening. His image would be all over the television tonight, causing legions of women to swoon.

Chloe had raved about Theo's looks, but he couldn't hold a candle to his best man. What had she called him? Akis something or other. He had a self-assured presence, bordering on an arrogance he probably wasn't aware of.

The maid of honor who'd danced with him earlier had looked pained when he'd left her side and made a beeline to Raina's table. Here Raina had tried so hard to be invisible during the reception. But at least no one recognized her.

So far the only photos taken of her were because

the best man with his Greek-god looks had helped
her out to the limo. Until now Raina had managed to
escape any notoriety. The paparazzi were following
him, not her. Chloe's beautiful day had gone perfectly
without a marring incident of any kind. If ever a bride
looked euphoric…

Grateful for the reception to be over, she let herself into the room. To her surprise there was a light
blinking on the phone. It couldn't possibly be Chloe.
Maybe it was the front desk. She used her crutches to
reach the bedside and sat down to find out if something was wrong.

When she picked up, she listened to the message
from Nora Milonis, Chloe's mother. She was sending
a car for Raina in the morning and insisted she spend
the rest of her time in Athens with them. *Be ready at
9:00 a.m.* Absolutely no excuses now that the wedding was over!

She'd known the invitation was coming. It warmed
her heart and put her in a much better mood.

Once she'd called for ice and was ready for bed,
she elevated her leg and turned on the TV. But her
mind wandered to the man who'd brought her home.

He spoke English with a deep, heavy Greek accent
she found appealing. The man hadn't done anything,
yet he'd disturbed her senses that had lain dormant
since she'd discovered her husband had been unfaithful to her. The way he'd looked at her both yesterday
and tonight had made her feel alive for the first time
in years and he hadn't even touched her!

Why this man? Why now? She couldn't understand
what it was that made him so fascinating to her. That
was the trouble. She didn't want to find him fasci-

nating because it meant a part of her wanted to see him again.

She'd planned to fly back to California soon, but her sprained ankle prevented her from leaving for a while. How wonderful that she'd be able to spend time with Chloe's parents after all! Raina needed family right now, even if it wasn't her own.

The doctor had warned her to keep it supported close to a week for a faster recovery. She'd planned to do work on her laptop and get in some reading.

Anything to keep her mind off Theo's best man.

CHAPTER TWO

"*Kalimera*, Galen."

The clerk's head lifted. "Kyrie Giannopoulos— what a surprise to see you in here this morning! I didn't expect a visit before next week."

Galen reminded Akis of himself at an earlier age. He was eager for the work and anxious to please. So far, Akis had had no complaints about him. "I came by to find out if you were on duty the day before yesterday when an American woman slipped and fell."

"Yes. Mikos and I were both here. How did you know?"

"That's not important. Tell me what happened."

Akis listened as his employee recounted the same story the exciting woman had told him last night. "Did she threaten to sue?"

"No. She claimed it was her fault."

"Did you fill out an incident report?"

"Yes. It's on the desk in the back room. I told the ambulance attendant the store would be responsible for the bill."

"You did exactly the right thing. Thank you."

Akis walked behind the counter and entered the small room, anxious to see what was written.

He reached in the Out basket and found the injury report.

June 3, 1:45 p.m.
Ginger Moss: American, age 26
Athens address: The Diethnes Hotel.
Customer fell on wet floor after purchasing some headache medicine. She limped in pain. I called an ambulance. She was taken to St. Michael's Hospital.
Signed: Galen.

Ginger... He liked the name very much. He liked everything about her *too* much. She'd caused him a restless night despite the fact that the whole wedding day had been exhausting. Ginger Moss had that effect on a man.

Akis had felt her magic and couldn't throw it off. Now that he was armed with her name, he planned to seek her out so he could get to know her better. Since he didn't know her agenda, he had no idea how long she'd be in Athens. The only way to find out was to head over to her hotel.

Galen poked his head in the door. "Is everything all right, boss?"

"You two are doing a fine job."

"Thanks. About that American woman who slipped and fell?"

Akis turned his head to look at his employee. "Yes?"

"Mikos had just mopped the floor before she came in. We did have the caution sign set out on the floor."

"Good." He nodded to his two employees and went

back out to the limo. "I'll walk to the Diethnes from here," he told the driver. "Follow me and wait in front until you hear from me again."

A few minutes later he entered the hotel lobby and told the concierge he'd like to speak to one of their guests named Ginger Moss. The other man shook his head. "We don't have a tourist staying here with that name."

Akis unconsciously ran a hand through his hair in surprise. "You're sure? Maybe if I explain that the woman I'm looking for was using crutches when I dropped her off here last night."

"Ah… The one with hair the color of a Titian painting and a figure like the statue in the museum. You know—the one of the goddess Aphrodite carrying a pitcher?"

Yes—that was the precise one Akis had envisioned himself.

He thought back to last night. She'd been elusive about everything. What kind of a game was she playing? He closed his eyes tightly for a moment, remembering her comment about him resembling a Greek god. *Touché.*

"Would you ring her room and tell her the man who helped her home last night is in the lobby and wishes to talk to her?"

His shoulders hunched. "I can't. She checked out an hour ago."

"You mean permanently?" he barked the question.

"Of course."

"Did she leave a forwarding address?"

"No. I'm sorry."

"Did she go by taxi?"

"I don't know. I was busy at the desk."

"What name did she register under?"

"Unless you have a judge's warrant, I can't tell you."

Trying to tamp down his frustration, he thanked the man and hurried outside to the limo where his driver was waiting.

"Shall I take you to the office?

"Not yet. I have a phone call to make first." Akis climbed in the back and phoned Theo's parents. He reached his friend's mother. After chatting for a moment about the perfect wedding, she mentioned Althea and her disappointment that Akis had needed to leave the reception so soon. Akis reminded her that something pressing in business had come up. Then he got to the point.

"Did you invite an American woman named Ginger Moss to the wedding reception?"

"Moss? No," she claimed after reflection. "That's an unusual name, and it certainly wasn't on our list or I would have remembered. Why?"

So that was the reason why Theo hadn't arranged for her to stay at the Grand Bretagne. "I'm trying to find her."

After a silence, "Is she the person who caused you to walk away from Althea so fast last night?"

Akis didn't mind her teasing insinuation. Theo's parents were like a second family to him. For the last year both of them had kept reminding him it was time he got married, too. "No. As I was leaving the ballroom, I ran into the woman who was on crutches and needed help out to a taxi."

"Hmm. Why don't you check with Chloe's parents? They must have invited her. If they haven't heard of her, either, maybe she was a friend of Chloe's or Theo's. Perhaps they invited her too late to receive an invitation."

"Maybe," he muttered. "She hadn't been at the church or *I* would have remembered," he said quietly. "Thanks. We'll all have to get together after they get back from their honeymoon."

"Wonderful, but don't you dare be a stranger while they're away!"

"I won't," Akis promised, but his mind was on the woman he'd asked to dance last night. He could have sworn there'd been feelings between them. Sparks. Some nuance of chemistry that had happened immediately while they were on the sidewalk and wouldn't leave him alone. Yet she'd run off this morning.

No matter what, he intended to find her. It bothered him that she'd given him the slip when she knew he wanted to get to know her better. Maybe it was his pride that made him want to prove she had feelings for him, too. One thing was certain. He wasn't going to let her disappear on him.

Without wasting another moment, he phoned Chloe's house. The housekeeper said she'd put through the call to Chloe's father because Kyria Milonis was occupied.

The more Akis thought about it, the more he decided this woman had to be a friend of Chloe's. Otherwise Theo would have talked about her long before now. He wouldn't have been able to help himself because even if he was head over heels in love with Chloe, this Ginger, or whoever she was, stood out from the rest.

Why had she sat at the last table near the doors last night? It was almost as if she hadn't wanted to be seen. Her behavior was a mystery to him. Vasso would be shocked by the strength of his brother's desire to find the tantalizing female. Nothing like this had ever happened before. No one was more shocked than Akis himself. In case she'd be leaving Athens soon, he had to work fast.

"Akis, my boy!" came the booming voice of Chloe's father. "Great to hear from you! We're going to miss the kids. The place feels empty. Come on over to the house for lunch. My wife will be thrilled. We'll eat by the pool."

The perfect place to vet Chloe's parents. "I'll be there soon, Socus. Thank you."

After getting settled on a patio lounger by the pool with her leg raised, Raina smiled at Chloe's mother who hovered around her like her grandmother used to do. She loved her friend's parents and drew great comfort from being with them. They couldn't seem to do enough for her.

"We were always sorry that you didn't come to live with us after Chloe's school year with you ended. It was all Chloe had talked about."

"I would have come, but as you know my grandmother wasn't well and I was afraid to leave her. Then I started college and met the man who became my husband. When our marriage didn't work out, I divorced him. Then, of course, my grandmother died and I needed to take care of my grandfather, who was diagnosed with stomach cancer. There was never a good time to come to Greece."

Chloe's father patted her hand. "You've had a great load on your shoulders."

"My grandparents raised me. I loved them so much and owed them everything. But I have to tell you, the year Chloe spent with me was the happiest of my life. It was like having a sister. My grandparents adored her."

Nora smiled with tears in her eyes. "She loved the three of you. Why don't you consider this your temporary home and stay with us for a time? There's nothing we'd like more. Chloe would be ecstatic."

"That would be wonderful, but I have a job waiting for me when I get back."

"You like your work?"

"Very much," but she was prevented from saying more because a maid appeared beneath the striped patio awning. She said something in Greek and suddenly the best man walked out on the terrace.

"Akis!" Nora cried with warmth in her voice.

Raina's heart skipped several beats. In a short-sleeved white crew neck and matching cargo pants, he robbed her of breath, with his rock-hard physique and arresting Greek features.

He hadn't seen Raina yet and said something in Greek to Chloe's parents with an aura of authority she was sure came naturally to him. He sounded intense, with no accompanying smile. After he stopped talking, they both started to chuckle and turned to Raina.

The man's dark head jerked around in her direction. His penetrating gaze caused her body to fill with heat. To her dismay she lay helpless on the lounger in another T-shirt and jeans with her leg propped, hardly an exciting sight. The look of shock on his face was priceless.

"You're here," he muttered, rubbing his chest absently. "I went to the hotel but the concierge said you'd already checked out. Theo's parents claimed they didn't know you, so I decided to come over here to find out if you were a friend of Chloe's."

The knowledge that he'd been trying to find her excited her. Again she was struck by his heavily accented English. For want of a better word, she found it endearing. Raina nodded to him, stunned that he'd gone to such lengths to find her. "Friends from a long time ago. Her parents sent a car for me this morning so we could visit."

"Which has been long overdue," Nora stated in English.

He still looked thunderstruck. Raina could read his mind. "Did you think I had invited myself to the reception?"

"No, but I got the feeling you didn't want to be noticed," he drawled. She had the feeling nothing got past him.

"While you two talk, I'll tell Ione to serve lunch out here." Nora got up from the deck chair and Chloe's father followed her, leaving them alone.

Raina swallowed hard. She never imagined seeing him again and wasn't prepared for this overwhelming response to the very sight of him.

He pulled up a deck chair and sat down next to her. His black eyes played over her from head to toe, missing nothing in between. Her pulse raced. "How's the pain this morning?"

"I took an ibuprofen and now it's hardly noticeable. At this rate I'll be able to fly home soon."

"What's the rush?"

"Work is waiting for me." *I don't dare spend any more time around you. I didn't come to Greece to meet a man who has already become too important to me.*

He leaned forward with his hands clasped between his hard muscled legs. "What kind?"

Oh, boy. She could tell she was in for a vetting. The less he knew about her, the better. She was afraid to be open with her feelings for fear of being hurt again. After having made a huge mistake in choosing Byron, she feared she didn't have wise judgment when it came to men.

Byron had been relentless in his pursuit of her. She'd been so naive and so flattered by his attention, she'd fallen into his grasping, narcissistic hands like an apple from a tree. His betrayal of her even before their marriage had scarred her for life, forcing her to grow up overnight.

Never again would she allow herself to be caught off guard, even if this man thrilled her to the core of her being. Raina would rather leave Greece without feeling any tug of emotion for this dark-haired stranger. He was already dangerous to her peace of mind.

"I work in a lab with a team of people." That was as much as she was willing to reveal. "What do you do for a living?"

He studied her intently. "My brother and I are in business. That's how I met Theo. So now that we have that out of the way, how did you meet Chloe?"

Raina could tell he was equally reticent to talk

about himself. That was fine with her. He could keep his secrets, whatever they were. "My senior year of high school, she came to live with me in California for the school year so she could learn English. That year there were three other students from other countries living with some of the students' families."

"Was it a reciprocal arrangement?"

"Yes. After graduation I was supposed to spend the next year with her family, but too many things at the time prevented me from coming here to live with them."

Needing some space to gather her composure before he asked her any more questions, she sat up and swung her legs to the ground. He anticipated her movements and handed her the crutches lying by the side of the lounger. "Thank you," she said, tucking them beneath her arms. "If you'll excuse me, please, I need to use the restroom."

"Of course."

Raina could see in his eyes she hadn't fooled him, but what did it matter. She hurried through the mansion to her suite of rooms. The fabulous Milonis estate had been built along neoclassical lines in its purest architectural form. So different from the home where she'd been raised in Carmel.

When she eventually returned to the patio, she discovered Akis in the swimming pool. Their lunch had been brought out to the patio table. While he was doing laps at tremendous speed, she sat down in one of the chairs around the table and dug into the salad filled with delicious chicken, feta cheese and olives.

Chloe's parents were nowhere in sight. Raina had hoped they'd come out to provide a buffer against his questions, but no such luck. Chloe's parents were a very hip couple she adored. Raina could see why. Too bad they thought they were aiding a romantic situation by staying away.

As her eyes looked out at the pool, Akis suddenly raised his head. The wet black hair was swept back from his forehead to reveal his extraordinary male features. The moment he saw her, he levered himself from the aquamarine water and reached for a towel, giving her more than a glimpse of his splendid body. He must have borrowed someone's black trunks. They hung low on his hips.

"Last night you resembled one of your disgruntled gods," she teased to fight her attraction. "Today you've morphed into Poseidon."

Akis finished drying himself off before he sat down in a chair opposite her and plucked a big olive from the salad his white teeth bit into with relish. Between his olive skin and black hair, he was a work of art if there was such a label to describe a beautiful man. To her consternation, everything he said and did intrigued her.

"Oddly enough you haven't changed since last night," he remarked. "The concierge said you resembled Aphrodite, a description that fits you in every detail except for your crutches."

She laughed to let him know she didn't take him seriously. To believe him would be a huge mistake. "Careful," she cautioned. "You might just turn my head if you keep up that malarkey."

One dark brow lifted. "Malarkey?"

"An English expression for nonsense."

His jet-black eyes came alive. "You mean my methods are working?" By now he'd devoured a roll and most of his salad.

"Absolutely. But since I won't be in Greece long, maybe your time would be better spent talking to someone of your own kind and background."

In an instant his jaw hardened. Uh-oh. She must have struck a nerve.

"My own kind?" The words came out more like a soft hiss.

She choked on her iced tea. What had she said to provoke such a reaction? "Surely you must realize I meant no offense. Perhaps the maid of honor wasn't to your liking last night, but I saw a lot of lovely Greek women at the reception—women who live here and would enjoy your attention."

Akis sat back in the chair. "Meaning you don't?"

"I didn't say that!" Their conversation had taken a strange twist.

"Let's start over again." He cocked his head. "We weren't formally introduced. My name is Akis Giannopoulos as you already know. What's yours?"

She took a deep breath. "Raina."

"Ah. Raina what?"

She shrugged her shoulders. "Does it matter when we'll never see each other again?"

"That's the second time you've used the same excuse not to tell me."

"I simply don't see the point." He grew on her with every moment they spent together. This wasn't supposed to happen!

An ominous silence surrounded them. "Obviously not. If you'll excuse me, I'm going to change clothes in the cabana."

She'd made him angry. Good. Raina wanted him to leave her alone. But as she watched him stride to the other side of the pool, she experienced a strange sense of loss totally at odds with her determination to separate herself from him.

Raina wanted to escape any more involvement because she had a premonition this man had the power to hurt her in a way not even Byron had done. Akis made her feel things she didn't want to feel. To give in to her desire to be with him could bring her joy, but for how long? When the excitement wore off for him, would he find someone else? Raina was afraid to trust what she was feeling. She quickly grabbed her crutches and hurried to find Chloe's mother who was in the kitchen.

"Thank you for the delicious lunch, Nora. Now if you don't mind, my ankle has started to ache again. I'm going to go to my room and lie down for a while. Please say goodbye to Mr. Giannopoulos for me. He came over to your home to visit with you and is still out in the pool."

Her eyes widened. "Of course. Can I get you anything?"

"Not a thing. You've done too much for me already. I just need to rest my leg for a while."

"Then go on." The two women hugged and she left the kitchen for her suite of rooms. In truth Raina needed to get her mind off Akis. Since she hadn't had family around for a long time, it felt wonderful to be spoiled by two people who showed her so much love. Hopefully when Raina went back outside later, she'd find Akis gone.

With Chloe and Theo touring the fjords in Norway

for the next two weeks, she hoped Akis wouldn't drop by until after the couple had returned from their honeymoon. After a few days' reunion in order to meet Theo, Raina would fly back to Monterey.

Akis took his time dressing. He knew instinctively Raina had said and done things to discourage him. Why? One of her stiletto-like jabs had worked its way under his skin and had taken hold.

How much did she know about him? Had she been insinuating that he wasn't good enough for her? Was it something Chloe had told her about his roots?

His own kind and background? Was he being paranoid?

Raina had rushed to explain what she'd meant when she'd told him he'd be better off spending time with his own kind and background instead of an American who'd be leaving soon. Even if he'd felt her sincerity and were willing to believe her explanation, the words had sunk deep in that vulnerable spot inside him and wouldn't go away.

He and Vasso were the brothers who'd climbed out of poverty without the benefit of formalized education. No college, no university degrees to hang on the wall. Akis wasn't well read or well traveled. He came out of that class of poor people who didn't have that kind of money, nor the sophistication. Whatever he and his brother had achieved had come through hard work.

No matter how much money he made now, it didn't give him the polish of someone like Theo who'd attended the finest university to become a banker like his father and grandfather before him. Akis could hold his own, but he was aware of certain inadequacies that would never change.

By now he got along fine in English, but being with her made him realize how much he didn't know about her language. He wasn't like Theo, who'd spent a year in England and spoke English with only a trace of accent.

Chloe could answer a lot of his questions, but she wasn't available and wouldn't be home for a fortnight. That presented a problem. Before long her former high school friend would be back in California. This woman worked in a lab? What kind? She could have meant anything.

His head was spinning with questions for which there were no answers. Not yet anyway.

When he left the cabana, he wasn't surprised to find Raina had disappeared on him. She couldn't get away from him fast enough. On his way into the house he ran into Nora. Though tempted to ask questions he knew she could answer, he didn't want to drag her into something that was strictly between him and Raina.

"The wedding was beautiful. Now you can relax for a little while. Thank you for lunch."

"You're always welcome here. You know that. Raina's ankle was hurting and she went to her room. She asked me to say goodbye to you."

"I appreciate that. She did seem a little under the weather."

He kissed her cheek and left the house for the limo where his driver was waiting. "Take me to the office."

During the ride he sat back trying to figure out what was going on with her. She'd told his employee at the store her name was Ginger Moss, but the concierge denied any knowledge of it. Why in the hell had she done that?

Once back at the Giannopoulos business complex off Syntagma Square, he walked through the empty offices to his private suite. It was a good thing it was Sunday. In this mood he'd probably bite the heads off the staff.

Vasso would be back tomorrow, but Akis needed to talk to him. His brother was busy overseeing a new store opening in Heraklion. If not for the wedding, Akis would have gone with him.

He rang Vasso's cell phone number. It was four o'clock in the afternoon. He should still be at the grand opening to make sure everything went smoothly. "Pick up, Vasso." But it went through to his voice mail. Akis left the message for him to call ASAP. While he waited to hear from him, he caught up on some paperwork.

When his brother hadn't phoned him by seventhirty, Akis couldn't take it anymore and decided to drive back to the Milonis estate. Before the night was out he would find out why she didn't want to let him into her life. Was it because she thought he was beneath her socially? Wasn't he good enough for her? If that was the case, then she needed to say that to his face.

Raina was different than any woman he'd ever met. He was deeply attracted not only to her looks but to her personality, as well. She could fight it all she wanted, but they had a connection. He just had to tear down that wall she'd put up. It was important to him.

Ione, the Milonises' housekeeper, met him at the

door and explained that Chloe's parents had gone out for dinner, but they'd be back shortly.

"What about their houseguest?"

"Thespinis Maywood is in the den watching television."

Maywood...

So she hadn't run away quite yet. Pleased by the information he said, "I'll just say hello to her, then. Thanks, Ione." Without hesitation he walked past her and found his way to the room in question. Having been over here many times, he knew where to go.

The door was already open so he walked in to find her lying on the couch in front of the TV with a couple of throw pillows elevating her leg. She was dressed in the same jeans and T-shirt she'd worn earlier.

"That was quite a disappearing act you performed earlier," he stated from the doorway.

Her eyes met his calmly, as if she'd known he would show up again and was amused by it. Challenged by her deliberate pretense of indifference to him he said, "What does one call you? Ginger when you're with strangers, but just Raina with close friends?"

A sigh escaped her lips. After turning off the TV with the remote, she sat up and moved her legs to the floor. "I take it you went to the store where I fell." She stared hard at him. "I must admit I'm shocked that the clerk would give you my name. That's privileged information."

"Agreed, but it was false information. In case you were worried, I happen to own that store."

"What?" Those incredible lavender eyes of hers had suddenly turned a darker hue. At last something had shaken her out of her almost condescending at-

titude. Did she really not know how he earned his living? Because of her relationship with the Milonis family, he found it hard, if not impossible, to believe.

"I read the incident report written up in the back room. You gave my employee the name of Ginger Moss, age twenty-six. What name will I find if I ask you to show me your passport? It will be important when I pay your hospital bill. They'll need more information to correct the discrepancy on the record."

"My insurance will reimburse you." She rested her hands on the top of her thighs. "I sometimes go by the nickname Ginger."

"Because of your hair?"

Her eyes fell away. "Yes."

"Even if I were to believe you, that's neither here nor there. I want to know why you felt you had to maintain your lie with me when you're a close friend of the woman who married my best friend."

The silence deafened him.

"I'll find out the truth before long. Why not be honest with me now and get it over with?" he pressed.

"Is that the only reason you came over here again?"

"What do *you* think?"

More color filled her cheeks. "I—I wish I hadn't told you where I'd fallen."

"Since I found you here at Chloe's, it's a moot point."

She stirred restlessly. "You want me to apologize?"

Akis had her rattled, otherwise she wouldn't have asked those questions. He rubbed his lower lip with his thumb. "You want the truth from me? Do you think that's fair when you've exempted yourself from being forthcoming with me?"

She moistened her lips, drawing his attention to them. All night he'd wondered what she'd taste like. "I meant no harm."

"If that's the case, then why the deception?"

"Look—" She sounded exasperated. Her cheeks grew more flushed as she got to her feet and fitted the crutches beneath her arms. "I haven't had a meaningful relationship with a man for a long time because it's the way I've wanted it."

He walked over to her. "But clearly there've been a lot of men who've wanted one with you. You think I'm just another man you can ignore without telling me why?" She looked away quickly, letting him know he'd guessed the truth. "A woman with your looks naturally attracts a lot of unwanted attention. It must be galling to realize that whatever you did to put me off, fate had a hand in my showing up at Chloe's home. Prove to me my interest in you isn't wanted and I'll leave now."

She looked the slightest bit anxious. "Akis—I just don't think it wise to get to know you better."

"Why? Because you haven't been honest with me and there *is* a man back home you're involved with?"

"No," she volunteered so fast and emphatically, he believed her. "There's no one. This conversation is ridiculous."

"It would be if I didn't know that you're interested in me, too. But for some reason, you're afraid and are using the excuse of having to fly to California to put me off. I want to know why."

"I'm not afraid of you. That's absurd."

"Last night you cheated me out of a dance. I don't

know about you, but I need to feel your mouth moving beneath mine or I might go a little mad with wanting."

"Please don't say things like that," she whispered.

"Because you know you want it, too?"

Her breathing sounded shallow. "Maybe I do, but I'm afraid."

"Of me?" He brushed his lips against hers.

"No. Not you. I'm afraid of my own feelings."

"Shall we find out if they're as strong as mine?" He wrapped her in his arms, crutches and all. His lips caught the small cry that escaped hers, giving him the opportunity to coax a deeper kiss from her. First one, then another, until she allowed him full access and the spark between them ignited into fire.

"Akis—" she cried softly before kissing him back with a hunger that thrilled him. He'd kissed other women, but nothing prepared him for the surge of desire driving both of them as they swayed together.

"I want you, Raina," he whispered against her creamy throat, "more than any woman I've ever wanted in my life." He came close to forgetting her sprained ankle until a moan sounded in her throat, prompting him to release her with reluctance and step away.

She steadied herself with the crutches for control. Those enticing lips looked swollen and thoroughly kissed. "That shouldn't have happened." The tremor in her voice was achingly real.

"But it did because we both wanted it." He took a quick breath. "I want to spend time with you, and from the way you kissed me, I know you want the same thing." His comment coincided with the arrival of Chloe's parents, who walked in on the two of them.

"Weren't you over here earlier?" Socus teased him in his native tongue. "No wonder our guest didn't mind that we had an important business dinner to attend."

Akis shook his head. "She didn't know I was coming over again."

"We're glad you're here, Akis," Nora said in English. "We don't want her to leave. Please do what you can to persuade her to stay until Chloe and Theo get back."

Socus chimed in. "If we had our way, we'd insist on your living with us for a long time, young woman."

Raina's eyes misted over. "You're such dear people and have been wonderful to me. But I'm afraid I have too many responsibilities at home to remain here for any length of time."

"Your ankle needs at least a week to heal before we let you get on a plane," Chloe's father declared. "But we can talk more about this in the morning. Good night, you two."

After they left the room Akis said, "Your ankle could use more rest. There's nothing I'd like better than to help you pass the time."

He sensed she knew she was defeated, but that didn't stop her from darting him a piercing glance. "What about your work?"

"My brother will fill in for me. We do it for each other when necessary." He stood there with his hands on his hips. "You look tired, so I'm going to leave. If I come over in the morning, will I still find you here?"

Her eyes flashed. "Perhaps the question should be, will you show up since you have a disparaging opinion of me?"

"You mean after you told me I should stick with my own kind and background?"

She stirred restlessly. "I can see you still haven't forgiven me for an innocent remark."

"There was nothing innocent about it. But the way you kissed me back a few minutes ago confirms my original gut instinct that you know something significant has happened to both of us. Good night, *thespinis*."

He left the house for the limo. On the way to his penthouse his cell phone rang. One look at the caller ID and he clicked on. "Vasso? How come it's taken you so long to get back to me?"

"Nice talking to you, too, bro."

His head reared. "Sorry."

"The phone died on me and I just got back to my hotel to recharge it. What's wrong? You don't sound like yourself."

"That's because I'm not."

"The opening went fine."

Akis was in such a state he'd forgotten to ask. "Sorry. My mind is on something else."

"Was there a problem at the wedding? I saw you on the evening news helping a beautiful woman on crutches into the limo."

So Vasso saw it. "She's the reason I called. When will you be back?"

His brother laughed. "I'll fly in around 7:00 a.m. and should be at the office by nine."

"If you're that late, I'm afraid I won't be there."

"That sounded cryptic. Why?"

"Something happened at the reception."

"You sound odd. What is it?"

"I've...met someone."

"I'm not even going to try to figure that one out. Just tell me what has you so damned upset."

"Believe it or not, a woman has come into my life."

"There've been several women in your life over the years. Tell me something I don't know. Are we talking about the woman on crutches?"

"Yes. This one is different." Both brothers had led a bachelor life for so long, not even Akis believed what had happened to him since he'd seen Raina on the street.

"Are you saying what I think you're saying?"

"Yes."

"You're serious."

"Yes."

Vasso exhaled sharply. "She feels the same way?"

His teeth snapped together. "After the way she kissed me back tonight, I'd stake my life on it."

"But you only met her last evening."

"I know. She looks like Aphrodite with lavender eyes."

"I'll admit she was a stunner." Laughter burst out of Vasso. "But you sound like you still need to sleep off the champagne."

"I swear I only had a sip."

"Come on, Akis. Quit the teasing."

"I'm not." For the first time in his life Akis was swimming in uncharted waters where a woman was concerned.

A long silence ensued. "How old is she?"

"Twenty-six."

"From Athens?"

"No. California."

"She's an American?"

"Yes. On the day of the wedding rehearsal, we almost bumped into each other on the sidewalk after I left Theo at the bank. I couldn't get her out of my head. On the night of the reception, to my surprise she was sitting at a table in the back of the ballroom.

"When I asked her to dance, she didn't understand because she said she didn't speak Greek. But she couldn't dance anyway because she was on crutches. I helped her out to the limo and took her to her hotel."

"Just like that you spent the night with her? You've never done anything like that before. Wasn't that awfully fast?"

"I didn't stay with her and you don't know all that happened. When I couldn't find her at the hotel today and learned she'd checked out, I checked with Theo's family. They hadn't heard of her so I decided to go over to Chloe's for help. When I went walked in, to my shock I found her relaxing at the side of the pool."

"She was at Chloe's?"

"Yes. It seems Chloe spent a school year with her back in high school on one of those exchange programs to learn English."

"How come you've never heard of her?"

"I once remember Theo telling me that Chloe had an American friend she lived with in high school, but I never made the connection."

"What's her name?"

"Raina Maywood. But when she fell and sprained her ankle in our number four store, she gave Galen a different name before going to the ER. I had a devil of a time tracking her down."

"Wait, wait—start over again. You're not making sense."

"Nothing has made sense since we first saw each other."

"Akis? Are you still with me?"

"Yes."

"What's your gut telling you?"

"I don't know," he confessed.

"Maybe she wanted to meet you. It wouldn't be hard to connect the dots. After all, she knows the circles Chloe's family runs in. Maybe when Chloe invited her to come to the wedding, she told her about Theo's best man and promised to introduce you."

"There's a flaw in that thinking, Vasso, because it didn't happen that way. By sheer chance I asked her to dance. Otherwise we would never have met. After I took her to her hotel, she made it close to impossible for me to find her."

"But she *did* end up at Chloe's, so it's my guess she hoped you'd show up there at some point. Even if that part of the evening wasn't planned, what if all along her agenda has been to come to the wedding and use Chloe's parents to meet you? Is that what you're afraid of? That she's after your money?"

"Hell if I know."

"It stands to reason Chloe would have told her all about Theo's best man. There's no sin in it, but the way things are moving so fast, don't you think you need to take a step back until more time passes? Then you can see what's real and what isn't. Think about it."

Akis *was* thinking. His big brother had touched on one of Akis's deepest fears. The possibility that somehow she'd engineered their meeting like other women in the past had done tore him up inside. He wanted to believe that everything about their meeting and the unfolding of events had been entirely spontaneous.

But if Chloe had discussed him with Raina, then her comment about his background made a lot of sense. He and Vasso were the brothers who'd climbed out of poverty to make their way in the world. They lacked the essentials that other well-bred people took for granted—like monetary help from family, school scholarships, exposure to the world.

They'd been marked from birth as the brothers who'd come out of that class of poor people who would be lucky to survive. Whatever he and Vasso had achieved had come through sheer hard work.

Akis could hold his own, but he was aware of certain inadequacies that would never change.

If in the past the situation had warranted it, he and Vasso had always given each other good advice. But this one time he didn't want to hear it even though he was the one who'd called his brother.

Akis didn't want to think Raina might be like Althea who was looking for a husband who could keep her in the style of Chloe's parents.

"Isn't that why you phoned me, because you're worried?" his brother prodded. "She's seen the kind of wealth Chloe comes from. You remember how crazy Sofia and I were over each other when we lived on the island without a drachma to our name?"

"How could I forget?"

"But she turned down my wedding proposal because she said she could do better. It wasn't until our business started to flourish that she started chasing me again and wouldn't leave me alone. At that point I wasn't interested in her anymore."

"I remember everything," Akis's voice grated. Both he and Vasso had been through the painful experience of being used. It had made them wary of stronger attachments. A few years ago when they'd set up two charities to honor their parents, one of the women they'd hired as a secretary to deal with the paperwork had made a play for Vasso. But it turned out she wanted marriage rather than the job.

Akis had run into a similar situation with an attractive woman they'd hired to run one of their stores. She'd called Akis one evening claiming there was an emergency. When he showed up at the store, it turned out the emergency was a ploy to get him alone.

Most women they met were introduced to them by mutual friends. After a few dates it was clear they had marriage and money on their minds. But the essential bonding of two minds and hearts of the kind he saw in Theo and Chloe's relationship always seemed to be missing.

"Sorry to be such a downer, but Chloe's friend did lie about her name, which I find strange. When are you going to see her again?"

"I told her I'd be over tomorrow."

"Did she tell you *not* to come?"

He grimaced. "No." But earlier she'd told him he'd be better off to find a woman of his own kind and background because she was leaving Greece. She'd been keeping up that mantra to hide what was really wrong.

"Okay. As I see it, maybe she's taking advantage of

her friendship with Chloe. Then again, maybe there is no agenda here. All I can say is, slow down."

Akis took a deep breath, more confused than ever over her mixed signals. Why would she have flown all the way to Greece, yet she hadn't attended the wedding of her good friend at the church? Bombarded by a series of conflicting emotions, he felt a negative burst of adrenaline, not knowing what to believe.

"I don't want to think about it anymore tonight. Thanks for listening. I'll see you in the morning." He clicked off.

Without that kiss he might have decided it wasn't worth it to pursue her further, except that he didn't really believe that. It had taken all his willpower not to chase around the corner after her with some excuse to detain her. But this evening he hadn't been thinking clearly. The need to feel her in his arms outweighed every other thought. *It still did...*

"Kyrie?" his driver called to him. "We've arrived."

So they had. Akis thanked him and climbed out of the limo. On his way up to the penthouse, he went over the conversation with his brother. Vasso had given him one piece of advice he would follow from here on out.

Slow down.

CHAPTER THREE

BY THE TIME Raina had unwrapped her ankle to shower on Monday morning, she had to admit it felt a lot better. Resting it had really helped because there was little swelling now. It didn't need to be rewrapped as long as she walked with crutches and was careful.

After dressing in a blouse and jeans, she brushed her hair and put on her pink lipstick. Every time she thought about Akis Giannopoulos, she got a fluttery feeling in her chest, the kind there was no remedy for.

Her lips still throbbed from the passion his mouth had aroused. For a little while she'd been swept away to a place she'd never been before. After having no personal life for so long, she supposed something like this had been inevitable. Maybe it was good this hormone rush had happened here in Greece. Before long she'd be leaving, so whatever it was she felt for this man, their relationship would be short-lived.

Since she couldn't do any sightseeing this trip, her only option was to stay at Chloe's. Such inactivity for a man like Akis would wear thin. When he found himself bored, he'd find a plausible reason to leave.

Breakfast came and went. She lounged by the pool

and read a book she'd brought. Every time Nora or a maid came out to see if she wanted anything, she expected Akis to follow. By lunchtime she decided he wasn't coming.

After kissing her as payback for the way she'd treated him last night, he'd left the house. It wouldn't surprise her if he'd had no intention of coming back today. Raina ought to be relieved. Once she'd eaten lunch with Nora, there was still no sign of him.

Hating to admit to herself she was disappointed he hadn't come, she went to her bedroom to do some business on the phone with her staff running the estate in California. No sooner had she gotten off the phone than the maid knocked on her door. "Kyrie Giannopoulos is waiting for you on the patio."

At the news her heart jumped, a terrible sign that he mattered to her much more than she wanted him to. "I'll be right there." She refreshed her lipstick before using her crutches to make it out to the pool area where Akis was waiting for her.

His intense black gaze swept over her while he stood beneath the awning in an open-necked tan sport shirt and jeans. His clothes covered a well-defined chest and rock-hard legs. Whether he wore a tux, a bathing suit or casual clothes, her legs turned to mush just looking at him.

"I would have been here sooner, but my business meeting this morning took longer than I'd supposed. The housekeeper told me you've already had lunch. Have you ever been to Athens?"

"I came here once with my grandparents when I was young, but remember very little."

"What happened to your parents?"

"They were killed in a light plane crash when I was twelve."

"How awful for you."

"I could hardly believe it when it happened. I suffered for years. We had such a wonderful life together. They were my best friends."

"I'm sorry," he whispered.

"So am I, but I was very blessed to have marvelous grandparents who did everything for me."

"Thank heaven for that." He eyed her thoughtfully. "Are you up to some sightseeing then?"

Her breath caught. "Much as I'd love to tour Athens, I can't. You didn't need to come over. A phone call would have sufficed."

"You can see Athens from my penthouse terrace." She blinked. "The city will be at your feet. I have a powerful telescope that will enable you to see its famous sights up close from the comfort of a chair and ottoman for your leg."

"Go with him, Raina," Chloe's mother urged, having just walked out on the patio. "Socus and I went up there one night. You can see everything in the most wonderful detail. The Acropolis at twilight is like a miracle."

Raina couldn't very well turn him down with an endorsement like that from Nora. "You've sold me. I'll just go back to the room for my purse." Reaching for her crutches, she hurried away with a pounding heart. Retrieving her purse, she headed for the front door, but Akis was there first to open it for her.

"Thank you," she whispered, so aware of his presence it was hard to think. Once he'd helped her inside the limo out in front, he sat across from her. "I know you want to rest your leg so I've told the driver to take us straight to the Giannopoulos complex."

"We could have stayed at Chloe's and played cards. It would have saved you all this trouble."

The compelling male mouth that had kissed her so thoroughly last night broke into a smile, turning her heart over. "Some trouble is worth it."

She looked out the window without seeing anything. Going to his penthouse wasn't a good idea, but her hectic emotions had taken over her common sense. Raina wanted to be with him. She would only stay awhile before she asked him to take her back to Chloe's.

The driver turned into a private alley and stopped at the rear of the office building. Akis helped her out and drew a remote from his pocket that opened a door to a private elevator. In less than a minute they'd shot to the roof and the door opened again.

Adjusting her crutches, Raina followed him into his glassed in, air-conditioned penthouse. No woman's touch here, no curtains, no frills or knickknacks. Only chrome and earth tones. It was a man's domicile through and through, yet she saw nothing of his dynamic personality reflected.

The best man who'd tracked her down despite all odds didn't seem to fit in these unimaginative surroundings. But she could understand his coming home to this at night. Glorious Athens lay below them from every angle.

"Come out to the terrace. I have everything set up for you."

The telescope beckoned beneath the overhang. Working her crutches, she stepped out in the warm air and flashed him a glance. "Were you an eagle in another life? I like your eyrie very much."

"As far as I know, this is the only life I've been born to, but I was hatched in a very different place as you well know."

She frowned. No, she didn't know. Akis was trying to rile her. In retaliation she refused to rise to the bait.

He took her crutches so she could sit on the leather chair and prop her leg on the ottoman. After putting the crutches aside, he placed the telescope so she could look through it while she sat there. "I've set it on the Acropolis and the Parthenon."

"The cradle of Western civilization," she murmured. "This is the perfect spot to begin my tour. Thank you." One look and she couldn't believe it. "Oh, Akis—I feel like I'm right there. How fabulous! A picture doesn't do it justice. Do you mind if I move this around a little? There's so much to see, I could look through it for hours."

"That's why I brought you here. Enjoy any view you want. Since it's heating up outside, I'll get us some lemonade."

She was glad he'd left. The brief intimacy they'd shared last night hadn't lasted long enough. The fire between them had been building since he'd shown up at Chloe's house. But he was only gone for a few minutes and returned with a drink for both of them. The second he came back out, her pulse raced.

He lounged against the edge of a wrought-iron patio table and played tour director for the next two hours. Akis was a fount of information, responding to all her questions.

No one watching them would know how disturbed

she was to be this close to such a man who on the surface appeared so pleasant. Underneath his urbane facade Raina knew he was just biding his time until she tired of sightseeing and he had her full attention.

When she'd eventually run out of questions, she sat back with a sigh. "Thanks to you, I feel like I've walked all over this city without missing anything important. I'll remember your kindness when I watch the city recede from my plane window."

Akis moved the telescope out of reach, then flicked her a probing glance. "Forget about returning to California. You've only seen a portion of Athens. What you haven't seen is what I consider to be the best part of Greece. I'm prepared to show it to you. I understand Chloe's parents have extended you an open invitation to stay for a while."

She shook her head. "Why would you want to do anything for me when it's obvious you have issues with me?"

"Maybe because you're different from the other women I've met and I'm intrigued."

"That's not the answer and you know it."

One black brow lifted. "You can't deny the chemistry between us. I'm still breathless from the explosion when we got in each other's arms last night."

Raina's hands gripped the arms of the chair. "So am I."

"After such honesty, you still want to run from me?" he said in a husky tone.

"Physical attraction gets in the way of common sense."

He folded his arms. "What is your common sense telling you?"

"I think your questions about me have fueled your interest."

"Is that wrong?"

"Not wrong, just unsettling. I know you've been upset with me since the night of the reception when I wouldn't tell you my name and gave your employee a different name. I already told you the reason why."

"Just not all of it," he challenged in that maddening way, causing her blood pressure to soar.

"What's the matter with you?" she cried softly. "Earlier today you accused me of knowing something about your origins, when in truth I know next to nothing about you except that you were the best man!" Her voice shook with emotion. "If there's some sinister secret you're anxious to hide, I promise you I don't know what it is."

His eyes narrowed on her features. "That's difficult for me to believe when you've been Chloe's best friend for years."

She nodded. "We became best friends and have seen and stayed in touch with each other over the years. I knew she was crazy about Theo months ago, but I only heard she was getting married a month ago. She was so full of excitement over the wedding plans, I didn't even know the last name of her fiancé's best man, let alone any details about you. If that offends your male pride, I'm sorry."

He shifted his weight. "I'm afraid it's you *I've* offended without realizing it. Shall we call a truce and start over? Nora wants us to come back and eat dinner with them by the pool. Afterward they're going to show us the wedding video."

"You can tell they're missing Chloe," she said.

"That's what happens when there's an only child."

Raina knew all about that and agreed with him. "Their family is very close. Just being with them this little bit makes me surprised they allowed her to leave home for the school year."

"If she hadn't been happy with you, I'm sure she wouldn't have stayed." While she felt his deep voice resonate, his gaze traveled over her. "Surely you can understand how much they want to pay you back for the way your family made her feel so welcome. If you want my opinion, I think you'll hurt their feelings if you fly to the States too soon, but it's your call."

Privately Raina feared the same thing. "I'm sure you're right. If I stay until Chloe and Theo get back, it'll give me a chance to rest my leg a little more." *More days to spend with Akis.*

Wasn't that the underlying factor in her decision just now, even though her heart was warning her to run from him as fast as she could? To love this man meant opening herself up to pain from which she might never recover.

"They'll be happy to hear it. Are you ready to go back?"

No, her heart cried, but her lips said "Yes."

After she finished her drink, he helped her with the crutches. Their hands brushed, sending darts of sensation running up her arms. He didn't try to take advantage, but it didn't matter. Every look or touch from him sensitized her body. As they left the penthouse for the drive back to the Milonis estate, she fought to ignore her awareness of him.

Later, after a delicious dinner, Akis took the crutches from Raina while she settled on the couch

in the den. Nora sat next to her while Socus started
the video. Akis turned off the light and sat in one of
the upholstered chairs to watch. Cries of excitement,
happiness and laughter from Chloe's parents punctu-
ated the scene of the wedding day unfolding before
their eyes.

The videographer had captured everything from
the moment Chloe left the house for the church. Parts
of the ceremony in the church left Raina in happy
tears for her dear friend. She just knew they'd have a
wonderful life together.

Other parts of the film covered the reception, including the dancing. The camera panned from the
wedding couple to the best man dancing with the maid
of honor. "You and Althea make a beautiful couple,"
Socus exclaimed.

Raina concurred. He was so handsome it hurt, but
the inscrutable expression on his face was distinctly
different from the adoring look on Althea's. Suddenly
the camera focused on the guests. Raina saw herself
at the table. Shock!

But there were more shocks when it caught Akis
accompanying her from the ballroom. She'd had no
idea they were being filmed.

Nora laughed. "Oh, Akis… Now I understand why
you didn't spend the rest of the evening with poor
Althea. You remind me of the prince at the ball who
avoided the stepsisters because he wanted to know the
name of the mystery woman on crutches and ended up
running after her." Socus's laughter followed.

In that instant Raina's gaze fused with a pair of jet
black eyes glinting in satisfaction over Nora's observation. Her body broke out in guilty heat.

"Wasn't I lucky that I found Cinderella at your house."

"We're very happy you did." Nora beamed.

"It saved me from prowling the countryside for the maiden with the crutches."

Chloe's mother chuckled. "Wait till Chloe and Theo watch this. They're going to love it."

"They will," Raina agreed with her before lowering her blond head. Chloe would appreciate the irony of the camera finding her friend from California in the crowd despite every effort Raina had made to stay away from the camcorders of the paparazzi.

While she sat there wishing she could escape to her bedroom, Akis got to his feet and turned on the light. "Thank you for dinner and an entertaining evening. Now I know Raina needs to rest her leg, so I'm going to leave."

"So soon?" Nora questioned.

"I'm afraid so. But I'll be by in the morning at nine. Earlier I told Raina I'd like to show her another part of Greece I know she'll enjoy while she's still recovering." His dark eyes probed hers. "But maybe you've decided you'd rather stay here."

He'd deliberately put her on the spot. Everyone was waiting for her answer. Not wanting to seem ungracious she said, "No. I'll be ready. Thank you."

"Good."

The pilot landed the helicopter on the pad of the Milonis estate. Akis could see Raina's gleaming blond hair as she stood on her crutches. It wasn't until you got closer that you noticed that hint of red in the strands. His gaze fell over her curvaceous figure that did wonders for the summery denims and short-sleeved small-print blouse she was wearing.

He opened the doors of the Giannopoulos company's recently purchased five-seater copter. "Let me take your crutches and handbag." Once she'd handed them to him, he put them aside, then picked up her gorgeous body by the waist. The instant there was contact, her warmth and fragrance enveloped him.

Without letting go of her, he helped her into the seat next to the window behind the pilot. That way he could keep an eye on her from the copilot's seat. "Are you all right?" Their mouths were only inches apart.

"Y-yes," came her unsteady voice before she looked away. A nerve jumped madly at the base of her creamy throat. The touch of skin against skin had affected her, too.

"Have you ever flown in a helicopter before?"

She nodded.

After laying the crutches on the floor, he put her purse in the storage unit, and then looked down at her.

"Are you all strapped in?"

"Yes. I'm fine. I just want to know where we're going."

"Are you afraid I'm planning to carry you off, never to be seen again?"

A secret smile appeared. "After the fierce look on your face as you headed toward my table at the hotel, the thought did occur to me."

Charmed despite his questions about what she was still hiding from him he said, "I'll give you a clue. We're headed for the Ionian Sea. Once we reach the water, I'll give you a blow-by-blow account using the microphone. But there's one more thing I have to do before takeoff."

Akis pulled out several pillows from a locker and hunkered down to elevate her leg. She wore sandals. His hands slid beneath her calf and heel to adjust the fit. He ran a finger over her ankle, pleased to notice she trembled. "There's no trace of swelling I can see," he said, eyeing her. "We'll make sure things stay that way today."

The urge to kiss her was overwhelming, but he restrained himself. Her thank-you followed him to his seat. He gave the pilot a nod, put on his sunglasses and strapped himself in. Before long Athens receded and they were arcing their way in a northwesterly direction. Over the mic he gave her a geography lesson and responded to her questions.

When they reached the island of Corfu surrounded by brilliant blue water, he had the pilot swing lower so she could take in the fascinating sight of whitewashed houses. Here and there he pointed out a Byzantine church and the remains of several Venetian fortresses.

He shot Raina a speaking glance. "I brought you here first. This is where Poseidon fell in love with Korkyra, the Naiad nymph."

"Ah. Poseidon…" Her lips curved upward. "Did Korkyra reciprocate his feelings?"

"According to legend she adored him and they had a baby named Phaiax. Today the islanders have the nickname Phaeacians. Another island in this group is fourteen miles south of here. We'll head there now."

"What is it called?"

"Paxos. When you see it, you'll understand why it's constantly photographed."

In a few minutes he heard a cry. "What a darling island!" That wasn't the word he would have chosen, but he was pleased by her response. "What kind of vegetation is that?"

"Olive groves. Some of the gnarled trees are ancient. The pilot will fly us over the western side and you'll see steep, chalky white cliffs. If you look closely, you'll spot its many caves along the coast line. When you go into them on a launch, they glow blue."

"How beautiful!"

"We have Poseidon to thank for its creation. He wanted to get away from stress on the big island of Corfu, so he used his trident to create this hideaway for him and his wife."

"Or maybe to hide his wife from Korkyra? What are you saying? That the stress of having a mistress and keeping his wife happy at the same time was too much, even for a god?" Like a discordant note, he heard brittle laughter come out of her. "That's hilarious!"

There was a story behind her hollow reaction, but now was not the time to explore it. "The Greek myths are meant to be entertaining. If you'll notice, there's another tinier island just beyond this one called Anti Paxos. When Poseidon wanted to be strictly alone, he came here to swim in the clear green water you can see below."

"I imagine that leading a double life would have worn him out."

Laughter burst from Akis.

"Wasn't *he* lucky to be a god and pick the most divine area in his immortal world to plan his next conquest." The pilot circled Anti Paxos for a closer look. "What a heavenly spot."

It was. Akis's favorite place on earth. He wanted to hide Raina away here, away from the world where the two of them could be together and make love for the rest of time.

Unfortunately they'd come to the end of the tour. He checked his watch. "We're going to head back to Athens via a little different route. We'll be crossing over a portion of Albania you should find fascinating. If you're thirsty or hungry, there's bottled water and snacks in the seat pouch in front of you."

"Um. Don't mind if I do. Would you or the pilot like something?"

That was thoughtful of her. "We're fine."

In a minute she said, "These almonds are the best I've ever tasted!"

"They're grown on these islands." Akis was addicted to them.

"How would it be to live right down there in paradise! If I did, I'm sure I'd become an addict."

Everything she said and did entrenched her deeper in his heart. She had a sweetness and vulnerability that made him want to protect her. Raina had become his addiction and already he couldn't imagine life without her. That's when he realized he was in serious trouble, but for once in his life he didn't care.

"If you'll extend your time in Greece, I can arrange for you to stay on Anti Paxos. Think about it and let me know after we get back to Chloe's house."

"Even if I could take time off from work, what about yours? Can you afford to be gone any longer?"

His heart leaped. So she *was* interested...

"My brother will cover for me."

"You're lucky to have him." She sounded sincere. "Is there more family?"

"No. Just Vasso."

"Is he younger? Older?"

The questions were coming at last. "Older by eleven months."

"You were almost twins!"

"Almost."

"Do you resemble each other?"

He turned to his pilot. "What do you think?" he asked in Greek. "Do Vasso and I look alike?"

The other man grinned before giving him an answer.

Akis translated. "He said, superficially."

"Is Vasso married?"

Why did she want to know that? "Not yet."

"Then maybe you should arrange for him to meet Chloe's bridesmaid."

His black brows furrowed. "I'm afraid my brother prefers to be the one in pursuit. What makes you so concerned for Althea?"

"Even Nora noticed how crestfallen she looked when you stopped dancing with her."

"According to Theo, she has lots of boyfriends."

"But she wanted *you*," Raina came back.

"Why do you say that?"

"I may have been farther away, but I could see her disappointment. Think how much she would have enjoyed a day like this with you."

"If you're trying to make me feel guilty, it isn't working."

She flashed him a quick smile. "Not at all. I was just thinking how fortunate I've been to be given a fantastic personal tour narrated by you. It's a real thrill."

"I'm glad you're enjoying it. But it's not over yet. We'll be flying over a portion of the Pindus National Park covered in black pines. The view from this altitude is extraordinary." While she studied the landscape, he'd feast his eyes on her.

For the next hour she appeared captivated by the unfolding scenery. Every now and again he heard a little gasp of awe as they dipped lower to view a new sight. Whatever his suspicions might have been in the beginning, her barrage of questions made him think her reactions to the beauty below them couldn't be faked.

Once they'd landed on the pad of the Milonis estate, he helped Raina down. Their bodies brushed, causing a tiny gasp to escape her lips. He knew exactly how she felt and didn't know how long he could stand it before he kissed her again.

Akis watched her disappear before he used the guest bathroom and phoned his driver to come to the house. He had plans for him and Raina later. After washing his hands, he walked out to the patio to phone his brother. No doubt he was still at the office. Akis needed to give him a heads-up that he wouldn't be coming in to work for a few days. He was taking a brief vacation in order to spend time with Raina.

To his frustration, his call went to Vasso's voice mail. Once again he had to ask him to call him back ASAP. Then he spoke to his private secretary to know if there were any situations he needed to hear about. But he was assured everything was fine. Vasso had been there until two o'clock, then he'd left.

After hanging up, he walked to the cabana and changed into a swimming suit. Akis needed a workout after sitting so long. Much as he wanted Raina to join him in the pool, he knew she couldn't. But on that score he was wrong. When he'd finished his laps and started to get out, he saw her at the shallow end, floating on her back. The crutches had been left at the side of the pool.

By rotating her arms, she was able to move around without hurting her ankle. He swam over to her, noticing her blond hair looked darker now that it was wet and swept back. The classic features of her oval face revealed her pure beauty. Those eyes shimmered like amethysts. *Incredible*.

"I'm glad you came out here."

"After today's tour, I thought I'd like to see what it was like to swim with Poseidon, god of the sea."

He sucked in his breath. "You're not afraid I might make you my next conquest?"

She kept on moving. "Do you think you can?"

He kept up with her. "After our kiss the other night, I think you know the answer to that."

"What will your wife say?"

"She doesn't rule my life."

"That would be the worst fate for you, wouldn't it? To be ruled by your passion for one woman? To be her slave forever?"

"Not if she's the right woman."

"How will you know when you've found her?" The pulse throbbing violently in the vulnerable spot of her throat betrayed her.

"I think I have. Stay in Greece until I can unveil all of the real you."

"The real me?"

"Yes. There's more to you than you want to let on."

A beguiling smile broke the corners of her mouth. "And what about you, swimming into my life? Who are you, really?"

He swam closer. "Who would you like me to be?" The blood pounded in his ears.

"Just yourself."

Raina...

She'd reached for the side of the pool and clung to it. "Akis," she said softly. "I'm frightened because my feelings for you are already too strong."

"Strong enough to meet me halfway and kiss me again?"

"I want to." Her voice throbbed. "But I'm worried I'll be enslaved by you."

Akis took a deep breath and moved through the water next to her. "Don't you know you're the one who has enslaved me? I need you, Raina."

Her eyes looked glazed. "You're not the only one," she confessed.

He clasped her to him and covered her trembling mouth with his own. This time he'd jumped right into the fire, heedless of the flames licking through his body.

Her curves melted against him as if she were made for him. He kissed her with growing abandon until he felt her hungry response. It wasn't like anything he'd ever known and he was afraid he'd never get enough.

"Raina," he whispered in a thick tone. "Do you have any idea how beautiful you are? How much I want you?"

She moaned her answer, too swallowed up in their

need for each other to talk. This was what Akis had been waiting for all his life, this feeling of oneness and ecstasy.

"Anyone for dinner?" came the sudden godlike voice of thunder.

Raina made a sound in her throat and tore her lips from his. "Socus has seen us."

"He has to know what's going on," Akis whispered against the side of her neck. "You're a grown woman."

"Yes, but I'm also a guest in their home. What must he think when we only met a few days ago?"

"That we're incredibly lucky and are enjoying ourselves."

She lifted anxious eyes to him. "Way too much." To his regret she eased away from him in her orange bikini to reach the steps of the pool. After grabbing her towel and crutches, she disappeared inside the house.

Akis threw his dark head back and drank in gulps of air. No doubt Chloe's father had seen the two of them locked together while the water sizzled around them.

Naturally Raina would bring out a protective instinct in the older man. She was their honored guest. Akis swam to the deep end. After levering himself over the edge, he headed for the cabana to shower and get dressed.

As he was pulling on his crew neck, his cell rang. He drew it from his pant pocket to look at the caller ID and clicked on. "Vasso? Did you get my message?"

"Yes, but we've got an electrical problem at the number ten store I've got to see about. I'm leaving the penthouse to take care of it now. Before you go away on vacation, I've left some papers for you to look at in the den."

"About that new property we were thinking about on Crete?"

"No. It's something else. Talk to you later." He hung up before Akis could question him further.

Something else? What exactly did that mean? Curious over it, Akis left the cabana in a slightly different mood than before and walked around the pool to the covered portion of the patio. Everyone was seated at the table waiting for him. Raina looked a golden vision wearing a pale yellow beach robe over her beautiful body.

"Ah, there you are," Nora exclaimed. "Now we can eat."

"I'm sorry to keep you waiting. My brother called me about a business problem. After dinner, I'll have to get back to the penthouse to deal with it." His gaze darted to Raina whose eyes were asking questions not even he could answer yet. "I'll phone you later about our plans for tomorrow." The night he'd planned with her would have to wait.

Raina watched Akis's tall, powerful body disappear from the patio in a few swift strides. Disappointment swept over her. She despised her weakness for remaining silent when he announced in front of Chloe's parents he'd call her later about plans for the next day. To them the silence on her part meant agreement and she'd be staying in Greece longer.

After the two of them had come close to kissing each other senseless out in the pool, he would naturally assume she couldn't wait to be with him again.

Socus had seen them kissing and had been left in no doubt what was going on between them.

That kiss had been her fault for taunting Akis. In some part of her psyche she'd wanted him to pull her into his arms. Otherwise she wouldn't have gotten into the pool. She knew she'd come to the edge of a cliff like the kind they'd flown over earlier in the day. One more false step and she'd fall so deep and hard for this man, she'd never recover. Raina couldn't forget a certain conversation with him.

What will your wife say?

She doesn't rule my life.

That would be the worst fate for you, wouldn't it? To be ruled by your passion for one woman? To be her slave forever?

Not if she's the right woman.

Raina didn't believe there was a right woman for a man as exciting and virile as Akis. In time he would tire of his latest lover and be caught by another woman who appealed to him. In an instant he'd go in pursuit.

The bitter taste of Byron's betrayal still lingered. It was time to end this madness with Akis. But she'd promised Chloe's parents she'd wait to leave Greece until after Chloe and Theo got home from their honeymoon.

Once dinner was over, she went to her room. Though it was early, she took a shower and got ready for bed. She knew Akis would phone her.

If you know what's good for you, don't get in any deeper with him, Raina.

CHAPTER FOUR

AKIS LET HIMSELF in the penthouse and walked back to the den. He saw some papers placed on the table next to the computer. They looked like printouts. His brother had handwritten him a note he'd left on top of the keyboard. Akis sat down in the swivel chair and started to read.

Don't get mad at me for what I've done. You're so damn honorable, I knew you'd let your questions about Raina Maywood eat you alive. So I decided to put you out of your misery and play PI so she can't accuse you of stalking her. For what it's worth, you're going to bless me for what I've done.

Start with the printout of the article from a California newspaper, then work through the rest. Any worry you've been carrying around about her intentions has flown out the window. There's so much stuff about her, it'll blow your mind.

When you told me her last name was Maywood and that she was a friend of Chloe's from California, it got me thinking about the two he-

licopters we purchased. No wonder Chloe's parents allowed her to stay with Raina, the granddaughter of a man who was one of the pillars of the American economy.

Dazed at this point, Akis picked up the top sheet dated nine months ago.

An American icon of aerospace technology is dead at ninety-two. Joseph Maywood died at his estate in Carmel-by-the-Sea after a long bout of stomach cancer. At his side was his beautiful granddaughter, Laraine Maywood, twenty-six, now heiress to the massive multibillion-dollar Maywood fortune. His wife, Ginger Moss, daughter of famous California seascape artist Edwin Moss, passed away from heart failure several years earlier.

Kaching, kaching, kaching.

Pieces of the puzzle were falling into place faster than Akis could absorb them. Nonplussed, he sat staring at the ceiling. She was an *heiress…*

Adrenaline gushed through his veins.

The X Jet Explorer, built by Pacificopter Inc., was a company owned by the Maywood Corporation in California, USA. Suddenly pure revelation flowed through him. Akis jumped to his feet, incredulous. She was *that* Maywood.

Absolutely stunned, he reached for the next printout dated four years back.

Scandal rocks world-renowned Carmel-by-

*the Sea, a European-style California village
nestled above a picturesque white-sand beach
and home to beautiful heiress-apparent Laraine Maywood Wallace of the Maywood Corporation.*

Wallace? He swallowed hard. She'd been married.
He looked back at the paper and kept reading.

*Reputed to be a lookalike for the famous
French actress and beauty Catherine Deneuve
in her youth, she has divorced husband Byron
Wallace, the writer and biographer involved
in a sensational, messy affair with Hollywood
would-be starlet Isabel Granger who was also
involved with her director boyfriend.*

Akis groaned.
Only now could he understand Raina's brittle
laughter during an earlier conversation. *What are you
saying? That the stress of having a mistress and keeping his wife happy at the same time was too much,
even for a god?* He could feel his gut twisting.
Vasso had left a postscript on his note.

*You've got a green light, bro. No more worry.
She's interested in you, not your money.*

He scanned the other sheets, astonished over the
two charities she'd started in California in honor of
her grandparents, including all she'd accomplished as
CEO of the Maywood megacorporation.
These revelations had turned him inside out. It

shamed him that he'd been so hard on her in his own mind when she'd suffered such pain in her life. The loss of her parents and grandparents...the betrayal by a man who had never deserved her...

"I hoped I'd find you here. How come you don't seem happier?"

Akis had been so absorbed and troubled, he hadn't heard his brother enter the den. He turned in his direction. "I didn't think you'd be back this soon."

"There was a power-grid failure, but it was soon repaired. I'm going to ask you again. What's wrong?"

He rubbed the back of his neck. "I feel like I've trespassed over her soul."

Vasso shook his head. "What are you talking about?"

"This information changes everything." It had been a humbling lesson that had left him shaken.

"Of course it does, but your reaction doesn't make sense."

"I can't explain right now." He squeezed Vasso's shoulder. "You're the best. I'll get back to you."

He left the printouts on the desk and hurried out of the penthouse, calling for his limo. Before he left for Chloe's house, he phoned Raina. She picked up on the third ring.

"Akis? I'm glad you phoned. We were all worried. Is everything okay?"

How strange what a piece of news could do to change everything. She was no longer a mystery in his eyes and the tone in her voice reflected genuine anxiety. The fact that he'd doubted her and had assumed she had an agenda, shamed him. It caused him to wonder how many women he'd falsely labeled when they were as innocent as Raina.

"That all depends on you." He gripped the phone tighter.

"So…there was no emergency with your business, or—or your brother?" Her voice sounded shaky.

Touched by her concern he said, "No. The problem was a power-grid failure that was soon put to right." This emergency was one closer to home. One so serious, he could hardly breathe. "I'm on my way over to talk to you."

"No, Akis. I've gone to bed."

"Then I'll see you tomorrow. We'll do whatever we feel like. I promise not to touch you unless you want me to. I've never met a woman remotely like you. I want to get to know you better, Raina. It would be worth everything to me."

Silence met his question.

"I'm not a god. As you found out in the pool, I'm a mortal with flaws trying to make it through this life. By a stroke of fate you were at the reception when I needed a woman who would dance with me. I haven't been the same since you lifted those violet eyes to me and told me you didn't speak Greek."

"I lied," she murmured. "I know about ten words."

His eyes closed tightly. "If you want nothing more to do with me, then say no in Greek and I'll leave you alone." It would serve him right. He didn't deserve her attention. He held the phone so tightly while he waited, it was amazing it didn't break.

"Neh," he heard her say.

"That means yes, not no."

"I know. I'll be here in the morning when you come

over. I admit I'd like to get to know you better, even if it goes against my better judgment. Good night."

An honest woman.

Akis released the breath he was holding. *"Kalineekta, thespinis."*

Raina spent a restless night waiting for morning to come. After hearing from Akis last night, she'd had trouble getting to sleep. She turned on television just as the news came on. All of a sudden she saw herself and Akis leaving the Grand Bretagne to get into the limo. It was already old news, but still playing because he was so gorgeous.

She shut off the TV, but couldn't shut out the memory of their kiss in the pool. When Akis had called her, she'd sensed a change in him. That edge in his voice had gone. There was a new earnestness in the way he spoke that compelled her to give in. Not only for his reasons, but for her own.

Besides his exceptional male beauty and the desire he'd aroused in her, she'd never met such a dynamic man. He'd gone to great lengths to entertain her while she had to stay off her leg. Only a resourceful person would give her a tour of Athens through a telescope and a sightseeing tour by helicopter, making sure she was comfortable.

He'd been generous with his time and was obviously successful in business with his brother. If she didn't know anything else about him, she knew that much. Chloe's parents seemed very fond of him. When it came right down to it, the big problem was the fact that he was Greek and lived here. Before long she had to go home.

But until that day came, she had to admit to a growing excitement at spending time with him. She couldn't remember the last time she'd taken a true vacation. Not since before her marriage to Byron.

Yes, it was taking a big risk to be with Akis, but she was tired of the continual battle to protect her heart. Before her grandfather had died, he'd warned her not to stay closed up because of Byron. She was too young to go through life an old maid because of one wretched man who didn't know the first thing about being a husband.

"Oh, Grandfather—I wish you were here. I've met a man who has stirred me like no other. Maybe he'll hurt me in the end, but I'll hurt more if I don't go with my feelings for him and see what happens."

If she let Byron win, then she was condemning herself to a life without love or children.

Raina had listened to her grandfather's wise counsel, but it wasn't until she'd been with Akis that his words had started to sink in.

Until the other night when he'd taken her back to the hotel, she'd felt old beyond her years, incapable of feeling the joy of falling in love or anything close to it. But being with Akis had made her forget the past and live in the moment for a little while. To date, no other man had been able to accomplish that miracle.

Akis thrilled her. He did. For once, why not go with those feelings? She wasn't about to walk down the aisle with him, but she could have a wonderful time for as long as this vacation lasted.

Without wasting time, she sat on the side of the bed and phoned the Maywood jet propulsion lab in Salinas where she worked. She asked to be put through to Larry.

"Raina! Great to hear from you. Are you back?"

"No. That's why I'm calling. I've decided to stay in Greece for a couple of weeks. Is that going to present any difficulties for you? I've got my laptop. If you need some problem solving done, I can do it from here."

"No, no. It's about time you took a long vacation. I take it you attended your friend's wedding."

"Yes. It was fabulous." Akis was fabulous.

"You sound different. Happier. That's excellent news."

"It's because I'm having a wonderful time. By the way, I was given a tour of the Ionian Islands in our latest X Jet Explorer. Take it from me, it's a winner in every aspect."

"Wait till I tell everyone! The Giannopoulos Company was our first buyer from Greece. They took delivery of two of them just a month ago."

Raina sprang to her feet in surprise. She'd assumed Akis had chartered a flight through one of the helicopter companies. "Giannopoulos?"

"Yes. Two brothers—like Onassis—who came from nothing and have become billionaires. How did you happen to meet up with them?"

Chloe had never mentioned a word. She'd been too caught up in her wedding arrangements. "Very accidentally," Raina's voice shook as she answered him.

"I've heard they have several thousand stores all over Greece."

Her hand tightened on the phone. *You sprained your ankle in one of them, Raina.*

Stunned by the news, Raina sank back down on the bed. The knowledge that Akis had his own money meant he was the antithesis of Byron, who couldn't make it on his own without living off a woman's money. Her grandfather's shrewd brain was instrumental in making certain Byron's extortion tactics for alimony didn't work.

As for Akis, whether he knew about her background or not, it didn't matter. Finances would never get in the way of her relationship with him. For the first time in her adult life she had no worry in that regard. Akis had his own money and was his own person.

"Thanks for letting me take more time off, Larry." Once she hung up, Raina felt so light-hearted she wanted to whirl around the room, but that wouldn't be a good idea yet. She couldn't risk taking a chance in delaying her recovery.

After getting dressed in a clean pair of jeans and blouse, she took time with her hair and makeup, wanting to look her best for him. Once ready, she left the bedroom on her crutches and headed out to the patio where the family always gathered for meals.

Her senses came alive to see Akis at the table with Chloe's parents while they ate breakfast. He wore a simple T-shirt and jeans. All she saw was the striking male who'd swept into her world, moving mountains to find out where she was hiding.

Well, maybe not mountains above the sea, she smiled to herself, remembering that he wasn't Poseidon. Right then she discovered him staring at her. The longing in his jet-black eyes told her he wanted her for herself. No other reason. He got to his feet and came round to relieve her of the crutches.

"Good morning, *thespinis.*" His deep voice sent curls of warmth through her body.

"It's a lovely morning," she said as he helped her to sit. The soap tang from his body assailed her with its fresh scent.

Socus smiled at her. "What are your plans for today?"

Her gaze switched to Akis who sat across from her. "I'm going to leave the decision up to my tour director."

His eyes gleamed over the rim of his coffee cup. "In that case you'll need to pack a bag because we'll be gone for a while. For the first couple of days we'll lounge by the water to give your ankle a good rest. After that we'll do more ambitious things."

"That's good for you to be careful," Nora commented.

"I'll make sure of it." Akis finished his meal. "When you're ready, we'll leave in the helicopter."

Raina took a certain pride in knowing she'd helped on the project that had tested it before it was ready for the market. Who would have dreamed she'd end up with Akis taking her for a tour in one he'd recently purchased for his business?

After eating some yogurt and fruit, she stood up. "I'll just go put some things in a bag."

Akis came around and handed her the crutches. In a few minutes they made their way out of the house to the helicopter pad. It was like *déjà vu*, except that this time Raina knew she and Akis were functioning on a level playing field where all that mattered was their mutual enjoyment of each other.

He helped her on board and propped her leg. Soon the blades were rotating and they were off. Raina hadn't asked where they were going. The thrill of being taken care of by a good man was enough for her to trust in his decision making.

After a minute he turned to her. "We're headed back to Anti Paxos."

"That island must have great significance for you."

"It's home to me when I'm not working. En route we'll fly over Corinth and Patras, old Biblical sites."

"I get gooseflesh just hearing those names. My grandparents took me to Jerusalem years ago. We didn't have time in Greece to see the religious sites. They promised we'd come back, but because of my grandmother's ill health, that promise wasn't realized."

"Then I'm glad you can see some of the ancient Biblical cities from the air."

For the next hour, the sights she saw including the islands of Cephalonia and Lefkada filled her with wonder.

"Do you recognize your birthplace?" he spoke over the mic.

She chuckled. "I thought I was born in Carmel, California."

"Then you've been misled. The goddess Aphrodite was reputed to be born on Lefkada." With his sunglasses on, she couldn't see his eyes, but she imagined they were smiling.

"That put her in easy reach of Poseidon."

"Exactly."

Before long they circled Paxos and still lower over Anti Paxos before the pilot set them down on a stone slab nestled on a hillside of olive trees and vineyards. Through the foliage she could make out a small quaint villa.

Enchanted by the surroundings, she accepted Akis's help as he lifted her to the ground and handed her the crutches. The pilot gave him her suitcase and purse to carry. They both waved to him before Akis led her along a pathway of mosaic and stone lined by a profusion of flowers to the side of the villa.

"What's that wonderful smell?"

"Thyme. It grows wild on the hillside."

The rustic charm and simplicity in this heavenly setting delighted her.

Once inside, she saw that the living room had been carved out of rock. A fireplace dominated that side of the cottage. The vaulted ceiling and beams of the house with its stone walls and arches defied description. Here and there were small framed photos of his family and splashes of color from the odd cushion and ceramics. She felt like she'd arrived in a place where time had stood still.

He opened French doors to the terrace with a table and chairs that looked out over a small, kidney-shaped swimming pool. A cluster of flowers grew at one end. Beyond it shimmered the blue waters of the Ionian in the distance. You couldn't see where the sky met the sea.

She walked to the edge of the grill-work railing. "If I lived here, I wouldn't want to go anywhere else. What a perfect hideaway."

He stood behind her, but he didn't touch her. He'd promised he wouldn't, but the heat from his body created yearnings within her. "I like living in a cottage. It suits my needs."

Unlike the penthouse, this place reflected his personality.

"How old is the original house?"

"Two hundred years more or less. If you want to use the bathroom, I'll take your bags to the guest room."

"Thank you."

In a few minutes she'd seen the layout of the house. The kitchen and bathroom had been modernized, but everything else remained intact like dwellings from the nineteenth century. She adored the little drop-leaf table and chairs meant for two, built into a wall in the kitchen. On the opposite wall was a door that opened onto steps leading down to the terrace.

A room for the washer and dryer had been built in the middle of the hallway between the two bedrooms. He had everything at his fingertips. She sat in one of the easy chairs and put her crutches down beside her. Akis brought a stool over to rest her leg, then he went to the kitchen and started getting things out of the fridge.

"I'm going to fix our dinner."

"If you'll give me a job, I'll help."

"Don't worry about it today."

"Akis? I don't know if you've heard the story of Goldilocks and the Three Bears, but this cottage reminds me of their adorable house in the forest."

"We Greeks have our own fairy tales. My favorite was the one our father taught me and Vasso about

Demetros who lived with his mother in a hut much like this one was once. When I come here to be alone, I'm reminded of it. He fell in love with a golden-haired fairy, but she wasn't happy with him and went away.

"Vasso and I must have heard that story so many times we memorized the words. Demetros would cry for the rest of his life, 'Come back, come back, my fairy wife. Come back, my fairy child. Seeking and searching I spend my life; I wander lone and wild.'"

Strangely touched by the story she asked, "He never found her again?"

"No. She belonged to a fairy kingdom where he couldn't go."

"That's a sad fairy tale."

"Our father was a realist. I believe he wanted us to learn that you shouldn't try to hold on to something that isn't truly yours or you'll end up like Demetros."

That's what Raina had tried to do when she first felt like she was losing Byron, who'd married her for money. It wasn't until the divorce she'd learned he'd been unfaithful even while they were dating.

No wonder their marriage hadn't worked. He thought he could have a wife, plus her money and another life on the side. Byron had belonged to his own secret world and could never be hers. Her choice in men before she'd come to Greece had been flawed.

As she glanced at Theo's best man, she realized she was looking at the best man alive. The knowledge shook her to the foundations. "Your father sounds like a wise man," she murmured. "Tell me about him."

"He came from a very poor family on Paxos." Ah,

she was beginning to understand why these islands drew him. "My grandparents and their children, with the exception of my father, were victims of the malaria epidemic that hit thousands of Greek villages at the time. By the early nineteen-sixties it was eradicated, but too late for them."

"But your father didn't contract the disease?"

"No. Sometimes it missed someone in a family. A poor fisherman living in a tiny hut in Loggos, who'd lost his family, took my father in to help him catch fish they sold at a shop in the marketplace. When he died, he left my father the hut and a rowboat. Papa married a girl who worked in the olive groves. Her family had perished during the epidemic too. They had to scrape for a living any way they could."

"It's hard for me to believe people can live through such hardships, but I know they do. Millions and millions, and somehow they survive."

"According to our papa, our parents were in love and happy."

"The magic ingredients. Mine were in love, too."

He nodded. "First Vasso was born, then I came along eleven months later. But the delivery was too hard on Mama, who was in frail health, and she died."

"Oh, no," Raina cried softly. "To not know your mother… I'm so sorry, Akis. I at least had mine until I was twelve."

Solemn eyes met hers. "But you lost both parents. It seems you and I have that in common."

"But you never even knew her. It breaks my heart. How on earth did you all manage?"

"Our father kept on working to keep us alive by

supplying olives and fish to the shop. When we were five and six years old, we would help him and never attended school on a regular basis. Life was a struggle. It was all we knew.

"The village thought of us as the poor Giannopoulos kids. Most people looked down on us. Then things turned worse when our father was diagnosed with lymphoma and died."

A quiet gasp escaped. "How old were you?"

"Thirteen and fourteen. By then the woman's husband who owned the shop had also died and she needed help. So she let us work in her shop and helped us learn English. She said it was important to cater to the British and American tourists in their language. We studied English from a book when we could."

"You learned English with no formal schooling? That's incredible."

He stared hard at her. "You're talking to a man whose education is sorely lacking in so many areas, I don't even like to think about it."

"I see no lack in you. Anything but."

"Give it time and my inadequacies will be evident in dozens of ways, but I digress.

"While Vasso waited on customers and did jobs the woman's husband had done, I would go fishing and pick olives. Then it would be my turn to spell him off. I don't think we got more than six hours sleep a night for several years."

"No time to play," she mused aloud.

He made an odd sound in his throat. "We didn't know the meaning of the word."

Raina hated to see him do all the work and got up

to help him. For the first time she didn't use crutches because the kitchen was so close.

"Careful," he cautioned.

"My ankle doesn't hurt."

"Just do me a favor and sit in the chair at the table. The food is ready. I'll bring everything over so we can eat." He'd cut up fresh melon and made a shrimp salad. Lastly came some rolls and iced tea.

"When did you have time to stock the refrigerator?"

He sat down opposite her. "I pay a boy to do errands for me when I come to the island."

"No housekeeper?"

"I prefer to do the work myself."

"You're a jack-of-all-trades as we say in English."

"What does it mean exactly? Whether you've been aware of it or not, I've been picking up a few expressions from you, but I'll admit I'm not familiar with that one."

"Jack is a common name and it means that you can do everything well. Now that you've given me some idea of your background, I understand why." The minute she said the word, she saw the slightest hint of emotion cause his lips to thin.

Realizing she'd stumbled on to something significant when he already felt vulnerable she said, "Akis? At the pool when I told you to talk to someone of your own kind and background, you thought I was being condescending. Admit it."

"The thought did cross my mind."

"Since I knew nothing about your upbringing until just now, will you believe me when I tell you I only said what I did because—"

"Because you sensed I was extremely attracted and it made you nervous." His dark eyes devoured her as he spoke.

She squirmed on the wooden chair. "You're right. Please go on and finish telling me your life's story. I'm riveted. The food is delicious, by the way."

"Thank you." He leaned forward. "The widow we worked for started to suffer from poor health and gave us more and more responsibility. One day an American came in and told us the place reminded him of the convenience-store chains in America. He said they were all over the country. We looked into it and started to make innovations."

"Like what?"

"To keep the shop open twenty-four hours, which we took turns manning. Besides stocking it with a few other items tourists needed, we let patrons cash checks and provided free delivery for those living or staying nearby. In time we'd saved enough money to buy half the store. When she had to stop working, we bought her out."

"That's amazing! How old were you?"

"I was eighteen. Vasso had turned nineteen and had to serve nine months in the army. While he was gone, I ran things. After he got back, it was my turn for military service. We both served in the peacekeeping forces and undertook the command of Kabul International Airport."

"It's a miracle neither of you was injured, or worse."

He shook his head, dismissing it too fast for her liking. What was it he wasn't prepared to share? "The real miracle was that overnight we started making real money. After the early years when most nights we went to bed hungry, it was literally like manna falling from heaven.

"After selling the hut, we moved to an apartment in Loggos right along the harbor. When the widow died, we purchased the property and undertook renovations. In time we'd made enough money to buy failing shops of the same type in Gaios and Lakka, the other towns on the island. We patterned them after the chains we'd investigated and called them Alpha/Omega 24."

She looked at him in amazement. "When I think of two brothers who had the will to survive everything and succeed, I'm in absolute awe over what you accomplished. How did you end up in Athens?"

"You really want to hear?"

"I can't get enough. Please. You can't stop now."

Not immune to her entreaty, Akis brought some plums to the table for their dessert before he spoke. "When our staff was in place at all three stores and we felt confident enough to leave, we took a ferry to Corfu. From there we flew to Athens, our first commercial plane trip."

"Late bloomers on your way to do big business." The warmth of her smile melted him. "Were you excited?"

"We were so full of our plans for future expansion, not much else registered. Without the backing of an established bank, we didn't have a prayer. After two days we found a shop for sale we wanted to buy and started talking to bankers. We were turned down by everyone."

Her eyes reflected the hue of a lavender field. "Obviously that didn't stop you."

"No. At the last bank on our list we met Theo Chiotis in the loan department. He was working his way up in his family's banking business. Maybe it was because we were all the same age and he could tell we were hungry, or maybe we just caught him on a good day, but he was actually willing to examine the books."

"Bless Theo," she murmured.

Akis nodded. "He asked a lot of questions and went with us to look at the property the next day. As we explained how we would remodel and showed him pictures, he said he would take the matter up with the bank director and get back to us. We had no choice but to return to Paxos and go about our business."

"How long did you have to wait?"

"A week."

"It must have felt like an eternity."

Unable to resist, he covered her hand resting on the table and squeezed it before letting it go. "He told us the bank would give us the loan for the one store. If it turned a profit, they'd consider loaning us more money for other stores in the future. But the loan was contingent on our offering our other stores as collateral."

"Of course. Akis—you had to have been overjoyed!"

He sat back in the chair. "Yes and no. Athens was a big city, not a little village. We had to gamble that Athenians as well as tourists would patronize us. In no time our number four store was up and running. Vasso and I took turns manning it. Literally overnight we started making a profit we hadn't even imagined and we never looked back. We call it our lucky store.

Would it interest you to know that's the store where you fell?"

A gentle laugh escaped her lips. "The concierge at the hotel recommended it so I could buy some headache medicine. After spraining my ankle, I didn't think I was so lucky."

"Fate definitely had something in store for us."

"Certainly for you since you and Theo became best friends."

"Theo had the good sense to fall in love with Chloe. If there'd been no Theo, you and I would never have met." Akis didn't even want to think about that possibility. "While I clean up, why don't you go in the living room so you can stretch out on the couch? There's an evening breeze coming in off the terrace."

"What's that other smell besides thyme?"

"It's the woody scent of the maquis growing here mixed with rock rose and laurel."

"I think you've brought me to the Elysian fields where Zeus allowed Homer to live out his days in happiness surrounded by flowers."

Everything she said reminded him that she was highly educated and had seen and done things only experienced by a privileged few. She knew things you only learned from books and academic study. That was part of what made her so desirable. What could he give her in return?

That question burned in his brain as he cleared the table and put things away. "I take it you don't mind being whisked here."

Her mouth curved into a full-bodied smile, filling him with indescribable longings. "Your only problem, Akis Giannopoulos, will be to pry me away when it's

time to leave. I love this island where you come to fill
your lamp with oil."

The things that came out of that beautiful mouth.

He took a swift breath. "Raina Maywood? Before
it's time for bed, it's time I heard the story of *your*
life."

CHAPTER FIVE

RAINA GOT UP before he could help her and walked into the other room, but she didn't dare lie down on the couch. The way she was feeling about Akis right now, Raina would ask him to join her and beg him to love her, so she opted for the chair.

He was a man a breed apart from other men in so many vital ways. What an irony that she'd tried to run from him that first night! What if he hadn't pursued her? The thought of never knowing him was like trying to imagine a world without the sun. She waited for him to come in the living room.

When he did, he stretched out on the couch, using the arm for a pillow. After hearing about his beginnings, she felt doubly privileged to be with him like this in his own private sanctuary. He turned his head toward her. "You haven't told me much about your parents."

Somehow Raina knew that question would come first. "I was blissfully happy until they died. Dad was an engineer."

"Your father had the kind of education I would have given anything for. And your mother?"

"She went to college, but became a housewife after

I was born. My most vivid memory of her was playing
on the beach. We built sand castles and talked about
life while my grandmother painted. I was blessed with
grandparents who were there for me when my parents
died. I don't know how I would have survived otherwise. They brought happiness into my life again, but
they knew I was lonely, even though I had friends.

"That's why they said I could have a student from
a foreign country come and live with us during my
senior year. I don't know how it happened that Chloe
was the perfect pick for me. It was so fun helping her
with her English. She was an only child, too, so we
just clicked from the beginning.

"My parents' house was near my grandparents
who lived close to the ocean. We had horses. I grew
up riding and loving it. When Chloe came, we rode
along the beach and we did a lot of hiking in the Big
Sur Mountains. We made all these plans about what
we'd do when I went to Greece. But after Chloe left,
my grandmother's heart started to act up and I was
afraid to leave her."

"I'm sorry," he murmured. "Was it hard to see
Chloe go?"

"Yes, but thankfully I had college and became engrossed in my studies."

He turned on his side toward her. "I missed out on
that experience a lot of people take for granted." Akis
sounded far away just then.

She smiled at him. "You didn't miss anything."
Mindful that his impoverished background had made
him the slightest bit sensitive, she said, "What you
learned growing up was something no professor or

textbook could ever teach you. Every student could
take lessons from your work ethic alone."

"Thanks, but I don't want to talk about me."

"I'm not patronizing you, Akis."

"I know that. Keep talking. I love to hear about
you. What did you study?"

"My father took after his father and his father before him. I guess a little of it rubbed off on me. I did
well in math and science so I went to graduate school
and studied physics. After that I went to work for the
Maywood Corporation at our jet propulsion lab in Salinas, not far from Carmel."

Incredulous, Akis jackknifed into a sitting position.
"Where the helicopters Vasso and I bought are man-
ufactured?"

Her eyes lit up in amusement. "My team did work
on its sensor system, one that spanned the electro-
magnetic spectrum using state-of-the-art instrumen-
tation."

He was aghast. "You rode in a helicopter whose
electronics you helped design and you never said a
word?"

"Maybe I didn't for the same reason you didn't tell
me your number-four store was only one of many."

They'd both been gun-shy of revealing themselves.
He got it. "I'm so impressed with the work you do,
I can hardly believe you've decided to prolong your
vacation here."

"If you want to know the truth, I've worried that
you've taken your tour director duty too seriously and
your brother might feel that you're neglecting business because of me."

After the information Vasso found on Raina, no doubt he was curious about what was going on and had left a message for Akis to call him. But he'd put off returning it because for the first time in his life, a woman filled his world and he couldn't concentrate on anything else.

"It's getting late, Raina. Before we go to bed, what would you like to do tomorrow?"

"Swim in that green water off your private section of beach. It tops anything I've seen in the Caribbean."

"I've never been to the Caribbean." It was yet another reminder of how worlds apart they were in experience. But her observation caused him to expel a satisfied breath. "That can be arranged. There are few cars on the island, but I have a run-down truck parked on the property to get me around if I need it. We'll drive down to the shore line. Getting there would be tricky with your crutches."

"After tomorrow I'm hoping I can throw them away."

"That can't come soon enough for me. I'm living to dance with you at a charming taverna in Loggos without being impaled." Her chuckle excited him. "We'll take the cabin cruiser over."

"Is the hut you were born in still there?"

"Yes. But today it's surrounded by a vineyard. The vintner uses it to store his tools and such."

"Did that bother you?"

"When Vasso and I found out what was planned, we were happy about it."

"You have amazing resilience." After a pause, "Can we explore one of those caves that glows blue?"

He was prepared to do anything for her. "Whatever your heart desires."

She got to her feet. "You'd better not say that around me. I might just take you up on it because this has been a day of enchantment and I'm border-line addicted already. Good night, Akis."

He watched her fit the crutches under her arms and make her way to the guest room. The urge to carry her to his room brought him to his feet. Needing some-thing constructive to do so he wouldn't follow her, he cleaned up the kitchen, then went out on the terrace to call Vasso. There was no answer. He left the message that he planned to be away from Athens with Raina for a few days. If there was a problem, let him know.

No sooner had he locked up and headed for his bedroom than the phone rang. He picked up on the second ring. "Vasso?"

"You're on vacation with her now?" Akis heard the incredulity in his voice.

"Yes."

"Where?"

"Anti Paxos."

"You're kidding! What has happened to you?"

Something that had already changed his life, but he couldn't say the words out loud quite yet. "Do you need me back at the office?"

"That's not the point. What's going on? Bottom line."

"I'm still trying to figure things out."

"Has she been honest with you?"

He sucked in his breath. "We're getting there."

"Akis—I'm really worried about you."

He didn't want to listen. "Why?"

"You've never been hurt soul-deep by a woman. The way you feel about her, she could be the first to do damage I don't even want to think about if it doesn't work out."

"You mean like Sofia did to you?"

"Yes, but I was younger then and got over it. I'm warning you to be careful."

"I thought you gave me the green light."

"So I did, but she's not just any woman. Hundreds of people depend on her as CEO. Don't forget she came for the wedding and has to go back."

Akis had forgotten nothing. The fear that she'd be able to walk away from him after their vacation was over would keep him tossing and turning during the nights to come. Once in a while the big brother in Vasso took over.

"What are you really trying to warn me about?"

"You've let her into your life where no other woman has gone. I guess I just don't want to see you get hurt. But don't mind me. Papa told me to look after you before he died. I guess I've forgotten you're a grown man now and can take care of yourself. Forgive me?"

"If you can forgive me for asking for a few more days off."

"What do you think?"

"I know it's asking a lot."

"Akis? Take care."

His brotherly warning had come too late. It had been too late by the time she'd flashed those violet eyes at him on the street.

After swimming for the better part of an idyllic day in aquamarine water so clear and clean you could see everything, Raina walked on white-gold silky sand to the little truck to go back to the villa. Akis had played gently with her, always careful so she wouldn't injure her ankle. He'd honored his promise to maintain his distance to the point she wished he hadn't carried it this far.

Once in the house, she washed her hair in the shower and blow-dried it. She'd picked up some sun and applied a frost lipstick, then donned a white sundress and sandals. All day she'd been waiting for evening. He was taking her to Paxos Island to show her where he'd grown up and worked. She brought her crutches, hopefully for the last time.

They drove to the only harbor on Anti Paxos, where he'd moored their cabin cruiser. In a lightning move he lifted her like a bride and placed her on one of the padded benches. While she put on a life jacket, he untied the ropes. She could hardly take her eyes off him, dressed in a collared navy knit shirt and cream-colored pants outlining his amazing physique.

He started the engine and they backed out of the slip at no-wake speed until they reached open water. Different kinds of boats dotted the marine-blue sea separating the two islands. Akis pointed out landmarks along the coastline till they reached Loggos. The small, quaint town with its horseshoe-shaped waterfront held particular significance for her. This was where Akis and his brother were born.

He found a slip along the harbor and berthed the cruiser. She removed the life jacket before he reached for her and set her down on the dock. Their bodies brushed, ramping up the temperature from a fire that had been burning steadily for days now.

"Here you go." He handed her the crutches. Once she was ready, they began an exploration of the beach-front with its tavernas and shops. He pointed out an apartment above one of the bars. "That was our first place to live after we sold the hut."

"I don't know your language, but I recognize the Alpha/Omega 24 sign up ahead. You lived close to your store."

"That's how we were able to be on duty day and night."

She turned to him. "I've got gooseflesh just being with you where the whole business began. Your number-one store. When you look back at the beginning, can you believe what you've accomplished this far?"

His smile quickened her heartbeat. "Watching your reaction makes it all worth it."

"I want to go inside."

"The interiors are the same, but we've kept the fa-cades of our various stores in keeping with the sur-roundings."

He was right. Once they stepped over the threshold, it was like entering the shop in Athens. There were several people in summer gear doing some shopping. A middle-aged man and woman beamed when they saw Akis and hurried over to him, giving him a hug, obviously holding him in great esteem.

Akis introduced Raina to the married couple who ran the store. Their gaze fastened on her with un-checked curiosity. They held a long conversation with Akis in Greek. At the very end he shook his head and ushered her back outside.

"What was that all about?"

He stared at her through veiled eyes. "Aside from

giving me a rundown about how business was going, they said you were very beautiful like a film star and that we looked beautiful together. They saw the news the other night where I was helping you out of the hotel into the limo. They wanted to know if you were my fiancée."

To be Akis's fiancée would be the ultimate gift after fearing it was all an unattainable dream. Heat filled her cheeks. "It's evident they're fond of you. So am I," her voice throbbed, "and I'm having a wonderful time with you. Where are we going to have dinner? I'm in the mood for fish."

"We'll go to the taverna ahead where you can eat beneath the olive trees. Their appetizers serve as an entire meal."

His choice didn't disappoint her. The waiter brought *mezes* made of octopus, salad, sardines, calamari, shrimp and clams. They feasted until they couldn't eat another bite. He taught her how to say the names of the fish in Greek. It was hilarious because her pronunciation needed help with *gareedes*, the name for shrimp, causing them both to laugh.

"I'm humbled when I realize you picked up English and are fluent in it. You're brilliant, Akis."

"We had to learn it out of necessity, no other reason."

"Those who know your story would call it genius. I lived with Chloe for nine months, but I didn't pick up her language. I'm ashamed to admit I didn't really try. *Your* genius is that you knew what you had to do and you *did* it against all odds."

"But my pronunciation needs help."

"No, it doesn't." She put a hand on his arm without realizing it. "I love the way you speak English. It's so sweet."

His black brows met together. "Sweet?"

"It's part of your unique charisma. There's nothing artificial about you. Never change."

He reached for her hand and kissed the palm. Full of food and so happy, she felt delicious sensations run through her body at the touch of his lips against her skin. She wanted, needed to be close to him.

"Vasso?" a female voice called out, causing Raina to lift her head in the direction of the lovely woman who'd come over to their table. She was probably Raina's age.

Still grasping her hand, Akis turned around to the person who'd interrupted them.

"Akis!" She looked shocked before her gaze strayed to Raina.

At that point he had to let go of her hand and stood up. "Sofia Peri," he said in English, "meet Raina Maywood."

The other woman nodded to Raina.

"Sofia grew up here at the same time with Vasso and me," he explained.

From the other woman's troubled expression, Raina suspected there'd been an uneasy history. "Akis and his brother must look a great deal alike for you to mistake him."

"Yes and no. How is he?"

"Busy running the office while I'm on vacation. How are you and Drako?" His gaze flicked to Raina. "Her husband owns the best fishing business on Paxos."

Sofia averted her eyes. "This has been a good year for us."

"I'm glad to hear it. Nice to see you, Sofia. Give my best to Drako."

"It was nice to meet you, Sofia," Raina chimed in.

Clearly Sofia wanted to prolong the conversation, but Akis had sat down, effectively bringing their meeting to a close. When they were alone once more Raina said, "She's a very pretty woman."

"A very unhappy one," Akis responded. "When Vasso got out of the military he asked her to marry him, but she turned him down because she was looking for a man who could give her all the things she wanted."

Raina read between the lines. "Now that you and your brother have prospered, she's wishing she hadn't turned him down?"

He sat back in the chair and nodded. "From his early teens, Vasso was crazy about her and she him, but she wanted more from life. There was a period when I feared he'd never get over the rejection. But he did."

She let out a sigh. "Thank goodness time has a healing effect."

His eyes searched hers. "You say that like someone who has been hurt."

The subject had come up. Better to get it out of the way now. "I married at twenty when I was young and naive. A writer ten years older than I came to the house to get details about a book he was writing on my grandmother's father, Edwin Moss. My great-grandfather was a seascape artist who's been gaining in popularity.

"Because Byron was older and brilliant, I was too blinded by his attention to realize he only wanted me for what my money could do to support his research and career. He told me he wanted to put off having children for a while."

"You wanted children?"

"More than anything. I didn't understand why he wanted to postpone it until he was trapped in a scandal with a grade-B film starlet from Hollywood and the director with whom she was having an affair. As you can imagine I thanked providence there was no child born to us who would be torn apart."

Akis's striking Greek features hardened.

"In court I learned Byron had been having relations with her before and during my marriage to him. It got ugly before it was over. My grandparents helped me through the ordeal. Without them I don't think I would have made it. Your brother was fortunate enough to be passed over. In the long run he's the winner."

"I couldn't agree more." Akis put some bills on the table. "Let's get out of here. Back along the shoreline near the dock is an outdoor club for dancing. We'll see how your ankle holds up without the crutches, but the second it starts to hurt, we'll leave."

Twilight had turned the island into a thing of incredible beauty. Between the water and the lights, Raina was caught in its spell. But for the crutches, she would have hung on to him, unable to help herself.

Many of the shops had closed for the night. "Look —your store is full of people. I'm so proud of what you've done I could burst."

"I'm afraid I'm going to burst if I don't get you in my arms soon."

He didn't know the half of it. Soon she could hear

live music coming from the club. They played every-thing from bouzouki to modern, jazz and rock. Some of the people sat around watching the lights of the harbor and the incoming ferry while they enjoyed a cocktail. Other couples had taken to the dance floor.

Akis put her crutches next to her chair and ordered them a local drink. "Come on." He reached for her hand and pulled her onto the floor. "I've waited as long as I can."

So had she. Today she'd been transported to an-other world and melted in his arms, dying for the le-gitimate excuse to get as close to him as possible. Her heart thudded so hard, she was certain he could feel it. Their bodies fit and moved as one flesh.

When he wrapped both arms around her to bring her even closer, she linked her arms around his neck and clung to him. The male scent of him combined with the soap he'd used in the shower acted as an aphrodisiac. Raina had no idea how long they'd been fused together when his lips brushed against her hot cheek. "How's your ankle?"

"What ankle?" she murmured back.

She felt his deep sigh. "When I was a young boy, we'd walk past this club on our way home from work every night. For years and years I used to watch the people sitting around drinking and dancing, unable to relate to their lives.

"It took money and leisure time, neither of which I had. A man needed decent clothes and shoes. But more than anything else it took courage I didn't have to walk in here with a woman and feel I was as good as anyone else."

Her eyes closed tightly. She was haunted by what

he'd told her. "How long did it take you to realize your own value and bring a woman in here to dance the night away?"

"I never did."

Raina's hands had a mind of their own and slid to his cheeks where she could feel the slight rasp of his hard male jaw. She forced him to look at her, trying to understand. "I'm the first?"

"I've been waiting for the right woman, but the way I'm feeling about you at this moment, I need to get us away from here now. Let's go." She knew how he felt and would have suggested it if he hadn't.

They walked back to the table. He handed her the crutches. After leaving money on the table, they left the club without having tasted their drinks.

The water felt like glass during the ride to Anti Paxos in the cabin cruiser. A sliver of a moon lit up the dark sky. Raina wanted this romantic night to last forever. When he pulled into the slip at the harbor, he turned to her. "How would you like to sleep out on the cruiser tonight?"

"Can we? I'd love it!"

"Tell you what. We'll drive to the house and pack a bag. I'll grab some food and we'll come back. Tomorrow we'll begin a tour of the different islands."

She removed her life jacket. "You're sure you want to do this for me when you've lived here all your life? Won't it be boring for you?"

"Being with you is like seeing everything for the first time because your excitement is contagious."

"This part of Greece is so glorious, I'm speechless, Akis."

"I'm in the same state around you. Come on." He

picked her up and carried her to the dock. They reached the truck and drove to the house in record time. At the house she changed out of her sundress and put on her lightweight white sweats. After packing bags and food, they returned to the cruiser. She really was doing fine without the crutches and had never known this kind of happiness before.

Being with Akis made her realize what a pitiful marriage she'd had with Byron, whose selfishness should have warned her she was making a terrible mistake. Theo's best man *was* the best man she'd ever known, and the most generous.

"We'll cruise over to my private beach and lay anchor until morning. The seats go back and make comfortable beds if you want to sleep on deck. Or you can use the bedroom below."

"I want to stay on top and look at the stars." That way they didn't have to be separated.

"Then that's what we'll do."

Euphoria enveloped Raina as they followed the shoreline to his area of the island. After cutting the motor, he dropped anchor. Theirs was the only boat around. He turned on the lights. It felt like they were on their own floating island. When she looked over the side, she could see beneath water so clear it didn't seem real.

She turned around with her elbows on the railing and smiled at him. "I feel enchanted. It's this place. The air's so warm and sweet, and the sky is like velvet."

His gaze swept over her. He'd turned on music and strolled toward her still dressed in the same clothes he'd worn earlier. Akis was so handsome, her mouth went dry. "I want to dance with you again. This time we don't have an audience."

Raina propelled herself into his arms and he swung her around. He murmured words into her hair she didn't understand. "What did you say?"

"That you smell and feel divine." He crushed her against him, running his hands over her back and molding her to him. They slow-danced until she lost track of time. His mouth roved her cheek until she couldn't bear it any longer. Needing his kiss like she needed air, she met his lips with her own. They became lost in a sea of want and desire.

"I could do this with you forever," he whispered against her warm throat. "My father told me it could be like this with the right woman."

She rose up on tiptoe and kissed his face one dashing feature at a time. "In my darkest moment, my grandfather told me the same thing and warned me not to lose hope. He and my grandmother were happily married for sixty-nine years."

Akis smiled down at her. "Imagine that." Twining his fingers with hers, he walked her to the banquette across the rear of the cruiser and pulled her onto his lap. He smoothed some strands of her hair tousled by the breeze. "If I were your great-grandfather, I'd paint you like this and name it Aphrodite by moonlight."

Raina buried her face in his neck. "If Rodin were alive, I'd commission him to sculpt you cavorting in the swells of your Hellenic world. Have you been to Paris?"

"No. But I've seen pictures of *The Kiss*. All the boys on the island liked looking at those kinds of pictures."

"I think everyone does. Do you think Rodin got it right?" she teased.

"As much as he could working with cold marble."

His comment sent a wave of heat through her body as she imagined them the models for the sculptor's famous work.

"You're all warmth." He lowered his head and kissed her until she was lost in rapture. A low moan passed through him. "Raina—I want to eat you up, every last centimeter of you. But if I do that, there won't be anything left for me tomorrow, so I'm giving you a chance to escape me. There's a comfortable bed waiting for you below where I won't be joining you. At least, not tonight."

He helped her off his lap. The last thing she remembered was the black fire of his eyes as he said good-night.

Her legs almost gave way from the blaze of desire she saw burning there and practically stumbled her way to the steps leading down to the galley. She was still out of breath when she finally climbed under the covers. Akis was the one who had the incredible self-control she lacked. Hers had deserted her the first time he'd taken her in his arms.

The frightening realization had come to her that to know his possession would change her life forever.

Forever...

Akis was a male force no woman could resist. There was no one else like him.

As Akis had done many times before, he slept on the top deck of the cruiser. But he couldn't sleep yet. When his father had talked about meeting the right woman he'd said, "Akis? You're only in your teens and you'll meet a lot of women before you're grown up. When you find *the* one, you must treat her like a queen.

"Your mother was my queen. I cherished and respected her from the beginning. She deserved that because not only was she going to be my wife, she was going to be the mother of our children."

There was no question in Akis's mind that at the age of twenty-nine he'd found *the* one. What tormented him was the fear she wouldn't think *he* was the one. How could he possibly measure up to the educated men she worked with and knew? Maybe that was why Vasso had cautioned him to be careful. Because he knew there was a vast chasm of knowledge separating Akis from Raina.

But when he awakened that morning, he felt the sun's warm rays on his face chasing away the disturbing fears that had come during the night. A burst of excitement radiated through him knowing Raina was only as far away as the bedroom below.

After he'd made breakfast in the galley, he called to her. He'd taken a swim first and was still dressed in his trunks. And needing a shave. She appeared minutes later looking a knockout in leaf-green shorts and a sleeveless white top. Those amazing lavender eyes smiled at him.

"I'm glad you're up, Raina. How are you feeling?"

"Fantastic. Something smells marvelous."

"It's the coffee." But she'd just come from the shower and brought her own intoxicating scent with her. "How's the ankle?"

"I've forgotten about it."

"Good. Come and sit down." He'd made eggs and put out fruit and pastries. "After we eat, I'll take us to Lefkada Island, your birthplace."

She chuckled and sat down in one of the pullout seats beneath the table. "Didn't we pass over it?"

He nodded. "Katsiki Beach will be a sight you won't forget. We'll swim to our heart's content."

She munched on a pastry and sipped her coffee. "I know I'm still dreaming and pray I never wake up."

"I'll do my best to ensure that doesn't happen."

Raina's expression turned serious. "You've been so good to me and have done all the work. I don't begin to know how to repay you. I've never been waited on like this in my life, but have done nothing to deserve it. Before our vacation is over I intend to wait on you."

"We'll take turns."

"While you pull up the anchor and get us underway, I'll start now by cleaning up the kitchen."

He walked around and kissed her luscious mouth. "See you on top in a few minutes." This was happiness in a new dimension. To make it last presented the challenge. If he wanted the prize, it meant not making mistakes along the way. Vasso's words still rang in his ears. *Slow down.*

Once he'd pulled on a clean T-shirt from his bag in the bathroom, he bounded up the steps to the deck and got everything ready. Raina appeared a few minutes later with a couple of beach towels and sunscreen. Beneath her beach robe he glimpsed the mold of her lovely body wearing her orange bikini and had to keep himself from staring.

"You'll need to put this on." He handed her the life jacket.

"Even if you swim like a fish, you have to wear one, too."

He flashed her a smile. "Tell you what. For you, I'll wear a belt." He opened a locker and pulled one out.

"Put it on, please."

"Nag, nag."

"Your command of English is remarkable."

"I heard the word enough times when an American husband and wife came in the store. His wife would tell him what she wanted and he'd walk around muttering the word under his breath."

Raina laughed so hard, her whole body shook. "Welcome to the US."

His black brows lifted. "I'm afraid it's the same here."

She nodded her head, drawing his attention to the gleaming red and gold strands of her hair in the sunlight. "Certain things between men and women will never change no matter the nationality."

"Like getting into each other's space until there's no air between them."

Raina had a tendency to blush. To avoid commenting, she poured the sunscreen on her hands to apply to her face and arms. "Would you like some?"

"Thanks, but my skin doesn't look like fine porcelain."

Her eyes traveled over his face. "You're right. You have an olive complexion that highlights your black hair and makes you...drop-dead gorgeous." She put the sunscreen on the seat.

His brows furrowed. "Drop-dead?"

"It's an American expression for a man who's so attractive, a woman could drop dead from a heart attack just looking at him. And there's another expression women use. They say 'he's jaw-dropping gorgeous.'" She touched his unshaven jaw with her left hand. "You know. Sometimes when you see something incredible and your mouth opens in shock?"

Studying the curving lines of her mouth almost gave *him* a heart attack. "You mean the way mine did when you looked up at me on the sidewalk? Does an American man say 'she's jaw-dropping gorgeous'?"

An impish twinkle lit up her eyes. "The phrase can be used to describe a woman or a man. And there's another more modern expression. 'He's hot.'"

"Which also works for a female. I've heard that one. Thank you for the vocabulary lesson. I'm indebted to you." But no matter how hard he could try to catch up to her intellectual level, he would never succeed.

"Maybe you can teach me some Greek, but I know it's a very difficult language to learn."

"You mean right now?"

"If you're willing."

"Then you'll have to sit close to me while I steer the boat."

She shot him a side glance. "How close?"

He gripped her hand and pulled her over to the captain's seat. After sitting down, he patted his leg. "Right here."

"Akis—" She chuckled. "You won't be able to drive."

"Try me."

As she perched on his leg, he grabbed her around the waist. "The first word I want to teach you is the most important. If you never learn another one, it won't matter." He started the engine and they skimmed across the water.

"What is it?"

"Repeat after me. *S'agapo.*"

She said it several times until she got the intonation just right. "How am I doing?"

"That was perfect."

"What does it mean?"

"Say it to Nora and Socus and surprise them. By their reaction you'll know what it means."

"S'agapo. S'agapo." She kissed his cheek and slid off his leg. "You're a terrific teacher, but you need to concentrate on your driving. We've been going around in circles," she teased.

"That's what you've done to me," he quipped back. "You have me staggering all over the place in a dazed condition."

"Then I'm going to leave you alone until we get to that beach you told me about."

"And then?"

"What do you mean?"

"You can't leave me hanging like that. Once we've arrived at our destination, I want to know what you propose to do to me."

She let out a devilish chuckle. "I'm considering several options, all of which require your complete attention."

The way Akis was feeling right now, they weren't going to make it another ten yards. "Shall we forget going anywhere and head back to my beach?"

Her smile filled all the lonely places inside him. "What kind of a tour director are you?"

"I can't help it if my first passenger surpasses any

sight I could show her. If you don't believe me, just watch the way men look at you when you walk by. I'm the envy of every male."

She rested her head against the seat, soaking up the sun. "Women do the same thing when they see you."

"I'm talking about you. Did you know the newspapers have printed photos of us leaving the Grand Bretagne? The headlines read, 'Who was the beautiful mystery woman seen with one of the Giannopoulos brothers?'"

She turned in his direction. "Chloe's wedding made the publicity inevitable. Knowing her like I do, I'm sure she didn't want it. She's the sweetest, kindest girl I've ever known."

"I couldn't agree more. Theo has a similar temperament. They're a perfect match."

"Isn't that wonderful? Tell me more about him."

"He's a vice president of the bank now."

"Good for him, but I want to know why you like him so much."

The more he got to know Raina, the more he realized how extraordinary she was, not only as a woman, but as a human being. "You're a lot like Theo. You look beyond the surface to the substance of a person."

He could feel her eyes on him. "I'm so glad he saw inside of you and was willing to take a risk for you. That's because you're such a good man."

"He's saved my back more than once."

"In what way?"

"We signed up for the military at the same time and served together."

Raina sat up. "How did you manage that?"

"His father had connections. I couldn't believe it when he was assigned to my unit."

"I take it that's where your friendship flourished."

"In unexpected ways. We grew close as brothers." He would have told her more, but talking about it would touch on a painful subject he didn't want to bring up today. "When he introduced me to Chloe six months ago, I worried she might not be good enough for him. But nothing could have been further from the truth."

Raina's eyes closed for a moment. She was so crazy about Akis, the thought of his breaking her heart caused her to groan.

"I had the same fear when she phoned to tell me about Theo. I knew her heart from long ago and didn't want any man breaking it. But getting to know you, I'm convinced he must be her equal, otherwise he wouldn't have come to be like family to you. I'm anxious to meet him when they get back from their honeymoon."

He had to clear his throat. "We'll definitely make that happen, but we've got a lot of living to do before then."

She sat back again. "I'm loving all this, but I'm afraid I'm keeping you from your work."

"I'm entitled to a vacation and have covered for Vasso many times."

"I haven't had a real one in years. It sounds like we're a pair of workaholics. But I have to admit work has saved my life since my grandfather passed away."

Akis filled his lungs with the sea air. "What do you say we forget everything and concentrate on having fun. We're coming to one of the most famous beaches in all of Greece."

Raina got up and wandered over to the side. "Those tall green hills are spectacular."

"You can't access them unless you climb up the eighty steep steps descending along the cliff. Your ankle is doing better, but I wouldn't suggest you try that activity for another few weeks."

"It's enough just to cruise around them. I can't get over how crystal clear the water is. Against the golden sand, you think you've arrived in a magical kingdom. I don't see any other people around."

"Without a boat it's difficult access. Most of the tourists come in July and August. For the moment we've got the beach to ourselves. I'll take us in closer. We can swim to the shore, then come back and eat on board."

"I can't wait!"

Neither could he. Akis needed her in his arms. When he'd found the right spot, he dropped anchor. She'd already taken off her life jacket. Soon she'd shed her top and shorts to reveal a bikini-clad body she filled out to perfection. Raina turned a beaming face to him. "See you on shore!"

A second later she climbed over the side and dove in. Now that her ankle had healed, he discovered she swam like a fish and had amazing stamina.

That's when a warning light came on in his mind, holding him back. His father's words came back to him again.

When you find the one, you must treat her like a queen. Your mother was my queen. I cherished and respected her from the beginning. She deserved that

*because not only was she going to be my wife, she was
going to be the mother of our children.*

As if in slow motion, he removed his life belt,
pulled off his T-shirt and plunged in after her. He
could hear her squeals of delight. "The water is so
warm! I've lived by the Pacific Ocean all my life, but
you always have to get used to the colder temperature. I could stay in this all day! There's no kelp or
seaweed. What's below us?"

"Rocks made of soft limestone."

She did a somersault and swam beneath the water.
He kept track of her until she emerged further away.
"They *are* soft." Her laughter was music to his ears before she started swimming parallel to the long shoreline.

He'd brought her here to spend time with her and
love her, but his father's words wouldn't leave him
alone.

CHAPTER SIX

RAINA TURNED AROUND and trod water while she watched Akis coming after her like a torpedo at high speed. While his strong arms cleaved the water, his powerful legs kicked up a fountain.

Her heart raced madly as he came to a stop in front of her and raised his dark head. She could never get enough of just looking at him. "I feel like a happy little girl who's finally out of school for the summer and has all day to play."

"Except that you don't look like a little girl. Do you have any conception of what kind of a problem that presents for me?"

The tremor in his voice told her what he was holding back through sheer willpower. 'It's not exactly easy for me, either. I've come out to play with a man."

Lines darkened his features. "How many men have been in your life?"

"You mean ones who were important?"

"Yes."

She might as well get it all said now. "There were two. Before Byron, there was a graduate assistant teaching my math class during my freshman year.

He held seminars for the most promising students and has since become a professor at a west coast college."

"What drew you to him?"

They swam around in circles, always facing each other. "His smarts. He had a different way of looking at a problem to solve it. I envied him that gift. He fed my ego by telling me I'd inherited my father's mathematical mind."

"Why didn't that relationship go anywhere?"

"I didn't find out he was married until I'd been dating him for a month."

"Did you sleep with him?"

"No. I was waiting for marriage."

"Raina…" She heard a tortured sound in his voice.

"It was over a long time ago. He didn't wear a wedding ring. At the end of the term I went to see if my grade had been posted. The head of the math department called me in and asked me if I knew Rod was married. I felt the blood rush to my feet. After I got my second wind, I thanked him for the information."

"What did you do?"

"Rod had a cubicle down the hall. We'd planned to go out to dinner that evening. I dropped in on him. He assumed I wanted to check on the time. I told him to do his wife a favor and take her out to dinner instead. And I added one more thing. I wouldn't be putting in a good word for him at the jet propulsion laboratory. Then I walked out and shut the door. That was the end of it."

A grimace darkened Akis's face.

"I made the same mistake with Byron by putting him on a pedestal. He was a published writer who'd traveled to Europe to do art research for more books.

I admired someone so intelligent and well-read. He was older and had knowledge on so many subjects. The fact that he wanted to do my great-grandfather's story was a huge plus.

"We could talk for hours about the art we loved. I thought we'd never run out of things to discuss. What I didn't see was his empty bank account and his proclivity for women he could prey on. Have you heard the expression 'once bitten, twice shy'?"

"No, but I don't need a translation," he stated.

"In my case I was *twice* bitten before I learned the lesson I'd been needing."

"Enough of the past, Raina. Let's swim back to the cruiser and have our picnic."

Relieved to get off the subject of her pathetic naivety, she swam next to him. He paced himself so she could keep up with him. He did everything right. How she loved him!

She *loved* him.

She loved him for who he was, nothing else. Raina could finally say it and not be afraid. She wanted to shout it to the world.

I'm in love with him.

Loving him wasn't a mistake.

When they reached the ladder, he got in the boat first, then helped her up and wrapped her in one of the beach towels. He kissed her on the side of her neck, on her chin and nose, her cheeks, eyelids, earlobes.

Before he reached her mouth she said, "I'm going to fix our lunch while you relax. After we're full, I'll give you a big kiss for dessert." Raina was afraid that if she stayed on deck with him another instant, she'd forget everything else.

"Coward," he whispered against her lips before letting her go.

She hurried down the steps to the bedroom and dressed in another pair of shorts and a top. There was nothing she could do about her hair until she showered later.

In the fridge she found the ingredients to fix a Grecian-style sandwich. She made a fresh pot of coffee and put everything on the table with a couple of oranges. Akis joined her. While they finished off their orange sections, he told her they were going to head to Cape Lefkas, the inhospitable part of the island with cliffs seventy meters high. The lighthouse was built on the old temple of Apollo. From there you could view incredible vistas including Kefallonia Island.

He got up from the seat first and pressed a passionate kiss to her mouth. "That's the sweetest dessert I ever tasted. Save me more because tonight I'll be starving."

Akis could have no idea of the depth of her hunger for him. She didn't know how much longer she could go on without loving him completely. If she did that, then she'd never want to leave him. But what did Akis want?

Her experience with Byron proved to her that living happily ever after with the same person you married didn't necessarily happen. She couldn't bear the thought of a long-term relationship not working out with Akis. For the moment they were in a short-term situation because soon she would have to go back to California and once again take on the weight of her responsibilities.

If he wanted a life with Raina to continue, could a

REBECCA WINTERS   129

long-distance relationship back and forth from Greece to California work? A week fit in here and another week there throughout the year with months of separation in between?

Raina knew she was getting way ahead of herself, but every second spent with him was condemning her to be fatally in love with him for the rest of her life.

There was one thing Raina refused to do. Become so desperate that she'd marry someone else who came along in the future just to be married and have children. She could meet dozens of men and none of them would ever measure up to Akis. If her grandfather were still alive and could know this bigger-than-life man, he'd understand why Raina would never be able to settle for anyone else.

Her only choice was to spend this precious time with the man she loved and see what happened. *Stop analyzing this to pieces, Raina.*

He wanted to show her *his* Greece, so go with it and let come what may. She'd come to Athens for Chloe's sake and had found joy beyond belief. If it meant that she could only experience it for a little while, then it was worth it. Casting any worries aside, she hurried up on deck and felt two arms grab her from behind.

"It took you long enough. I've been waiting for this." He turned her around and lowered his head, covering her mouth with his own. Once again she was swept away. They'd started devouring each other when Akis unexpectedly lifted his lips from hers. "I can't get enough of you, Raina."

She let out a shaky breath. "I'm in the same condition."

His hands gripped her shoulders. "I thought I could do this, but I can't."

When she saw the torment in his black gaze, she shuddered. "What's wrong?"

With a sound of reluctance, he let go of her. "I'd intended to vacation with you, but it's not working. Do you mind if we go back to the house?"

Raina took a step away from him. "Is it me? Something I've done?"

His answer was a long time in coming. "It's nothing you've done. I want to make love to you more than you can imagine, but I don't have the right."

Afraid her legs wouldn't support her, she found the nearest banquette so she could sit. Filled with anguish, she couldn't look at him. "What are you talking about?"

"You're wonderful, Raina, and you've changed my life to the point I don't know where I am."

She threw her head back. "Since you asked me to dance at the reception, my life hasn't been the same, either. Taking a vacation probably wasn't a good idea, but I'll never regret the time we've spent together. If that's what you want, then by all means let's go back to Anti Paxos."

His face was an expressionless mask. "It isn't what I want, but I don't see another alternative for our situation."

She didn't know what was driving this latest decision. But if by situation he meant that not making love to her had ruined the trip for him, then she agreed there was no point in prolonging it.

"All right." In a quick move she reached for the life jacket and put it on. "While you get us under way,

I'll go below to clean things up in the kitchen and pack."

He didn't try to stop her. After getting the work done, she stayed below the whole time and rested her leg on the bed, knowing he would prefer to be alone. Her pain had gone beyond tears. When he cut the motor, she realized they'd returned to the harbor and was surprised the return trip had been so fast. There was only a slight rocking movement of the boat now that he'd pulled into the slip.

She heard footsteps in the hallway and checked her watch. It was seven-thirty. He peered inside the bedroom with an indecipherable expression in his dark eyes. "I'll take your bag to the truck. Are you ready?"

"Yes." Raina got up and followed him to the deck. "Just a minute. I need to stow the life jacket." Once she'd taken it off and put it under the bench, she reached for the hand he extended to help her onto the dock. She thought he'd let go, but he kept it grasped in the warmth of his until he helped her into the truck in the parking area.

They drove in silence to his villa nestled in the greenery. It already felt like home to her. When it came time to say goodbye to this place, the wrench would be excruciating. She got out with her purse and started ahead of him along the path leading to the house. No longer needing the crutches she'd left behind, she climbed the steps to the back door. Akis let them in.

He walked her to the guest bedroom and put her bag down. "While you freshen up, I'll start dinner." Whatever emotions had been building inside him, he hadn't made her privy to them.

"I won't be long."

She headed for the bathroom to shower and wash her hair. After using a towel to dry it, she put on her sundress. Raina had picked up a lot of sun. Even with the sunscreen, her skin felt tender. The straps of the dress wouldn't hurt so much.

Once she'd brushed her hair, she put on lipstick and felt ready to face Akis. Before the night was over she knew there'd be a conversation and she was dreading it. When she walked into the living room, she saw that he'd opened the terrace doors. The table had been set on the patio.

He flicked her a glance and told her to come and eat. Akis had put another salad together along with fruit, rolls and coffee. He helped her into her chair and took a seat opposite her. "You picked up a lot of sun today."

"I know. I'm feeling it now."

"Skin like yours needs special care."

Don't keep it up, Akis. I can't take it.

She'd lost her appetite, but ate a little of everything so she wouldn't offend him. "Thank you for taking me to Lefkada. I loved every minute of it, including the helicopter tours."

He eyed her over the rim of his coffee cup. "Do you still remember the word I taught you?"

"*S'agapo.* I promise to try it out on Chloe's parents as soon as we fly back." When there was no response, Raina got to her feet. She couldn't stand their stilted, unnatural conversation. "Since we're both through eating, I'll clear the table. I can't tell you how nice it is to be able to walk around without crutches."

"I can only imagine."

After two trips to the kitchen, she returned to the terrace, breathing in the fragrant air. It filtered through the house, arousing her senses. This was all too much. "If you'll excuse me, I'm going to phone Nora. I promised her I'd call her, but I forgot last night. I don't want her worried."

Akis had gotten to his feet. "Don't take too long. After you've assured her you're all right, come back to the living room. I want you with me. We need to talk."

He wanted her with him? She didn't understand him. Her heightened pulse rate refused to go back to normal. "Nora may not even be available. If not, I'll leave a message."

As it turned out, the call went through to the Milonises' voice messaging. She told them Akis had brought her to Anti Paxos and they'd been out in the cruiser to Lefkada. After saying she'd see them soon, she hung up and returned to the semidark living room. Akis was still out on the terrace.

His arms were stretched out against the railing, presenting a hard muscled silhouette against the starry sky.

"Akis?" she called quietly from the doorway.

He turned so he was facing her. "I made a promise to you before we flew here. But today I was so terrified I was going to break it, I had to do something to stop myself. The only thing I could think of was to bring you back here while I got myself under control."

She swallowed hard. "Did it occur to you that I wanted you to break it?"

"Yes," he said in a gravelly voice. "But I don't think you know what you're saying. If I touch you, I won't be able to stop. I want you so badly, I'm trembling. I thought I could vacation with you and handle it, but it isn't possible to control what I'm feeling. Tomorrow I'll take you back to Chloe's."

Her heart rebelled at his words. "What are you afraid of?"

"I don't want an affair with you and then have to say goodbye."

Raina could hardly breathe. "Why does it have to be an affair?"

"Because I want to make love to you. But you're the kind of woman a man wants to marry before he takes her to bed."

"And you don't want marriage because you prefer to remain a bachelor. Is that what you're saying?"

His chest rose and fell visibly. "More to the point, you wouldn't want to marry me. I could never be your equal."

"Why would you say something like that? I know we haven't known each other long. But if you feel as strongly about me as I do you, what is there to prevent us from marrying? Is there some dark secret you've been hiding?"

His hand went to the back of his neck. "Not a secret, but I'm not marriage material for a woman like you."

A slight gasp of pain escaped her lips because he'd delivered the words with a chilling finality. "What do you mean a woman like me? If this is your unique way of letting me know up front that marriage isn't in your future, I get the message. You're the one who brought it up, not me."

"After the pain your ex-husband put you through, I'm trying to be totally honest with you."

"Except you haven't told me why you're not marriage material. What am I to think about a cryptic comment like that?" Her anger flared. "However honorable you're trying to be, you have no clue about what I'm thinking or what drives me."

He moved closer until she could see his black eyes glittering. "I know a lot more about you than you think. You're the gorgeous young heiress to the Maywood fortune, the darling of the paparazzi from coast to coast. The Maywood estate in Carmel is one of the wonders of your state. Your corporation is one that helps keep the economy of California afloat. Your philanthropic projects are well known."

His admission stunned her so much she couldn't talk.

"According to the newspapers, besides your important work at its jet-propulsion laboratory, you run the entire corporation like a captain runs his ship, involved in every aspect. I happen to know that the Maywood tactical defense-system group works on air-defense issues, particularly air-vehicle survivability where the vulnerability of the US Air Force is concerned. Do I need to go on?"

By now her body was trembling. "So you've done your homework on me. I guess that means Chloe didn't keep her promise to me after all." The knowledge stung.

His expression grew fierce. "What promise?"

"That she wouldn't tell her husband-to-be that her old scandal-plagued heiress friend was coming to Greece. Did you know she'd asked me to be her maid of honor? Much as I would have loved to do that, I told her it wouldn't work. It was her special day. I didn't want my being there with all my baggage to ruin it for her. That's why she chose Althea."

Akis shook his head. "Neither Chloe nor Theo said anything to me. You've got this all wrong."

"Then how did you find out about me? No one was supposed to know I was coming. In order to keep the press from creating chaos at her wedding and swarming around me instead of focusing on her at the church, I chose to slip into Greece unnoticed.

"Out of consideration for her I flew on a commercial airline and stayed in a budget hotel in order not to be recognized. We agreed that I'd attend the reception as one of the guests. She made sure that there would be a place for me to sit at one of the tables in the rear of the ballroom while I watched."

"I believe you, Raina. Now you need to listen to me. I found out about you from a completely difference source."

"What source would that be?" Her voice sounded shrill, even to her own ears. "It's finally making sense that you singled me out for a dance in the ballroom. I honestly believed it was pure accident that we met. You were the best man and as such, *you* took on the job of entertaining me. I can hear the conversation now."

"Stop, Raina. It was my brother who told me about you."

She blinked in shock. "What do you mean, your brother?"

"He knew I had a lot of questions about you and he did some digging without my permission."

Adrenaline filled her system. "You two really do watch out for each other. What happened? When he found out my secrets and told you, did you decide to give me a thrill and ask me to dance?

"Was it because I'd had such a bad time of it with that awful husband of mine, you took pity on me? I was so vulnerable, you knew I wouldn't turn down the best man. And once again I was so desperate for attention, I bought it. No matter what I said or did, you kept coming and refused to be put off."

"If you'll let me explain—"

"Explain what?" She was borderline hysterical. "For the first time in my life I thought, here's a man who wants to get to know me better, just for me and no other reason! What a joke!

"You have no idea what a heady experience it was to see you barge in on Chloe's parents looking for me." Tears trickled down her hot cheeks. "Here I thought something extraordinary had happened that night. But all along you put on an exhibition that rivaled anything Poseidon could have done with all his power."

"*Raina*—"

"I have to hand it to you, Kyrie Giannopoulos." She kept on talking, too fired up to stop. "All this time you've been toying with me, shoring me up while I was in Greece because I was a pathetic mess. But it shook you up when I brought up the *m* word. That idea became too real to you."

"You don't know what you're talking about."

"No? Who better to take on the responsibility than the best man Akis? My sprained ankle gave you the perfect excuse to see to my comfort, but you played your part too well and it has rebounded on you."

She was running out of breath. "Let me tell you something. I never want to be someone's project." The tears were gushing now, but she didn't care. "I suppose I should be grateful to your brother. It's taught me there's absolutely no one in this world I can trust. For the first time in his life, my grandfather was wrong."

"Don't say anymore," he whispered from lips that looked as pale as his face.

"I won't. I'm through and am ready to leave."

"*Agape mou—*"

But she was too far gone to acknowledge his cry that came out in Greek. "Tomorrow I'll go back to Chloe's. You can remain here and you won't have to lift a finger for me. You've done more than enough. Who could have been more qualified than a Giannopoulos to carry the water without complaint?

"In case you don't understand the expression, it means you took on the job of giving this old maid a thrill out of the kindness of your heart. Congratulations to you and your brother who've gotten everything you want out of life, yet can still throw a few crumbs to those less fortunate."

Akis stood there dumbfounded while she ran down the hall to the guest room and shut the door. Because of his fear that he didn't have the credentials to be the kind of husband she deserved, he was afraid to propose marriage to her. But he'd handled this all wrong and had said things that had turned the most heavenly day of his life into a nightmare.

He couldn't let another minute go by allowing her to believe the worst about him. This was all his fault and he had to make it right no matter the cost.

As he walked down the hall, he could hear gut-wrenching sobs. The sound tore him apart. He rapped on the door. "Raina? I need to talk to you."

She refused to answer. He couldn't blame her, but there was no way he was going to let this go without her knowing the truth. Relieved that he'd never had the door fitted with a lock, he opened it and stepped inside.

Raina lay across the bed with her face buried in her arms, still dressed in the white sundress. Her body shook with tears that tortured him. He stole across the room and half lay on the bed facing her. Acting on instinct he slid a hand into her glossy hair.

"You've said a lot of things and I heard you out. Now it's my turn."

"You don't get a turn. Please leave me alone."

He smiled despite his pain. "I can't do that. You're going to have to listen to me even if you don't want to. Trying to peel away the layers of misunderstanding is going to take some time. But before we start over, there's one matter I need to clear up right now.

"Whatever secret you asked Chloe to keep, I swear to you she kept it so well that Theo never breathed a word of anything to me. Furthermore I didn't know of your existence until I arrived at Nora and Socus's house. They told me the beautiful woman with the sprained ankle I was looking for was Chloe's friend from America and that you were going to stay with them for a while."

He waited for a response. When it didn't come he said, "Did you hear what I just said? You'll have to take my word for it that everything going on with you and me was purely accidental."

In a surprise move she rolled onto her back with a

tear-blotched face, forcing his hand to slide from her hair. "If that's true, then when did your brother manage to tell you all about my life?"

"Not until the next night when Vasso phoned about the downed power grid. He told me he'd left some papers for me at the penthouse I should look at before I left on vacation. But he didn't explain the nature of them. I had to leave you when it was the last thing I wanted to do.

"You have to understand he's the older brother and has always had this thing about looking out for me. After I told him I'd met this amazing woman, it made him nervous because I've never been this taken with a woman in my life. He realized how important you were to me already. When he connected the Maywood name with our helicopter purchase, he searched the internet and wanted me to see what he'd found."

She groaned. "I can't get away from the notoriety no matter what I do."

"You did with me. What thrilled me was that you didn't know anything about me, either.

"In a world that worships money, Vasso and I are constantly stalked by the press. Their voracious hunger to pry into our lives has been a nightmare.

"Don't you see, Raina? For once in our lives, you and I were simply two ordinary people who met by accident and were seized by an attraction we couldn't control or dismiss."

Raina gazed at him in the semidarkness with her soul in those violet eyes. "To be fair, I discovered who you were in a roundabout way. When I called the lab to tell them I was going to prolong my vacation, I inadvertently informed Larry that I'd just ridden in our newest model helicopter and that it performed beautifully.

"That's when he told me that the famous rags-to-riches billionaire Giannopoulos brothers were the first from Greece to purchase them. Suddenly everything made sense…the Giannopoulos Complex and penthouse, this house set on property only people with great wealth can afford, a state-of-the-art cabin cruiser."

He put his arm around her and pulled her close. "You never said a word," he murmured against her lips.

"Neither did you."

"I didn't want anything to ruin our relationship."

"Neither did I."

He cupped her face in his hands. "Except for the last few minutes in the living room, I've never been happier in my life."

"Akis—" She moaned his name before he couldn't stand it any longer and plundered her mouth over and over again. She met him with an avid eagerness he could only dream about. For the next while they communed in the most primal way. Time passed as they bestowed kiss after kiss on each other until he was held in the thrall of ecstasy.

"You're my heart's desire, Raina," he murmured into the curve of her neck. "But I don't want to make a wrong move with you. No one needs to tell me you're not just any woman. I knew it the second we met."

Out of breath, she lifted her head and rolled away from him. Sitting on the edge of the bed she said, "When I came to Greece, I never imagined something like this happening. I was ready to leave the reception when you asked me to dance. It seemed like some trickery of magic that the best man found his way to my table. I'd watched you all evening.

"But even with all these emotions, I still feel like my happiness is going to be taken from me."

"Why?"

"Because I don't know if your feelings are as intense as mine, that they'll last…"

He got to his feet. "Don't you know I suffer from the same fear? We've both been taken by surprise. I don't want to do anything to ruin it. Before this goes any further, there's something I need to tell you about me that could alter your feelings where I'm concerned."

"In what way?"

"You told me you were hoping to have children after you got married, but children weren't part of your husband's plan."

Exasperated, she stood up. "What does that have to do with our situation? We're not contemplating marriage."

"You have no idea what's on my mind." Did that mean he'd entertained the thought? Her heart skipped a beat because tonight she'd wished he'd been her husband and they were on their honeymoon. "Even so, you deserve to know the truth about me."

She felt a moment of panic. "What truth?"

"I'm simply trying to say that if we were to become intimate, you wouldn't have to worry about getting pregnant."

She hugged her arms to her waist. "Because you wouldn't want children whether in or out of wedlock?"

"I didn't say that. While I was in the military, I

came down with mumps. I'm one of the thirteen percent of men who developed mumps-related orchitis. It rendered me sterile."

A quiet gasp escaped. "You weren't vaccinated?"

"Afraid not."

"But that was ten years ago. Today there are any number of specialists in that field. Have you been to one recently?"

"No. I've never had a reason to be worried about it. But after you told me the history with your husband, I know having children means everything to you."

And no doubt to him.

Her heart bled for him. "I'm so sorry, Akis. Have you had this conversation with the other women in your life?"

"There've only been a few, but the answer is no."

"Why not?"

"Because no woman ever made me want to carry her off where I could get her alone to myself for the duration."

His admission just described her condition, causing her body to quiver in reaction. "I'm touched that you would reveal something so personal to me."

She had to assume that the only reason he'd told her these things was so she wouldn't be expecting a marriage proposal at the end of their vacation. There was always adoption, but he wouldn't want to hear that from her. The painful conversation had gone in a different direction. Needing to change the subject she said, "Where are we going to go exploring tomorrow?"

His head jerked upward. "You've changed your mind about going back to Chloe's?"

"You know why I said it, but if you'd rather I did…"

In the next breath he grasped her upper arms and drew her to him. "You know damn well I want to spend as much time with you as I possibly can until you have to go back to California."

"That's what I want, too." Without conscious thought she pressed her mouth to his, wanting him to know her feelings for him ran deeper than he knew.

He kissed her long and hard before lifting his head. "I'm going to let you go to sleep. Tomorrow over breakfast we'll come up with an itinerary. If there's something you want to do, we'll do it."

CHAPTER SEVEN

If there's something you want to do, we'll do it.

Akis's words went round and round in Raina's head for the rest of the night. He was a conflicted man. On the one hand he didn't want to make love to her because she was the kind of a woman you married first.

On the other hand, Akis seemed convinced that her desire for a baby prevented him from entertaining marriage to her or any woman for that matter. He'd set up an impossible situation where Raina couldn't win.

He'd all but broken down and told her he was in love with her. Every sign was there. If she could penetrate that part of his psyche and make him realize his sterility didn't matter to her in the way he thought…

She would reason with him. Marriage was a risk. How many women got married and then found out that they had a problem that would prevent them from getting pregnant? Those situations happened to thousands of couples.

After moving restlessly for most of the night, an idea came to her and she was able to fall asleep. The next morning she awakened with a firm plan in mind. She freshened up and dressed in shorts and a small print blouse.

Before she'd left California she'd packed a pair of sneakers, but hadn't used them while she'd been here. Glad she was prepared, she put them on, eager to give them a workout today.

As usual, Akis had gotten up ahead of her and had breakfast waiting on the patio. He got up from the chair where he was drinking coffee. "Good morning, *thespinis.*" His eyes played over as he helped her to be seated.

"It's another beautiful morning. Does it ever get cloudy here?"

He smiled. Akis was so attractive, her heart literally jumped. "It rarely rains in June. You've come at the perfect time."

"I'm so lucky, and this looks delicious, as always." She started with eggs and a roll covered with marmalade. "No wonder Chloe chose this month to be married. Where are they going to live? Do you know?"

"They've bought a home in the northwest area of Athens called Marousi."

"I'll bet Chloe is so excited to set up her own house. She has a real eye for decor." Even back in high school her friend had dreamed of being married and having children, but Raina stayed away from that subject.

Akis flicked her a glance. "Have you decided where you'd like to visit today?"

"I have. I'd like us to take the cruiser to Paxos. When we went there before, I had to use crutches. Today I feel like walking and would like to visit all your old haunts like your first home, the school where you went when you had time. How about the home where your mother grew up? Could we visit the church where your parents were married?"

He averted his eyes. "None of it is that exciting."

"Maybe not to you, but I can't think of anything I'd rather do more. Unless it brings back painful memories. Does it?" she asked quietly.

"Not at all, but I supposed you wanted to see some of the other islands like Kefallonia."

"Maybe tomorrow, or another time."

Akis seemed engrossed in thought. While he finished his coffee, she cleared the table, anxious to get underway. This could be the most important day of her life if all went well.

In a few minutes he announced he was ready to leave. She grabbed her purse and left the house with him. "I love this old truck, Akis."

"It has seen a lot of wear transporting baskets of olives to town over the years."

"How did you come by it?"

"I bought it off a farmer who was happy for the money."

She eyed him intently. "Knowing you I bet you paid him ten times what it was worth."

A tiny nerve throbbed at the side of his temple. "What makes you think that?"

"You're a generous person by nature."

"You don't know any such thing."

Why couldn't he accept a compliment? "The way you treat me tells me the important things about you."

He lapsed into silence while they drove to the harbor to take out the boat. Maybe she shouldn't have suggested they travel to Loggos.

Once they reached the dock, she fastened her life jacket and sat across from him. He started the engine and they were on their way. "Akis? We don't have to go to Paxos if you don't want to."

"It's fine," he said without looking at her.

No, it wasn't, but he was determined to take her there. Raina made up her mind to enjoy this journey back in time with him. She ached to know all the private little things about him that made him the marvelous man he was.

The few framed photos in his house showed his parents, a young, attractive man and woman. There were two baby photos of him and Vasso. Adorable. Her heart pained for the circumstances that had taken their mother's life early. Her eyes filled with tears.

What a great father they'd had. One who'd worked night and day for them and had taught them how to be men. Though she couldn't meet his parents, she yearned to picture their life together. How proud they would be of their sons.

"Raina? Are you all right?"

"Of course."

"I can see tears."

"The sun got in my eyes."

The trip to Loggos didn't take long. This part of the famous island looked like a crown of dark green with jewels studding its base. Akis pulled into a slip to moor the cruiser. She discarded the life jacket and got out to help him tie the ropes to the dock.

She looked up at him, trying not to feast her eyes on him dressed in tan chinos and a dusky-blue crew neck. "Where should we start?"

He'd been studying her features through veiled eyes. "The old hut is on this side of the village, but it's a brief walk by trail. We might as well go there first."

Excitement built up inside her to be exploring his backyard, so to speak. They walked through the lush grove of olive trees interspersed with cypress trees. He'd grown up here, played here. At least he had to have played here a little until he was put to work at five years of age.

Before long they came to a clearing where a vineyard sprawled on the steep hillside before her eyes. She took a deep breath before following him along a path through the grape vines to the hut made of stone. It was even smaller than she had imagined.

Akis! He'd been born right here!

A man working the vineyard called out to him. Akis said something in Greek and a conversation ensued. He turned to Raina. "The owner says we're welcome to go inside."

She was too moved to say words. He opened the wood door and they walked into a stone house with windows and a wood floor. Twenty by thirty feet? There were no partitions, only a lot of vintner equipment and stakes. A counter with a sink was in the other corner.

"This is it, Raina. Our living room was over in that corner, our beds on the other side. That door over there leads to a bathroom of sorts. We had to pump water to fill the old bathtub. The best way for me and Vasso to get clean was to bathe in the sea."

"Were you able to keep any furniture?"

"It wasn't worth it. When the owner took over, he must have gotten rid of it."

A lump lodged in her throat. "Grandpa always said home is where love is. You can't get rid of that."

Akis turned to her and put his hands on her shoulders. He squeezed them, but didn't say anything. They stayed like that until he gave her the sweetest kiss on the mouth. Then he grasped her hand and they went outside.

"We'll climb up the hillside and along the ridge. The church is perched at the top. Because of the foliage you can't see it from here."

He let go of her as they walked through the rest of the vineyard and came to the trail. Pretty soon she saw the glistening white Greek church ahead of them standing alone, small and elegant. Raina looked back to the sea with a sweep of forest-green olive groves running toward it. She'd never seen such scenery.

"What's that white complex in the distance near the water?"

"The Center Vasso and I had built. It's a hospital and convalescent center for people with lymphoma who can't afford that kind of care. All in honor of our father."

"He raised such wonderful sons, he deserves the recognition. Did you go to church all the time?"

"Papa took us when he could."

"When was the last time you came here?"

"Vasso and I come every year and visit our parents' graves on their wedding anniversary in July. They're buried in the cemetery behind the church."

"If I'd known I would have brought flowers."

"We don't have to worry about that. See all those yellow flowers growing wild beneath the olive trees? The broom is in bloom. We'll pick an armful."

Akis left the path. She followed him and within a minute they'd picked a huge bunch. She buried her face in them. "They smell like vanilla."

He flashed her a white smile. "One of my favorite scents."

Soon they reached the church and walked around to the back. He stopped in front of his parents' headstone filled with Greek writing and dates. There was an empty can left in the center. Akis reached for her flowers and put them with his before lowering their stems into the can. "There's no water, but they'll stay beautiful until tomorrow."

She stood still while he remained hunkered down for a minute. Then he got up and they walked around to the front of the church. After the dazzling white outside, Raina had to take a minute for her eyes to adjust to the darker interior. It smelled of incense. Akis cupped her elbow and they moved toward the ornate shrine.

"There's no one here."

"The priest lives close by on the outskirts of the village. He'll come toward evening to conduct mass for the workers."

"This church is so lovely and quiet. While you sit, do you mind if I walk around to look at the wall icons?"

He slanted her a glance. "I'll come with you." To her delight he gave her a short history of each one before they walked outside the doors into the sunlight. The rays were so bright, she reached in her purse for her sunglasses.

"Let's head down to the village and have lunch at my favorite taverna. Elpis, the older woman who owns it, knew my parents before I did."

Raina chuckled over his little joke. Deep inside she was filled with new excitement to meet someone with whom he had a past connection. "I bet you're her favorite visitor."

"When Vasso and I were young, she cooked *l oukoumades* fresh every day and saved half a dozen for us to eat on the way home from work. She knew we couldn't afford them."

"I love that woman already. What are they?"

"Donuts soaked in honey and cinnamon. She'll serve you one. No one on the island makes them like she does."

Raina was so happy, she was surprised her feet touched the ground as they made their way down to the harbor. He pointed out the school where he and Vasso attended when they could. His life story was incredible.

The second they appeared at the blue-and-white outdoor café she heard a woman call out to Akis and come running. She hugged and kissed him in front of the people sitting at the tables. This woman had done her part for two young boys who'd lost their mother and had to work so hard.

When Akis introduced her to Raina, the older woman with gray in her dark hair eyed her for a minute and spoke in rapid Greek. Raina asked him what she said. His eyes narrowed on her face.

"You are a great beauty."

"That was kind of her."

For the next half hour they were plied with wonderful food while several tourists took pictures of them. Raina winked at him. "You've been found out. Smile pretty for the camera, Akis."

"Every eye is on you," came his deep voice.

Pretty soon Elpis appeared with a sack for Akis.

Raina knew what was in it. "Efharisto," she said to the older woman who kissed her on both cheeks.

"You are his fiancée?"

Raina didn't have to think twice. "I want to be."

A huge smile broke out on her face. "Ahh." She looked at Akis and said something in Greek, poking him in the chest.

After she went back inside he pulled some bills out of his wallet and put them on the table. His black brows lifted. "Are you ready to leave?"

"If I can get up. I ate so much, I'm afraid I'm nailed to the chair."

He came around to help her. By the lack of animation on his face, she couldn't tell if he'd understood the expression or not. The whole time more people were taking pictures of them with their phones. Akis was a celebrity. A lot of people had seen pictures of the Milonis wedding on TV, but he and his brother had been in the news long before that because of what they'd achieved in business.

The sun had grown hotter. When they boarded the cabin cruiser and took off for Anti Paxos, Raina welcomed the breeze on her skin. She stood at the railing all the way to the smaller island, wondering what he thought about her comment to Elpis. It appeared to have caught Akis off guard. That had been her intention. She needed him to know how she felt. But his silence had unnerved her. By the time they'd made it back to his house, she'd started to be afraid.

After setting down her suitcase, he put the sack of donuts on the counter and stared at her. "Do you have any idea what you said to Elpis?" His voice sounded unsteady.

She clung to one of the chair backs. "Yes. I'm in love with you, Akis. I couldn't hold it in any longer. It was evident how deeply Elpis cares for you, and I didn't want her to think that I just sleep with you. If I embarrassed you I'm so sorry," she whispered. "The fault's on me."

He cocked his dark head to the side. "What if I were to take you up on it?" His eyes were slits. "Aren't you afraid I might be your third mistake?"

The question produced a moan from her. "No. For once in my life I know clear through to my soul that you're the real thing." Her voice shook. "The only fear I have is that you don't have that same profound feeling for me. I saw the expression in your eyes when I blurted that I wanted to be your fiancée. I could read it so clearly.

"It was as if you'd said to me, 'Raina? We've been having a heavenly time together, but to take it to the next step is a completely different matter.' Deep in your heart of hearts you yearn to find a woman who's like the woman your father married—someone sweet and innocent with no divorce in her background."

"That's not true!"

"Oh, yes, it is. I understand why your brother was concerned enough to find out what he could about me. Some foreign woman with scandal in her past flies into Athens and disrupts the tenor of your lives. I never had a sibling. But knowing the story of you and Vasso, any woman either of you chooses will impact both your lives because you're family. I envy you that."

He moved closer, putting his hands on his hips in that potent male way. Her heart thudded mercilessly in response. "Let's talk about what I bring to your life.

As I told you the night of the reception, my brother and I are in business together. That's the sum total of our existence."

Her eyes misted over. "You bring so much, I don't know where to start."

"Why not start with the obvious. You run an empire."

She shook her head. "*I* don't do anything. My grandfather put people in place who do all the work. Since his death I've been the titular head. If I walked away from it tonight, there wouldn't be as much as a ripple. As for my job in the lab, there are dozens of scientists who'd fill my spot in a heartbeat."

His jaw hardened. "You're telling me you could leave it all behind? Just like that?"

Raina tried to swallow. "That's what I'm telling you. My parents and grandparents are gone. There's nothing to hold me." She couldn't control the throb in her voice. "To put it all in the hands of the capable people already in place and come to you would be my greatest joy."

His eyes closed tightly for a moment. "We couldn't even have a baby that could grow up to run the Maywood Corporation one day."

"We could have several babies through adoption who could one day head the Giannopoulos Company. You could call it Giannopoulos and Sons, or Daughters."

A strange, anguished sound came out of him. "I could swear the gods are playing a monstrous trick on me."

Her spirits sank. "In other words, Aphrodite is a monster in disguise."

"No, Raina. Your grandfather left you a legacy you can't ignore."

"I won't ignore it, but you're making an erroneous assumption. The difference between you and me is this…I didn't create the Maywood Corporation with my bare hands. I didn't do one thing to build it from scratch a hundred years ago. I'm a recipient of all the hard work that my great-great-grandfather started. That's all.

"But you and your brother started your company from scratch. You poured blood, sweat and tears into it every day, *all* day for years. It's your monument to your parents who gave you life and a father who taught you what was the most important thing in life."

"So what are you saying?" he ground out.

"That you can't leave your brother to live with me in California. You wouldn't want to and I wouldn't want you to. Furthermore I hate the idea of flying back and forth so we can see each other for a weekend here and there. It would be ludicrous.

"Since I don't want an affair, either, the simple solution is to live here with you for as long as you want me. I'd rather be married to you, but if you can't bring yourself to do that, then I'll be your lover and deal with it. As long as I know where I stand with you, no one else's opinion matters to me."

"It *does* matter." He sounded exasperated.

"Then what you're saying is nothing will fix our problem, so I should plan to go back to California? If that's the case then so be it." She wheeled around and grabbed her suitcase.

"Where are you going?"

"To change into my swimming suit and enjoy your pool. I need to work off the calories from our delicious lunch. Thank you for allowing me a glimpse of your early beginnings. It meant the world to me. Let me know when you're ready to pack in this vacation and get back to work. I can be ready in no time at all."

He followed her down the hall to the bedroom. "Will you stay until Chloe gets back?"

So he *was* anxious to get back to Athens. "Where else?" she said over her shoulder and plopped her suitcase on the bed. "I don't want to disappoint her parents."

"Do you want to leave in the morning? I'll send for the helicopter."

Her back was still to him. "That's entirely up to you." She opened the lid and pulled out her bathing suit.

"Don't be like this, Raina."

She whirled around. "Like what?"

"You're not thinking with your head. No one with a background like yours just walks away from everything because the man she loves lives on another continent."

She drew in a quick breath. "This one does, but you don't know me well enough to understand. If I leave California for good, money will continue to pour into my personal account Grandpa set up for me. Most of that money will be used to do research for a cure for stomach cancer and heart disease.

"As for everything else, I'll be available over the phone whenever one of the heads of the various departments wants to discuss a problem. I'll step down as CEO but remain on the board. If there's a vote to be cast that requires my physical presence, then I'll fly over. That's it. Not at all complicated."

He stood in the doorway unconsciously forming his hands into fists. "What about the estate? How could you contemplate leaving your home?"

Her chin lifted. "Before I ever heard from Chloe that she was getting married, I'd decided to move to a condo and turn the mansion and estate into a hospital. One wing for heart failure patients and the other for stomach cancer patients who can't afford health care. When I fly back to Carmel, I'll get the process going."

"You'd get rid of everything and live in a condo?" He was clearly incredulous.

"I already told my grandpa what I was going to do when he was gone. He gave me his blessing. I don't need an estate. To live one day in every room would take me a year."

She hoped he'd laugh, but his expression was inscrutable. "Look at this villa—it's the perfect size for you. That's why I love it so much. When you took me to the penthouse, I couldn't see you in it."

"Vasso and I use it out of necessity when we do business and have to stay on site in Athens."

"Ah, that explains it. Where does he live?"

"In a villa about this size on Loggos. But it's a beach house on the other side of the village."

She blinked. "You see? He doesn't need masses of square footage to be happy, either. Why do you think I would be any different?"

"But to come here and live isn't you."

His arguments were getting to her. "Because I'm a lousy linguist? I know I only know twelve words and don't pronounce them well, but I can learn. Just like you learned English!"

"We had to learn it in order for our business to succeed."

"Well, I'll have to learn Greek for marriage to you to be successful. What's the difference?"

"What kind of work would you do here?"

"If you opened up a new store along the harbor here on Anti Paxos, I could help manage it. If you hired another clerk, I could learn Greek from him."

He shook his head. "A job like that isn't for a woman like you."

"Akis—you have a strange idea of who I am. I'm flesh and blood and need work like everyone else. I think it would be fun. Your mom and dad worked together."

"That was different."

"How?"

"Because you're a physicist!"

"That's not the only thing I do. I'm a master scuba diver and could give lessons to people on the island."

"You never told me that," he accused.

"Because it never came up."

"Be serious, Raina. You'd go crazy being stuck here."

"Not if you came home to me at night."

"I can't always be here."

There was an edge of resolution to his delivery. A brittle laugh rose from her lungs like a death cry.

"I'd hoped you would want me here so much that I could convince you. But it hasn't happened, so you win. There's still some daylight left. Why don't you send for your helicopter and we'll fly back to Athens by dark. I'll phone Chloe's parents and alert them."

His lips had thinned to a white line. "Is that what you want?"

"You know what I want, but it doesn't matter. Go ahead and call your pilot. I'll take a swim, but I'll be ready when he arrives. Now if you don't mind, I'd like my privacy to change."

At first she didn't think he was going to leave. She could feel the negative vibes emanating from him. If he didn't go, she was in danger of screaming the house down.

Finally he disappeared and she got ready for her swim. For the next hour she played in the pool and lay back on the lounger. She had no idea what Akis was doing. Until the last second she prayed he hadn't sent for the helicopter. But then she heard the faint sound of rotors and knew it was coming. A stake driven through her heart couldn't have done more damage.

"Raina—you're back!" Chloe's mother clasped her with love and gave her kisses on both cheeks. "You've gotten a lot of sun."

"We've been so many places. It was wonderful." She hooked her arm through Nora's and they walked through the house to the guest bedroom. They'd left Akis and Socus having a private conversation at the helicopter pad.

"I have good news for you."

"What is it?"

"Chloe and Theo are having such a wonderful time, they're going to extend their honeymoon another week. Which means you have to stay with us longer than you'd first thought. She knows you're here and won't hear of your leaving Greece until after they get back."

Raina gave her a hug. "How about this? I'll fly home in the morning to do business. But I'll fly back when Chloe and Theo have arrived and we'll have our reunion."

"You promise?"

"Of course. I plan to leave early in the morning. Since it's getting late, I'm going to go to bed now."

"I'll have breakfast waiting for you before you leave."

"You don't need to do that."

"I want to."

"Thank you, dear Nora." She hugged her hard, already feeling a loss so excruciating, she didn't know how she would handle it.

After Nora left, Raina got ready for bed. The nightmare flight from the island with a taciturn Akis had pretty well destroyed her. When they'd landed on the pad, he'd helped her down and had whispered goodbye to her.

Just like that he'd let her go from his life. His words about Althea at the reception came back to haunt her. *You saved me from being caught. For that, I'm in your debt.*

"You're welcome," she whispered to the air before she buried her face in the pillow and sobbed.

As soon as the helicopter took off for the penthouse, Akis phoned his brother. Vasso picked up on the third ring. "How's the vacation going?"

"It isn't. Everything's over."

"What do you mean? Where are you?"

"I'm headed for the penthouse."

"I'll meet you there in ten minutes."

Akis hadn't been in the apartment five minutes before his brother arrived, but he'd already poured himself a drink. He held up the glass. "Want to join me?"

"No. You look like hell. Sit down and talk to me."

"There's nothing to say. I just said goodbye to Raina. She's going back to California in the morning."

Vasso sat down next to him. "Why?"

"It won't work."

"What won't work?"

"Us!"

"Doesn't she love you?"

He poured himself another drink. "She says she does."

"So what's the problem?"

"Look at me, Vasso!"

"I'm looking."

"Do you see a man who's worthy of her?"

Vasso's brows knit together. "Worthy—give me a definition."

"I'm not in her league and couldn't be in a hundred years. She's everything I'm not. In time she'll start to notice all that's missing and fall out of love with me. I couldn't handle that, so I let her go tonight." Exploding with pain, Akis got up from the couch. "I've got to go."

"At this time of night?"

"I need to be alone. I'm going to fly back to Anti Paxos."

"I'll come with you."

"No. I release you of the promise you made Papa to watch out for me. It's time I took care of myself."

"Wait—"

"Sorry, bro. I need to be alone."

It wasn't until Raina heard her phone ring in the middle of the night that she realized she'd been asleep.

She came wide awake and grabbed it off the night stand without looking at the caller ID. "Akis?" she cried.

"I'm sorry, Raina. It's Vasso Giannopoulos."

His big brother was phoning her? Her heart ran away with her. She clutched the phone tighter. "What's happened to him? Has there been an accident?"

"Not an accident, but he needs help and you're the only one who can fix this. I know it's three in the morning, but I had to call you. When he left me at the penthouse, he was in the worst state I've ever seen in my life."

"Where is he now?"

"He flew back to Anti Paxos. I heard him mutter something about being afraid you were leaving Greece forever."

She took a deep breath. "I am. I have to be at the airport in three hours to make my plane."

"Then it's true." Vasso's voice sounded a little different than his brother's, but he spoke English in the same endearing way.

"He said goodbye to me earlier when he dropped me off at Chloe's. I took it as final."

After a brief silence he said, "This is my fault for telling him about you. I did it because I wanted him to stop worrying about you. I don't know what has gone on between you two, but I have serious doubts he'll be able to handle it if you leave."

"He told me what you did, but that's not what is wrong. It's a long story. He took me to eat dinner at the taverna Elpis owns. When she asked me if I loved him, I said I wanted to be his fiancée."

"You *what*?"

Raina didn't blame him for being totally shocked. "Don't worry. He shut me down. I think it's because he got mumps and because of his sterility can't give me or any woman a child. He wants to do the honorable thing and give me a chance to marry a man who can."

"I don't believe that's the reason," he bit out, sounding like Akis just then.

"If it isn't, then I don't know what it could be."

"Look, Raina. I don't mean to interfere, but you can't leave yet."

"There's no point in staying. I fought him all day long trying to break him down so he'd really listen to me. That hurts a woman's pride, you know?" Tears crept into her voice.

"His pride is much worse. Do you love him?"

She got to her feet. "I love him to the depth of my soul."

Raina heard a sharp intake of breath. "Then go after him to that place inside of him and wear him down until you get the answer you're looking for."

She bit her lip. "He's given me his answer."

"No. It's a smoke screen for what is really bothering him. Trust me. If you love him like you say you do, don't give up."

"That's asking a lot."

"I'll send a helicopter for you first thing in the morning."

Her nails bit into her palm. "I'm afraid."

"Your fear couldn't be as great as his. He's not as secure as he lets on."

"Why do you say that?"

"Because I've known him longer. And I'm afraid of what will happen if you disappear from his life. I'll have the helicopter there at six whether you decide to take it or not."

He clicked off and left her pacing the floor for what was left of the night. It would mean telling Chloe's parents that she would going to Anti Paxos before she flew back to the States.

For the next two hours she went back and forth deciding what to do. At five o'clock she called to cancel her flight and the limo. When she left the bedroom with her bag, she went straight out to the patio to tell Chloe's parents her plans had changed. Only Nora was up, pouring coffee.

"There you are. I'm still having a hard time letting you go."

"Nora—my plans have changed."

"What do you mean?"

"I've cancelled everything and am going to fly to Anti Paxos to talk to Akis. We had a problem yesterday. In good conscience I can't fly home until we've talked again. Forgive me for making you get up early."

"I was awake." She smiled and gave her a hug. "The path to love is filled with obstacles."

Raina eyed her hesitantly. "Am I that transparent?"

She laughed. "Come on and sit down. As my husband remarked the day Akis came barging out here looking for the woman with the sprained ankle, the second you saw each other, no one else existed but the two of you. It was fascinating really because we'd noticed Akis running from Althea at the reception."

"I know. I felt so sorry for her."

"To our knowledge, Akis has never chased after a woman in his life. Yet the minute he saw you at the table, everything changed in an instant. I wondered when it was going to happen to him. Those two devilishly handsome brothers have been free agents for so long, it's had us worried.

"Their distaste for publicity has caused them to retreat from all the lovely women who'd love to have a relationship with them. But you've been surrounded by publicity, too, so you understand how stifling it can be."

Raina nodded. "I was afraid some member of the press would recognize me at Chloe's wedding and ruin her wedding day. That's why I chose to wait until the reception to make an appearance."

Nora patted her hand. "Chloe told us everything. She's always said you're the sweetest, kindest person she's ever known. Socus and I found that out years ago."

If Nora didn't stop, Raina would be in tears again. "So are all of you."

While she forced herself to eat breakfast for Nora's sake, she heard rotors in the distance. Her heart turned over. Vasso was as good as his word. Maybe he knew something she didn't. At this point she was running on faith and nothing else. He knew Akis better than anyone in the world and he was urging her to go to him.

Socus joined them for breakfast. Nora filled him in

before the three of them walked out to the pad with her
suitcase. After several hugs, she climbed on board and
waved to them before the helicopter whisked her away.

Athens passed beneath her, the Athens she'd seen
through the telescope from his penthouse. Tears ran
down her cheeks unchecked. She loved him so terribly. What if Vasso was wrong and Akis wanted nothing more to do with her? But Raina couldn't think
about it.

CHAPTER EIGHT

AKIS DIDN'T KNOW where to go with his pain. Vasso
hadn't been able to help him. For once in their lives
the brother he relied on had no answer for him. This
was a crisis he had to figure out on his own. Vasso
had helped him get to the helicopter at the complex
and told the pilot to fly him to Anti Paxos.

When he reached his house, he headed straight for
the truck. He didn't care it was dark out. He needed
work. It had been his salvation for years. He'd clean
the cabin cruiser until he dropped.

Midmorning he grew so tired he staggered down
the steps to the cabin. One of Raina's crutches resting
against the wall had fallen across the floor, causing
him to trip. He collapsed onto the bed so exhausted
and emotionally drained he stayed right where he'd
fallen. The next thing he knew it was late afternoon.
He could tell by the position of the sun through the
window slat.

Groaning, he turned on his back. Not since the serious case of mumps that almost killed him had he
felt this ill. But it was a different kind of sickness that
started in the very core of his being. By now Raina
would be flying somewhere over the US to her home

of three hundred and sixty-five rooms. He'd gotten rid of her all right. He'd done everything to make certain she'd never come near again.

His stomach growled because it was empty, but he wasn't hungry. He hadn't eaten since their meal at the café yesterday when Raina had told Elpis she wanted to be his fiancée. To be that open and honest in front of the older woman had knocked him sideways. He still hadn't recovered.

When she'd told him she'd be his lover if that's what he wanted, he'd felt shame that he'd been so cruel to her. He'd seen her heart in those fabulous violet eyes. They haunted him now. He looked around the cabin. All he saw was emptiness.

Life without Raina wasn't life.

He couldn't comprehend how he'd gotten through it this far without her. Life would have no meaning if he didn't go after her and beg her forgiveness. Grovel if necessary. It terrified him that she might refuse to see him. She would have every right.

The first thing to do was make arrangements for their company jet to fly to Corfu. He'd leave for the States from there. He pulled out his cell phone and made the call, then he headed to the bathroom for a shower and shave, but he only made it as far as the hallway when he smelled coffee and ham of all things.

Akis had been in a traumatic state last night. His brother must have come to check up on him. Calling out his name he went to the kitchen and came close to having a cardiac arrest.

"Raina—"

She stood at the counter whipping up eggs. Her blond head swerved in his direction. "You look terrible. By the time you've taken a shower, dinner will be ready. I'm fixing you an American breakfast. Did you know breakfast is my favorite meal? I could eat it morning, noon and night."

He rubbed the back of his neck in disbelief that she was really here. "You're supposed to be on your way home."

"Well as you can see, I haven't left Greece yet. Vasso phoned and asked me to peek in on you before I go. He seemed to think you needed help."

Akis couldn't believe it. "Vasso actually phoned you?"

She nodded. "From the look of you, I can see why. Hurry. We're having omelets and they only taste good right out of the skillet. Cooking is another one of my accomplishments."

Raina had so many accomplishments, it staggered him. Still in shock that she was here on the cruiser instead of a jet liner, he showered and shaved in record time. He kept casual clothes on board in the drawer. After dressing in a pair of jeans and a T-shirt, he hurried back to the kitchen, afraid he'd been dreaming and she wouldn't be there.

"You look a little better. Sit down and I'll feed you." She slid the omelets onto two plates with ham and placed them on the table.

"How did you get here?"

"When I saw that the truck was gone, I walked to the harbor and there it was. I climbed on board and found you passed out on the bed. I thought maybe you'd had too much to drink."

"I rarely drink."

"So I went back on deck and walked around the village to buy a few groceries and a pan. You were still asleep when I returned. To pass the time I got busy and made some brownies."

"What are they?"

"A chocolate dessert."

"Now that I think about it, I can smell it. This omelet with the ham is divine, by the way."

"That's because you're hungry. I'll report back to Vasso that your appetite has returned." He watched her get up and put some chocolate squares on a plate before she brought it to the table. "If you're still starving, you can fill up on these."

One bite and he was hooked on them. In no time at all he'd eaten all five.

"They're good, aren't they? The convenience stores carry them. They sell like hotcakes."

"Like hotcakes?"

"Or pancakes. Same thing. Americans love them, but you can never stop with just one. If you sold them in one of your Alpha/Omega 24 stores, you'd be shocked how fast they'd disappear."

"Raina—" He couldn't take anymore. "We need to talk."

"I think we've said it all. Now that some food has brought you back to life, I can leave in good conscience."

"Where do you think you're going?" He got to his feet to bar the way.

"Now that I've made my pit stop for your brother, I'm walking back to the house. Vasso's helicopter is waiting to fly me to Corfu. I'll let him know his worry over you is unfounded and I'll take the plane home from there."

"First you're going to come to the bedroom with me where we'll be more comfortable."

"Oh. Now you've decided I can be your lover? Sorry. I'm taking that offer back."

A grimace broke out on his face. "There's only one reason why I haven't asked you to marry me."

"Because you can't give me a baby. I know."

"That's not it." He picked her up around the hips and set her on the counter. "This is better. Now you're on eye level with me." Akis could feel her trembling. "Look at me, Raina."

"I don't want to."

"I don't blame you. After the way I've treated you, you have every right to despise me. The truth is, I'm not an educated man with diplomas covering my walls. I don't know all the things you know and have learned."

"*That's* the reason you were willing to let me go? Just because some pseudoacademic can talk to me about the differences in Pointillism between Seurat and Signac means absolutely nothing to me!"

"You see? I don't know who they are. I don't know what Pointillism is."

"You think I want to talk to you about that?"

"If we went to a party at one of your friends, they'd see my deficits in a hurry and you'd wish you'd never brought me."

"Oh, Akis—if I took you to one of my parties, the women would fall all over themselves just to hear you speak English with your unforgettable Greek accent. The men would take one look at you knowing they couldn't measure up to you, and they'd be so jealous of your business acumen, they'd croak."

"Croak?"

"Yes. Like a frog."

"Don't tease me, Raina. You're brilliant. I can't do math, I can't speak intelligently about art or literature. I'm not well read and haven't traveled the globe. Chloe and Theo have most everything in common. They suit each other in so many ways. But you and I are poles apart.

"I couldn't take it if we married and you grew bored with me. You told me Byron made a wonderful companion. Even though he betrayed you, he had a cultural background that stimulated you in the beginning. I can't give you that and I'm afraid I'll lose you."

She lifted wet eyes to him. "So you decided to push me away before you gave us a chance to find out what our life could be like? Do you know you could teach a class on Greek history and mythology that would blow everyone's mind? I know your worth, Akis. You know things no one else knows. You can't let that be the thing that keeps us apart!"

He cupped her face in his hands. "I was afraid at first, but no longer. I want to be all things to you. You're my heart's blood. I don't want to take another breath if I can't be with you. I love you, Raina. I love you," he cried against her lips. "I want you for my wife if you'll have me."

"If I'll have you— Oh, Akis…" She launched herself into his arms. He carried her out of the kitchen and down the hall to the bedroom. When he laid her down, she pulled him to her. "I love you, my darling," she murmured over and over again between kisses. "I wish we were already married."

"So do I, but I know a man in high places who can arrange a special license for us tomorrow. We can be married at the church on Paxos. I'll arrange it with the priest."

"You don't want a big wedding?"

"Never. Do you?"

"I did all that once before. What I want is to be your wife and hibernate with you for several months before anyone knows except Chloe's family, and Vasso, of course."

"I owe him for getting you here. How did he manage it?"

"His call at three in the morning got my attention in a hurry, but he didn't have to beg me. The thought of leaving you was so terrible, I doubt I would have gotten on the plane." By this time she'd broken down in tears of joy.

"Don't you know I love our differences? No woman could love you the way I do, Akis. I'm so in love with you, a lifetime won't be enough to show you how much. We were meant to be together, my love."

"I know that," he admitted. "My psyche knew it at the reception. One look into your eyes and the hairs began prickling on the back of my neck. They've never stopped."

"I knew I was crazy about you when you ran to my table in desperation." Their joyous laughter turned into moans of need as their mouths met and clung. Time had no meaning as their legs entwined and they tried without success to appease their unquenchable desire for each other. Akis felt as if he'd been born for this moment.

An all-consuming need to prolong this ecstasy

caused him to burn out of control. For the next while he found himself drowning rapturously in her over-whelming response. It was so marvelous to feel this alive, to touch her, love her. She was all warmth and beauty.

But Akis knew that to stay in the bedroom any longer would mean they'd never come out. He relinquished her mouth. "We need to go back to the house and make our plans, Raina. I want to be married before I make love to you for the first time. My father told me it was the best way to start out a marriage. I'd like to be a good son and honor his final advice to me."

"Then we will, but you're going to have to be the one with the willpower. Mine has deserted me. *S'agapo, Akis.*"

His breath caught. "You know what it means?"

"When you told me it was the most important word I would ever say in Greek, I figured out what it meant and have been dying to try it out on you. How did I do?"

He drew her off the bed and crushed her in his arms, rocking her back and forth. "You sounded like a native just now."

"Then there's hope for me. I plan to learn your difficult language or die in the attempt."

"Don't talk about dying on me," he begged. "Not ever, and not in jest. This is the first day of our new life together. Kiss me one more time before we leave. I need you the way I need our Greek sun to shine. You're my life force, Raina. Do you hear me?" He shook her gently.

"I think you have that turned around. You swept

across the dance floor to my table, and then you swept
me out of the hotel, crutches and all." She looked into
his eyes. "My beloved Poseidon, I'll love you forever.
Do you hear me?"

CHAPTER NINE

Six weeks later

RAINA HURRIED INSIDE the villa with all her packages and put them down on the couch in the living room. Before she did anything else, she needed to call Akis and let him know her plans had changed. But she got his voice mail and had to leave a message.

"Darling? I know I told you I'd be at the penthouse when you got back from Crete, but I decided that since it's Friday, I'd rather we spent the weekend at the villa so I'll see you when I see you. Hurry. *S'agapo.*"

She had no idea when he'd hear the message, let alone when he'd be home. It was already ten after five. Between her shock and excitement since her morning appointment at the doctor's office in Athens, she wouldn't be surprised if she were running a temperature.

To get ready for tonight she'd stopped at an internet café to look for the picture she wanted. When she found it, she printed it off. Next, she went to a high-fashion boutique and found the perfect Grecian gown of lilac chiffon that tied over one shoulder.

After running by a florist's shop, she headed for the hair salon near the Grand Bretagne hotel and asked the stylist to make her hair look like the picture on the printout and twine the small lavender flowers in it. From there she went to a shop to buy a dozen vanilla-scented candles. Last but not least, she stopped at a boutique for infants and bought a beautiful baby book, which she had wrapped.

Once her errands were done, she returned to the penthouse and took the helicopter to Anti Paxos.

Time was of the essence. She made his favorite chicken salad with olives and feta cheese and would combine it with crusty rolls and fresh fruit. With the dinner ready, she went out on the patio to set the table. In between the potted plants she placed the candles, and put the last three for a centerpiece. She hid the baby book behind a big clay pot filled with azaleas.

Now to get dressed. After her shower she put on the gown. While she was tying it at the shoulder, her cell rang. Giddy with joy, she reached for it and saw the caller ID. "Darling?" she cried the second she picked up.

"I just got your message. Vasso and I are headed for the island now. You didn't want to go out on the town tonight?"

"Not really. Do you mind?"

"What do you think? If I had my way, we wouldn't go anywhere else."

"I'm glad you feel that way. Are you hungry?"

"Starving."

"How soon do you think you'll be here?"

"Fifteen minutes. You sound like you've missed me."

She was breathless. "I know it's only been two days, but I feel like it's been a month!"

"I'm never going to spend another night away from you. Not having you in bed with me was torture I don't want to live through again."

"Neither do I. Hurry home and be safe." *We have a future awaiting you never thought was possible.*

It took a few minutes for her to light all the candles. The flames flickered in the scented air, sending out their marvelous fragrance Akis said he loved. Twilight had fallen over the island. She'd just lighted the table candles when she heard the blades rotating.

He'd be here any second. She walked to the terrace entrance to wait. In a minute she heard him call out, "Raina? Where are you?"

Taking a deep breath she said, "I'm out on the patio."

Her gorgeous husband appeared in the living room wearing a sport shirt and trousers, but he stopped short of coming any closer. She could see he was almost dumbstruck. Good. That was exactly the reaction she'd hoped for.

His black eyes had a laser-like quality as they examined her from the flowers on her head to the gold slippers on her feet. She saw desire in that all-encompassing gaze and almost fainted.

"You've been away, so I wanted to make your homecoming special. Tonight you're going to stay with me or I'll think you've forsaken me. Come and eat while I serve you. I have a special surprise."

She heard him whisper her name, but he looked absolutely dazed. She loved him so much she could hardly stand it.

"Would you like your surprise first, or later?"

His hand passed over his chest. "I don't think I could handle another one. The way you look tonight standing there like a vision from Mount Olympus, I'm having trouble breathing."

Raina sent him a come-hither smile. "That's more like it. I thought maybe you'd forgotten me."

He started to look nervous. "Is there something wrong?" She could see an anxious expression in his eyes. It was sweet really. Her darling husband was so wonderful, she needed to put him out of his misery.

"Of course not. You're always so generous and take such perfect care of me, can't your lover do something special for you without you worrying?"

His chest rose and fell visibly, evidence that he needed an answer. Afraid to carry this charade any further without an explanation he could live with, she walked over to the flowerpot and pulled out the wrapped package.

"If you'll sit down at the table with me, I'll give this to you."

Instead of the happiness she'd expected, he looked stricken. "It's our six-week anniversary. I planned to give you your gift tonight while we were out to dinner in Athens. But I left it at the penthouse."

"There's plenty of time for you to give it to me. Right now why don't you open yours." She walked over to the table and put the present on top of his plate, then she sat down opposite him.

Akis moved slowly, like he was walking through water. Then he sank down in the chair stiffly and reached for it, but he kept looking at her. Why was he behaving like this? She couldn't understand it.

When he pulled the baby book out of the wrapping, she thought he'd paled, but it was difficult to tell in the candle light. His black brows furrowed. "What kind of a joke is this?"

With that question, she finally understood how much he'd suffered because he thought he could never be a father.

"It's no joke. I've been nauseated every morning for the last week. I asked Chloe to get me in to see her OB this morning in Athens. He took a blood test. I'm pregnant with your baby."

His head reared. He stared at her. "But that's impossible."

"I told my doctor the same thing. He said that mumps for a certain percentage of men cause a drop in their sperm count. But research has come a long way since ten years ago when you came down with them. Since then, he says you've recovered." She put a hand on his arm and squeezed it. "You had to have recovered because I'm pregnant."

When the truth finally sank in, the chair scraped on the tile. He shot out of it and came around to pick her up in his arms, holding her like a bride. "We're going to have a baby! *Raina*—"

He carried her through the house to their bedroom and followed her body down onto the bed. His mouth kissed her so long and hard, she could scarcely breathe. "My precious love." Over and over he kissed every inch of her face and hair. The tie on her shoulder had come undone. She felt moisture on her skin. By now they were both in tears.

"I didn't know it was possible I could be this happy, Akis."

"I still can't believe it." His hand slid down her body to her stomach, sending darts of delight through her. He leaned over to kiss her through the chiffon. "Our baby is inside you."

"Incredible, isn't it. Do you want a boy or a girl?"

"Don't ask me a question like that. I don't care. I only know I want you to take care of yourself. I couldn't bear to lose you."

She hugged his head to her breast, kissing his black hair. "Please don't be afraid for me. I'm not your mother. I won't die after giving birth. I'm strong and in perfect health. The doctor has given me a prescription for nausea. I've had all day to consider names. I can't think of a girl's name yet, but I know what I want if we have a boy."

He lifted his head. His eyes were filled with liquid. "Tell me," he whispered, kissing her mouth.

"Patroklos Giannopoulos after your father. We can call him Klos for short. I looked up his name. It means glory of the father. It's a perfect name to revere the man who fathered you and Vasso."

"It might be a girl," he murmured, kissing her neck to hide the emotions she knew were brimming out of him.

"Of course. But I draw the line at *Phaiax.*"

All of a sudden that delightful, rumbling sound of male laughter poured out of Akis. He rolled her on top of him. "My adorable Naiad nymph. If we have a daughter, we'll name her Ginger after her earthly great-grandmother who raised you to be the superb woman you are."

"Hmm." Raina drew her finger across his lower lip. "Ginger Giannopoulos. I love it. Almost as much as

I love my husband who has given me a priceless gift. Darling—I know what this news means to you. I also know that you and Vasso share everything. Go ahead and call him, then I'll have your whole attention."

A half smile broke the corner of his mouth. "Am I that transparent?"

"It's a beautiful thing to see two brothers so devoted to each other. Your joy will be his. Here. Use my phone." It was lying on the bedside table.

Their conversation was short and so touching, she teared up again. When he hung up, he crushed her in his arms. "Thank God my brother phoned you in the middle of the night."

She clasped him to her. "I know now that Grandpa was inspired when he told me not to close off my heart. He knew something I didn't. I love you so much. I'm the luckiest woman on earth. The doctor says I probably got pregnant on our wedding night."

"Have you told Chloe?"

"No. I simply asked her to give me the name of her OB since I needed a prescription for birth control. I think news like mine should be reserved for the man who's made me the happiest woman in the world."

"We haven't seen them since the wedding. Let's invite them over on Sunday and tell them together."

"I'd love it, but right now I want to concentrate on you. Do you want to eat first?"

"Not yet. I need to inspect my pregnant wife from head to toe."

Heat swept into her cheeks. "You already did when you saw me standing on the patio."

"I'll never forget the sight of you in this gown with

those flowers in your hair and the air fragrant with vanilla. But there are other sights meant for me and me alone. Come here to me, Raina."

"I'm here. *S'agapo*, my wonderful, fantastic Akis."

* * * * *

A WEDDING FOR
THE GREEK TYCOON

REBECCA WINTERS

CHAPTER ONE

August 9, New York City

THE BEARDED OLDER DOCTOR looked at Zoe. "Young woman. You've been cancer-free for eight months. Today I can say without reservation that it's definitely in remission. We've already talked about the life span for recovering patients like you. But no one can predict the end of life for any of us."

"I know," she said as he continued to explain the survival expectancy statistics for patients like her. But she'd read about it all before and didn't really listen. The adage to take it one day at a time and rejoice for another day of life was the motto around the hospital.

Zoe's physical exam had gone without incident. Her labs looked great. But she would never outgrow her nervousness. Fear lurked in her that the next time she had to have a checkup, the cancer would have come back. She couldn't throw it off.

The therapist at the center had given her a book to read about dealing with the disease once it had gone into remission. Depression bothered many patients who feared a recurrence and that was a problem they needed to deal with. Since Zoe was a prime example, she could have written that section of the book herself.

But for today she was filled with relief over the lab results. In fact she was so overjoyed with the news she had difficulty believing it. A year ago she'd been told she had a terminal case, but now... She looked at the doctor. "So what you're saying is—it's really gone."

His brows furrowed. "Believe it, girl."

She believed it for today, but it would come back.

"I'm pleased that the terrible fatigue you felt for so long is now gone. You seem much stronger physically and emotionally. Your therapist and I believe you're ready to leave the center today if you wish."

That was the news she'd been waiting for. She had plans and there was no time to lose.

"Here's hoping that from now on you can live a normal life."

Normal... It would never be normal when she knew the cancer would return. But she smiled at him. "How can I thank you for everything you've done for me?"

"You already have by working so hard to get well. You have a beautiful spirit and are an inspiration to the other patients here in the hospital. All the friends you've made here will miss you."

Tears stung her eyes. "I'll miss them more." With this checkup behind her, she could put her plan into action.

"I doubt that."

Zoe folded her arms to her waist. "My bill has to be astronomical. If it takes me the rest of my life, I'm going to pay back every cent of it."

"It's been taken care of by the generosity of the Giannopoulos Foundation Charity."

"I'm aware of that." So aware, in fact, she needed to thank the members of the Giannopoulos family personally and one day she would. "But everyone who works here is an angel, especially you. I don't know what I ever did to deserve such care."

When she'd been admitted to the hospital, she'd read the material given to every patient. The first time she'd gone to the chapel inside the hospital she'd read the plaque. It had been named for the Church of Agii Apostoli in Greece.

In honor of Patroklos Giannopoulos and his wife Irana Manos who survived the malaria outbreak on Paxos in the early 1960s.

In honor of her brother Kristos Manos who survived the malaria outbreak and emigrated to New York to build a new life.

In honor of Patroklos Giannopoulos who died from lymphoma.

"I'm here by the grace of the foundation here in New York too," the doctor reminded her. "It was established for Greek Americans with lymphoma who have no living family or means for the kind of help you've needed. There are some wonderful, generous people in this world. Do you have a place to go?"

"Yes. Father Debakis at the Sacred Trinity Greek

Orthodox Church has taken care of everything. I've known him since I was young. Throughout my ordeal he's been in constant contact with me. I owe him so much, and Iris Themis too. She's from the humanitarian council at Sacred Trinity and has arranged to take me to their homeless shelter where I can stay until I find a job and a place to live. All I have to do is phone her at her office."

"Splendid. As you know, you'll need another checkup in six weeks, either here or at another hospital depending on what's convenient. It will include a blood test and physical exam for lumps. But you can contact me at any time if you have concerns."

Zoe dreaded her next checkup, but she couldn't think about that right now. Instead she stood up to give him a hug. "Thank you for helping me get my life back. You'll never know what it means."

After she left his office, she hurried through the hospital and walked along the corridor that led to the convalescent center. She had a room on the second floor. Having lost her family, this had been her home for twelve months.

In the beginning, Zoe didn't dream that she'd ever leave this place alive. At first the man she'd been dating had called her often, but the technology company Chad worked for transferred him to Boston and the calls grew fewer and fewer. She understood, but it hurt her to the core. Even if he'd told her he was crazy about her, if he could leave at the darkest moment of her life, then she couldn't expect any man to accept her situation.

Though there were family friends from her old

neighborhood who phoned her every so often, the inmates had become her choice friends. With all of them
being Greek American, they shared stories of their family histories and had developed a camaraderie so strong
she didn't want to leave them. It was here that her whole
life had passed before her.

Once inside her room, she sat down on the side of
the bed and phoned Iris. They planned to meet in front
of the convalescent center in a half hour. One day Iris
and the priest would receive their crowns in heaven.

Zoe had emerged from her illness wanting to help
people the way they'd helped her. College could wait. If
she could go to work for the Giannopoulos Foundation,
that was what she wanted to do. Of necessity Zoe would
have to approach Alexandra Kallistos, the woman who
managed this center, but any experiences with her were
unsettling. The other woman was standoffish. Whether
that was her nature, or if she just didn't care for Zoe,
she didn't know.

Earlier today when they'd passed each other in the
hall, Ms. Kallistos hadn't even acknowledged her.
Maybe it was because Zoe was taking up a bed someone else needed, but the therapist had insisted she
still needed to be here. Because she'd lost her parents
and required more time to heal mentally, the arrangements had been made for which Zoe would be eter-
nally grateful.

Ms. Kallistos had an office at the hospital and was
officially in charge. All the staff, doctors, nurses, thera-
pists, lab workers, X-ray technicians, orderlies, kitchen
help, volunteers and housekeeping people reported to

her. She was a model of efficiency, but Zoe felt she lacked the bedside manner needed to make the inmates comfortable enough to confide in her.

Alexandra was a striking, brown-eyed, single Greek American woman probably in her early thirties. Her dark brown hair flounced around her shoulders. She wore fashionable clothes that made the most of her figure. But she seemed cold. Maybe that wasn't a fair judgment, but the thought of approaching her for a position made Zoe feel uneasy.

If there was a problem, maybe Father Debakis would have better luck in bringing up the subject of Zoe working here.

August 10, Athens, Greece

Vasso Giannopoulos was nearing the end of the audits on the Giannopoulos Complex in Athens, Greece he co-owned with Akis, his younger married brother, when he heard his private secretary buzz him. He'd been looking over the latest inventories from their convenience stores in Alexandroupolis.

"Yes, Kyria Spiros?"

"Ms. Kallistos is on the line from New York. She's calling from the hospital in New York, asking to speak to you or your brother. Do you want to take it, or shall I tell her you'll call her back later? I know you didn't want to be disturbed."

"No, no. You did the right thing." The Giannopoulos Hospital and Convalescent Center were located in Astoria. But why she would be calling when he was scheduled to meet with her tomorrow seemed odd. His head lifted. "I'll speak to her."

"Line two."

He picked up the phone. "Alexandra? This is Vasso."

"I'm sorry to bother you, Vasso. I thought I could catch you before you fly here. You're very kind to take my call."

"Not at all."

"Everyone knows that you and your brother established the Giannopoulos Greek American Lymphoma Center here in New York several years ago. This is the fourth time that I've been contacted by a major television network to devote a piece to your lives.

"The managing director of the network wants to send a crew here to film the facility and interview some of the staff. More importantly they want to interview you and your brother for the featured documentary. I told him I would pass this along to you. I know you've turned them down before, but since you'll be here tomorrow, would you be interested in setting up an appointment?"

Vasso didn't have to think. "Tell the man we're not interested."

"All right. When can I expect you to arrive?"

"By two at the latest. I appreciate the call. *Yassou.*" As he rang off, Akis walked in the office. "Hey, bro. I'm glad you're back. Alexandra just phoned. One of the networks in New York wants to do a documentary on us."

"Again?" Akis shook his head. "They never give up."

"Nope. I told her to tell them no."

"Good. How soon are you leaving for New York?"

"I'm ready to head out now. I plan to meet with some of our East Coast distributors early in the morning. Then I'll go over to the hospital and take a look at the books."

"While you do that, I'll finish up the rest of the inventories for the northern region. Raina will help. She's a genius with accounts. You won't have anything to worry about."

"How's her morning sickness?"

"It hardly ever bothers her now."

"Glad to hear it."

"Before you leave, I have a question." Akis eyed him with curiosity. "How did your evening go with Maris the other night?"

"So-so."

"That doesn't sound good. We were hoping she might be the one who brings an end to your bachelor existence."

"Afraid not. She's nice and interesting, but she's not the one." He patted Akis's shoulder. "See you in a couple of days."

Vasso hadn't been dating Maris that long, but already he knew he needed to end it with her. He didn't want to lead her on. But Akis's comment had hit a nerve. Both of them had been bachelors for a long time. Now that Akis was married, Vasso felt an emptiness in his life he'd never felt before. His brother was so happy these days with his new wife and a baby on the way, Vasso hardly recognized him.

August 12, New York City

"Vasso!"

"How are you, Alexandra?"

The manager got to her feet. "It's good to see you."

"I walked through the hospital and convalescent center first. Everything seems to be in perfect order. My congratulations for running an efficient center we can be proud of."

"Thank you. I know you're busy. If you want to go over the books in here, I can order lunch to be brought in."

"I've already eaten. Why don't I look at the figures while you're out to lunch? If I see anything wrong, we'll discuss it when you get back."

"All right. Before I leave, I wanted to tell you about a young woman who applied here for a job yesterday. I told her she didn't have the education or background necessary for the kind of work we do at the center.

"Later in the day I received a phone call from Father Debakis at the Sacred Trinity Church here in Astoria. He knows this woman and finds her a very capable person. He wanted to know if he could go to someone higher to arrange for an interview. I wrote the priest's number on my sticky note in case you want to deal with him."

"I'll take care of it now. Thanks for telling me."

"Then I'll leave and be back in an hour."

"Take your time." Vasso's curiosity had been aroused by the mention of the priest. As she reached the door he said, "I want you to know my brother and I are very pleased and grateful for the work you do to keep this center running so smoothly."

He heard a whispered thank-you before she left the office. Vasso phoned the number she'd left and asked to speak to Father Debakis. Then he sat back in the chair.

"It's an honor to speak with you, Kyrie Giannopoulos. I'm glad Ms. Kallistos passed my message along. Since I don't wish to waste your time, I'll come straight to the point." Vasso smiled. He liked brevity. "A very special twenty-four-year-old Greek American woman named Zoe Zachos here in Queens would like to work for your charity. I've taken it upon myself to approach you about it."

"I understand Ms. Kallistos had reservations about hiring her."

"When I spoke to her on Zoe's behalf, she said this young woman doesn't have the credentials and flatly refused to consider interviewing her for a position. I disagree strongly with her assessment and hoped to prevail on you to intercede in this matter."

Vasso and Akis had flown to New York ten months ago to find a new manager after the old one had to give it up due to ill health. Alexandra had come to them with outstanding references and was the most qualified of all the applicants because she'd had experience working in hospital administration.

Akis, who'd been in business with Vasso from childhood, had flown to New York five months later to check on her. So far neither he nor Vasso had a problem with the way she'd been doing her work. She must have had good reason not to take the other person's application.

"Obviously this is important to you."

"Very." Vasso blinked in surprise at the priest's sobriety. "Perhaps she could be interviewed by you?"

He sat forward. "That isn't our normal procedure."

"Ah…" The disappointment in the priest's voice wasn't lost on Vasso, who'd been taught by his deceased father to revere a priest.

His black brows furrowed. "May I ask why you have such strong reasons for making this call?"

"It's a matter of some urgency."

The hairs lifted on the back of Vasso's neck. After the priest put it that way, Vasso didn't feel he could refuse him. "Tell me about her background."

"I think it would be better for you to discover that information yourself."

At this point Vasso was more than a little intrigued. In all honesty he found himself curious about the unusual request. "How soon could she be at Ms. Kallistos's office?"

"Within two hours."

"Then I'll be expecting her."

"Bless you, my son." The priest clicked off while a perplexed Vasso still held the phone in his hand. For the next hour and a half he pored over the books. When Alexandra returned, he told her everything looked in order and listened to some of her suggestions to do with the running of the hospital.

During their conversation, a polite knock sounded on

the closed door. He turned to Alexandra. "That would be Zoe Zachos. If you'll give us a half hour please."

After a discernible hesitation she said, "Of course." She showed remarkable poise by not questioning him about it. He watched her get up and open the door. "Come in, Zoe," she said to the blonde woman before she left them alone.

Zoe? That meant Alexandra knew her.

Vasso didn't know exactly what to expect other than he'd been told she was twenty-four years old. He got to his feet as the young woman came into the office.

"Kyrie Giannopoulos?" she said, sounding the slightest bit breathless. "I'm Zoe Zachos. I can't believe it, but somehow Father Debakis made this meeting possible." In an instant a smile broke out on her lovely face. "You have no idea how grateful I am to meet you at last."

Tears had caused her translucent green eyes to shimmer.

When she extended her hand to shake his across the desk, he saw a look of such genuine gratitude reflected in those depths, it reached places inside him he didn't know were there.

"Please, Thespinis Zachos. Sit down."

Her lissome figure subsided in one of the chairs opposite the desk. She was wearing a print blouse and khaki skirt, drawing his attention to her shapely body and legs below the hem. She had to be five-six or five-seven.

"I'm sure he told you that I'd like to work for your foundation."

He felt an earnestness—a sweetness—coming from her that caught him off guard. "He made that clear."

She clasped her hands. "When he spoke on my behalf with Ms. Kallistos, she said I didn't have the kind of background she was looking for."

"But Father Debakis feels that you do. Tell me about yourself. Why would you want to work for the foundation as opposed to somewhere else, or do another type of work entirely?"

"He didn't tell you?" She looked surprised.

"No. He's a man of few words."

"But he makes them count," she said with a smile that told him she'd had a running relationship with the priest.

Vasso agreed with her assessment. The priest had an amazing way of making his point. It had gotten Vasso to conduct this interview, which was out of the ordinary. "Why not start at the beginning, *thespinis*?"

She nodded. "I've been a patient here with non-Hodgkins lymphoma for the last year and was just released on the ninth of this month."

A patient...

Knowing what that meant, he swallowed hard. Vasso had thought of several reasons for the possible conflict between the two women. He thought back to a year ago when another manager had to resign because of health issues. When they'd hired Alexandra, Zoe Zachos had already been a patient here. The two had seen each other coming and going for months. But it didn't explain the problem that caused Alexandra to turn down Zoe's request.

"I was thrilled to be told I was cured."

The joy in her countenance was something Vasso would never be able to describe adequately. "That's wonderful news," he said in a thick-toned voice.

"Isn't it?" She leaned forward with a light in those marvelous green eyes. "It's all because of your family. The foundation you established literally gave me back my life!" The tremor in her voice resonated inside him.

He had to clear his throat. "To hear your testimonial is very gratifying, Thespinis Zachos."

"There's no way to pay you back monetarily. But I would love to work for you in some capacity for the rest of my life. I'm a good cook and could work in the hospital kitchen, or in the laundry, or give assistance to those convalescing. Give me a job and I'll do it to the best of my ability. The trouble is Ms. Kallistos told Father Debakis that without a college degree and no experience in the health field, there was no point in interviewing me.

"She wondered if I might not be better suited to becoming a nun if I wanted to be of service to others." A *nun*? "I'm sure she was just teasing. Father Debakis and I laughed over that. I'm hardly nun material. But I do want to make a difference."

Vasso's anger flared. Not so much at Alexandra as at himself and Akis. At the time they hired her, both he and Akis had decided she had the best credentials for the important position even if she was younger. But Vasso could see there was a great deal more to finding the right person for this particular job than what was put on paper. Since Zoe had been a patient here for such a long time, surely Alexandra could have shown a little more understanding.

"Whatever was said, you have a great advocate in Father Debakis. How did you come to know him?"

"My parents owned a Greek *taverna* and we lived in the apartment above it here in Astoria near the Sacred Trinity Church. Father Debakis was serving there when I was just a young girl and always took an interest in our family. If it hadn't been for him, I'm not sure I'd be alive today."

"Why do you say that?"

An expression of unspeakable sorrow brought shadows to her classic features, changing her demeanor. "A year ago I'd gone to a movie with some friends from the neighborhood. We walked home after it was over. It was late. My parents would have been in bed."

She paused before saying, "When we got there, it looked like a war zone. Someone said there'd been an explosion. I ran towards the fire chief who told me an arsonist had planted a bomb in the back of the laundry next door to my parents' *taverna* where I sometimes helped out part-time. Fire spread to the *taverna*'s kitchen. Everything went up in smoke. My parents died. So did the owners next door who'd run the laundry for many years."

"Dear Lord." Vasso couldn't fathom it.

"Everything burned. Family photos, precious possessions, clothes—all was gone. I've always lived with my parents and worked in the restaurant kitchen to save money while I went to college. The scene was so horrific, I collapsed. When I came to, I was in the ER at the local hospital. Father Debakis was the first person I saw when I woke up.

"He told me the doctor had examined me and had discovered a lump in my neck." Vasso saw her shudder. It brought out a protective instinct in him he hadn't felt since he and Akis were on their own after their father died. Though Akis was only eleven months younger, their dying father had charged Vasso to look after his younger brother.

"Honestly, I'm still surprised I didn't die that night. I wanted to. I was convinced my life was over. He, along with Iris Themis, one of the women on the church humanitarian council, wouldn't let me give up.

"They are wonderful people who did everything to help me physically and spiritually in order to deal with my grief. The diagnosis of cancer added another level of despair. My parents and I had never taken a handout from anyone. For them to shower me with clothes and toiletries lost in the fire besides being there for comfort, meant I felt overwhelmed with their generosity."

Vasso got up from the chair, unable to remain seated. Father Debakis had told him she was a very special young woman.

"Before the fire and my illness, I'd planned to finish my last semester of college to get my English degree. I'd even thought of going on to get a secondary school teaching certificate. Because I had to work at night and go to school during the day, my education had to be strung out."

A sad laugh escaped her lips. "At twenty-four I would have been one of the oldest college graduates around, but the enormity of losing my parents this last year along with the lymphoma has changed my focus."

"It would change anyone's." When Vasso's father had died of the disease, the world he and Akis had grown up in was changed for all time. They'd adored their father who was too poor to get the medical treatment needed. As he slipped away from them, they'd vowed never to feel that helpless again.

He watched as she re-crossed her elegant legs. "While I was still at the hospital, I met with a cancer specialist who discussed my illness with me. My student insurance would only cover a portion of the costs. There was only a little money from my parents' savings to add to the amount owing.

"With their insurance I was able to pay off my student loan. What I had left was the small savings in my bank account that wouldn't keep me alive more than a couple of months. I was trapped in a black abyss when Father Debakis and Iris came to get me and bring me here.

"I was told the center existed to help Greek Americans with lymphoma who had few sources of income to cover the bulk of the expense. They took me into the chapel where I read what was written on the plaque."

As she looked up at Vasso, tears trickled down her flushed cheeks. "At that moment I knew the Giannopoulos family truly were Samaritans. You just don't know how grateful I am." The words continued to pour out of her. "As long as I'm granted life, I want to give back a little of what your foundation has done for me. It would be a privilege to work for you and your family in any capacity."

As long as I'm granted life.

What had Father Debakis said? It was a matter of some urgency.

Zoe Zachos's revelations had left Vasso stunned and touched to the soul. He sucked in his breath. "Are you in a relationship with anyone?"

"I had a boyfriend named Chad. But he got a job offer in Boston around the time of the fire. I urged him to take it and he did. We've both moved on. So to answer your question, no, there is no special person in my life."

Good grief. What kind of a man would desert her in her darkest hour?

"Where do you live right now?"

"I'm at the church's shelter. I'm planning to find an apartment, but I hoped that if I could work at the center here, then I would look for a place close by."

"Do you have transportation?"

"Yes."

"And a phone?"

"Yes." She drew it from her purse. "Iris will pick me up here as soon as I call her."

He pulled out his cell. "Let's exchange phone numbers." After that was done he said, "Before the day is out you'll be hearing from me."

She got to her feet. "Thank you for giving me this opportunity to talk to you. No matter what you decide, I'm thankful I was able to meet one of the Giannopoulos family and thank you personally. God bless all of you."

All two of us, he mused mournfully. *Four* when he included Raina and the baby that was on the way.

After she left the office, Vasso went back to the desk

and sat down to phone Akis. He checked the time. Ten o'clock in Athens. His brother wouldn't have gone to bed yet. He picked up on the third ring.

"Vasso? Raina and I were hoping we'd hear from you before it got too late. How do things look at the center?"

He closed his eyes tightly. "Alexandra has everything under control. But something else has come up. You're not going to believe what I have to tell you." For the next few minutes he unloaded on his brother, telling him everything.

"When we created the foundation, it felt good. It was a way to honor *Papa*." In a shaken voice he said, "But one look in her eyes taught me what gratitude really looks like—you know, deep down to the soul. I've never been so humbled in my life."

"That's a very moving story," Akis responded in a serious tone. "What do you think we should do? Since Alexandra has made her opinion obvious for whatever reason, I don't think it would work to create a position for Thespinis Zachos under the same roof."

"I'm way ahead of you. What do you think if we hired her to work at the center on Paxos?"

He could hear his brother's mind ticking away. "Do you think she'd be willing to relocate to Greece?"

"I don't know. She has no family in New York, but she's very close to Father Debakis and one of the women working for the Church's humanitarian program."

"What about a boyfriend?"

"Not at the moment. But I'm sure she has friends she met at college. There was the mention of friends she'd been out with the night of the fire."

"She's definitely one of the survivors of this world. What does she look like?"

How to describe Zoe Zachos…? "I can't explain because I wouldn't do her justice."

"That beautiful, huh?" Akis knew him too well. After a pause, "Are you thinking of asking her if she'd like to move to Paxos?"

It was all he'd been thinking about since she'd left the office.

"Just be careful, Vasso. I know you inside and out. If she does take you up on your offer of a job, you're going to feel responsible for her. Be sure that's what you want."

He lowered his head. Funny how circumstances had changed. Vasso used to be the one watching out for Akis. Now his little brother had taken over that role. It gave him a lot to think about, but there wasn't time if he expected to phone her before nightfall. "I'll consider what you've said. *Yassou.*"

On his way out of the office, Alexandra was just coming in. "You're finished?"

"That's right."

She looked surprised. "Are you staying in New York tonight?"

"No. I'm flying back to Athens." The beauty of owning a private jet meant he could sleep at night and arrive where he needed to be the next morning.

"I see. What have you decided about Ms. Zachos?"

"You were right. Her skills can best be used elsewhere." Her bilingual abilities in English and Greek played only a tiny part of what she could bring to the job. "That's what I'll tell Father Debakis. Keep up the good work, Alexandra. My brother and I are relying on you."

Relief broke out on her face. "Thank you. I hope the next time you come you'll arrange to stay longer."

Vasso nodded before leaving the center. After he got in the limo, he phoned the priest.

"Father? This is Vasso Giannopoulos. I've just come from the center and am pressed for time. Could I meet with you and Thespinis Zachos in your office ASAP?"

"That can be arranged. I'll ask Kyria Themis to bring her immediately."

"Excellent. In lieu of her parents who died in the fire, I look to you as someone who has her deepest interest at heart. I understand she has revered you from childhood. What I'd like to do is present an employment offer to her. I believe it's vital that you are there so she can discuss it with you." He paused, then said, "She regards you as her mentor."

"She's so grateful to everyone who helped her; her dearest wish is to work for your foundation. She lost everything. Now that she has survived, she wants to give back what she can."

"After talking to her, I believe that's true. I'll see you soon."

He hung up and asked the limo driver to take him to the Greek Orthodox Church a few blocks away.

CHAPTER TWO

ZOE DIDN'T KNOW what the meeting with the priest was all about. The incredible-looking man she'd met at the hospital earlier had told her he'd phone her before the day was out. Since leaving that office, she'd wondered if he'd really meant what he'd said.

But any concern in that department vanished the second she caught a glimpse of his black hair through the opening of the study door. Her pulse quickened for no good reason the second a pair of jet-black eyes beneath black brows zeroed in on her.

Both men stood when she walked in wearing the same skirt and blouse she'd worn earlier. She only had three or four outfits because no more was necessary living at the hospital. But now she needed to do some shopping for a wardrobe with the money she still had left in her bank account.

Over the years Zoe had been in the priest's study many times with other people, but she'd never laid eyes on any man as gorgeous as Vasso Giannopoulos. The thirtyish-looking male possessed facial features and a hard-muscled body that were as perfectly formed as her favorite statue of Apollo she'd only seen in pictures. No other man could possibly compare.

Her first meeting with him had been so important, she hadn't had the luxury of studying him the way she could now. He was probably six foot two and topped the priest by several inches, having an authority about him not even Father Debakis possessed. The dark gray suit toned with a lighter gray shirt gave him a rare aura of sophistication.

"Come in and sit down, Zoe. Kyrie Giannopoulos requested that I be in on this visit with you."

"Thank you." She found an upholstered chair next to the couch where he sat.

Father Debakis took his place behind the desk. He nodded to the younger man. "Go ahead and tell her why you've asked for this meeting."

Vasso sat forward to look at her with his hands resting on his thighs. Her gaze darted to his hands. He wore no rings. "After you left the hospital, I phoned my brother to tell him about you and your situation. We would be very happy to have you come to work for the foundation, but the position we're offering would be on the island of Paxos in Greece."

Zoe decided she had to be dreaming.

"Have you ever been there?"

She shook her head. "No, though I did go on a two-week university tour to England right before the fire broke out. As for our family, we took trips up and down the East Coast and into French Canada."

After a quick breath she said, "My great-grandparents left Florina in Macedonia to escape communism after the Greek Civil War and came to the US in 1946. It was in New York my father met my mother whose family were also refugees. They'd planned to take us on a trip back there for my graduation present, but it didn't happen."

"Maybe now it can," he said. "The center here in New York is fully staffed, and it might be a long time before there's a vacancy. But our center on Paxos has needed an assistant to the manager since the last one left to take care of a sick parent."

Zoe could feel her pulse racing. "You've established another hospital?" That meant she wouldn't have to work under Ms. Kallistos?

"Our first one actually. My brother and I have interviewed a number of applicants, but the manager hasn't felt he could work with any of them."

He? "What makes you think he would feel differently about me?"

"I have a feeling he'll welcome you because you have one credential no one else has possessed to date. It's more important than any college degree."

Her heart was pounding too hard. "What's that?"

"Compassion. You've lived through the agony of having been diagnosed with lymphoma, being treated for it and beating it. The year you've spent in the center here has given you the most valuable knowledge of what it's like to know you have the disease, and to have survived."

"Still, Ms. Kallistos said—"

"Let me finish," he cut her off, not unkindly. "For

that kind of learning experience, you've paid a terrible price. Yet it's that very knowledge that's needed to work with patients because you conquered the disease. Everyone in the hospital will relate to you and your presence alone will give them hope."

"She does that at the hospital every day," the priest inserted.

Her throat swelled with emotion. "What's the manager like?"

"Yiannis Megalos served as a rear admiral in the Greek Navy before his retirement."

A man who'd been an admiral. How interesting. "Then he must run a very tight ship."

The smile he flashed turned her heart over. "He's an old family friend and came to us about a position with the foundation after losing his wife to cancer, in order to work through his grief. In that respect you and he already share something vital in common by having a burning desire to help. I don't need to tell you his organizational skills and his work with the wounded during his military career made him an excellent choice."

"He sounds remarkable."

"Yiannis is a character too," he added on a lighter note. She felt his eyes travel over her. "If I have any concerns, it's for you. Leaving New York to live in a new country is a huge decision to make. If you've got anyone special you don't want to leave, that could prove difficult."

She shook her head. "There's no one."

"Even so, you may not feel that you can uproot yourself from friends. It might be hard to leave those here at the church who've helped you. That's why I wanted Father Debakis to be here in case you want to discuss this with him in private."

"Of course I'll miss everyone, but to be given a chance to work for your foundation means more to me than anything."

"We can come to terms over a salary you'll feel good about. You'll need a place to live. But all of those matters can be discussed once you've determined that you want this position. Talk it over with Father Debakis. Take as long as you need."

Zoe was so thrilled to have been offered a job it took a minute for her to comprehend it. She fought back her tears. "I'll never be able to thank you enough for this offer, not to mention the generosity of your family's foundation."

He got to his feet. Again she felt his scrutiny. "Be sure it's what you want," he warned in a more serious tone of voice. If she didn't know anything else, she knew deep down this was what she wanted and needed. "In the meantime I have to fly back to Athens tonight. You can phone me when you've made your decision."

Seize the moment, Zoe. "Before you leave, could I ask you a few more questions?"

"Of course."

"What's the weather like right now?"

"It's been in the low eighties all summer and won't drop to the seventies until later in September. Usually the night temperature is in the sixties."

"It sounds too good to be true. Are there shops near the hospital to buy clothes?"

"The center is on the outskirts of the small seaside village of Loggos. There are a few tourist shops, but I'd suggest you do your shopping in Athens first."

"Then that solves any problems I'll have about luggage. I lost everything in the fire so I'll replenish my wardrobe there."

He paused in the doorway, looking surprised. "Does this mean you've already made up your mind?"

She eyed the priest then glanced back at the other man. "I can't wait!"

"I can see you're a woman who knows her own mind." She thought his eyes might be smiling. "Under the circumstances, let's go out for dinner where we can talk over details. I'll drive you back to your shelter then leave for the airport."

She turned to the priest. "Oh, Father Debakis…I'm so happy I could take flight."

He chuckled. "I believe you could."

Vasso knew he'd never forget this moment. It was a nice feeling to make someone happy. He smiled at the priest. "It's been a pleasure to meet you."

"And mine, Kyrie Giannopoulos. Bless you."

"Shall we go, *thespinis*?"

After they walked out to the limo, he asked her to recommend a good place to eat.

Zoe swung around. "There's a Greek diner called Zito's a few blocks over. They serve lamb kebabs and potatoes so soft you can taste the lemon."

That sounded good to him. He told the driver who headed there, then concentrated on the charming female seated across from him. "We need to talk about your travel arrangements. There are dozens of flights to Athens every day. Once we know the date, I'll book a flight for you."

"Thank you, but I'll take care of that. This is so exciting, I can't believe it's happening."

Her excitement was contagious. He hadn't felt this alive in a long time. Once inside the diner they were shown to a table for two. The minute they were seated and Zoe ordered for them, she flicked him a searching glance.

"While I've got you here alone, I need your advice. If I were to take Kyrie Megalos a small gift from New York, what would he like?"

His lips twitched. "He collects naval memorabilia from all over the world."

That gave her a great idea. "Thanks for the tip."

"You're welcome. Before any more time passes, I need to know about your financial situation."

"I don't have one. I'm broke." A laugh escaped her lips, delighting him. "That doesn't mean I have no money, but it wouldn't be enough to keep me alive for more than a few months. That's why I can't wait to start work.

"When I look back, I'm pretty sure I know the reason why Ms. Kallistos didn't want me to work there. I took up a bed in the center for eight months after my first cancer-free checkup. That's because I was allowed to live in the hospital's long-term facility for the last eight months and get therapy to help me with grief issues."

Vasso surmised that was only one of the reasons Ms. Kallistos had problems with Zoe. No woman could compete with this female's effervescent personality. Her reverence for life sucked you in.

"After the chemo and bone marrow transplant, I was given all the time there I needed to recover, for which I'm grateful. I don't even have to wear a wig now. No one would ever guess that I'd once lost all of it."

Without her blond hair that had a slightly windblown look, she would still possess stunning classic features. "You seem the picture of health. If a long stay at the center was what made the difference in your recovery, then I applaud the therapist's decision."

She nodded. "I finally got it out of my doctor that the therapist was worried about my recovery. Losing my parents was so horrendous I had gone into a deep depression, and he could see I needed counseling. That part was certainly true. I was an only child and way too connected to them at the hip. They were wonderful and worked so hard, I tried to do everything I could to help them. In one night my whole world evaporated."

"That's the way my brother and I felt when our father died of lymphoma. The world we knew had gone away. Luckily we had each other."

"My therapist explained that if I'd had a sibling, it might have made a big difference. He made me realize why I had such a hard time letting them go. Grief hits everyone differently. In my case I was a twenty-four-year-old woman crying like a child for her parents. You don't know how much fun they were. We were best friends."

"Akis and I had the same relationship with our father." Everything she told Vasso rang so true with him about his own life he had trouble finding words. "I'm glad the priest prevailed on me to interview you. He's very persuasive."

Another quick smile appeared. "He is that. The other day when the doctor saw me for my six-weeks checkup and told me I was still cancer-free, something changed inside of me. I didn't want to stay there any longer and realized I'd come out of the worst of my depression. Father Debakis knew about my wanting to work for your foundation. So for you to give me a chance is like another miracle." Her voice trembled. "Thank you for this opportunity. I promise I won't let you down."

"I'm sure you won't."

The waiter brought their food, but Vasso hardly noticed what he was eating because emotions got in the way of anything else. Their conversation had reminded him of the father he and Akis missed. Their dad had treated them like buddies. He had laughed and joked with them.

Vasso always marveled over how smart he was. Their father knew everyone and had taught them to treat other people with respect. That was how you got ahead. He and Akis remembered everything their father had told them.

She finished her meal before looking up at him. "Your money saved my life and it's saving the lives of everyone at the hospital. Not just the patients, but the staff too. My oncologist is thrilled to be working there.

You and your family have done more for others than you will ever know."

"I hear you, Zoe. Now no more talk about gratitude. Because you'll be living on Paxos, I know of several places you can rent. By the time you reach the island, I'll have lined up some apartments for you to look at."

"That's very thoughtful of you, but I can do that myself."

"I'm sure you could, but you'll need a place close to the center and they're not easy to come by."

"Then I take your word for it. Thank you."

"If you've finished, I'll run you by the shelter."

She got up from the table. "I'll phone you as soon as I've made my flight plans."

"I'll be expecting your call and we'll go from there."

As he walked her out to the limo, he felt as if he too had undergone a life-changing experience. Of course he realized the foundation was helping many people. But for the first time since he and his brother had established the two centers, he had a personal interest in one of the former patients who had recovered.

She'd been so open about her family it triggered memories for him about his father and the life the three of them had enjoyed together before he'd died. Despite their poverty they'd had fun, too. He'd forgotten that aspect until Zoe started talking about her life. Because of her comments about family, he was seeing his own past through fresh eyes. Her story tugged at his heart and Vasso found he was no longer the same emotionally closed-up man who'd flown to New York on business.

August 17, Athens, Greece

Prickles of delight broke out on the back of Zoe's neck as the plane made its descent through a cloudless sky toward the runway. From her coach-class window seat she looked out at the sea, the islands. Closer still she made out the clay-roofed houses lining Athens's winding roads. This was Vasso Giannopoulos's world.

A sense of wonderment accompanied these sensations because she still couldn't believe she was coming to a place where she'd never been before and would be working. No doubt her ancestors experienced the same feelings when they arrived in the US, ready to embark on a new life.

How easy her life was by comparison! Instead of reaching the US by ship, she was on an airliner. Instead of having to undergo a holding time for immigrants, she'd been given safe passage right through to the Athens airport where she'd be taken care of. A job was waiting for her. So was the man who'd made all this possible. He was so wonderful she couldn't believe how lucky she was to have met him.

Kyrie Giannopoulos and his family were responsible for everything that had happened to her since she'd been admitted to the Giannopoulos Center in Astoria a year ago. Somehow he'd made it possible for her to work for his foundation. He'd said he'd be waiting for her when her plane landed.

The thought of seeing him again gave her butterflies. Surely meeting him a second time wouldn't cause her legs to almost buckle as they'd done the first time.

The mere sight of such a magnificent-looking man had haunted her thoughts whether she was awake or asleep.

After the plane touched down and taxied to the hangar, the seat belt came off and Zoe reached for her secondhand overnight bag. She followed the other passengers out of the plane to the terminal lounge where they went through customs. Her bag was searched. After she'd presented her passport and answered a few questions, a female airline attendant came up to her.

"You're Zoe Zachos?"

"Yes?"

"Come with me, please."

She got on a cart and was driven some distance to an elevator that descended to the ground floor. After another little ride the airline employee stopped the cart in front of a door. She got out and opened it. "Your ride is waiting out there."

The second Zoe walked through the door onto the tarmac where the hot sun beat down she saw a limousine in the distance. Once again her legs seemed to go weak when she spotted her benefactor lounging against the passenger side wearing sunglasses. This morning he'd dressed in a light blue sport shirt and tan chinos. He looked so wonderful she moaned before she realized he could have heard her.

"Thespinis Zachos, welcome to Greece."

No man should be this handsome. Zoe felt out of breath. "Thank you for meeting me."

"Of course. I hope you had a good flight." He took her bag and opened the rear door for her to get in.

"It was fine."

He went around the other side and got in with her bag so they sat across from each other. The interior smelled of the soap he must have used in the shower. Her reaction to him was over the top. Maybe there was something wrong with her.

"My driver will take us to the complex where my brother and I work. We'll stay in the penthouse. It's where we entertain guests and business people who must stay overnight. Tomorrow we'll fly to Paxos."

The limousine moved into the center of Athens. Another time and she might enjoy the scenery more, but right now she couldn't concentrate. After what he'd just told her, Zoe felt like a tongue-tied high school girl with a giant-sized crush on a man so far out of her league it was outrageous.

Glomming onto the safer subject of business she said, "Does Kyrie Megalos know you've hired me?"

"Not yet. I want him to meet you first."

She eyed him directly, but couldn't see his eyes behind the glasses. "Something tells me you're pulling the same thing on him that Father Debakis pulled on you." Vasso laughed hard. "He may not want me to be his assistant."

"In that case he'll give you another position. Don't worry. He won't suggest that you join a nunnery."

Laughter escaped her lips. His sense of humor was very appealing. "I shouldn't have said anything about Ms. Kallistos's remark. It wasn't kind of me."

"She should have known better than to say anything, so put it out of your mind."

"I have. Do you mind if I ask you some questions? Would you please tell me what kind of business you're in? I don't have a lot of information about you apart from your philanthropic work."

They'd driven into the heart of the downtown traffic. "If you'll look out your right window, you'll see a store coming up that says Alpha/Omega 24."

Zoe searched each shop. "Oh—there it is! *Everything from A to Z.* It's like one of the 7-Elevens in the States!"

"It's store number four, the first store we opened on the mainland."

"So you're a convenience store owner! Where are stores one through three?"

"On Paxos. My brother and I started our own chain years ago. They've spread throughout Greece."

"Now you're forcing me to guess." She eyed him with an impish expression. "Do you have as many as a hundred perchance?"

"We reached the hundred mark in Thessalonika."

Zoe gulped. "You weren't kidding, were you? Does your chain spread as far as Florina?"

"Farther, but it might interest you to know we have a store in Kozani. It's not far from the home of your ancestors."

She'd just been teasing, but he'd come back with an answer that filled her with awe. "So how many stores do you have altogether? Wait—don't answer that question." Heat filled her cheeks. "I'm being rude to pry. Forgive me."

"I don't mind. 2001, including the one we recently opened in Crete."

Zoe had tried to imagine the kind of money it took to run both centers. Now that she knew what kind of wealth was behind the foundation, she was blown away by the generosity of these men. "You really are perfect," she whispered.

"You have a lot to learn," he quipped, making her smile.

By now the limousine had turned down an alley and stopped at the side of a big complex. He got out with her bag and came around to help her. He had a remote on his key chain that opened the door to an elevator. They rode it to the top. When the door opened, she entered a glassed-in penthouse where she welcomed the air conditioning.

"If you'll come with me, I'll show you to the guest bedroom." She followed him through a hallway to a room with a fabulous view of Athens.

"What an incredible vista! Am I the luckiest woman in the world to sleep here tonight or what? You're far too good to me."

"We do this for business people who come to be interviewed for store manager positions."

"But I'm not exactly the kind of business person that generates a profit for you. I promise I'll do my best to help the patients at the hospital."

"I have no doubt of it." He put her overnight bag on the floor. "The en-suite bathroom is through that door. This area of the penthouse is all yours until we leave for Paxos. Now I'm sure you want to freshen up and relax, but first let me show you the kitchen."

She walked down the hallway to the other part of

the penthouse with him. "There's food and drink waiting for you if you're hungry. Please help yourself to anything you want while I go down to the office and check in. If you need me, just phone me, but I won't be long. After lunch we can go shopping if you're up to it."

"Thank you, Kyrie Giannopoulos." He was beyond kind and so many other things she'd lost count.

"Call me Vasso."

She smiled. "I'm Zoe."

He'd removed his sunglasses. "Zoe Zachos. Has anyone ever called you ZZ?"

Another laugh broke from her. He had a bit of an imp in him. "No. You're the first."

She felt the warmth from his black eyes long after he'd left the penthouse. Before doing anything else she walked over to the windows in the living room. The site of the Acropolis seemed as surreal as the whole experience of meeting Vasso Giannopoulos for the first time.

He had to be a very busy man, yet he'd taken time out to interview her himself. His insight about the emotions she would experience by moving to Greece revealed he was a man of empathy and compassion. Because of his goodness, her life was already being transformed.

CHAPTER THREE

"KYRIE GIANNOPOULOS?" VASSO'S secretary spoke to him
as he was passing through to his office. "Your brother
said he'd be in after lunch. You've had two calls this
morning from Maris Paulos who said it was urgent you
get back to her."

In order to maintain his privacy, he gave out his cell
phone number only to a few people. It forced Maris to
reach him through his secretary. Until she'd mentioned
Maris's name, Vasso hadn't thought about her.

"I'll call her now. Just so you know I'll be out of the
office tomorrow. Akis will handle anything that comes
up. If there's an emergency, he'll call me."

"Yes, sir."

Vasso went into his private office and rang Maris.
After apologizing for not phoning her before his quick
trip to New York, he asked if they could meet later
that night. He'd stop by her condo. She sounded happy.
That worried him because he didn't plan on seeing her
after tonight. But Maris deserved the truth. She wanted
more out of their relationship, but he didn't have it inside to give.

With that taken care of, he sequestered himself in his office for a couple of hours to do paperwork. Then he phoned Zoe.

"I'm glad you called. I've eaten lunch and was just leaving to go shopping."

"Then I'll take you."

"Oh no. You've done enough for me."

She was so different from other women he'd known whose interest in money seemed to be at the forefront. Both he and Akis felt the women they met were always assessing the worth of the Giannopoulos brothers, a real turnoff. But the Zoe he'd met so far seemed the exact opposite of a woman with that kind of hidden agenda.

"But you don't know where to go to shop."

"I'll be fine. I've lived in a big city all my life."

Vasso chuckled at her show of independence. "I realize that. But it would please me to accompany you this once. I'm coming upstairs now."

He was aware how grateful she was for everything. Pleased that she wasn't too tired, he arranged for his driver to meet them in the alley and drive them to the Attica department store near Syntagma Square.

She must have showered because she smelled sweet like a fragrant rose, dressed in a different skirt and blouse, when he helped her out of the limo. "You'll find everything you want here at a good price," he explained. "Shall we start in the luggage department? You'll need a large suitcase."

Her sculpted mouth curved into a smile. "You're reading my mind."

He liked the three-piece set of luggage she picked with a gold fleur-de-lis design on a dark red background. Vasso asked the clerk to find an employee to take their purchases out to the limousine waiting in front of the store.

Women's clothing was on the next floor. Zoe stopped him before they approached the counter. "Tell me something honestly. I saw Ms. Kallistos coming and going for a whole year. She only wore dresses or skirts and blouses. Would you suggest the same thing for me?"

"For work, yes. But you'll want other kinds of clothes, too. The island has a lot to offer when you're off of work. Among other things like jeans and shorts, you're going to need some good walking shoes and a bathing suit. Maybe a sweater or jacket when the nights cool down. Paxos is a different world from New York."

"I realize that. After living in the asphalt jungle, I'm relishing the quiet of a sun-filled island with no skyscrapers."

"You're going to undergo a big change. Tell me something. Do you have a laptop?"

"I had one for college, but it got destroyed in the fire."

"I was afraid that might be the case."

"Stop, Vasso. I know what you're going to say. I have enough money to buy another one."

"I believe you, but the foundation supplies all the equipment, so I have an idea. While you shop for clothes, I'll go to the electronics department and get you a computer. You'll need it when you're not at the center. It shouldn't take me long then I'll come back here for you."

"That sounds good. When we're through shopping, I'd like to take you to an early dinner. It will be on me. I'm afraid I won't have much money left to spend, so I'll let you pick a place my pathetic bank account can afford."

Those shimmering green eyes had him mesmerized. "I know just a spot in the Plaka. You'll love it."

"The old part of Athens," she mused. "To think I have Greek blood running through my veins, yet I've never been here. I promise to hurry because I can't wait to explore." Zoe's eagerness to live life made him see it through new eyes. "My father didn't like to go shopping with my mother because she took so long. I'll try not to be like her."

Amused by the comment he said, "Take all the time you need." He and Akis had grown up in a one-parent household, so he didn't know what it would be like to hear two parents going at it back and forth.

He left her talking to a saleswoman and headed for another part of the store. Besides a laptop, Vasso wanted her to have a new iPhone. He was still amazed by the extent of her loss, and even more astounded that she wasn't bitter or angry. She didn't know how to feel sorry for herself. That trait alone increased his admiration for her.

Fire had snatched away everything from her, including her parents. She was forced to build a life all over again. The woman was a survivor in more ways than one. He couldn't imagine another woman of his ac-

quaintance who would be eager to throw herself head-
long into an undetermined future.

She was beautiful inside and out. By some miracle
the lymphoma hadn't taken her life. Her gratitude was
over the top, yet it was that very quality that drew him
to her. You couldn't compare her to anyone else. She'd
maintained a great sense of humor even after the ordeal
she'd been through, which put her in a class by herself.

As Vasso had discussed with Akis, he was happy
they'd honored their father by creating the foundation.
But at the time, neither of them had any idea that their
money would be responsible for Zoe getting the medical
care she'd needed to whip the terrible disease. Today he
was thankful they'd had both centers built so he could
give her the job she wanted.

She's becoming important to you.

An hour later he found her and they walked out of
the store with their arms loaded. They were greeted by
a rash of photographers and journalists taking pictures
and calling out questions. Someone had tipped the paparazzi off that he'd come to the store. Vasso was fu-
rious this had happened, but Zoe seemed to handle it
well by ignoring them. He helped her into the smoked-
glass limo.

"You must be a celebrity," she said in a quiet voice.

"Anyone's a celebrity if they have money."

"There's a lot more to their interest in you than that!"

"It's because Akis and I came from a life of poverty. The media has been following us around for several years."

"How ghastly." He heard a sigh come out of her. "But

I think it's because you've done something extraordinary with your lives. To impart your fortune for the good of humanity puts you in a class all by yourselves. Surely you must realize how much people admire you for that. It's a great compliment to you, even if you don't like the publicity."

"Trust me, I don't," he muttered. "Let's forget them. I'm just sorry I couldn't protect you from them."

"I can understand that you don't relish being mobbed."

She understood a lot of things that made him feel closer to her. He was beginning to desire her company more and more. "It's one of the reasons why I don't spend all my time in Athens."

Her gaze darted to him. "I don't blame you. Under the circumstances, can we go back to the penthouse to eat dinner? Now that they've seen you, they'll probably follow us to the Plaka. If I can't pay for our meal, I can at least cook for you."

"I didn't bring you here to cook."

"You don't know how much I miss it. I was at the center for a whole year. No place of my own to have fun in the kitchen. Yours is a cook's dream, believe me! But please don't misunderstand me," she cried softly. "I just meant that now I'm well, I look forward to doing the things that once brought me pleasure. That is if you'll let me."

How could he say no to that? "Of course."

"If I say so myself, my parents' *taverna* brought in a lot of customers because of my mother's recipes that go way back."

Vasso couldn't hear enough about her life. "What was her specialty?"

"She had several, but my favorite main dish is *burek*."

His brows lifted. "You can make Macedonian *burek*?"

"So you like it?" Her eyes smiled.

"I had it once in Kozani and loved it."

"I'd like to make it for you if you'll let me loose in your kitchen. We'll see how it compares. But you need to start with an appetizer and some Mastika liqueur over ice. You probably don't have any of that on hand."

"Our number-four store should carry it. We'll stop there on the way back."

She reached in her purse and wrote something on a piece of paper before handing it to him. "Do you have all these items?"

He checked the list: dough ingredients, minced lamb, white cheese, spinach, *kasseri* yellow cheese, olives and tomatoes. They'd need to pick up at least half the items on her list. Vasso alerted his driver, then focused on her. "I'm already salivating."

"So am I." She chuckled. "There's nothing I'd love more than to fix you one of my family's specialties."

"Are you homesick for New York already?" He'd been worrying about that. To live on Paxos was going to be a huge adjustment for her.

"I'll never stop missing my parents, but there's nothing in New York for me now so I won't be missing it. Yet being able to cook up a meal in your kitchen will be a little like old times with my folks."

Her tremulous answer tugged on his emotions. He

had a longing to comfort her. "I can relate. So many times I've wanted to discuss business with our father."

"Every time I went into the hospital chapel, I would read the words on the plaque and wonder about him. When did he die?"

"Sixteen years ago."

She shook her head. "You were so young to lose him. That must have been terribly hard on your mother."

Vasso cleared his throat. "She died soon after I was born."

A slight gasp escaped her. "I had no idea. That means your father raised you and your brother alone. Did you have grandparents?"

"They died too, but that's another story."

"Will you tell me about it?"

"Maybe. Over dinner." Just then the limo pulled in front of the store. "I'll be right back." He got out and hurried inside the crowded interior.

"Boss?"

"*Yassou*, Galen. I'm here to pick up a bottle of Mastika liqueur."

"I think we've got one left. It's been on the top shelf in back for a while."

"The older, the better."

"I'll get it."

"Let me." Vasso found it and the other items needed. After putting some bills on the counter he said, "Talk to you later."

When he got back in the limo with the groceries, he handed the bottle to Zoe. "Is this what you wanted?"

She looked delighted. "I can't believe you stock it

here. No wonder your stores have been such a huge success. This is my lucky day. Now I'm going to have to produce a meal that will win the Giannopoulos seal of approval."

He laughed, realizing that she had a knack for bringing that out in him. When she'd walked into Alexandra's office last week, he hadn't been prepared for the effect this utterly feminine woman would have on him. But the first impression she'd made on him, with her wavy blond hair, had brought a spring-like newness into his life.

When they arrived at the penthouse, they loaded everything into the elevator and rode to the top. Before long they'd taken everything to her bedroom. Then they gravitated to the kitchen where he helped her gather all the ingredients to make their dinner.

It was fun working side by side. "This is a brand-new experience for me."

"How come?"

"I've never brought a woman to the penthouse, let alone allowed her to take over the kitchen."

"You're kidding! Not one girlfriend?"

"I have a confession to make. After Akis and I started making real money, we worried whether the women we met only wanted us for what we could do for them. We refused to bring them here. It was safer to take them to dinner. That probably sounds very cynical to you."

"No. Not after what you've told me about your life. There's a lot of avarice in the world. I imagine anyone who has the kind of money you make would have trouble trusting someone who wanted to get close to him."

"Akis had the same trust issues, but he's married now. When he first met Raina, he fell hard. But his fear of not being loved for himself caused him all sorts of pain."

"How did they meet?"

"She flew over to attend the wedding reception of her Greek friend Chloe who'd lived with her in California. Akis had been the best man. After running away from the maid of honor who was after him, he picked on Raina to dance with him until he could get out of the room safely. That accidental meeting changed his life."

Zoe chuckled. "When did he know she was the real thing?"

"He always knew it in his heart, but he needed a nudge. I did some research on her and learned she was Raina Maywood."

"What? Isn't she the famous American heiress to the Maywood fortune?"

He nodded. "When Akis found out, everything changed. He knew that she wasn't after his money, but he had another problem."

"Why?"

"He didn't feel good enough for her. Our lack of formal education made him worry that she'd soon grow bored of him. On the night she was leaving to go back to California, I called her and begged her to go to him. She was broken up, not understanding why he couldn't accept that she loved him. Luckily she took my advice and convinced him he was her whole world. They got married fast and I've never seen him so happy."

"Was that a little hard on you?"

He looked in those compassionate green eyes. "You have a lot of insight, Zoe. Until they said their vows, I never realized how connected we'd been throughout our lives. When you told me how close you were to your parents, you were describing me and Akis.

"I felt lost at first, but slowly that feeling started to dissipate. Raina has been a joy and makes my little brother so happy I can't imagine life without her now. With a baby on the way, Akis isn't the same man."

"A baby? That's wonderful!"

"When Akis and I were young and struggling, we couldn't have imagined this day."

She flashed him a smile. "And now there's a lot more to come. Your lives are a miracle, too."

The things she said…

They kept working in harmony. Zoe definitely knew her way around a kitchen. By seven o'clock, they sat down at the dining room table to eat the best home-cooked food he'd ever tasted.

They started with the Mastika poured over ice and served with a grilled *krusevo* cheese pie for an appetizer. The *burek* was out of this world. Layers of dough with white cheese, minced lamb and spinach garnished with tomatoes and onions marinated in a special herb sauce. It was so good he ate more than he normally did at a meal.

"You could open your own *taverna*, Zoe."

"What a lovely compliment. Before I decided to go

to college, I actually thought about it, but my parents insisted I try college first. You know the rest. Then the day came when the world as I knew it went away."

Vasso didn't want her to think sad thoughts. "We can be thankful you didn't go away with it or I wouldn't have been treated to such a feast."

"You're just being nice."

"Not true. Now it's my turn to pay you back by doing the dishes while you get your bags packed. Tomorrow we'll have breakfast here and fly to Paxos."

That was the plan, but he discovered he was loving her company so much he wanted to keep her here in Athens for a while and show her around. It shocked him that he could feel this attracted when they'd known each other for such a short while. How had he existed all this time before she came into his life?

"Before I do that, I want to hear about your grandparents. It's sad to think you didn't have them in your life either." She started clearing the table. It thrilled him she didn't want to leave him quite yet.

"Both sets of grandparents came from Paxos."

"Ah. I'm beginning to understand why the island has been so important to you."

"The grandparents on my father's side and their children—with the exception of our father—were victims of the malaria epidemic on Paxos. In the early sixties it was eradicated, but they didn't escape it."

"Amazing that your father didn't get the disease."

"No. Pockets of people were spared. No one knows why. Maybe he was naturally immune. A poor fisherman who lived on Paxos took care of my father. Together they caught and sold fish at the market in Loggos.

"After the fisherman died, our father continued to fish in the man's rowboat. It was in town he met our mother. She and her brother Kristos survived the epidemic that had killed her family. He emigrated to New York to find a new life, but was killed crossing a busy street."

"How awful. That explains his name on the plaque!"

"Yes. Apparently my mother grieved when he left Greece. In time she and my father fell in love and got married. She worked in the olive groves. Together they scraped to make ends meet any way they could.

"I was born first. Then Akis came along eleven months later. But the delivery was too hard on *Mama* who was in frail health and she died."

He could see Zoe was trying not to break down. "It pains me that neither of you knew your mother. That's so tragic. I at least didn't lose my parents until a year ago, so I have all the memories of growing up with them."

His eyes met hers. "In ways I think your pain has been much worse. We never knew her. She didn't know about her brother getting killed, which was a good thing. We were so young when she died we had no memories except the ones our father told us about. But you lived, laughed and cried with your parents for your whole life, doing everything together. That's a loss I can't comprehend."

"Thanks to the therapy provided by your generosity, I'm doing fine these days. Truly your father had to be a saint to manage on his own. No wonder you wanted to do something extraordinary to honor his name."

"To be sure, he was our hero. I was six when we helped him in the store where he sold the fish. Neither Akis nor I went to school regularly because we needed the money too badly. Poverty was all my father knew. I know it hurt his pride that we boys were known as the poor Giannopoulos kids.

"Most people looked down on us. But no one could know the depth of our pain when he was diagnosed with lymphoma and died. At that point we only had each other in order to survive. *Papa* asked me to look out for Akis."

Zoe gasped. "How old were you?"

"Thirteen and fourteen."

"Overnight you two had to become men."

"All we knew was that we only had ourselves in order to survive. The man who owned the store died and his wife needed help. We asked if we could stay on and work for her. By then the woman was used to us and she really needed the help. So she let us work in her store.

"Akis and I traded off jobs. He'd wait on the customers while I went fishing and picked olives. Then we'd turn the schedule around. We worked long hours."

"When did you fit in some time to play, let alone attend school?"

"Not very often."

"I'd love to meet Akis."

"That can be arranged. But enough about me. Now I want to change the subject. Have you ever ridden in a helicopter?"

She shook her head, still haunted by what he'd told her. "No. I've always wondered what it would be like."

"Does the thought of it make you nervous?"

"Kind of." A hint of smile broke the corner of her mouth. "Ask me tomorrow when I actually have to climb inside it."

"Once you get used to it, you won't want to travel any other way."

"I'll have to take your word for it." After a hesitation... "Vasso?"

He'd started loading the dishwasher. "What is it?"

"You've been so kind to me my debt to you keeps growing. I told Father Debakis what I'm going to tell you. If it takes me the rest of my life, and it probably will, I intend to pay back every cent your foundation spent on my behalf.

"Every inmate at the center would like to tell you of their gratitude in person. You've saved the lives of many people who had no hope. It's staggering the good you've already done." Her lower lip started to tremble. "You're wonderful."

Her words moved him. "If I started to tell you all the things I think about you, there wouldn't be enough hours."

Color rushed into her cheeks. "You're full of it, but it's nice to hear."

"How could the man you had been seeing before the fire have walked away?" he whispered. That question had been gnawing at him since she'd first told him she'd had a boyfriend.

"I don't know." She half laughed as she said it. "He broke my heart when he made the decision to move to Boston. I went through a lot of pain, but with hindsight I can see he didn't love me in that heart-whole way or he couldn't have left.

"After several months I decided I was lucky. If there'd been no fire, would he have eventually asked me to marry him? I don't have an answer. But the fact remains that he wanted to go to Boston more than he wanted to be with me. I certainly don't blame him. To be with a terminally ill patient would mean he had to forget his dreams. That's asking too much of a man unless he's met the love of his life."

"Was he the love of *your* life?" Vasso needed to hear her answer.

"Let me put it this way. I had boyfriends. Some meant more to me than others. But I met Chad while we were both on that study abroad program in England. That was his graduation-from-college present. It threw us together for two weeks. You can learn a lot about someone on a trip like that. We had fun and didn't want it to end after we returned to New York.

"The more I saw of him, the more I thought maybe he could be *the* one. But the circumstances that brought me to this hospital put an end to the relationship we'd enjoyed. Now you know the story of my life."

"But not the pain you suffered when he didn't stay with you."

She took a deep breath. "It was awful. I won't lie about that. If ever I needed someone who loved me that was the time. But his love wasn't the forever kind. That was a hard lesson to learn. It taught me not to put my faith in a man." She looked up at him. "That's as honest as I know how to be."

The man had been a fool. Vasso's black eyes burned into hers. "Just look what he missed. Thank you for telling me."

"I've probably said too much." After taking a few steps away from him, she turned around. "Thanks for listening. I've talked your ear off."

"It was my pleasure. Just so you know, I have to go out again for a little while. I'll try not to disturb you when I come back in."

"Please don't worry about me. Good night." In the next instant she'd disappeared into the other part of the penthouse.

While Vasso stood there overwhelmed by tender new feelings she brought out in him, his cell rang. He pulled it from his pocket. When he saw it was his brother, he clicked on. "Akis?"

"I thought I'd check in. How's everything going with Thespinis Zachos?"

He held his breath. "Fine."

Low laughter bubbled out of Akis. "Come on. It's *me* you're talking to."

"I'm aware of that. I took her shopping, then we had dinner and now she's gone to bed. Tomorrow morning we'll fly to Paxos."

"I can read between the lines, bro. Let's try this again. How are things really going?"

"The press intruded as we left the department store, so we came back to the penthouse and she cooked dinner. It was probably the best Macedonian food I've ever eaten."

"I guess that makes sense considering her parents ran a *taverna*."

"She only has one more semester before she receives her college degree in English, but Alexandra didn't know about that. It's just as well Zoe will be working on this side of the Atlantic. Tonight she told me she wants to meet you and thank you for saving her life. If you want my opinion, she'll charm Yiannis until she has him eating out of her hand."

"It wouldn't surprise me considering she's already accomplished that feat with you. A woman cooking in our kitchen? That has to be a first. I guess it's too late to tell you to go slow, the same advice you once gave me. *Kalinihta*."

"*Kalinihta*."

Zoe was still on his mind when he arrived at Maris's condo twenty minutes later. "Vasso—you're finally here!" she said after opening the door. "I've missed you."

But when she would have reached for him, he backed away.

A hurt look entered her eyes. "What's wrong?"

Vasso hated to do this, but for both their sakes he needed to break things off with her. Zoe filled his thoughts to the exclusion of all else, but that made him anxious when he remembered how he'd once felt about Sofia.

As for Maris, he didn't like hurting her when she'd done nothing wrong, but as he'd told his brother, she wasn't the one. Still, he couldn't help feeling a little guilty about doing this to her.

"Let's sit down."

"I don't want to." Her chin lifted. "Why do I get the feeling you're here to tell me it's over with us?"

Being a journalist, she had good instincts and was always out for the truth. "To be honest, while I was in New York I had a chance to think. I don't believe there's a future for us and I thought it would be better to tell you now. I like you very much, Maris. We've had some good times, but—"

"But you're ready to move on," she interrupted him.

"Surely you know I don't mean to hurt you."

"One of my friends told me this was how it would end with you, but I didn't want to believe her. So who's the new woman in the life of the famous Vasso Giannopoulos?"

He stared her down. "Would you have preferred that I told you this over the phone?"

She had the grace to shake her head. "No. It hurts no matter what."

Vasso admired her honesty. "I've enjoyed the times we've spent together and I wish you the very best in the future."

Maris walked over to the door and opened it. "I'm afraid I can't wish you the same, but one day I'll get over it. I thought we had a real connection. Being with you has meant everything to me. Too bad it was one-sided. *Adio,* Vasso."

He left for the penthouse. After reflecting on what had just happened at Maris's condo, he realized this had been the story of his life since Sofia Peri had rejected his marriage proposal. That was ten years ago after he'd finished his military service. It had taken a long time to get over the pain of her marrying someone else. From then on he'd buried himself in business with Akis.

Over the last few years he'd been with different women when time permitted, but he'd ended every relationship prematurely and had pretty well given up on finding his soul mate.

Then Zoe Zachos had walked in Alexandra's office, causing his heart to beat so hard he hadn't been the same since. In the last twenty-four hours her effect on him had been staggering.

After getting used to being in a helicopter, Zoe was entranced by everything she saw. They passed over so many historic places in the Ionian Sea she'd only read about in books or seen in the movies she was awestruck.

From the copilot's seat, Vasso looked back at her through his sunglasses. Today he'd dressed in a white crewneck and white cargo pants. It wasn't fair one man out of millions could be so attractive. Using the mic he said, "We're coming up on Paxos."

She looked down from the window. "But it's so tiny!"

"It's only seven miles by three. Too small for an airport which is just the way all of us who live on the island like it."

Zoe leaned forward. "What do you mean *we*?"

A dazzling white smile greeted her gaze. "As I told you last night, my brother and I were born here. We had the center built here. *My* home is here."

Her heart pounded so hard she was afraid he could hear it. "*This* is where you live when you're not in Athens or traveling for business?"

"That's right."

In shock that she'd be working so close to this fantastic man's home, she turned to the window once more.

"We're flying to the center now. I've phoned Yiannis to expect me. Once inside his office you two can meet and talk about the position."

As the helicopter dipped, she made out several fishing villages with colorful harbors. Lower and lower now, she took in the lush deep greenery of olive trees sprinkled with pastel-colored clusters of small villas. Quaint waterside cottages came into view. One stretch of fine white sand scalloped the green coves and gave way to another seaside village. On the outskirts now she realized they were headed for a sprawling white complex peeking out of the olive groves.

She held her breath as they were about to land. This time it set down on the hospital roof, but she wasn't as nervous as when the helicopter had lifted off the penthouse roof.

"Are you all right, Zoe?"

"Yes. I was just thinking how my parents and I would have loved transportation like this all the years we lived in New York City. I'm spoiled already."

But the minute the words were out of her mouth, it made her realize she did too much talking. He brought that out in her. Now that they'd landed, she didn't want to prolong the conversation and unbuckled her seat belt.

She thanked the pilot and climbed out of the helicopter wearing one of her new outfits. The navy cotton dress with the white print had a crew neck and sleeves to the elbow. It was summery light, yet had a certain classy look she felt would be appropriate for the job.

When Vasso walked her to the stairs that led to an elevator, she felt his gaze travel over her. Hopefully he approved of her choice of dress. But the second Zoe entertained the thought she was irritated with herself that he was on her mind way too much. The fact that his home was so close to the center meant she'd probably see him more often than she would have imagined. It shouldn't thrill her so much.

"This is a private elevator," he explained as they entered. "The hospital takes up three floors. On the second floor there's a walkway to the three-floor convalescent center. Yiannis's office is on the main floor off the foyer at the main entrance."

They exited the elevator and walked along the corridor of one wing, passing a set of doors with stained-glass inserts signifying the chapel. Zoe looked around. "I love the Hellenic architecture." Their eyes met for a moment. "It flows like the sculpture of a Greek temple."

Her comment seemed to please him. "When we had it built, we tried to preserve the flavor of the island. The kitchen and cafeteria are in the other wing. The eating area extends outside the doors to the patio overlooking the water."

"A hospital built in the middle of paradise," she mused aloud. "If I'd been privileged to recover here, I know I would have lived on the patio. To be near the sea would be heavenly."

When they came to the foyer filled with exotic plants and tubs of flowers, he smiled warmly at a woman probably fifty years old who appeared to run the reception area. "Hebe." He kissed her cheek.

The other woman beamed. "Yiannis said you were coming. It's always good to see you."

"The feeling is mutual. Kyria Lasko, I'd like you to meet Thespinis Zoe Zachos from New York City. She's here for an interview with Yiannis."

"Ah? I hope it means what I think it means." Her friendly brown eyes were so welcoming Zoe was able to relax a little.

"How do you do, Kyria Lasko?" She shook hands with her.

"Call me Hebe."

After being around a cold Alexandra for a whole year, Hebe Lasko was like a breath of fresh air. "Thank you."

"Hebe is the head of our business office located down the other hall," he explained, "but she's been doing double duty as Yiannis's assistant."

Zoe turned to him. "You mean this front desk is where I would work?" she asked quietly.

He nodded. "Yiannis's office is through that door behind the desk. Let's go."

She followed him around the counter where he knocked on the door and was told to enter. Vasso ushered her inside and her first thought was that she'd entered a room in a naval museum.

There were models of ships on the shelving and several framed photographs of the former military leader in dress uniform. Other small photographs showed him with his striking wife. What an attractive man he was with gray hair and dark brown eyes!

As the two men embraced, she noticed he was shorter than Vasso and was dressed in a short-sleeved white shirt and dark trousers. They exchanged comments and his hearty laugh filled the office. Then his eyes swerved to Zoe.

"So, Vasso… I see you've brought along a visitor. A very lovely one at that. Is this some kind of announcement you're making?"

CHAPTER FOUR

THE INFERENCE COULDN'T have been more obvious. Zoe tried to repress a groan.

"In a way, yes! I've found you the assistant you've been needing. Yiannis? Meet Thespinis Zoe Zachos. She was born and raised in New York City, and she's a bilingual Greek American. I was so impressed with her I plucked her away and brought her here. I'm going to leave the two of you to get acquainted and take a look around the facility, but I'll be back."

He disappeared so fast Zoe felt like the foundation had just been knocked out from under her.

The older man smiled at her. "Sit down, Zoe. How come you're still *thespinis*?"

He immediately reminded her of her father who was always outspoken. "I haven't met the right man yet."

He frowned before taking his seat. "What's wrong with the men in New York?"

"I'm afraid the problem lies with me."

"What are you? Twenty-two?" he asked with a teasing smile.

"I'll be twenty-five next weekend."

His brows lifted. "That old." Laughter broke from her. "All right. Let's start from the beginning. Vasso wouldn't do this to me if he weren't a hundred-percent sure you're the person I'm looking for to help me run this place. Tell me about your background."

Without going into too much unnecessary detail, she told him about her family and education. When she got to the part about the fire, she managed to stay composed. Then she told him about her lymphoma and the year she'd spent at the center.

"My family priest knew how much I wanted to work for the center to pay back all it had done for me. When the doctor gave me another clean bill of health, Father Debakis arranged for Kyrie Giannopoulos to interview me. He said your assistant had to leave and you were looking for a new one."

The older man suddenly sat forward. "You're cancer-free?"

"At the moment, yes. But there's no guaran—"

"Forget that," he broke in on her. "You're exactly what's been needed around here. How long before you have to go back to New York?"

"I—I don't plan to," she stammered. "I told Kyrie Giannopoulos I'd like to work for the foundation for the rest of my life. It will take that long to pay his family back for all they've done for me. If I'm given a job here, this is where I'll plant new roots."

"You're hired, Thespinis Zachos."

Zoe couldn't believe it. "But you hardly know anything about me."

"Of course I do. Vasso wouldn't have brought you

here if he had any questions. This center needs input. Who better than you to see what we're doing right or wrong? When I was in the navy, we had informers who quietly gathered information helpful to the brass. With you around, I'm already feeling like I'm back on duty with a crew I can count on."

To hide her joy that he'd accepted her on Vasso's say-so alone, she reached in her tote bag and pulled out a seven-by-seven-inch box wrapped in paper showing various American naval frigates. "This is for you." She handed it to him. "I would have given it to you whether I got the job or not."

Yiannis eyed her in surprise before opening it. "What's this?" He pulled out a creamware mug and read aloud the words printed in dark red ink. *"We have met the enemy and they are ours."*

"That's the image of Edward Preble," she explained. "He was a naval hero at the time of the war in Tripoli. Kyrie Giannopoulos told me you're a naval hero and have collected naval memorabilia. I knew he meant Greek memorabilia, but I thought you could add this mug as a piece to show your appreciation for an American naval hero. A little diversity makes things more interesting, don't you think? If nothing else, you could drink coffee from it."

He burst into laughter at the same moment Vasso joined them. "It looks like you two are getting along famously."

Yiannis lifted the mug. "Did you see this?"

"No."

"Take a look. Our new employee just presented me

a gift to add to my collection." Vasso shot her a knowing glance before he took it to examine.

The retired admiral sat back in his chair, eyeing the two of them with satisfaction. "The only thing I need to ask now is: how soon can you come to work? I needed you yesterday. Poor Hebe has been run ragged doing the job of two people."

Zoe liked him a lot already. For years she'd worked with her parents at the *taverna*. It would be nice to feel useful again with someone dynamic like him. Despite his grief over the loss of his wife, he had a buoyant spirit.

"Tomorrow morning? Today I need to find a place to live."

"Tomorrow at eight-thirty it is. You've made my day."

She got to her feet. "You've made mine by being willing to give me a chance. I can't thank you enough and I'll try not to make you sorry." Zoe shook his hand and headed for the door. She needed to use the restroom she'd seen down the hall.

After she emerged, Vasso caught up to her. "We'll fly back to my house for the car and drive into Loggos. When we reach the village I thought we'd stop for lunch and check out several furnished apartments I told you about. Hopefully one will suit."

Things were moving so fast she could hardly think. "Do all the people working at the center live in Loggos?"

"They come from all over the island, but Loggos is a good place for you to start out. The only bus picks up passengers in front of the main *taverna* and will bring you to the center. It makes three stops a day there in front of the fountain, so you'll always have a ride home. I suggest you give it a month. If it isn't to your liking, you can live wherever you want on the island, but you'll need a car. I'll help you with that when you're ready."

"Thank you, but I don't have a driver's license, Vasso. If I decide to buy a car, then I'll have to take lessons first." He'd already spoiled her so completely she would never be out of his debt. Vasso was so caring and concerned—the differences between him and Chad were like day and night.

The flight back to his house passed in a blur. There was too much to absorb. She couldn't take it all in. Once again she felt the helicopter dip and fly toward a charming, solitary white beach villa with a red tiled roof. They landed on a pad in the middle of a copse of olive trees, causing her breath to escape. There was no doubt in her mind this was Vasso's sanctuary.

She spotted a dark gray Lexus parked nearby.

Once the rotors stopped spinning, Vasso unbuckled the seat belt. While he removed her luggage, she jumped down so he wouldn't have to help her and reached for the train case. Without waiting for him, she headed for his car.

"Zoe? The house is in the other direction. Where do you think you're going?"

"To get in your car. I'm assuming I'll be able to move into an apartment today and don't want to put you out any more than necessary."

"We're not in that big a hurry."

"*I* am. Once I have a place to live and am on the job, I'm going to feel free. I don't expect you to understand. But being the recipient of so much generosity for so long has become a burden, if that makes sense. I hope I haven't offended you."

"Not at all."

Zoe tried to sound matter of fact about it, but it was hard to hide the sudden alarm that had gripped her. Vasso was already bigger than life to her. She'd been in the penthouse that he and his brother used for business. She'd even cooked a meal there! Because she was a future employee, Vasso had opened every door for her.

But to enter his home would be crossing a line into his private world she refused to consider. She might like it too much. No way did she dare make a move like that. Already she was afraid that her feelings for him might interfere with their professional relationship.

Yiannis Megalos had made an assumption about her and Vasso the second he'd seen them walk in the office. She could imagine how it looked. Obviously Vasso had gone out of his way to do something unprecedented to accommodate her desire to work for the foundation. But this last favor to help her get settled had to be the end of it. Her self-preservation instinct had kicked in to guard her heart.

If she came to depend on Vasso, how did she know he wouldn't be like Chad in the sense that he wasn't invested in the relationship to the extent that she was? Zoe refused to put her trust in a man again where it came to her heart. There was no point anyway since her cancer could be coming back. Better to concentrate on her work and give it her all. In the end she'd be spared a lot of heartache.

She waited for Vasso to bring the rest of her luggage to the car. He used a remote to open the doors and put the luggage in the trunk. Zoe took advantage of the time to get in the front seat.

When he got behind the wheel, he turned to her. Suddenly they were too close. She was so aware of him she could hardly breathe. "Why do you think you would be putting me out?"

Until now she hadn't felt any tension between them, but after what he'd just said, she feared she'd irritated him after all. "Because you've done so much for me, it doesn't make sense that you'll have to come back here later for my luggage."

"I'm in no hurry. Have I led you to believe that?"

She moistened her lips nervously. "No. Of course not. You're such a gentleman you'd never make anyone uncomfortable. But you and your brother run a huge corporation. Everything was going smoothly until you were asked to interview me. I know Father Debakis laid a big guilt trip on you, so don't try to deny it."

"I wasn't going to."

She took a breath. "Thank you. Since then you've had to deal with me. As if I'm not already indebted to you several hundred thousand dollars."

"Zoe—have you considered the situation from our point of view? Our father died a terrible death while Akis and I stood by helplessly. To know that the foundation has helped someone like you means everything to us. It's a pleasure to see you get back on your feet."

Her head bowed. "You're the two best men I know."

"That's nice to hear. What do you say we drive to the village? After lunch you can take a look at the furnished apartments available. One is over a bakery, the other over a gift shop."

She flicked him a worried glance. "A bakery?"

The second Zoe's question was out, Vasso realized where he'd gone wrong and gripped the steering wheel so hard it was a miracle he didn't break it. "Forgive me for forgetting where you'd lived." She'd never forget the fire that had traveled to the kitchen of her parents' *taverna*.

"We'll cross that one off the list. You'll like Kyria Panos. She's a widow who's been renting the apartment over the gift shop since her son got married. You'll have your own entrance in the back. The only drawback is that it's a one-bedroom apartment."

"I don't need more than one."

"You're so easy to please it's scary."

"Not all the time."

"Give me an example."

"If I told you some of my hang-ups, you'd send me back to New York on the next flight."

"How about just one?"

"A couple of my girlfriends wanted me to room with them in college, but I'd always had my own space at home and didn't want to give it up. They teased me about it and tried to talk me into it. But the more they

tried, the more I didn't like it. I guess I'm really a private person and get prickly when I sense my space is
being invaded. That's why I lived with my parents."

"There's nothing wrong with that. But maybe the day
will come when you won't want to be alone."

"If you're talking about marriage, I'm not planning
on getting married."

"Why?"

"I like my life the way it is." She turned to him. "I
really like the way it is right now. I don't want some
man bossing me around. One of the older patients at the
center used to tell me about the fights she had with her
husband. For the most part my parents got along great,
so I couldn't relate to this woman's life. He pecked at
her all day long."

Vasso's black brows lifted. "Pecked?"

"Yes. You know. Like a hen pecks at her food. That's
what he'd do to her about everything. What she bought,
what she ate, what she did with her spare time. Peck,
peck, peck."

Laughter pealed out of Vasso. "Most of the older
women in the center made similar comments about
married life. I decided I was well enough off being on
my own."

"My brother loves married life."

"Maybe that's true, but what does his wife have to
say when he's not listening?"

She heard a chuckle. "I have no idea."

"Maybe it's better you don't know." He laughed
louder. She loved hearing it. "I could see in Yiannis's
eyes that he wonders why you aren't married, Vasso.

Admit you don't want some wife leading you around by the nose."

"Now there's a thought."

She laughed. "I'm only teasing." No woman would ever do that with a man like him. The female who caught his eye would be the luckiest one on the planet. No way did she dare dream about a romantic relationship with Vasso.

If it didn't work out, she wouldn't be able to handle it. Just admitting that to herself proved that her feelings for Vasso already ran deeper than those she'd had for Chad. The two men weren't comparable. No one could ever measure up to Vasso.

"You may be teasing, but I can hear the underlying half truths."

Time to change the subject. "Tell me about my landlady, Kyria Panos. Did she henpeck her husband?"

"As I recall they did a lot of shouting, but for the most part it was good-natured."

"That's nice. I bet you know everyone around here."

"Not everyone," he murmured, "but Akis and I rented an apartment along this waterfront when we started up our business years ago, so we're friends with many of the owners around here."

Vasso started the engine and drove them through the olive groves to the village. An hour later, after they were filled with spinach pie and ouzo lemonade, he carried the last of Zoe's luggage up the stairs to the furnished apartment. The front room window overlooked the horseshoe-shaped harbor. The minute he saw Zoe's expression, he knew she liked the view and the typical blue-and-white décor.

She smiled at him. "This place is really cozy and so colorful. I love it, and it's all mine."

After what she'd recounted earlier about needing her space, he could believe she was serious. But it bothered him that she was so happy about it.

"I'm glad you like it. Our number-one store is just a few doors down. You can grab breakfast there while you're waiting for the bus."

"If I do too much of that I'm going to get fat, but I want you to know I'm ecstatic to be here," she exclaimed. Vasso couldn't imagine her with a weight problem, not with her beautiful face and body. Her green eyes lifted to his. "Cinderella may have had a fairy godmother, but I've had the perfect godfather who has granted my every wish. Now that your mission has been accomplished, I release you to get back to your life."

Zoe could tease all she wanted, but he sensed she wanted him to leave. The hell of it was he didn't want to go. Since she'd flown to Athens, he'd been a different person and couldn't spend enough hours with her. She was so entertaining he never knew what was going to come out of her mouth next. The thought of her ever being interested in another man disturbed him more than he wanted to admit.

He'd only scratched the surface of her life, but she'd drawn the line at entering his home. Why? Was it because she didn't trust him after what Chad had done to her? Did she see every man through the filter put there by the other man's defection? Was she afraid of marriage because of that experience?

She didn't bat an eye over renting an apartment with one bedroom. Did that mean she really did like to be alone? He could hear Akis commenting on the subject. *Are you still feeling responsible for her, or is there something more eating at you?*

Vasso had to admit there were a lot of things eating at him. He sucked in his breath. "If you need help of any kind, I'm only as far away as the phone."

"You think I don't know that?" She walked him to the door. "I'm sure we'll see each other again. Hopefully by then Yiannis will have a good word for me."

As Vasso had predicted to Akis, she already had Yiannis eating out of her hand.

"Stay safe, Zoe."

"You, too."

He heard the slight wobble in her voice. It stayed with him as he left the apartment, taking with him the haunting image of her blond hair and sparkling eyes, not to mention the white-on-navy print dress that clung to her figure.

Once he reached the car, he took off for his villa. But he was too upset by emotions churning inside him to stay on the island till morning. If he did that, he'd be tempted to drop by the apartment with some excuse to see her again. Instead he alerted the pilot that he was ready to fly back to Athens.

After the helicopter touched down at the penthouse, he checked any messages his private secretary might have left. Apparently Akis had dealt with everything important. Grabbing a cup of coffee, he went back to his office to dig into the inventories still left to get through. But first he texted his brother.

I'm back in the office working. Zoe Zachos is living in the apartment above Kyria Panos's shop. All is well with Yiannis.

Not two minutes later his brother phoned him back. "Have you contacted Maris?"

"Yes."

"That's good. She phoned several times yesterday wanting to know about you."

"Sorry."

"I get it. So how are things with her?"

"I broke it off with her last night."

"I guess that doesn't surprise me. Whatever happened to 'slow down'?"

Vasso let out a morose laugh. "Look where it got *you*."

CHAPTER FIVE

August 26

ALREADY IT WAS FRIDAY. Five days without seeing Vasso felt like five years. In the time they'd been together, they'd confided in each other about the very personal things in their lives. He knew information about her she hadn't shared with anyone else. Zoe loved being with him. She ached for his company. He brought excitement into her life.

But she'd better get used to separations because the foundation was only a small part of the huge company he ran with his brother. And the more she heard about their generosity, the greater her need grew to do all she could to help in such a humanitarian effort.

Over the last five days Zoe had been able to introduce herself to every inmate except the twenty-four-year-old guy from Athens named Nestor. The resident therapist was worried about him. He'd been undergoing chemo in the infusion clinic and was in a depressed state, refusing to talk to anyone.

The therapist told her Nestor had been a receptionist

at a hotel that went bankrupt. He couldn't find a job and after a few months became homeless. Two months later, he was diagnosed with lymphoma. He usually lived on the steps of a Greek Orthodox Church but spent a lot of time under the nearby bridge with his other home-less friends.

This was the case of another kind priest who got in contact with the center on Paxos and arrangements had been made to get him admitted. Zoe found out that the helicopters owned by the Giannopoulos brothers helped transport patients like Nestor from all over Greece when there was no other solution.

Through Yiannis she learned more about Vasso and Akis. Born to poverty, they'd built a billion-dollar busi-ness in such a short period of time it stunned the Greek financial world. That was why the media was always in their face. It explained why Vasso made his home here on Paxos. Evidently his younger brother lived on the nearby island of Anti Paxos.

Just thinking about Vasso caused her breath to catch.

Already she was finding out that the homeless pa-tients were afraid there'd be nothing for them to look forward to once they had to leave the center. That was an area needing to be addressed. Zoe had known the kind of depression that was drawing the life out of Nestor. Now that lunch was over, it would be a good time to visit him.

She took some oranges and plastic forks with her. When she reached his room she found him half lying in a recliner wheelchair. Every room had a sign that said,

"Reality is never as dark as the places your brain visits in anticipation." How true.

"Nestor?"

He opened his eyes. They were a warm brown. Despite his bald head, he was good looking, or would be if he were animated.

"If you're too nauseated to talk, I've been there. Mind if I sit down?" She pulled a chair over to him and set the items on the table. "I'm new here. My name's Zoe. I just got out of the hospital in New York City after being there a year. I had lymphoma too."

That brought a spark. "You?"

"I thought I'd be dead by now, but it didn't happen. I also lost my family in a fire, which made things much worse. I understand you don't have family either."

"No. My grandfather raised me, but he died."

"Well we're both very lucky that the Giannopoulos Foundation exists. They've given me a job here. What kind of a job do you want when you leave?"

"I won't be leaving," he murmured.

"Of course you will. As my priest told me, God didn't come to my rescue for nothing. I know how the nausea can make you think you'll never be better. But it will pass. I brought you some things that helped me.

"If you open and smell an orange before you eat, the aroma will make the food tolerable. At least it worked for me. Also, the metal forks and spoons sometimes make you gag. Try eating your food with a plastic fork and see if it makes any difference."

He eyed her with curiosity. Good!

"See you soon. Maybe one of these days we'll go

outside on the patio and have a game of cards. I'll bring a scarf and some snacks. I have an idea you'd make a dashing pirate. You know, young-Zorba-the-Greek style."

She left the room and continued on her rounds until the end of the day. Yiannis wanted her to be his eyes and ears. Besides keeping up on the paperwork, he expected her to make suggestions to improve their services. What was missing? That's what he wanted to know.

Now that she'd been hired full time, they would take turns covering for each other Saturday and Sunday. This coming weekend was his turn to work. Suddenly Zoe had more freedom than she knew what to do with.

When she walked out to catch the bus, the fountain of Apollo was playing. Again she was reminded of Vasso who, like the sun god in his chariot, was so handsome it hurt. She needed to get her mind off him. In the morning she'd take a long hike around the island.

On Sunday, she and Olympia, one of the cooks from the hospital, were going to take the ferry to Corfu from Loggos. While Olympia met with her relatives, Zoe planned to do some sightseeing on her own and was looking forward to it.

A group of workers got on the bus with her. They were already friendly with her and chatted. One by one they got off at different stops. Zoe was the only one who rode all the way into the village. By now the driver named Gus knew her name. Though she might be in Greece rather than New York, there was the same atmosphere of community she'd loved growing up.

When Zoe got off the bus, she headed for one of the *tavernas* that served *mezes* along the harbor front. At twilight the lights from the boats and ferry twinkled in the distance. It was a magical time of night.

Most of the tables outside were taken by tourists, but she finally found an empty one. She'd been anxious to try the various fish appetizers to see how they compared with her mother's cooking. The waiter brought an assortment of octopus, shrimp, sardines, calamari and clams.

Maybe she was biased, but she thought her mom's were better. Then again maybe she was missing her family. How they would have loved to come here for a vacation.

Don't look back, Zoe. You're the luckiest girl in the world to have been given this opportunity. You've been handed a second chance at life. You've been able to realize your dream to work for the Giannopoulos Foundation. You're living in one of the most beautiful spots on earth.

"Such a beautiful young woman sitting alone at the table looking so sad is a sin. Even if it isn't all right, I'm going to join you."

She'd know that distinctive male voice anywhere and looked up in shock. "*Vasso—*"

"Sorrow on a night like this is a tragedy."

Zoe made an odd sound at the sight of him. Tonight he'd dressed in a black silk shirt and tan trousers. Afraid she was staring hungrily at him, she averted her eyes. "I was just doing a little reminiscing about my parents. You caught me at the wrong moment."

He took a seat opposite her at the round table. His nearness did strange things to her equilibrium. "What's on that mind of yours?"

The waiter came, but Vasso only ordered a cup of coffee. She knew he was waiting for an explanation. "I've been sitting here counting my blessings."

"That sounds like you. So you're not missing home then?"

She sat back in the chair. "I stay in touch with my friends through email. As for Chad, he took my advice and is out of my life."

Her heart skipped a beat. "It was the right decision for both of us. Otherwise I wouldn't be sitting here on the island Kyria Panos calls the jewel of the Ionian, eating dinner with my benefactor. If you saw me in a sad mood just now, I was thinking how much my parents would have loved this island and how they longed to visit Florina. But my mother would whisper that these sardines were overly seasoned."

Following his chuckle, he took a sip of the coffee the waiter had brought to the table. "What are your plans for this weekend? I talked to Yiannis and learned it's your turn to be off work until Monday."

She glanced around as if she were afraid to look at him. "We've decided to alternate weekends. The security guards will take turns to cover for us while we sleep there."

"According to him you're turning the place around already."

"Yianni is just being nice."

"So it's Yianni now?" he questioned with a smile.

"The first time I called him that by mistake, he said his wife always dropped the 's' and he ordered me to keep doing the same thing."

"It's clear he's happy with you." Vasso finished his coffee. "How do *you* like your job by now?"

CHAPTER SIX

CHAPTER SIX

"I LOVE IT!" Zoe's eyes sparkled like the aquamarine sea around Akis's villa on Anti Paxos. "There's this one patient named Nestor I want to tell you about. But only if you have the time."

"I'm off work for the weekend too. If there isn't something you need to do, why don't we drive to my house to talk? There's a lineup of tourists from the ferry who would appreciate this table."

When she reached in her purse to pay the bill, he checked her movement and pulled out his wallet to do the honors.

"I don't expect you to pay for me."

"Not even when it's your birthday?"

She gasped slightly, but then she shook her head. "Why am I not surprised? You know everything about me."

"Almost everything," he teased. "This one is the big twenty-five. I remember having one of those five years ago."

"Did you celebrate with someone special?"

"If she'd been special, she and I would still be together."

She eyed him frankly. "Your fault or hers?"

"Most definitely mine."

"Don't tell me there hasn't been one woman in your life who meant the world to you?"

He helped her up from the table and they walked along the waterfront to the parking area near the pier. "Her name was Sofia Peri. I asked her to marry me."

After a measured silence, "How long ago?"

"When I was twenty. But the business Akis and I put together hadn't gotten off the ground yet. She needed a man with substance."

Zoe stared up at him before getting in his car. "Just look what *she* missed…"

Touché.

He closed the door and went around to the driver's seat to get in. They drove the short way to his house in companionable silence. "Where does that road go?" she asked before they reached his villa.

"To the pier where I keep my boat."

She turned to him. "Can we drive down to look at it?"

"If that's what you want." He made a right turn that led to the water's edge where she saw his gleaming cruiser.

There was an enchantment about the night. A fragrant breeze lightly rippled the water. This was Vasso's front yard. "It must be fabulous to go everywhere you want by water. Of course you go by helicopter too, but I can't imagine anything more fun than finding new coasts to explore."

Vasso shut off the engine and turned to her. "I had

those same thoughts years ago. When the rich people pulled into our little harbor to eat and buy things from the store where Akis and I worked, I always wondered what that would be like. That was long before it became an Alpha/Omega 24 store."

Her heart ached for how difficult his life had been. "Is that how you met the woman you proposed to? Was she a tourist who came in?"

"No. She lived in the village. We went to the same church and the same school, even though Akis and I were absent most of the time. Her parents didn't approve of me, but she defied them to be with me."

Zoe felt pained for him. "Was she your childhood sweetheart?"

"You could say that. I assumed we'd get married one day. We were crazy about each other, or so I thought. It helped me get through some difficult times, especially after our father died. Akis and I continued to work there and had saved enough money to buy it from the owner. By then I was nineteen and had to do my military service.

"While I was gone, we wrote to each other and made plans. At least *I* did. But I didn't realize that while I was away, she'd started seeing a local fisherman's son who was making a good living. She never once mentioned him to me until my return. The news that she'd fallen for someone else pretty well cut my heart out."

Zoe didn't know what to say. "My relationship with Chad never got as far as yours." The normal platitudes wouldn't cover it to comfort him because in truth, the woman sounded shallow. If she chose ready money over the true value of Vasso Giannopoulos whom she'd loved for years, then he was well out of it.

"Are you saying you were never intimate with him?"

"No. I was taught to wait for marriage. Guilt kept me from making that mistake. Thank goodness it did since Chad and I weren't meant to be. But I'm truly sorry about Sofia."

"That's past history. Fortunately for me, it was Akis's time to go into the military. I had to do the job of two people to keep our business running. By the time he got back, we went all out to make a success of our lives. Both of us were sick of being looked upon as the impoverished Giannopoulos boys who rarely went to school and had no education. I believe it was harder on Akis, but he's very sensitive about it."

"The poor thing," she said quietly. "Neither of you knew your mother who could have comforted both of you. I can't comprehend it."

"Our father made up for it."

"That's obvious. The two centers you've built in honor of him say everything." Her throat had started to swell. "If I could meet him, I'd tell him he raised the best sons on earth."

"If I keep listening to you, I just might believe it. As long as we're here, would you like to go for a boat ride?"

"I thought you'd never ask," she admitted on a laugh.

"I'll take us on a short drive to the harbor. It's very picturesque at night."

Zoe got out of the car before he could come around to help her and started walking to the boat dock. She turned to him. "What can I do to help?"

His white smile in the semi-darkness sent a rush of warmth through her body. "If you want to undo the rope on this end, I'll take care of the other."

His cruiser looked state-of-the-art, but small enough for one person to manage. She did her part, then stepped in and moved over to the seat opposite the driver's seat. Never in her wildest dreams would she have imagined spending her twenty-fifth birthday driving around an island in the Ionian Sea with a man as incredible as Vasso. If she was dreaming, it didn't matter. She was loving every minute of it.

He stepped in with a male agility that was fascinating to watch and handed her a life jacket to put on. As he started to sit down she said, "You have to wear one too. I'm not the world's greatest swimmer. If I had to save you, it would be kind of scary."

His deep chuckle seemed part of the magic of the night. When they were both buckled up, he started the engine and they went at wakeless speed until they were able to skirt the cove. Zoe got up and stood at the side. Other boats were out, but all you could see were their lights and other lights on the island.

She turned around and braced her back so she could look at Vasso. "I've been thinking about your childhood. Did they offer a class in English when you did go to school?"

He slanted her a glance. "Yes, but we were rarely there. Our major knowledge came from talking to the English-speaking tourists. The owner of the store gave us a book to learn from. Our father told us we had to learn it in order to be successful."

"My parents spoke English and I was lucky to be taught at school from day one. If I'd had to learn it from a book the way you did and teach myself, it wouldn't have happened, believe me."

"You would if it meant your living."

Her life had been so easy compared to Vasso's, she didn't want to think about it. "I'm sure you're right."

"What kind of books did you read?"

"For pleasure?"

He nodded.

"English was my major, but I have to admit I loved all kinds of literature. In my mind you can't beat the French for turning out some of the great classics. My favorite was Victor Hugo's *Les Misérables* about Jean Valjean, who listened to the priest and did good. One of my classmates preferred Dumas's *Count of Monte Cristo* whose desire for revenge caused him not to listen to the priest."

Vasso slowed the boat because they'd come to the harbor where she could fill her eyes with its beauty. "I've seen the films on both stories. We'll fly to Athens and take in a film one day soon, or we could go dancing if you'd like."

Zoe smiled. "That sounds fun, but finding the time might be difficult." *Don't torture me with future plans, Vasso.* "I have my work cut out here."

In that quiet moment Vasso reached out and caressed her cheek with his free hand. His touch sent trickles of delight through her nervous system. "Yiannis has been thanking me for dropping you on his doorstep. I do believe everyone is happy." In the moonlight his heart-melting features and beautiful olive skin stood out in relief. "Shall we go back to the house?"

More than anything in the world Zoe wanted to see his home, but there were reasons why she had to turn him down. He was her employer, but there was much more to it than that. She'd found herself thinking about him all week, wishing he'd come by the hospital. For her to be looking for him all the hours of the day and evening meant he'd become too important to her already.

She could feel her attraction to him growing to the point she found him irresistible. This shouldn't be happening. If she fell in with his wishes, she could be making the worst mistake of her life. And it would be a big one, because there was no future in it.

"I'd better not, but thank you anyway. This has been a thrill to come out in your cruiser. I've loved every second of it, but I've got a big day planned tomorrow and need to get to bed."

The oncologist had told her that because of her type of lymphoma, the odds according to the Follicular Lymphoma International Prognostic Index indicated she'd live five years, maybe more. No one could guess when there'd be a recurrence.

With that in mind, she needed to keep her relationship with Vasso professional. She was already having trouble separating the line between friendship and something else. By touching her cheek just now he'd stoked her desire for him. He'd mattered too much to her from the beginning and her longing for him was getting stronger.

Whatever the statistics said, Zoe was a ticking time

bomb. The breakup with Chad had been hard enough to deal with. But knowing the disease would come back had made her fear another romantic involvement. The only thing to do was stay away from any sign of emotional attachment that could hurt her or anyone else. Zoe had her work at the center and would give it her all.

On their way back to the car she hoped she hadn't offended him. He'd been so kind to find her at the *taverna* and help her celebrate her birthday. Yet once again she felt tension emanating from him, stronger than before.

When he helped her in the car he said, "Tomorrow I'm planning to look at a new property. I'd like you to fly there with me. It'll be a chance for you to see another part of Greece. We'll only be gone part of the day. Once we're back, you can get on with your other plans."

The blood pounded in her ears. "That wouldn't be a good id—"

"Humor me in this, *thespinis,*" he cut her off. "Since I came empty-handed this evening, let it be my birthday present to you."

She averted her eyes. "Did Yianni put you up to this?"

"No. I actually thought it up all by myself." On that note she laughed and he joined in. "I like it when you laugh."

Zoe didn't dare tell him how his laugh affected her... the way his black eyes smiled, the way he threw his head back, the way his voice rumbled clear through to her insides making them quiver. Oh no. She couldn't tell this beautiful Greek god things like that.

Her resistance to him was pitiful. "How soon did you want to leave?"

"I'll come by your apartment at eight-thirty."

If he was going on business, then she needed to dress for the occasion. When he went out in public he was targeted by the paparazzi. She wanted to look her best for him.

"What's on your mind?" he asked when he pulled up in back of the apartment.

"Things that would bore a man."

"Try me," he challenged with fire in his eyes.

"What lipstick should I put on, what shoes to match my dress, what handbag will be better. Decisions, decisions. See what I mean?"

He scrutinized her for a moment. "I see a lovely woman. What she wears doesn't matter."

"I'm a fake. If you saw me without my hair you'd have a heart attack." She'd said it intentionally to remind him who she was, and got out of the car. "Someday I'll lose it all again when I have to undergo another session of chemo, so I'll enjoy this momentary reprieve while I can. Thank you for this unexpected evening. I'll be waiting for you in the morning. Good night, Vasso."

She let herself in the back door, but was so out of breath it took a minute before she could climb the stairs. Even if her fairy godfather hadn't needed the reminder, *she* did.

Tomorrow has to be your last time with him, Zoe. Absolutely your last.

After a shower and shave, Vasso put on tan trousers and a silky, claret-colored sport shirt. While he fixed himself his morning cup of coffee, his phone rang. It was his brother.

He picked up. "*Yassou,* Akis."

"Where are you?"

"At the house."

"Good. Raina and I were hoping you'd come over this morning and have breakfast with us. We haven't seen you in two weeks."

"Thanks, but I'll have to take a rain check on that."

After a pause, "What's going on?"

"I'm off on business in a few minutes."

"We already closed the deal on the store in Halkidiki."

He rubbed the back of his neck. "This is something different."

"Then it has to involve Zoe Zachos. Talk to me."

Vasso let out a frustrated sigh. "I've been helping her settle in."

"And that includes taking her on a business trip?" His incredulity rang out loud and clear.

Vasso checked his watch. "I'm going to be late picking her up. I'll explain everything later. Give Raina my love."

The question Akis was really asking went to the core of him. But he couldn't talk about it. Once they got into a conversation, his brother would dig and dig. Zoe had said the same thing about him. They weren't brothers for nothing, and Akis wouldn't stop until he'd gotten to the bare bones. Vasso wasn't ready to go through that. Not yet...

Pieces of last night's conversation with Zoe had shaken him.

I'm a fake. If you saw me without my hair you'd have a heart attack. Someday I'll lose it all again, so I'll enjoy this momentary reprieve while I can.

Chilled by the possibility of the lymphoma recurring, Vasso started the car and drove to her apartment, unaware of the passing scenery.

When Chad heard I'd been told my disease would probably be terminal, he couldn't handle it. I told him I didn't want him to have to handle it and begged him to take the job offer in Boston and not look back. He took my advice.

Chad's pain would have been excruciating to realize he might lose her. But Zoe had to have been in anguish over so many losses.

Vasso's thoughts flew to his father when he'd been on the verge of death. The sorrow in his eyes that he wouldn't be able to see his sons grow to maturity—the pain that they'd never known their mother—the hope that they would never forget what a wonderful woman and mother she'd been—

Tears smarted his eyes. Not so much for the pain in his past, but for Zoe who didn't know what the future would bring. Their light conversations only skimmed the surface of what went on underneath. Her declaration that she never planned to marry was part of the babble to cover up what was going on deep inside of her.

All of a sudden he heard a tap on the window and turned his head. It was Zoe! He hadn't realized he'd pulled to a stop outside the apartment door. She looked gorgeous in a simple black linen dress with cap sleeves and a crew neck. The sun brought out the gold high-lights in her hair.

He leaned across the seat to let her in. She climbed in on those well-shaped legs and brought the smell of strawberries inside. Her lips wore the same color and cried out to be kissed. Her eyes met his. "*Kalimera,* Vasso."

"It's a beautiful morning now, *thespinis*. Forgive me for staring. You look fabulous."

Color rose into her cheeks. "Thank you. After getting caught off guard by the paparazzi in Athens, I thought I'd better be prepared to be seen in the company of one of Greece's major financial tycoons."

Vasso took a deep breath. "I hope that's not the case today. Have you eaten breakfast?"

"Oh yes. Have you?"

"Just coffee."

Her brows met in a delicate frown. "That's all you had last night."

Zoe managed to notice everything. He liked it. He liked her. *So much in fact he couldn't think about any-thing else.* "I'm saving up for lunch," he said and drove the car back along the tree-lined road to his house where the helicopter was waiting.

"Where are we going?"

"I've decided to let it be a surprise. You'll know when we land at the heliport."

Before long they'd climbed aboard the helicopter and lifted off. Vasso put on his sunglasses and turned on the mic. When he looked over his shoulder he saw that Zoe had put on sunglasses too. She was beautiful and could easily be a famous celebrity. But he was glad no one knew about her. He liked the idea of keeping his find to himself.

He gave her a geography lesson as they flew north-ward to Macedonia. She knew more Greek history than most people of his acquaintance. Once they neared the desired destination, the land became more mountainous. He could tell her eyes were riveted on the dark green landscape that opened up to half a dozen magnificent lakes. Further on a sprawling city appeared. The pilot took them down and landed in a special area of the airport. When the rotors stopped whirling Vasso said, "Welcome to Florina, Zoe."

She looked at him in wonder. "Are you serious?"

"When you told me your parents had wanted to bring you here for your graduation, it gave me the idea."

"So you don't really have business here?" she asked in a softer voice.

"I didn't say that."

Zoe shook her head and took off her sunglasses. "You do too much for me, Vasso."

"I'd hoped for a better reaction than a lecture."

"I didn't mean to sound like that. Forgive me."

"Come on. I have a limo waiting to take us sightsee-ing." He got out first then helped her down. The urge to crush her warm body in his arms was overwhelm-ing, but he held back.

The limo was parked nearby. He helped her inside, but this time he sat next to her. "I've asked the driver to take us on a small tour. When I told him your great-grandparents lived here until the outbreak of the Greek

Civil War, he promised to show us some of the histori-
cal parts of Florina and narrate for us over the mic."

She looked out the window. "I can't believe this is
happening."

"I'm excited about it, too. I've never spent time in
this area and am looking forward to it."

"Thank you from the bottom of my heart," came
her whisper. When he least expected it, Zoe put a hand
over his and squeezed it for second. But as she tried
to remove it, he threaded his fingers through hers and
held on to it.

"I think I'm almost as excited as you are. The cycle
of the Zachos family has come full circle today. Seventy years ago your ancestors left this town to get away
from communism. Now their great-granddaughter is
back to put down her roots in a free society. That's no
small thing."

"Oh, Vasso."

In the next instant she pressed her head against his
arm. While the driver began his narration—unaware
of what was going on in the rear—Vasso felt her sobs
though she didn't make a sound. Without conscious
thought he put his arms around her and hugged her to
him, absorbing the heaves of her body. He could only
imagine the myriad of emotions welling up inside her.

After a few minutes she lifted her head and faced
straight ahead. "I hope the driver can't see us. Here
he's going out of his way to tell us about the city, and
I'm convulsed."

"He knows this tour has more meaning for you than
most tourists so he'll understand."

"You always know the right thing to say."

For the next half hour the driver took them past buildings and landmarks made famous by the prominent filmmaker Theo Angelopoulos.

"Since the last war I don't imagine the homes my great-grandparents left are even standing," she confided.

"Probably not." Vasso asked the driver to drop them off at a point along the Sakoulevas River. "Let's get out and walk to Ioannou Arti Street so you can get a better view of the twentieth-century buildings along here. There's an archaeological museum we can visit."

She climbed out and put her arm through his as they played tourist. It felt so natural with her holding on to him like this. He could wish this day would go on forever.

"This is fabulous, Vasso. I had no idea the city was so beautiful. To think maybe my great-grandparents walked along this very river."

"Maybe it was along here they fell in love."

Zoe looked up at him in surprise. "I had no idea you're such a romantic at heart."

"Maybe that's because you bring it out in me." Obeying an impulse, he lowered his mouth and kissed those lips he'd been dying to taste. It only lasted a moment, but the contact sent a bolt of desire through him. She broke the kiss and looked away before they walked on.

The limo met them at the next street and they got back in. "If you've had enough, I'll tell the driver to run us by a market the Realtor told me was for sale. He tells me there's a *taverna* nearby where we can try out *burek*. We'll see if it compares to your mother's recipe."

"I'd love that."

Vasso alerted the driver and soon they pulled up in front of a store selling produce. He got out and helped Zoe down. Together they walked inside the busy market. The city was certainly big enough to support one of their stores. But he was curious to know the figures and approached the owner.

"While I talk to him, take a look around and see if there's something you want to buy to take back to the apartment."

She smiled. "Take as long as you need."

Zoe strolled around, eyeing the fruits and vegetables brought in by local farmers. Vasso noticed the customers eyeing her, even the owner who could hardly concentrate when asked a simple question.

When Vasso had learned what he wanted to know, he went in search of Zoe and found her at the back of the market buying a bag of vegetables.

"Don't they sell peppers in Loggos?"

Her face lit up. "No. These are sweet Florina red peppers. My mother remembered her mother and grandmother cooking these. They aren't like any other peppers in the world. I have the recipe. When we get back to Loggos, I'll cook some for you with feta cheese and we'll see if they live up to their reputation. The eggplant looks good, too."

His pulse raced at the thought of going back to Zoe's apartment. "Then let's grab a slice of *burek* at the *taverna* two doors down now, and eat a big meal this evening."

"That sounds perfect."

She hadn't said no. Their day out wasn't going to end the second they flew back to Loggos. That was all he cared about.

After telling the owner he'd be in touch with the Realtor, Vasso carried her bag of precious peppers and eggplant as they walked along the pavement to the outdoor café. He ordered *burek* and Skopsko beer for both of them.

When she'd eaten a bite, he asked for her opinion.

"I'm more curious to know what you think, but you have to tell the truth. If you like it better than mine, it won't hurt my feelings very much."

He burst into laughter and ate a mouthful of the pie. Then he ate a few more bites to keep her in suspense. She was waiting for an answer. Those green eyes concentrated solely on him, melting him to the chair. "It's good. Very good. Yours is better, but I can't define why it's different."

She leaned forward. "You mean it?"

Good heavens, she was beautiful. "I don't lie, *thespinis.* Let's drink to it." They touched glasses, but she only drank a little bit of hers while Vasso drained the whole thing. Food had never tasted so good, but that was because he was with her and was filled with the taste of her. He wanted more and suspected she did too otherwise she wouldn't be talking about their spending the rest of the day together back on Loggos.

"Excuse me while I freshen up before we leave."

Two hours later they arrived back at Zoe's apartment. While she got busy preparing the peppers, Vasso followed her directions for *moussaka*. "I'm glad you're staying for dinner, Vasso. There's something important I want to talk to you about."

Vasso darted her a piercing glance. His heart failed him to think she had an agenda. Was that the reason he'd made it over her doorstep tonight, and not because she couldn't bear to say good-night to him?

"What is it?"

CHAPTER SEVEN

"I DIDN'T FINISH telling you about one of the patients named Nestor. The poor thing doesn't think he's going to get better. He's depressed, but it isn't just because he's undergoing chemo. He lives with the fear that because he was homeless when he was brought in, he has no work to go back to even if he does recover.

"I've discovered that several of the older patients are afraid they won't get their jobs back if their disease goes into remission. So I was thinking maybe in my off hours I could set up a service to help those patients find a job."

"A service?" One dark brow lifted. "Have you discussed this with Yiannis?"

"Oh no. This would be something I'd do on my own. But I wanted to see what you thought about it."

He put the *moussaka* in the oven. "It's a very worthy project. Maybe even a tough one, but you're free to do whatever you want in your spare time. Surely you know that."

"So you wouldn't disapprove?"

Vasso frowned. "Why would you even ask that question?"

She carefully peeled the skins off the roasted peppers. "Because the people I approach will ask what I do for a living and your foundation will come up. You're a modest man. I don't want to do anything you wouldn't like."

He lounged against the counter while she prepared the peppers to cook with olive oil, feta cheese and garlic. "You couldn't do anything I wouldn't like."

Her gaze shot to his. His compelling mouth was only inches away. She could hardly breathe with him this close to her in the tiny kitchen. "You shouldn't have said that. I'm full of flaws."

His lazy smile gave her heart a workout. "Shall we compare?"

"You don't have any!"

"Then I'll have to break down and reveal a big one."

"Which is?"

"This!" He brushed her mouth with his lips. "When a beautiful woman is standing this close to me, I can't resist getting closer." He kissed her again, more warmly this time.

"Vasso—" She blushed.

"I told you I had a flaw."

She turned from him to put the peppers in the oven. When she stood up, he was right there so she couldn't move unless he stepped away. "I'd like to spend the day with you tomorrow. We'll tour the island and go swimming on a beach with fascinating seashells. What do you say?"

He could probably hear her heart pounding. She'd promised herself that after today, she wouldn't see him again unless it was for professional reasons.

Thank heaven she had a legitimate excuse to turn him down.

"Thank you, Vasso. That's very sweet of you, but I can't. I'm going to Corfu in the morning with Olympia."

Those black eyes traveled over her features as if gauging her veracity. "I might have known you'd strike up a friendship with her. She worked in the food services industry before coming to us."

Zoe nodded. "We have that and more in common."

He took a deep breath and moved away. "I'm sad for me, but glad for you to be making friends so fast."

"I found out she bikes with her husband. So they're going to lend me one of their bikes and we'll take rides around the island after work and on our free weekends." She'd added that to let him know her calendar was full.

Another long silence followed, forcing her to keep talking. "Everyone here has been so friendly. I already feel at home here. After moving heaven and earth for me, your job is done. You don't have to worry about me anymore."

Still no response. Needing to do something physical, she set the little breakfast table. After making coffee, she invited him to sit down while she served him dinner. When he still didn't say anything, she rushed to fill the void.

"I'll never forget the gift you gave me today. Seeing the city of my ancestors meant more to me than you will ever know."

"It was a memorable day for me, too," he murmured. "I want to spend more days like this with you, Zoe. I'd love to go biking with you."

"Between our busy schedules, that could prove difficult." She put the *moussaka* on the table and stood at his side to serve him a plate of peppers. "Tell me what you think about Florina's most famous vegetable."

He took one bite then another and another and just kept nodding.

That was the moment Zoe knew she was in love with him. The kind you never recovered from. To her despair, the thing she hadn't wanted to happen *had* happened. She adored him, pure and simple. His kisses made her hunger for so much more. His touch turned her inside out with longings she wanted and needed to satisfy. *Oh, Vasso... What am I going to do about you?*

Before Zoe blurted that she loved him, she sat down and ate with him. "Um... These really are good."

"You're a fabulous cook, and I've never tasted better *moussaka.*"

"You put it together, so you get the credit."

After Vasso drank his coffee, he flashed her a glance. "The next time we're together, I'll cook dinner for you at my house and I won't take no for an answer."

Zoe let the comment slide. The way he made her feel was toppling her resistance. As she got up to clear the table her cell rang. She reached for her phone lying on the counter.

"Go ahead and answer it," he urged her when she didn't click on.

She shook her head. "It's Kyria Themis. I'll call her back after you leave."

"Maybe it's important, so I'll go."

Much as she was dying for him to stay, she knew this

was for the best. Their friendship needed to remain a friendship, nothing more. The kiss he'd given her today had rocked her world. That's why the less they saw of each other, the better.

She walked him to the door. "Good night then, Vasso. This day was unforgettable."

So are you, Zoe.

Vasso got out of there before he broke every rule and started to make love to her. In his gut he knew she wanted him, too. Desire wasn't something you could hide. Whether in the limo or the car, the chemistry between them had electrified him.

Though he didn't doubt she'd already made plans for tomorrow, he sensed she was deliberately trying to keep their relationship platonic. But it wasn't working. Despite her determination not to go to his house, she'd invited him to the apartment tonight and had cooked dinner for him.

There were signs that she was having trouble being too close to him. He'd noticed the little nerve throbbing at the base of her throat before he'd moved out of her way in the kitchen.

While she'd stood next to him to serve dinner, he'd felt the warmth from her body. It had taken all his willpower not to reach around and pull her onto his lap. She was driving him crazy without trying.

On the drive to his house he made a decision to stay away for a few days and let her miss him. He had no doubts it would be harder on him, but work would help him put things in perspective.

Tomorrow he'd do a tour of the stores where he needed to meet with the new store managers to make certain they were following procedure. That would take him the good part of a week. In the meantime Akis would be free to meet with their food distributors in Athens for the critical monthly orders.

Once he was home he phoned his brother to tell him his plans. Before hanging up he said, "I met with the owner of a produce market in Florina today who wants to sell. The Realtor has named a figure that's too high. I think I can get the asking price down, but wanted to know your feelings about us putting up a store there."

"I always trust your judgment, but why Florina? What were you doing there?"

He gripped the phone tighter. "I flew Zoe there for her birthday. Her great-grandparents emigrated from there to America in the mid-forties. Before her parents could take her there for a college graduation present, they died in the fire."

His brother was quiet for a minute. "*Vasso—*"

"I know what you're going to say."

"Since you've already disregarded my warning to take it slow, I was only going to ask if there's a boy-friend in the picture."

"He bailed on her when he found out her disease would probably be terminal."

"That, on top of all her pain," his brother murmured in commiseration. "It would have taken a committed man."

He exhaled sharply. No one knew that better than Vasso. If Chad had loved her enough, he wouldn't have let her talk him into walking away. He could say the same for Sofia who hadn't had the patience to wait until things got financially better for him. Today he rejoiced that he and Zoe were still single.

"How is she working out with Yiannis?"

"They're trading off weekends and he lets her call him Yianni. That's how well they've hit it off. Let me tell you about her latest idea."

After he'd explained, Akis said, "I must admit a job referral service for the patients is a brilliant idea. When are Raina and I going to meet her?"

"I was hoping next Friday evening before she has to go on duty for the entire weekend."

"Do you want to bring her to our house?"

"I fear that's the only way it will work. She isn't comfortable coming to mine yet."

"Then you *have* heeded my warning to a certain extent."

Akis couldn't be more wrong. "Let's just say that for now I'm letting her set the pace. But I don't know how much longer I can hold out."

"Before you do what?"

"Don't ask that question yet because I can't answer it. All I know is I like being with her." *That was the understatement of all time.* "I'll talk to you later in the week. *Kalinihta.*" He clicked off and got ready for bed.

Once he slid under the covers, Akis's probing question wouldn't leave him alone. Until Vasso knew what Zoe really wanted, he couldn't plan on anything. She'd been hurt by Chad who hadn't seen her through her life-changing ordeal. To have a relationship with Zoe meant earning her trust. He'd begin his pursuit of her and keep at it until she had to know what she meant to him.

After a restless night, he flew to his first destination in Edessa and emailed her to let her know what he'd been doing. He did the same thing every night. By the time Friday came, he couldn't get back to Paxos soon enough. Before he drove to the center, he stopped by the number-one store to check in with the managers and buy some flowers.

"Vasso?" a female voice spoke behind him.

He turned around. "Sofia."

Her brown eyes searched his before looking at the flowers. "I was hoping to see you in here one of these days. Can we go somewhere private to talk?"

After she'd turned down his marriage proposal, there'd been times in the past when he would have given anything to hear her say that she'd changed her mind and wanted to marry him. How odd that he could look at her now and feel absolutely nothing. Meeting Zoe had finally laid Sofia's ghost to rest.

"Why not right here? I'm on my way to the center, but I can spare a few minutes. How are you?"

"Not good. I've left Drako."

Somehow that wasn't a surprise to him, yet it brought him no pleasure. Akis had told him he'd seen her in town a few months ago and she'd asked about Vasso. "I'm sorry for both of you."

Her eyes filled with tears. "Our marriage never took and you know the reason why. It was because of you. I've never stopped loving you, Vasso."

He shook his head. "I think if you look deep inside, you'll realize you were young and ambitious. Drako was already doing an impressive fishing business."

"I was a fool."

"I'm sorry for both of you."

"All this time and you've never married. I know it was because of me, and I was hop—"

"Sofia," he cut her off. "I moved on a long time ago."

"Are those flowers for someone you care about now?"

"They're for the woman I love," he answered honestly. Her face blanched. "You have children, and they need you more than ever. Now if you'll excuse me, I have to get to the center. I wish you the best."

He waved goodbye to the owners and hurried out to the car needing to see Zoe. By the time he reached the center he was close to breathless with anticipation. But first he went by Yiannis's office to let him know he was there. The older man told him she was out on the patio with several of the patients.

"When you have the time, I'll tell you about all the changes she's made around here for the better. We're lucky to have her, Vasso."

"I agree. Will it be all right with you if I steal her away for an early dinner?"

"Of course."

"Good."

Without wasting another second he hurried down the hall to find a container for the flowers, then he headed for the doors leading to the patio. She'd arranged four round umbrella tables to be close together with two patients at each one in their recliner wheelchairs. One man and one woman to a table. All wore some kind of head covering and all were playing cards. Zoe was obviously running the show using a regular chair.

She hadn't seen him yet. He stood watching in fascination for a few minutes.

All of them had to be in their late forties or were older, except for one man who looked to be in his twenties. He wore a red paisley scarf over his head like a pirate. As Vasso moved closer, he could tell the younger man was fixated on Zoe. Why wouldn't he be? She was by far the most beautiful and entertaining female Vasso had ever seen. Today she was wearing a soft yellow blouse and skirt.

They were all into the game and the camaraderie between them was apparent. This was Zoe's doing. He reached for a regular chair and took it over to put down next to her. "Can anyone join in?"

He heard her quiet intake of breath when she glanced up at him with those translucent green eyes. "Kyrie Giannopoulos—this *is* a surprise. Please. Sit down and I'll introduce you."

One by one he learned their names. They were profuse in their thanks for his generosity. "We're having a round-robin that's timed," Zoe explained. "Nestor here is on a winning streak." She smiled at the younger man.

"Then don't let me interrupt," he whispered, tamping down his jealousy. "I'll just sit here and watch. Maybe later you'll tell me why the emails you sent back to me were so brief."

For a moment their eyes met. He saw concern in hers. Before the night was out, they were going to talk.

It appeared Nestor couldn't take his eyes off her. When he could see that Vasso wasn't about to leave, the younger man glared at him beneath veiled eyes. The fact that he was recovering after chemo didn't stop the way he studied her face and figure. Was Zoe interested in him?

Vasso couldn't prevent another stab of jealousy, but when he thought about it that was absurd. If there was a bond between them, it had to do with the fact that both Nestor and Zoe had their illness in common. They had an understanding that drew them together. If she suspected the younger man's infatuation, she didn't let it show.

Soon a couple of the nurses came out to take the patients back to their rooms. But Nestor declined help and wheeled his chair out of the room.

"Don't forget movie night tonight!" she called to them. "I'm bringing a treat!"

"We won't forget!" said one of the older men.

Vasso watched her clear up the cards. She was nervous of him. Did he dare believe that she was equally thrilled to see him, and that's why she'd been caught off guard? He desperately wanted to believe she was in love with him, too.

"What's this about movie night?"

She nodded. "During my chemo, there were nights when I couldn't sleep and wished there were something to do. I asked Yianni about it and he told me to organize it. Anything that could increase everyone's comfort was worth it."

Zoe never ceased to amaze him. "You're already revolutionizing this place. What time is your movie night?"

"After nine-thirty. That's when the demons come."

He didn't want to think about the demons she'd lived through. "In that case I'd like you to have an early dinner with me first. Please don't turn me down. My brother and his wife want to meet the new assistant manager. They've invited us over. Maybe you can get Raina to unload about Akis's imperfections. Maybe he pecks at her, too."

She laughed, causing her nervousness to disappear for the moment. "As if I'd ask her a question like that!" There was green fire in her eyes. "I'll have to let Yianni know I'm leaving for a while."

"I've already asked if it's all right, but if you'd rather not leave the center, just tell me. We can arrange dinner with them for another time."

"No." She shook her head. "That sounds lovely. I've wanted the opportunity to thank Akis. How soon do you want to leave?"

"As soon as you're ready. We'll leave from the hospital roof."

"Let me just freshen up and then I'll meet you at the private elevator in ten minutes."

"Before you go, these are for you." He handed her the flowers.

"Umm. Pink roses. They smell divine."

"They smell like you. I noticed the scent the first time you climbed in the limo."

Color filled her cheeks. "Thank you, Vasso. They're beautiful."

"Almost as beautiful as you."

She averted her eyes. "You shouldn't say things like that to me."

"Not even if I want to?"

"I'll just run to my desk and put them on the counter, then I'll join you."

He could have no idea how much the flowers meant to her. She loved him… Too many more moments like this and all her efforts to keep distance between them would go up in smoke.

After receiving his newsy emails all week, to be given these flowers had her heart brimming over with love for him. It was clear he wasn't about to go away, and now he was whisking her off to his brother's villa.

She was filled with wonder as the helicopter flew over the tiny island next to Paxos. Vasso pointed out the vineyards on Anti Paxos. "If you notice the surrounding water, it's Caribbean green. Your eyes are that color, Zoe."

Every comment from him was so personal it made it harder for her to keep pushing him away. *That's because you don't want to, Zoe. You're in love and you know it.*

As they descended to a landing pad, she could see that the water *was* green, not blue, putting her in mind of emerald isles she'd never seen except in film. Vasso helped her down and kept a hand on the back of her waist as they made their way toward the small stone villa.

"Look at these flowers!" Zoe exclaimed. "It's breath-taking." They lined the mosaic stone pathway.

"Vasso?" she heard a female voice call out.

"Nobody else!" he called back.

In the next instant Zoe caught sight of the lovely American woman who'd married the other Giannopou-los son. She was a blonde, too. Zoe's first impression was that she glowed with health. Vasso had told her they were expecting a baby.

"Zoe? This is my favorite sister-in-law Raina."

"Your only one," she broke into English, rolling her violet eyes. "I'm so glad you could make it." Raina shook her hand before hugging Vasso. "Akis just got back from Athens and will join us after he gets dressed. Please come in. We've been excited to meet you."

Zoe followed her into the most amazing living room. A fireplace had been built in a wall carved out of rock. Between the vaulted ceiling and arches, the stone villa reminded her of pictures from the old family photos that had gone up in flames. The curtains and pillows added marvelous colors of blue and yellow to the décor. Zoe loved it.

"While Vasso goes to find Akis, come out on the ter-race, Zoe, and have some lemonade with me."

They walked past the open French doors where the terrace overlooked a kidney-shaped swimming pool. Glorious shades of red, purple and yellow flowers grew in a cluster at one end. Beyond it the sea shimmered. "You live in paradise, Raina."

Her eyes sparkled with glints of blue and lavender.

"Every day I wake up and can't believe any place could be so beautiful."

"I know. When Vasso took me on a helicopter ride, I thought I had to be dreaming."

"May we never wake up." Raina Giannopoulos had a charming manner Zoe found refreshing. "Come and sit. I've wanted to meet you ever since we heard you were coming to Greece to work." She smiled. "Don't get me wrong. I love it here, but I miss talking to another American once in a while. Do you know what I mean?"

Zoe liked her very much already. "I know exactly. It's nice to speak English with you."

"I'm working on my Greek, but it's slow in coming."

"I may be Greek in my DNA," Zoe confided, "but I'm American in my heart."

"I thought I was, too, before I married Akis. Now the Greek part has climbed in and sits next to it."

Zoe laughed while Raina poured them both a glass of lemonade. "Before the guys come out, may I tell you how much I admire you for handling everything you've been through? My grandfather died of stomach cancer and my grandmother from heart failure. I watched them suffer and can only imagine your agony."

"It's over now."

Raina nodded. "You don't know it, but both brothers have been very touched by your story and are astounded by your desire to pay them back. Their father meant the world to them. Until you came along, I don't think either of them realized what good they've really done."

"I know," Zoe whispered, moved by her admission

about her grandparents. Raina had known a lot of pain
too. "It's hard for Vasso to accept a compliment. I'm
afraid all I do is thank him. I'm sure he's sick of hearing about my gratitude."

"If that were the case, you wouldn't be here now."

"That's the thing. He got me this job so fast he
couldn't know how important that is to me. One day
my lymphoma will come back, so I want to do all I can
for as long as I can."

She saw a shadow pass over Raina's face, but before
anything else was said, two black-haired men with striking features came out on the terrace, dressed in casual
trousers and sport shirts.

Zoe stared at Vasso's brother, then turned to his wife.
"I didn't realize how closely they resemble each other,"
she whispered. "I thought Vasso was the only Greek
god flying around Greece in a helicopter."

"Do you want to know a secret?" Raina whispered
back. "When I first saw Akis on the street in Athens,
he seemed to be the incarnation of the god Poseidon
come to life from the sea."

"I thought you met at a wedding reception."

"That's true, but we almost bumped into each other
first on the street."

Zoe smiled. "And you never recovered."

"Never."

"Would you believe my first thought was that Vasso
was the sun god Apollo? The statue in the fountain
at the center looks just like him. With a husband like
yours, it makes you wonder if you're going to give birth
to a gorgeous god or a goddess, doesn't it?" After that

comment they both laughed long and hard, cementing their friendship.

The men came closer. "What's so funny, darling?"

While Zoe sat there blushing, Raina smiled up at her husband. "We were discussing the baby's gender."

"What's funny about that?" Vasso wanted to know. His intense gaze had settled on Zoe. She knew he wouldn't let it go without an answer.

"Maybe Raina will give birth to a little Poseidon carrying a trident. That's why we laughed."

A knowing look entered Akis's eyes before he kissed his wife on the cheek. "My choice would be an adorable Aphrodite like her mother."

The two of them were madly in love. Zoe could feel it. She was terribly happy for them and about the baby on the way. Zoe would never know that kind of joy. To get married, let alone have a baby, when she knew her cancer could come back wasn't to be considered.

She could see the hunger in Vasso's eyes when he looked at his brother's family. It was killing Zoe, too, because marriage and babies weren't in the cards for her. They couldn't be.

"Akis, let me introduce you officially to Zoe Zachos. Yiannis tells me he doesn't know how they ever got along without her."

"So I've heard." Akis came around and shook her hand. "Apparently your round-robin card game was a huge hit today. We'll have to lay in some chips to make things more interesting for your future poker games."

"That would be fantastic! Thank you. Before another moment goes by, I have to thank you for allowing me to work at the center. I've been given a second chance at life and will always be indebted to you and Vasso." Zoe fought to hide the tears quivering on the ends of her lashes.

She put up her hands. "I'll only say one more thing. I know you're God-fearing men because of your father's example. Christ said that when you've done it unto the least of these, you've done it unto me. Well, I'm one of the least. It's my joy to give back what I can."

Vasso stared at her for the longest time before Raina told the men to sit while she put on an American dinner California-style in Zoe's honor. Fried chicken, potato salad and deviled eggs along with Raina's Parker House rolls recipe.

Zoe had never enjoyed an evening more. Vasso told them about their trip to Florina and discussed the wisdom of putting in a store there. The time passed so fast she protested inwardly when she looked at her watch and saw that she needed to get back to the center.

Raina walked her out to the helicopter. Zoe smelled a haunting fragrance coming from the flowers. "I've never seen Vasso this animated since I met him. He never used to laugh the way he does now. It must be your effect on him. We'll do this again soon," Raina promised.

No. There couldn't be another time. Zoe wouldn't be able to stand being around these wonderful people again when it hurt so much. "Thank you for making me feel welcome, Raina. I've loved it. Vasso told me how you two met. Apparently Akis was running from the maid of honor at the reception and asked you to dance."

"Did he tell you I'd just sprained my ankle and was on crutches?"

"No."

"I was glad I couldn't dance with him because I didn't want anyone to know I was there. The paparazzi were outside waiting. Chloe's wedding was the event of the summer for the media."

Zoe nodded. "They mobbed Vasso the day we went shopping at the department store in Athens. With them always being in the news, it doesn't surprise me that women are after those two brothers. It's really a funny story about you two. Akis is a lucky man. For your information, you could open up your own restaurant serving the food we ate tonight."

The other woman hugged her. "After I heard from Vasso what a great cook you are, that's a real compliment."

Vasso came from behind and opened the door so she could climb in.

"Thanks again, you two. It was wonderful meeting you."

He followed her in. Once they'd fastened their seat belts, the rotors whined and they climbed into the twilight sky.

Zoe could see Vasso's profile in the semidark. He was a beautiful man who'd taken over her heart without trying. She was prepared to do anything for him. That meant weaning herself away from him. He deserved to meet a woman who had a lifetime ahead to give him love and bear his children.

Because of the foundation, she'd been granted five

years, maybe a little more, to live life until her time ran out. But it would be a selfish thing to do if she reached out for love. It would be asking too much to deliberately marry a man and have his baby, knowing she would have to go through another period of illness before leaving them. Zoe refused to do that to any man.

"Zoe? We're back at the hospital." Vasso's low voice brought her back to the present.

She thanked the pilot and got out of the helicopter. When Vasso started toward the elevator with her, she turned to him. "I had a marvelous evening and loved meeting your brother and his wife."

"You and Raina really seemed to hit it off."

"She's terrific. Between you and me, your brother doesn't have anything to worry about. She's crazy about him. No talk of his pecking at her."

Vasso grinned.

"It's obvious they have a wonderful marriage. Now I need to go inside and set things up. You don't need to come all the way to make sure I'm safe."

His dark brows furrowed. "Why are you pushing me away, Zoe?"

After taking a deep breath, she folded her arms to her waist. "Let's be honest about something. Our relationship has been unique from the beginning. The normal rules don't apply. You've done everything humanly possible to help me relocate to a new life, but I'm acclimatized now. For you to do any more for me will make me more beholden to you than ever. I don't want that."

"What if I want to be with you, and it has nothing to do with anything else?"

Zoe lowered her head. "If that's true, then I'm flattered."

"Flattered," he mouthed the word woodenly. "That's all? So if you never saw me again, it wouldn't matter to you?"

"I didn't say that," she defended in a throbbing voice.

"Then what *did* you say?"

"You're trying to twist my words." She pressed the button that opened the elevator door. When she stepped in, he joined her.

"Why are you running away from me?"

"I'm not! I'm supposed to be back at work."

"Work can wait five minutes. I want an answer."

"*Vasso*—"

"Yes? I'm right here. Why won't you look at me? I lived for your emails, but you didn't open up in them."

Her cheeks felt so hot she thought she must be running a temperature. "Because… I'm afraid."

"Of me?" he bit out, sounding angry.

"No—" She shook her head. "Of course not. It— It's the situation," she stammered.

"If you're afraid I'm going to desert you the way Chad did, then you don't know me at all."

"I never said that."

"But it's what you were thinking. Admit it."

"You've got all this wrong, Vasso."

"Then what are you worrying about?"

"*Us!*" she cried.

"At least you admit there *is* an us," he said in a silky

tone. In the next breath he reached for her and slid his hands to her shoulders, drawing her close to his rock-hard body. "You're trembling. If it's not from fear, then it means you know what's happening to us. I'm dying to kiss you again. But this time we're not standing in the middle of Florina for all to see."

She hid her face in his shoulder. "I'd rather you didn't. We'll both be sorry if you do."

"I'll be sorry if we don't. Would you deny me the one thing I've been wanting since we met?"

All this time?

"Help me, Zoe," he begged. "I need you."

His mouth searched for hers until she could no longer hold out. When it closed over hers she moaned. Thrill after thrill charged her body as they began kissing each other. One led to another, each one growing deeper and longer. She was so lost in her desire for him she had no awareness of her surroundings.

Vasso's hands roved over her back and hips, crushing her against him while they strained to get closer. She was so on fire for him it wouldn't surprise her if they went up in flames. This wasn't anything like her response to other men, to Chad. All Vasso had to do was touch her and she was swept away by feelings she'd never thought possible.

"Do you have any idea how much I want you?" His voice sounded ragged. "Tell me now how sorry you are." His mouth sought hers again, filling her with sensation after sensation of rapture. But his question made it through the euphoric haze she was in and brought her back to some semblance of reality.

"Vasso—we can't do this any longer," she half gasped, struggling for breath.

"Of course we can."

"No." She shook her head and backed away from him. "I don't want a complication like this in my life."

"You see me as a complication?" he ground out.

"Yes. A big one. You're my ultimate boss. I'm here because of you. We crossed a line this evening, but if we stop right now, then there's been no harm done. I look upon you as a blessed friend and benefactor. I don't want to think of you in any other light."

His face looked like thunder. "Don't make me out to be something I'm not."

"You know what I mean. I need to be here on my own and work out my life without any more help from you. I don't have to explain to you how much I already love it here. But when Father Debakis asked you to interview me, he had no idea what a kind and generous man you really are or how far you would go for the welfare of another human being."

"You're confusing my human interest in you with the attraction we feel for each other, which is something else altogether. Admit the chemistry has been there from the beginning."

"How can I deny it after the way we kissed each other? But it doesn't change the dynamic that I'm an employee of the Giannopoulos Foundation. It would be better if we remain friends and nothing more. You admit you've had other girlfriends. I'm positive there will be more. When another woman comes into your life who sets off sparks, you'll be able to do something about it without looking back."

His black eyes glittered dangerously. "What about you?"

She threw her head back. "I told you the other day. I'm not interested in romance. I want to make a difference in other people's lives. In ways, Ms. Kallistos had the right idea about me after all."

"What rubbish. You know damn well you don't believe what you're saying. I know you don't, but for some reason I have yet to figure out, you've decided to be cruel."

"Cruel?" Her face heated up. "I'm trying to save both of us a lot of pain."

She heard a sharp intake of breath. "You're so sure we'll end up in pain?"

"I *know* we will."

He shook his dark head. "What do you know that I don't?"

Zoe didn't want to say the words. "Think about it and you'll see that I'm right. There's another Raina out there waiting for you to come along. She won't be an employee and she'll be able to give you all the things you've been longing for in your life. Trust me in this. Your turn is coming, Vasso. You're a dear man and deserve everything life has to offer."

Frown lines darkened his handsome features. "Why do I feel like you're writing my epitaph?"

No, my darling. Not yours. Zoe swallowed hard. "I'm not the woman for you."

A haunted expression entered his eyes. "You're not making sense."

"In time, it will be clear to you. Good night, Kyrie Giannopoulos. From now on that's how I'll address you coming and going from the center."

He pushed the button that took them down to the main floor. "Since I'm your boss, I'll accompany you to the entertainment center to offer help if you need it."

Oh, Vasso...

When they reached the game room, there were twelve patients assembled with several nurses standing by. "We've been waiting for you, Zoe," one of the women called out.

Nestor shot her a glance. "Did you forget the treat?"

"Of course not. It's something we chemo patients enjoyed when I was convalescing at the other center. I'm curious to know if you'll like it. But you have to be patient while it cooks."

"What are you going to pull out of your magic bag now?" Vasso said *sotto voce*.

After their painful conversation, his teasing comment made her smile. She ached with love for him and moved over to the microwave. "See these?" Zoe picked up a packet of popcorn lying on the counter.

"They don't sell this in Greece," Vasso murmured.

"True. I brought a supply in my bag when I flew over."

She put a packet in the microwave and pressed the button. In a few seconds the kernels started to pop. Her eyes met Vasso's as that wonderful smell started to permeate the air. When it stopped, she opened the door and pulled out the filled bag. Taking care, she opened it.

Vasso had first dibs. After eating some, he started nodding and took a handful. He couldn't stop with just one and kept eating and nodding. Zoe knew it was a winner and smiled. "I'll let you keep this bag and I'll do another one."

She started cooking it. "Since you're the bird down in the mine and you're still breathing, they'll be willing to try it."

His burst of rich male laughter warmed her heart.

"You think it'll catch on?" she asked.

"Like wildfire. In fact we'll have to stock these in our stores."

"You'll have to tell your managers to cook a batch to entice the customers."

His black eyes smoldered. "You've enticed *me*, Thespinis Zachos."

The popping stopped, but her heartbeat pounded on. She hurriedly pulled out the bag. Vasso took over and opened it before passing it around to those who were willing to try it.

In a louder voice she said, "The popcorn helped some of us at the other center. But if you're too nauseated, then wait till next Friday night," she urged. "Now I'll turn on the film. It's the one that got the most votes to watch. *The Princess Bride* in Greek."

Everyone started clapping.

Vasso turned off the overhead light and came to stand by her with a lazy smile on his face. "Where did you find that?"

"When I went to Corfu with Olympia. This film is a winner with everyone. Have you seen it?"

"No. Any chance of my cooking another bag while we watch?"

If Vasso was trying to break her down, he was doing a stellar job. Those roses had been her undoing. "You don't have to ask me if you want more popcorn. You're the boss."

CHAPTER EIGHT

EVERYTHING HAD BEEN going fine until Zoe reminded Vasso that she worked for him. But that was okay because he wasn't going to let her get away with ignoring him. She would have to put up with him coming to the center on a regular basis. Little by little he would wear her down until she confessed what was going on inside her.

Throughout the entertaining film, he noticed Nestor watching her rather than the movie. One day the younger man would be better. Since Zoe had voiced her concern, Vasso had been thinking about him. Their company had two thousand and one store managers throughout Greece. On Vasso's say-so, any one of them would take Nestor on as an employee.

When the movie was over and the lights went on, the nurses started wheeling the patients back to their rooms. Vasso volunteered to take Nestor. He felt Zoe's questioning glance on him while she straightened up the room. He kept on going and soon they'd entered his hospital room where Vasso sat on the chair near the table.

"You didn't have to bring me," Nestor murmured. "Thank you."

"You're welcome. Before I leave, I wanted to discuss something with you. I know you're in the recovery phase of your illness. When you're ready to be released, I'm curious to know where you want to go."

"I was born and raised in Athens."

"But I understand you have no family now."

"No," he said, tight-lipped.

"If you could do anything, what would it be?"

"Anything?" Vasso nodded. "I'd like to go to college, but that would be impossible."

At Nestor's age, Vasso had wanted the same thing, but he and Akis were too busy building their business. There was never the right time. "Maybe not."

The younger man looked shocked.

"There are scholarships available for hardworking people. If I arranged for you to get a job in Athens, you could attend college at night."

Nestor's eyes opened wider. "That would be amazing, but I don't know if I'm going to get well."

"I understand you're better today than you were a week ago. Have faith and we'll talk again when the doctor okays your release."

He left Nestor thinking about it and headed for the private elevator. There was nothing he wanted more than to find Zoe and talk to her. But she needed her sleep so she could be in charge tomorrow and Sunday. The one thing that helped him walk away tonight was knowing she wasn't going anywhere. She loved her job and he would always know where to find her.

For the next week he kept busy coordinating work with Akis and continued to send emails to Zoe. He knew his brother wanted to ask him more questions, but Akis kept silent. That was good because Vasso didn't want to get into a discussion about Zoe. They debated the pros and cons of putting up a store in Florina, but didn't come to a decision. The city wasn't growing as fast as some other areas.

On Friday afternoon he flew back to Paxos. After a shower and shave, he put on casual clothes and headed over to the center. Seven days away had made him hungry for the sight of her. But first he checked in with Yiannis who sang Zoe's praises. "We can be thankful all is well with that young woman."

"Amen to that." He expelled a relieved sigh. "I'm going to go over the books with Kyria Lasko in accounting if you need to find me." Vasso knew he wasn't fooling the admiral, but he appreciated the older man for not prying into his personal life.

Two hours later he walked down the hall. When he couldn't see Zoe at the front desk, he headed for the entertainment center. Friday night was movie night. He had a hunch she was in there setting things up for later. But when he went inside, he only found a couple of patients with a nurse.

"Have you seen Thespinis Zachos?"

"She just left, but she'll be back at nine-thirty."

Vasso thanked her and left the hospital in his car. En route to the town center he phoned her. By the time she picked up, his pulse had jumped off the charts.

"Vasso?"

She sounded surprised. He'd missed her so much just the sound of her voice excited him. "I'm glad you answered. Where are you?"

After a pause, "At the apartment."

"No bike riding today?"

"No. Our plans fell through. Her husband hurt his leg biking, so she's home taking care of him this weekend."

"Sorry to hear that. I flew in earlier and worked with the accountant at the center. I didn't see you anywhere. Have you eaten dinner?"

"Not yet."

"I'd like to talk to you about Nestor. Would you like to meet me at Psara's? I don't know about you but I'm craving fish."

He could hear her thoughts working. "That's the *taverna* down near the parking area?"

"Yes. I'm headed there now if you'd like to join me. But if you have other plans, I'll understand."

"No—" she exclaimed, then said no in a quieter voice. "Nestor told me you talked to him last week."

"That's right."

"You...planted a seed."

Good. "If you want to discuss it, I'll be watching for you." Without waiting for a response, he clicked off and pulled into the parking. He got out and hurried toward the *taverna* to grab a table before the place filled up. Being that it was a Friday night, the paparazzi were out covering the waterfront. Celebrities from Athens often came to Loggos for dinner. Vasso couldn't escape.

In a few minutes, every male young or old stared at the beautiful blonde woman making her way toward him. She'd dressed in a leaf-green blouse with a white skirt tied at the waist. He experienced the same sense of wonder he'd felt when he'd seen her the first time. She was like a breath of fresh air and walked with a lilt on those fabulous legs.

When Vasso stood up to pull out her chair for her, several journalists caught her on camera. She couldn't have helped but see them. "Ignore them," he muttered. "Pretty soon they'll go away."

"Not as long as you're here." But she said it with a smile. "I knew I was taking a chance to be seen with you."

"You're a brave woman, but then we already know that about you." His comment brought the color flooding into her cheeks.

The waiter came to pour coffee and take their order. They both chose the catch of the day. Once they were alone again, he studied her classic features. "Thanks for answering my emails. You've kept me abreast of everything going on at the center. But you never share your personal feelings. How *has* your week gone?"

"Every day is different. I couldn't be happier," she said through veiled eyes. "What about yours?"

"I can't complain as you know from my messages to you, but thanks for asking."

Considering what it had been like to get in each other's arms last week, this conversation was a mockery. But he'd play her game for a while longer. "How much did Nestor tell you?"

Now that he'd changed the subject to something important to her, she grew animated. "He mentioned that you talked to him about a scholarship so he could go to night school. He's been in disbelief that you really meant it."

Vasso sucked in his breath. "I would never have brought it up if I weren't serious. Earlier this week I talked to the manager of our number-four store in Athens. He'd be willing to give Nestor a job. I have no idea if he would want to work in a convenience store after being employed at a hotel, but—"

"I'm sure he would!" she cried out excitedly. "Oh, Vasso—there's been a light in his eyes that hasn't been there until now. It's because of you."

No. That light had to do with Zoe. She ignited everyone she met. "How much more chemo does he have to go through?"

"He's had his last treatment. The doctor has high hopes for his recovery."

"In that case I'll come to movie night tonight and tell him."

His news made her so happy he realized she couldn't tell him not to come. "Hope will make him get well in a hurry."

The waiter chose that moment to bring their dinner. When he walked away Vasso said, "That's the idea, isn't it. We all need hope."

That little nerve at the base of her throat was pulsing again. She started to eat her fish. "Between you and Father Debakis, I don't know who will deserve the bigger reward in heaven."

"Your mind is too much on the hereafter," he teased. "I'm quite happy with life right here."

She flushed. "So am I. It's just that I'm so than—"

"Don't say that anymore, Zoe. I'm quite aware of how you feel. I want to talk about how we feel about each other. I can't stay away from you. I don't want to. So we need to talk about where we're going to go from here. I *know* you feel the same way about me."

Her head lifted and their gazes collided. "I admit it, but you'd have to be in my shoes to understand why it wouldn't be a good idea for us to get any more involved."

"I can't accept that."

Zoe's expression sobered. "You're sick of hearing the same thing from me, aren't you?"

If he dared tell her what he really thought, she'd run from him. He couldn't handle that. "I'm not saying another word while we're the focus of other people."

One journalist had stayed longer to get pictures of the two of them. Vasso shot Zoe a glance. "If you're through eating, let's head for my car and ruin that guy's evening."

Her sudden laugh always delighted him. He put money on the table and got up. She was still chuckling when they reached the Lexus and he helped her inside. Zoe looked over at him as he drove. "Even paradise has its serpents."

"They have to earn a living, too."

Her eyes rounded. "You feel sorry for them?"

"No, but I understand that the need to make money in order to survive makes some people desperate enough to take chances."

"You're right, of course. I've never been in that position." She glanced at him. "I've never gone to bed hungry in my life." There was a catch in her voice. "Because of your foundation, I've been taken care of in miraculous ways. Sometimes I'm overwhelmed by your generosity."

Vasso couldn't take it anymore. "Overwhelmed enough to do me a favor?"

"I'd do anything for you. Surely you know that by now."

"Then come to my house after movie night is over. There's something I have to discuss with you, but we'll need privacy."

He heard her quick intake of breath. "That sounds serious."

"It is. Don't tell me no. I couldn't take it."

Zoe trembled, wondering what had happened to put him in this cryptic mood. If he was unhappy with some of the innovations she'd made at the hospital, all he had to do was tell her up front. Maybe Yianni had confided that she wasn't working out, but he didn't have the heart to tell her to her face because he was such a sweetheart.

When they reached the center, he parked the car and they entered through the front door.

She saw the clock. "It's almost time. I need to hurry to the game room and set up."

"Go ahead. I'll be there in a minute."

Did he want to talk to Yianni again?

Zoe went to the restroom first so she could pull herself together. She had the idea he was going to discuss her future here at the foundation. Could he be going to let her go? Fear stabbed at her. Maybe coming to work for him hadn't been a good thing after all. The passion enveloping them last week had only muddied the water. Tonight things were crystal-clear.

If Father Debakis hadn't intervened, she wouldn't be in this precarious position now. It wasn't his fault, of course. If she hadn't been so desperate to repay her debt, she wouldn't have caused all this trouble.

That's what Vasso had been alluding to earlier. Desperation was responsible for all kinds of mistakes. Her biggest one had been to accept his offer to relocate to Greece and continue taking his charity for the rest of her life.

Of course she was earning a salary now, so she hoped that wasn't what it looked like to him. She buried her face in her hands, not knowing what to think.

She wished her mother were around to talk to her about this. The great irony about that was the fact that if her parents were still alive, Zoe wouldn't be thousands of miles away from home. She'd be finishing college and getting on with her life, never knowing of Vasso's existence. Instead she'd dumped all her problems on Vasso who hadn't asked for them in the first place.

Zoe was terribly conflicted. She'd acted besotted in his arms, but as he'd reminded her, the emails she sent back to him didn't say anything about her feelings. In her heart she'd been watching for signs of him all week. When he hadn't come to the center before tonight, she was desolate. But she couldn't have it both ways, not when she'd told him she wanted to keep their relationship professional.

What a laugh she must have given him. No doubt he saw her as the worst kind of needy female. If she kept this up much longer, he'd be forced to find her something else to do in order to get her out of his hair. But he was such a good man he would never fire her without a new plan.

When she'd washed the tears off her face, she headed for the entertainment center. Eight patients showed up. The other four had just been through another session of chemo and wouldn't rally for a few days.

Vasso had singled out Nestor. While he thrilled him with a job offer, she popped more popcorn and started a movie. This time it was the Greek version of an old film, *Zorba the Greek*. The audience would complain that Anthony Quinn was Mexican, not Greek then they'd pull the crazy plot apart. Hopefully it would entertain them enough for a little while to forget how sick they felt.

By the end of the film, no one wanted the evening to be over. It proved to her that movie night worked. While the nurses took the patients back to their rooms, she tidied the place. But when she followed Vasso out of the center to his car, her heart felt as if it weighed a stone. She dreaded what was coming and her legs felt like dead weights.

On the drive to his house she turned to him. "How did your conversation go with Nestor?"

Vasso let his wrists do the driving. "He sounded just like you when I told him I'd find him an apartment near the number-four store. That way he could walk to work and take the bus to the university after he was released. I don't think he could see the film through the tears."

No. Nestor's gratitude would know no bounds for their benefactor, but she refrained from saying anything because Vasso didn't want to hear it.

Zoe tried to gear up for what was coming. How awful that a conversation with him would take place in his house, the one personal area of his life she'd tried to stay away from. She loved it already just seeing it from the air.

He drove around the back of it. It had been built near the water's edge. They entered a door into the kitchen area with a table and chairs. Though small like a cottage, huge windows opened everything up to turn it into a beach home, making it seem larger. No walls.

Everywhere you looked, you could see the sea. All you had to do was open the sliding doors and you could step out on a deck with several tubs of flowers and loungers. Beyond it, the sand and water were at your feet.

A circular staircase on one side of the room rose to the upper floor. It had to be a loft. The other end of the room contained the rock fireplace with a big comfy couch and chairs.

"Would you like a drink?"

She shook her head. "Nothing, thank you."

"Let's take a walk along the beach. The sand feels like the finest granulated sugar. I do my best thinking out there. We'll slip off our shoes and leave them inside. You can wash your feet later at the side of the deck."

After she did his bidding, she followed him outside. Night had descended. A soft fragrant breeze with the scent of thyme blew at her hair and skirt. She knew it was thyme because there was the same smell at the center. Yianni had explained what it was. He was a walking encyclopedia of knowledge.

She could talk to him the way she did with Father Debakis. The wonderful man had great children who looked after him, but he'd loved his wife to distraction and talked to Zoe about their life together. How heavenly to have enjoyed a marriage like Yianni's.

When they'd walked a ways, Vasso stopped and turned to her. The time had come. Her body broke out in a cold sweat. To her shock, he cupped her face in his hands and lifted it so she had to look at him. Zoe couldn't decipher the expression in his eyes, but his striking male features stood out in the semidarkness.

"I want to start over."

She blinked. "What do you mean?"

"I mean, I'd like us to do what two people do who have met and would like to get to know each other better."

After everything she'd been thinking as to what might be the reason why he'd brought her here, Zoe was incredulous. "That's the favor?"

"I know it's a big one. Last week you made it clear you didn't want anything more than friendship from me, but we moved past that after your arrival in Greece. I want to spend this weekend with you and all the weekends you're available from here on out."

The ground shifted.

She was positive she'd misunderstood him.

"Did you hear me?" he asked in an urgent voice.

"You *can't* be serious." She grasped his wrists, but he still cradled her face in his hands.

"Why are you acting like this, Zoe?"

"Because you're carrying your sense of responsibility to me too far."

"Does this feel like responsibility?" He lowered his mouth to hers and kissed her long and hard until she melted against him. Zoe was delirious with desire after being away from him for a whole week. "Tell me the real reason you're fighting me," he said after lifting his head. They were both out of breath. "I know you're attracted to me. You told me there's no one else in your life." The warm breath on her mouth sent a fire licking through her body.

"There isn't, but Vasso—" she moaned his name, "I can't be with you. If I had known this was going to happen, I would have changed my mind and stayed in New York. I would have found another place to work."

His brows met. "You don't mean that. You're lying to cover up what's really wrong."

Making a great effort, she eased herself out of his arms. "You're a very intelligent man. If you think hard about it, you'll know why this won't work. My cancer is in remission, but no one knows when it will come back."

She heard him suck in his breath. "Guess what? Tomorrow I could go down in the helicopter and never be seen again. It could happen. But if I looked at life like that, nothing would get accomplished."

"A possible helicopter crash one day compared to a recurrence of cancer are two different things."

He raked his hands through his hair. "No. They're not. No matter what, life is a risk."

"But some risks are more risky than others, Vasso. To get close to you is like buying something you want on time. One day—much sooner than you had supposed—you'll have no choice but to pay the balance in full. It will be too heavy a price to have to come up with all at once. I won't let you get into that position."

This time his hands slid up her arms. "You honestly believe you're going to die soon? *That's* what this is all about?"

"Yes. But I don't know the timetable and neither do you. What I do know is that you watched your father die of the same disease. No one should have to live through the trauma of that experience a second time in life. You and your brother have fought too hard to come all this way, only for you to get involved with a time bomb, because that's what I am."

He drew her closer. "Zoe—"

"Let me finish, please? I saw the love Akis and his wife share. With a baby on the way they're totally happy. He doesn't have to worry that Raina is going to be stricken by the inevitable.

"Don't you understand? I want you to have the same life *they* have. No clouds on the horizon. To spend time with me makes no sense for you. I'm a liability and I made Chad see that. He was smart and did the right thing for both of us."

Vasso's features darkened. "How was it right for you?" his voice grated.

"Because I would have been more depressed to watch

his suffering over me when I could do nothing to alleviate it. Just think about what it felt like when your father was dying, and you'll understand exactly what I'm talking about. It would have been so much harder on me if Chad had been there day and night. I couldn't have handled it."

"I'm not Chad." His hands slid to her shoulders. "Did you love him?"

Vasso's question caught her off guard. "I…thought I did. There are all kinds of love."

"No, Zoe. I'm talking about that overpowering feeling of love for another person that goes so deep into the marrow, you can't breathe without it."

He'd just described her feelings for him and pulled away before he read the truth in her eyes. "I don't want to talk about this anymore. If it's all right with you, I'd like to go home."

She turned back and hurried toward the deck where she could wash the sand off her feet. By the time he'd caught up to her, she'd gone inside and had slipped on her shoes.

"Before we go anywhere, I need to tell you something important, Zoe. Will you listen?"

They stood in the middle of the room like adversaries. Spiraling emotions had caused her to shake like a leaf. "Of course."

"Something unprecedented happened to me when I flew to New York to interview you. I didn't ask for it, but it happened. I haven't been the same since. Like you with Chad, I thought I loved Sofia. She'd always been there. We'd been a couple for such a long time, it just seemed normal for us to get married.

"Luckily, she got impatient. While I was in the military, she couldn't wait for me. Though I didn't know it at the time, she did me the greatest service in the world because it was apparent she wasn't the one for me.

"After surviving that hurdle, Akis and I led a bachelor existence for years. When Raina came into his life, it was as much a shock to me as to him. He'd been with other women, but she knocked him sideways without even trying, and transformed his life. I can promise you that if she'd been a recovering cancer patient, it would have made no difference to him."

"That's what you say because it's what you want to believe." She shook her head. "I can see there's no way to get through to you on this."

"You're right. There's only one solution to end our impasse."

"Exactly. By ending it now."

"I have a better idea in mind."

Zoe couldn't take much more. "I need to get back to the apartment."

"I'll take you, but I want you to think very seriously about my next words."

She reached for her purse and started for the kitchen. "Will you tell me in the car?"

Without waiting for him, Zoe went outside and walked along the path to his Lexus. Afraid to have contact, she quickly got in and shut the door.

Vasso went around to his side of the car and started the engine. But before he drove them to the road, he slid his arm along the seat so that his fingers touched the ends of her hair. Immediately her body responded, but she refused to look at him.

"We need to get married."

Her gasp reverberated in the interior. "*Married*—"

"The sooner the better. According to your timetable, we might have five years together before everything comes to an end. I want to give you children. I'd rather take those five years and live them fully with you, than walk away from you now and leave us both in pain."

"I won't be in pain," she defended in a quiet voice while her heart ran away with her at the thought of having his baby.

"Well, I will." He tugged gently on her hair strands. "After the way you kissed me back tonight, I know for a fact you'll be in pain, too. I don't need an answer yet, but I'll look for one soon."

"No—" she whispered in agony. "You mustn't."

"If I'd let the *no*s and the *mustn't*s get in the way, I wouldn't be where I am today. You and I don't have the usual problems that beset couples. We know who we are and exactly what we're getting into. We've learned how precious life is. We've been made brutally aware that there are no guarantees for the future, only what we're prepared to build together."

She swallowed hard. "What it proves to me is how far you would go to honor the wishes of Father Debakis."

"He has nothing to do with this!"

"Then why would you be willing to make the ultimate sacrifice by marrying me and giving me a home when you know I have a very short life span."

"Because I love you."

"I love you, too, but I wonder if you remember the warning you gave me in New York. You said, 'Be sure it's what you want.' How sad someone didn't warn you to be sure it was what *you* wanted."

"You're putting up a defense because of your own insecurities." He drove the car to the road and they headed for the village.

"Vasso, you don't want to marry me. We're both temporarily attracted to each other. You're like any red-blooded bachelor might be, but you're not in love with me. I refuse to be your personal project.

"I came here to work and pay you back for your generosity. Wouldn't it be a great way to show my gratitude by becoming your wife? Then you'd be forced to take care of me for however long I have left.

"Forget children. No way would I want to leave a baby for you to raise on your own. Your father did that. I won't allow history to repeat itself. You and Akis have been through so much, you deserve all the happiness you can find.

"Sofia Peri didn't know what she was doing when she let the most marvelous man on earth slip through her fingers. If you'd married back then, you'd probably be a father to several darling children. I should never have come here."

Yianni had gotten along fine before Zoe had arrived. The center would run smoothly whether she was there or not. If she flew back to New York, she could get a job as a cook. When she'd saved enough money she could finish her last semester of college. Then she could get a job teaching school and send money to the foundation every month. It was the best plan she could think of under the circumstances.

When she got back to the apartment, she'd phone Father Debakis and have a heart-to-heart with him. He was probably at dinner and could talk to her when he was through. The priest would understand her dilemma and give her the guidance she needed because heaven help her, she couldn't make this decision without his blessing.

Vasso drove around to the back of the shop. She opened the door before he came to a stop. "Thank you for bringing me home. You made Nestor a happy man tonight."

"And what about you?"

"You already know what I think."

"We're not finished, Zoe."

"How can I convince you that this just won't work?"

"I didn't realize you were so stubborn."

"Then be thankful I'm not the marrying type. You've dodged a bullet. Good night."

CHAPTER NINE

For the next week Vasso worked like a demon, traveling from city to city to check on stores while Akis worked out of the Athens office. After the last conversation with Zoe, he knew she needed time to think about their situation without being pressured.

Now that it was Friday evening, he couldn't stay away any longer and flew to Paxos. She would be on duty this weekend and couldn't run away from him. After they watched a movie with some of the patients, he'd get her alone to talk until he convinced her they belonged together.

At five to six he tapped on Yiannis's half-open door and walked in. Zoe wasn't out in front, but he didn't expect her to be.

He found the admiral pouring himself coffee from a carafe brought in on a cart from the kitchen. The older man was using the cup Zoe had given him. He turned to Vasso. "Ah. You're here at last."

By his sober demeanor Vasso sensed something was wrong. "Did I miss a call from you?"

"No, no." He walked back to his chair. "Sit down so we can talk."

Not liking the sound of that, he preferred to remain standing. Yiannis looked up from his desk. "I have a letter here for you. It's from Zoe. She asked me to give it to you when you came by and not before."

His heart plummeted. He took the envelope from him, almost afraid to ask the next question. "Where is she?"

"She flew back to New York on Tuesday."

The breath froze in his lungs.

"On Sunday she came over, white as a sheet, and submitted her resignation. Zoe's the best assistant I could have asked for, but the tragic expression on her face let me know she's been suffering. She told me she was so homesick she couldn't stay in Greece any longer. The sweet thing thought she could handle being transplanted, but apparently it was too big a leap. Kyria Lasko is helping me out again."

His agony made it hard to talk let alone think. "I'll find a temporary accountant from headquarters until we can find the right person to assist you," he murmured.

"You'd better sit down, Vasso. You've gone quite pale."

He shook his head. "I'll be all right. Forgive me. I've got things to do, but I'll be in touch."

Vasso rushed out of the hospital and drove to the village at record speed. He parked the car and ran along the waterfront to the gift shop. The second Kyria Panos saw him she waved him over with an anxious expression. "If you're looking for Thespinis Zachos, she's left Greece."

He felt like he was bleeding out. "I heard the news when I was at the center earlier. Let me pay her bill."

"No, no. She paid me. Such a lovely person. Never any trouble."

Not until now, Vasso's heart cried out.

He thanked the older woman and drove back to his house. After making a diving leap for the couch he ripped open the envelope to read her letter. She'd only written one short paragraph.

> *Forgive me for accepting your offer of employment. It has caused you so much unnecessary trouble. I'm desolate over my mistake. One day I'll be able to start paying you back in my own way.*
>
> *My dear, dear Vasso, be happy.*

Blind with pain, he staggered to the storage closet and reached for his bike. He'd known pain two other times in his life. A young teen's loss of a father. Later a young man's loss of his childhood sweetheart. This pain was different.

Zoe thought she could spare him pain by disappearing from his life. But with her gone, he felt as if his soul had died on the spot. Vasso didn't know how he was going to last the night, but he couldn't stay in the house.

He took his bike out the back door and started cycling with no destination in mind. All he wanted to do was keep going until he got rid of the pain. It was near morning when he returned to his house and took himself up to bed.

The next time he had cognizance of his surroundings, he could hear Akis's voice somewhere in the background urging him to wake up. He couldn't figure out where he was. How had he made it upstairs to his bed?

His eyelids opened. "Akis?"

"Stay with me, Vasso. Come on. Wake up."

He groaned with pain. "Zoe left me."

"I know."

"Did you see her letter?"

"That, and your bike lying on the ground at the back door."

He rubbed his face with his hand and felt his beard. "How did you find out?"

"Yiannis called me yesterday worried about you."

"What's today?"

"Sunday."

He opened his eyes again. "You mean I've been out of it since Friday?"

"Afraid so." His brother looked grim. They'd been through every experience together. "You've given me a scare, bro. I was worried you might have driven yourself too hard and wouldn't wake up. Don't ever do that to me again."

Vasso raised himself up on one elbow. "A week ago I asked her to marry me. Friday night she left her answer with Yiannis. I wanted her so badly I pushed too hard."

"It's early days."

"No. She left Greece to spare me. Zoe's convinced the disease will recur."

Akis sighed. "Raina picked up on that the night you came for dinner."

"For her to give up the job she wanted was huge for her. There's no hoping she'll come back."

"Why don't you get up and shower, then we'll fly to my house. Raina has food ready. Once you get a meal in you, we'll talk. Don't tell me no. This is one time you need help, even if you are my big brother."

September 23, Astoria, New York

"Zoe? Come in my office."

She knew what the doctor was going to say and was prepared for the bad news. This was her first checkup since she'd left the hospital six weeks ago. The month she'd spent in Greece was like a blip on a screen, as if that life had been lived by a different person.

She'd decided not to call Father Debakis. No one at the church knew she was back in the US. Zoe prayed Ms. Kallistos hadn't seen her slip in the hospital and would never know about this appointment.

Zoe had made up her mind she wouldn't depend on the charity of others ever again. While she was staying at the YWCA, she'd been going out on temporary jobs to survive. There was always work if you were willing to do it. This was the life that had put Nestor in a depression. She could see why.

If any good had come out of her experience on Paxos, it had been to introduce him to Vasso who had not only saved his life through his charity, but had made it possible for him to go to college.

Vasso... Zoe's heart ached with a love so profound

for him she could hardly bear to get up every day and face the world without him.

"Zoe? Did you hear me?"

She lifted her head. "I'm sorry. I guess I was deep in thought."

He frowned. "You've lost five pounds since you were released from the hospital. Why is that?"

"With the recurrence of cancer, that doesn't surprise me."

"What recurrence?"

Zoe shook her head. "You don't need to be gentle with me, doctor. Just tell me the truth. I can take it."

He cocked his head. She had to wait a long time before he spoke again. "I'm beginning to think that if I told you the truth, you wouldn't recognize it, let alone believe me. I *am* a doctor, and I've sworn an oath to look after the sick."

"I know," she whispered.

"But you think I'm capable of lying?"

She bit her lip. "Maybe not lying, but since you work with cancer patients, I realize you're trying to be careful how you tell a patient there is a death sentence in the future."

He leaned forward. "We all have a death sentence awaiting us in life. That's part of the plan. In the meantime, part of the plan is to live life to the fullest. Something tells me that's not what you've been doing."

Those were Vasso's words. It sent prickles down her spine.

"There's no recurrence of cancer, Zoe. I'm giving you another clean bill of health."

"Until another six weeks from now, then it will show up."

He made a sound of exasperation. "Maybe you weren't listening to me the first time I told you this. In people like you with none of the other complicating factors, the statistics prove that about ninety-one out of every one hundred people live for more than five years after they are diagnosed. And seventy-one out of every one hundred people live for more than ten years. Some even live to the natural end of their lives."

She'd heard him the first time, but she hadn't been able to believe it. *Was it really possible?*

"Since you're cancer-free and in perfect physical shape, I want to know the reason for your weight loss. It has to be a man."

She struggled for breath. "You're right."

"Tell me about him."

Zoe had refused to give in to her feelings since returning from Greece. But with the doctor who'd been her friend for a whole year pressing her for an explanation, she couldn't hold back any longer and blurted everything in one go. The tears gushed until she was totally embarrassed.

"Before I see my next patient who's waiting, do you want to know what *I* think, girl?"

Girl? He hadn't called her that in a long time. Surprised, she looked at him, still needing to wipe the moisture off her face. "What?"

"You're a damn fool if you don't fly back there and tell him yes. I don't want to see you in my office again unless you have a wedding ring on your finger!"

September 25, Athens, Greece

When the ferry headed toward the familiar docking point at Loggos, Zoe was jumping out of her skin with nervous excitement. She'd taken the cheapest one-way night flight from JFK to Corfu and caught the morning ferry to Paxos Island. While on board she changed into walking shorts and sneakers. Everything else she owned was in her new suitcases. Luckily the largest case had wheels, making it easier for her to walk along the waterfront to the gift shop.

Kyria Panos looked shocked and anxious when Zoe entered her store. "I didn't know you were back. If you want the apartment, I've already rented it. I'm sorry."

"Don't be. That's good business for you! I just wondered if I could leave my luggage here. I'll pay you and be back for it by the end of the day."

"You don't have to pay me. Just bring it behind the counter."

"You're so kind. Thank you."

"Did you know Kyrie Giannopoulos tried to pay me for your rental?"

"No, but that doesn't surprise me." There was no one in this world like Vasso. "I'll buy one of these T-shirts." She found the right size and gave her some euros. "Mind if I change in your bathroom?"

"Go ahead. Whatever you want."

Having deposited her luggage and purse, she left and was free to buy her favorite snack of a gyro and fruit at Vasso's number-one store. Once she'd eaten, she rented a bike from the tourist outfit at the other end of the pier and took off for Vasso's beach house.

Though she hadn't lived on Paxos for very long, it felt like home to her now. The softness of the sea air, the fragrance, it all fed her soul that had been hungering for Vasso. Raina had said it best. "I thought I was American too before I married Akis. Now the Greek part has climbed in and sits next to my heart." Zoe could relate very well.

She had no idea if Vasso would be home or not. If she couldn't find him, she'd bike to the center and drop in on Yianni. He was a sweetheart and would be able to help her track him down without giving her presence away. She wanted, needed to surprise Vasso. It was important she see that first look in his eyes. Just imagining the moment made it difficult to breathe.

The ride through the olive groves rejuvenated her. Every so often she'd stop to absorb another view of the azure sea and the white sailboats taking advantage of the light breeze. She removed her helmet to enjoy it. While she was thinking about Vasso, she saw the local bus coming toward her. It slowed down and a smiling Gus leaned out the window.

"*Yassou*, Zoe! Where have you been?"

"In New York, but I'm back to stay!"

"That's good!"

"I agree!"

After he drove on, she put her helmet back on and started pedaling again. She went through alternating cycles of fear and excitement as she contemplated their reunion. Zoe wouldn't allow herself to be bombarded with negative thoughts again. She'd weathered too many of them already. Because of a lack of faith, she'd wasted precious time, time she and Vasso could have had together.

Zoe stopped every so often to catch her breath and take in the glorious scenery. She had no way of knowing if he'd be at the house, but it didn't matter. This was his home. He would return to it at some point, and she'd be waiting for him.

Akis looked at Vasso. "What do you think about him?" The last person they'd interviewed for the assistant's job at the hospital went out to the lounge to wait. Over the last week there'd been a dozen applicants for the job before him.

"I think he's as good as we're going to get."

"His disability won't present a problem and he's ex-military. Yiannis will like that."

Vasso nodded. Neither of them wanted to admit Yiannis had been so unhappy about Zoe's resignation he'd found something wrong with anyone they'd sent for an interview. He'd rather do the extra work himself.

"Will you tell him? I need to get back to the house if only to find out if it's still standing." Since the Sunday Vasso had awakened to a world without Zoe in it, he'd been living at the penthouse when he wasn't out of the city on business. He got up and headed for their private elevator.

"Hey, bro." Akis's concern was written on his face. "Come over for dinner tonight."

"Can I take a rain check?" Akis and Raina had done

everything to help, but there was no help for what was wrong.

"Then promise you'll keep in close touch with me."

"Haven't I always?"

"Not always," Akis reminded him.

No. The Friday night he'd read Zoe's goodbye letter, everything had become a blur until Akis had found him on Sunday morning. By now he'd gotten the message that she had no regrets over leaving him. None.

While he'd waited in the hope that he'd hear from her, he'd gone through every phase of pain and agony. Maybe it would never leave him. Desperate for some relief, he flew to Paxos. When the helicopter dropped him off, he got in his car. After buying some roses in town, he headed for their family church on the summit.

A breeze came up this time of day, filling the air with the scent of vanilla from the yellow broom growing on the hillsides. He pulled off the road and got out. The cemetery was around the back. Sixteen years ago he and Akis had buried their father next to their mother. They'd been young and their grief had been exquisite. In their need they'd clung to each other.

Vasso walked around and placed the tub of roses in front of the headstone. Then he put a knee down and read what was inscribed on the stone until it became a blur. As if it had been yesterday, he still remembered a conversation they'd had with their father before he'd died.

"You're only in your teens and you'll meet a lot of women before you're grown up. When you find *the* one, you must treat her like a queen. Your mother was my queen. I cherished and respected her from the beginning. She deserved that because not only was she going to be my wife, she was going to be the mother of our children."

Tears dripped off Vasso's chin.

"I've found my queen, *Papa,* but her fear of dying early of the same disease as you has made it impossible for us to be together. I don't know how you handled it when our mother died, but somehow you lived through the grief. If you could do it, so can I. I'm the big brother. I *have* to.

"Wouldn't you know Akis is doing much better than I am because he's found the love of his life? They're going to have a baby." His shoulders heaved. "I'm so happy for them. I want to be happy, too. But the real truth of it is…I *have* to find a way for that to happen, *Papa,* otherwise this life no longer makes sense."

Vasso stayed there until he heard the voices of children playing on the slope below him. That meant school was out for the day. He'd been here long enough and wiped the tears with the side of his arm. It was time to drive back to the house and take stock of what he was going to do with his life from here on out.

Something had to change. To go on mourning for something that wasn't meant to be was destructive. He had a business to run. One day soon he'd be an uncle to his brother's child. Vasso intended to love him or her and give all the support he could.

After reaching the car, he drove home with the windows open, taking the lower road that wound along the coastline. As he rounded a curve he saw a cyclist in the far distance. It was a beautiful day. Vasso didn't wonder that someone was out enjoying the sea air.

But when the helmeted figure suddenly disappeared from sight, Vasso was surprised. There was only one turnoff along this particular stretch of road. It led to his beach house. Curious to know if he had a visitor, or if the cyclist was simply a tourist out sightseeing, he stepped on the gas.

When he reached the turnoff, he came close to having a heart attack. Despite the helmet, Vasso could never mistake that well-endowed figure or those shapely legs headed for his house.

It was Zoe on the bike!

He stayed a few yards behind and watched the beautiful sight in front of him, trying to absorb the fact that she was back on the island.

The way she was pedaling, he could tell she was tired. At some point she must have sensed someone was behind her. When she looked over her right shoulder, she let out a cry and lost control of the bike. In the next second it fell over, taking her with it.

Terrified she could be hurt, Vasso stopped on a dime and jumped out of the car. But she'd recovered before he could reach her and was on her feet. His eyes were drawn to the English printed in blue on her white T-shirt with the high V-neck. *I'd rather be in Greece.*

If this was a private message to him, he was receiving it loud and clear. The way she filled it out caused him to tremble.

"Zoe—I'm so sorry. Are you hurt?"

Those shimmering green eyes fastened on him. "Heavens, no. I'm such a klutz."

She looked so adorable in that helmet and those shorts, he could hardly find his voice. "Of course you're not. I should have called out or honked so you'd know I was behind you. But to be honest, I thought maybe I was hallucinating to see you in front of me."

He watched her get back on the bike. "I was coming to visit you."

His heart pounded like thunder. "This has to be perfect timing because I haven't been here for several weeks."

"I probably should have phoned you, but after I got off the ferry earlier, I just decided to come and take my chances." She flashed him one of those brilliant smiles that melted his insides. "Beat you to the house!"

He had a hundred questions to ask, but whatever the reason that had brought Zoe back to Paxos, he didn't care. It was enough to see her again. Something was very different. Her whole body seemed to sparkle with life.

She rode toward the house with more vigor than before, convincing him she hadn't hurt herself. He got back in his car and drove slowly the rest of the way. Zoe reached their destination first and put on the kickstand. She was waiting for him as he parked his car and got out.

"Where are you staying?"

"I don't know yet. Kyria Panos let me leave my luggage with her."

His mind was reeling. "You must be thirsty. Come in the house and we'll both have a soda."

Another smile from her turned his insides to butter. "You're a lifesaver."

They walked to the back door. Using his remote to let them in the house, he said, "The guest bathroom is behind that door at the far end of the kitchen."

"Thanks. I'm a mess."

The most gorgeous mess he'd ever seen. While she disappeared, he took the stairs two at a time to the loft and changed into shorts and a T-shirt. Before she came out, he hurried down to the kitchen in sandals and produced some colas from the fridge for them.

When she emerged she was *sans* the helmet. Her blond hair was attractively disheveled. Vasso wanted to plunge his fingers into it and kiss the very life out of her. Her flushed skin, in fact every single thing about her, was too desirable. But he'd learned a terrible lesson since the day she'd left Greece. He'd pushed her too hard, too soon, and wouldn't be making that mistake again.

He handed her a drink. "Welcome back to Greece." He clicked his can against hers and swallowed half the contents in one long gulp. "I like your T-shirt."

"The second I saw it, I had to have it and bought it from Kyria Panos earlier. She let me change shirts in her bathroom."

"You've made a friend there."

She sipped her drink. "Everyone is a friend on this island. Gus waved to me from the bus while I was riding on the road to your house."

"I take it you haven't seen Yiannis yet."

"No. If I couldn't find you, I was planning to bike to the center."

"You look wonderful in those shorts, Zoe."

She blushed. "Thank you."

"I'm used to seeing you in skirts and dresses."

"I know. They make a nice change. You look wonderful, too."

He didn't know how long he could resist crushing her in his arms, but he needed answers. "Shall we go out on the deck?"

"I'd love it."

They walked over to the sliding doors. She sat on one of the loungers while he pulled a chair around next to her. "Tell me what happened when you went back to New York."

He listened as she gave him an account. They were both circling the giant elephant standing on the deck, but he needed to let her guide this conversation if he wanted to know the reason she'd come back. If she was only here for a few days, he couldn't bear it.

"While I was there, I had to go in for my six-weeks checkup."

This was too much. Vasso broke out in a cold sweat and got up, too restless to sit still. He turned on his heel. "Were you given a death sentence and a date? Is that why you're here? To thank me one more time and say a final goodbye?"

"Vasso—" She paled and shot to her feet.

"Because if you are, I could have done without this visit. You know damn well why I asked you to marry me. Can you possibly understand the pain you've inflicted by turning up here now?" The words had gushed out. He couldn't take them back.

"Do you want to hear the exact quote I got from my doctor?"

"Actually I don't." She seemed determined to tell him, but he couldn't go through this agony again and started for the doorway into the house.

She followed him. "He said, 'There's no recurrence of cancer, Zoe. I'm giving you another clean bill of health. In people like you with none of the other complicating factors, it's possible you'll live a full life.'"

Vasso wheeled around. "But you still don't believe him."

"You didn't let me finish. I told him about you and me."

He closed his eyes tightly. "Go on."

"The doctor said, 'You're a damn fool if you don't fly back there and tell him yes. I don't want to see you in my office again unless you have a wedding ring on your finger'!" Zoe moved closer to him.

"Little did he know he was speaking to the converted. After being the recipient of a miracle, I realized I would be an ungrateful wretch if I didn't embrace life fully. He reminded me that we are all facing a death sentence in life, but most of us don't have a time frame.

"Vasso—I came back because I want to spend the rest of my life with you. You have to know I love you to the depths of my being. I want to have children with you. I want the privilege of being called Kyria Giannopoulos, the wife who has a husband like no other in existence.

"You have no idea how handsome and spectacular you are. I lost my breath the first time I laid eyes on you, and I've never completely recovered. You're probably going to think I'm crazy, but I'm thankful I came down with the disease. It brought me to you. If you'll ask me again to marry you, I promise to make you happy because I'm the happiest woman alive to be loved by you."

He could feel the ice melting around his heart. "So you don't think I want you to be my wife because I feel responsible for you?"

"No, darling. I only said that because I was so afraid you couldn't love me the way I loved you. I know you're not perfect, but you are to me," her voice trembled.

"Then come here to me and show me."

She flew into his arms. When he felt them wind around his neck, he carried her in the house and followed her down on the couch. *"Agape mou...*I'm so in love with you I thought I was going to die when I read your letter.

"You're the woman my father was talking about. You're *the* one. I knew it when you walked in the center's office bringing spring with you. I'll never forget that moment. The fierce beating of my heart almost broke my rib cage. You're so sweet and so funny and so fun and so endearing and so beautiful and so kind and so compassionate all at the same time. I love you," he cried. *"I love you, Zoe."*

He broke off telling her all the things she meant to him because her mouth got in the way. That luscious mouth that thrilled him in ways he'd never even dreamed possible. They couldn't get enough of each other. Her body melted against him. Their legs entwined and they forgot everything except the joy of loving each other at last.

If it hadn't been for his phone ringing, he didn't know when they would have surfaced. He let it ring because he had to do something else first.

"Maybe you should get that. It could be important," she whispered against his jaw.

"I'm pretty sure it's Akis calling to find out if I'm all right."

A frown marred her lovely features. "He loves you so much."

"I almost lost it when I read your letter. Akis found me here two days later. Just so he won't worry and come flying over here to find out if I'm still alive, just answer me one question, then I'll listen to the message. Will you marry me, Thespinis Zachos? We've already been through the sickness and health part. Will you be my love through life? I adore you."

Her eyes glistened with tears. "You already know my answer. I have a secret. The morning I got off the plane and found you waiting to pick me up at the airport, I wanted to be your wife. I couldn't imagine anything more wonderful." She buried her face in his neck. "You just don't know how much I love you."

He gave her another fierce kiss before getting up to find his phone on the table. "It's from my brother."

"Call him so he won't worry. I'll wait right here for you."

Without listening to the message, he called him back. "Thanks for returning my call, bro."

"I'm glad you phoned. How would you like to be the best man at my wedding?"

"*What?*"

"She's back and we're getting married as soon as we can."

Akis let out a sound of pure joy then shouted the news to Raina who was in the background and gave her own happy cry. "Tell that Zoe I love her already."

Vasso stared down at her. "I will. She's easy to love."

"I only have one piece of advice. Remember what *Papa* said."

He knew. Treat Zoe like a queen. "I remember."

"Come on over for dinner so we can celebrate."

"You mean now?"

"Now! And you know why." Vasso knew exactly why. "We're expecting you." Akis clicked off.

Vasso hung up and leaned over Zoe. "We're invited for dinner."

"I don't want to move, but considering it's your brother...." She sat up and kissed him passionately. "You two have been through everything together. I get it."

He knew she did. "We'll go in the cruiser. I'll phone Kyria Panos and tell her we'll be by for your luggage later tonight."

CHAPTER TEN

October 16, Paxos Island

"IRIS!" ZOE CRIED out when she saw Akis help her old friend from New York out of the helicopter that had landed on the center's roof. She ran to her and they clung. "This is the best present I could have. You've been like a mother to me. I'm just so thankful you could come for the wedding."

"I wouldn't have missed it. Neither would Father Debakis."

Zoe's eyes lit on the priest who was getting out of the helicopter. The two of them had flown over yesterday and had stayed at the penthouse.

She left Iris long enough to run to the great man she owed her life to. "Oh, Father—I'm so glad you could come to marry us."

He hugged her hard. "It's my privilege. I had a feeling about the two of you a long time ago."

"Nothing gets past you."

Akis walked over to them. "Come on, everyone. Let's get on the elevator. Raina is waiting to help you into your wedding dress. Yiannis will drive you and Raina to the church. I'll drive everyone else in my car.

"Needless to say my older brother is climbing the walls waiting for the ceremony to begin. For his sake, I beg you to hurry, Zoe."

The best man's comment produced laughter from everyone and brought roses to Zoe's cheeks. She had to pinch herself that this was real and that she was getting married to Vasso.

When they reached the main floor, Zoe hurried along the hall to a private room where Raina was waiting.

"They've arrived!"

"Thank heaven! I've had three phone calls from Vasso. If he doesn't see you soon, he's going to have a nervous breakdown."

"Well we can't have that."

Zoe got out of her skirt and blouse and stepped into the white floor-length wedding dress. Raina had dared her to wear the latest fashion. It was strapless, something she would never have picked out on her own. But Raina insisted she was a knockout in it. This was one time she needed to render her soon-to-be husband *speechless*.

"Oh, Raina. It's so fun having you to help me. What I would have given for a sister like you."

"I feel the same way. Today I'm getting her. We're the luckiest women in the world."

"Yup. In a little while I'll be married to a god, too."

"They really are," Raina murmured. "But you've

still got your perfect figure while I'm beginning to get a bump."

"If you ever saw the way Akis looks at you when you're not aware of it, you'd know you and the baby are his whole world."

"Today the focus is on you. I have something for you, Zoe. Vasso asked me to give this to you."

With trembling hands, Zoe opened the satin-lined jewelry box. Inside lay a strand of gleaming pearls. A card sat on top. *"For my queen."*

She looked at Raina in puzzlement. "He thinks of me as his queen?"

Raina nodded. "Akis gave me the same kind of pearls with the same sentiment on his card. When I asked him about it, he told me that his father had told them the women they would choose would be their queens and they needed to treat them like one."

"What a fabulous father he was. Vasso has always treated me like that."

"So has Akis. Now hold still while I put this around your neck."

Zoe's emotions were spilling out all over to feel the pearls against her skin. She'd already done her hair and applied her makeup. She wore pearl studs in her ears.

"Now for the crowning glory." Raina walked over and put the shoulder-length lace mantilla over her head. "When you get to the church, pull it over your face. You know? I think I'd better have an ambulance standing by. After Vasso sees you, anything could happen."

"You're such a tease."

"I'm only speaking the truth." She turned and opened

a long florist's box. Inside was a sheaf of flowers. Raina laid it in the crook of Zoe's arm.

"Aren't they lovely!" Her eyes took in the all-white arrangement: white roses, cymbidium orchids, hydrangeas and stephanotises. "My mother would have planned a bouquet just like this for me. She loved white flowers."

"Don't we all." They both breathed in the heavenly scent.

Zoe eyed her dearest new friend. "You look absolutely stunning in that blue silk suit." Raina wore a gardenia in the lapel.

"Except that I had to undo the zipper to get into it. I think I can get away with it for as long as we're at the church." She smiled at Zoe. "Ready?"

"Yes," she said emotionally.

They left the room and headed for the main entrance. When they walked outside by the fountain Zoe saw Yianni. He looked splendid wearing his former naval uniform. "You're a sight for sore eyes, Zoe."

"So are you. I can see why your wife grabbed you up the second she met you."

"You look radiant today." He kissed her forehead then pulled the edge of the veil down to cover her face.

"Thank you for standing in for my father."

"It's an honor. Now let's get you in the car and be off. Your fiancé is waiting for you. I've had two phone calls from Vasso. He's going to have a coronary if we don't arrive soon."

Zoe laughed and got in the rear of the limo. Raina helped her with her dress. Yianni checked to make sure everything was secure then he drove them through the olive groves and up the steep hillside to the glistening white church at the summit. It made an imposing sight overlooking the sea.

This was the church where Raina and Akis had been married by his family priest. Their parents had been buried in the cemetery behind it. This was the place where history had been made and was still being made today by another Giannopoulos son.

Father Debakis would be doing the honors with the other priest's help. This was right out of a fairy tale.

The closer they got, she could see dozens of cars lining both sides of the road leading to the church. Akis and his best friend Theo had taken care of the invitations. Zoe feared there wouldn't be enough room in the church to accommodate everyone.

Vasso had told her not to worry. The priest would leave the front doors open and set up chairs for those people who couldn't get inside. A real Greek wedding was a high point no one wanted to miss.

When they came around the bend she could see dozens of beautifully dressed guests seated at tables outside with white ribbons on the chairs. But that wasn't all. Behind the chairs were throngs of people willing to stand.

Raina and Theo's wife Chloe had made the arrangements for the food, which would be served on the grounds after the ceremony, followed by singing and dancing. She promised they wouldn't run out of food, but when Zoe saw the amount of people congregated, it shocked her.

Yianni drove past the cars and circled around to the front steps of the church. Suddenly all Zoe could see was Vasso. He stood at the open doors waiting for her in a formal midnight-blue suit with a white rose in the lapel. She couldn't hold back her cry when she saw him. No man was ever created like him.

Once the limo came to a stop, he walked toward her with a loving look in his black eyes that lit up her whole body. Yianni came around the door to help her out. But it was Vasso who grasped her hand and squeezed it.

Raina took the flowers from her and walked behind them with Yianni while Vasso led her into the church. She'd been in here several times in the last few weeks and thought it an exquisite jewel. The smell of incense and flowers greeted them as they moved toward Father Debakis, decked out in his priestly finery. The interior was so full people who hadn't found a seat were lined up against the walls.

Both she and Vasso wanted a traditional wedding to honor their parents. Her heart pounded so hard she knew he could feel its beat through her hand. When they arrived at the altar, he leaned over and lifted the veil. The love pouring from his soul was evident in those gorgeous black eyes.

If ever there was a time to faint, it was now. But she didn't feel light-headed. She felt a spirit of joy wash over her as they grasped hands and entered into this sacred ritual that would make him her husband.

They went through the different stages of the ring

ceremony until it came to the union of the bride and groom with the crowning. This was the part she'd been looking forward to. The priest took two crowns with ribbons from the altar table, blessed them, then put the crowns on their heads.

"Oh, Lord our God, crown them with glory and honor."

The other priest exchanged their crowns over their heads to seal the union. He read from the Gospel account of the wedding in Cana. After a prayer, he passed the common cup for them to take a sip of the wine. This was the part that meant they shared equally in the process of life. Father Debakis then led them around the table three times.

This was where her heart beat wildly as the two of them stared at each other while they made circles. A hint of a smile broke the corners of Vasso's mouth. Zoe felt this part of the wedding ceremony was terribly romantic, but she'd never admit it to anyone but him. He looked so handsome with the crown on she wanted a picture of him just like that.

When they faced the priest again, he removed their crowns. His eyes rested kindly on Vasso. "Be magnified, O Bridegroom, as Abraham." Then he looked at Zoe with such tenderness she was deeply moved. "And you, O Bride, be magnified as was Sarah, and live a long, fruitful life."

He'd added those words meant just for her. Once again she was overcome with gratitude that out of the shadows, she'd emerged into a light greater than the one she could see with the naked eye.

Father Debakis placed a Bible in both their hands and said a final prayer. He smiled at them. "Congratulations, Kyrie and Kyria Giannopoulos. Just think, Vasso," he whispered. "If I hadn't called you…"

"I don't want to think about it, Father," he whispered back. He put his arm around Zoe's waist and they faced the congregation. She'd never seen so many smiling faces in her life, but one stood out above the rest.

It was Akis. He and Vasso exchanged a silent message that was so sweet and said so much Zoe could hardly breathe with the love she could see between the two of them.

Suddenly Vasso lowered his mouth to her ear. "Let the fun begin."

Raina came forward to hand her the sheaf of flowers. After she stepped away, Zoe and Vasso started walking down the aisle. Everyone was here. Olympia and Nestor had come from the center. She smiled at Kyria Lasko, Kyria Panos, Gus the bus driver, Iris, and her doctor from the center in Astoria.

With each step, people said Vasso's name; they were the managers from some of their stores, family friends, their mutual friends, two of the helicopter pilots, the woman called Elpis who'd given the boys free sweets when they were young. The list went on and on. When they reached the rear of the church and stepped outside, there was cheering and music. People rushed to congratulate them.

The paparazzi were out in full measure, but Zoe didn't care. She was too happy to be married to her heart's desire to have a care in the world. They had their own videographer there to record the proceedings of the day.

"Give us a kiss with your husband, Kyria Giannopoulos."

"Gladly!" She turned to Vasso. There was a wild look in his eye before he caught her to him and kissed the life out of her in front of everyone. They were a little drunk with happiness. The taste of his mouth was sweeter than any wine. She would never be able to get enough of it. Anyone could see that.

Part of her felt a fierce pride at the turnout. If she had a megaphone and dared, she'd love to say, "Look at these poor Giannopoulos boys now! Eat your hearts out!" But of course she couldn't say or do that.

The caterers had arrived and had set up more tables to accommodate the huge crowd. With the musicians in place, the dancing began. Yianni grabbed Zoe's other hand and several dozen people joined to form a line. They danced through the tables while everyone threw rice. The excitement had made her heady.

Every time Vasso's fiery eyes met hers, her heart palpitated right out of her chest. She knew what he was thinking. It was all she could think about. Their wedding night.

Zoe had been waiting all her life for the time when she would marry. She actually wanted to call Ms. Kallistos one day and tell her that *she* was the person responsible for the miracle that had come into Zoe's life. But on reflection it wouldn't be a good idea.

Vasso had hired Alexandra and there was no doubt in Zoe's mind the manager had been crazy about him from day one. Through Akis she'd learned that Sofia Peri had left her husband and wanted Vasso back. Zoe couldn't blame her for that. Today she could feel sorry for every woman alive who wasn't married to her Apollo.

Today she'd met so many people who thought the world of Vasso and Akis. If their father were still alive, he would be so proud of them. *And their mother...* Zoe had seen the few pictures they had of her. She'd been a beauty. That's why the two brothers were so gorgeous.

Oh, Vasso. I can't wait until we're alone. Really alone.

The party went on several hours. Toasts were made to the happy couple. As Zoe danced with Akis, Vasso danced with Raina. Then she saw the brothers signal each other. The next thing she knew Akis whirled her toward the limousine where Yianni was parked in front of the church.

Akis opened the rear door and hurried her inside. Vasso came around the other side and slid in next to her. The second his door closed, the limo started moving. Everyone saw them leave and gave out shouts. But Zoe was caught in Vasso's arms. His mouth came down on hers and the world whirled away. When he lifted his lips, she realized the car had come to a stop outside Vasso's beach house.

He opened the door and stepped out. Then he helped her. The second she was on her feet he picked her up and carried her in his arms. "Thank you, Yiannis."

The car drove off, leaving them alone. "I've been dreaming about doing this for weeks, Zoe."

"So have I, darling."

Vasso unlocked the back door with the remote and carried her over the threshold. He didn't stop until he'd gained the loft. "I've never been up here before," she said as he twirled her around.

"That was the plan. Thank heaven the long wait is finally over."

"I love you, my darling Vasso. *I love you.*"

After they'd made love throughout the night, Vasso's beautiful wife fell asleep around five o'clock, but he was still wide awake. Adrenaline rushed through his system like a never-ending fire.

Her wedding dress lay over one of the chairs, her mantilla on the dresser with her wedding flowers. Their scent filled the loft. He'd thrown his wedding suit over another chair. The white rose was still in the lapel.

She was the most unselfish lover he could ever have imagined. For the next little while he lay on his side holding her loosely in his arms so he could study her beautiful features. He still couldn't believe she was his wife, all signed, sealed and delivered to be his, now and forever.

Her mouth was like a half-opened rose, lush with a red tint, like a strawberry. He needed to taste her again and again and never stop. As soon as he started to kiss her in earnest, she made a little moan and her eyes opened.

"Vasso—I dreamed I was kissing you, but I really *am* kissing you."

He laughed deep in his throat. "I wanted to kiss you

good morning. It wasn't nice of me to wake you up, but I'm so in love with you, I don't think I'll ever be able to leave you alone."

"Please don't, or I won't be able to bear it." She rolled over and kissed him so deeply that age-old ritual started again. They didn't come up for breath for several more hours.

Vasso finally lifted his mouth from hers. "Did I tell you yet how gorgeous you looked in that wedding dress? I could hardly breathe when you got out of the limo."

"Raina said I should wear it to give you a jolt."

"You did a lot more than that. Every man at the wedding would have given anything to be in my place. She has the right instincts. Raina's so good for Akis."

"I love her already."

"So do I."

"You kind of stopped traffic yourself. Have I told you yet how good you are for me? You make me thankful to have been born a woman. Seriously, Vasso, I'm so wild about you I think maybe there's something wrong with me."

"I'll never complain." He kissed every feature. "So you don't mind that I'm invading your space?"

"I must have been crazy when I said that."

"It's because you never lived with a man and didn't know it's the only way for a man and woman to experience true joy. These last few years I knew that the most important element in my life was missing. But not anymore." He crushed her body to his, kissing her neck and throat. "Where do you want to go on our honeymoon?"

"Right here with you."

"We could go anywhere," he murmured against her lips.

"I know. What do you say we wait to take a trip after we find out we're going to have a baby."

Vasso smoothed the hair off her forehead. "You want a baby soon?"

"You know I do. I'm so envious of Raina and Akis. There's no reason to wait. You heard what Father Debakis said. Be fruitful."

He rolled her over and looked deep into her eyes. "Maybe he already knows something we don't."

"I know. Exciting, isn't it?"

"In that case we'll just stay here until we get it right."

She cupped his face and pulled him down to press a passionate kiss to his mouth. "I was hoping you'd say that. If you think I'm shameful, I don't care. I need you with every particle of my being."

His expression sobered. He kissed her hands and moved them to either side of her head. "Don't you know you've made me whole? A thrill went through me when you circled the altar with me. I felt your love binding me tighter and tighter."

"I had that same wonderful feeling," she cried softly. "Our ceremony was holy, but it was also very romantic."

He smiled. "Only you could come up with the perfect description. That's because there's only one perfect you. You're the light of my life, *agape mou*. Kiss me again, Kyria Giannopoulos."

Three hours later he heard his cell vibrate. Only one person would be texting him.

Zoe smiled. "That has to be your brother. I love how close you are. Put him out of his misery and tell him we're deliriously happy."

Vasso reached for the phone on the bedside table. "He says to turn on the news. Do you want to watch?"

"No. I don't need to see my beloved husband on TV when I've got him right here in my arms."

"That's just another one of the thousand reasons I love you more than life itself." He buried his face in her neck, crying her name over and over again.

* * * * *

* * *

HER GREEK DOCTOR'S PROPOSAL

ROBIN GIANNA

A huge thank you to my SWs, Sheri, Susan, Natalie, Margaret and Mel. You helped me through some tough times with steadfast support and love. I appreciate it, and all of you, so, so much!

CHAPTER ONE

LAUREL EVANS GASPED as the pinhead-sized gleam of gold revealed itself, winking at her through the layers of dirt she'd painstakingly removed. Even mostly still buried in this pit they'd dug on Mount Parnassus, the glow was unmistakable.

Laurel's heart danced wildly in her chest as she grabbed her pick and brush, forcing herself to go slow as she gently worked to free the treasure. It took only a moment to realize it was something small, not the item she'd hoped to find, and she shoved down her brief disappointment. Oh so carefully, she used the delicate tools until the ancient find was finally loosened completely from the earth it had been long buried in.

A ring. Likely worn and possibly loved by someone thousands of years earlier. Even the smallest pieces of pottery, tools and partial bits of art they'd unearthed, reassembled and cataloged in the past weeks stepped up her pulse, but this? Nothing beat the thrill of finding a treasure like this one.

No, scratch that. There was one thing she could think of that would be way beyond thrilling, and the weeks were ticking away on her hopes of finding it. Of getting it on the cover of archaeological magazines all over the world, along with her parents' faces, crowning the pages of her

PhD dissertation, and ensuring funding for the next project that would get her own belated career launched at last.

She closed her fingers around the ring in her palm and breathed in the dusty, sweltering air. Too soon to panic. There were still a few weeks left before the end of this dig, and she, the rest of the crew and volunteers just needed to work harder and smarter. She looked up the mountain where the ruins of Delphi lay hidden from her view. Why couldn't the oracle still be there to advise her where the heck the mythical treasure might be deeply hidden on this mountain?

Laurel wanted to show Melanie what she'd found, but as she looked around at the crew working the numerous rectangular pits dug into the mountainside she didn't see her anywhere. Where could the woman be? Usually she was up early and on the mountain to enthusiastically guide her and the volunteers. Could she have gone to the caves with Tom? Seemed unlikely she wouldn't tell Laurel she'd be working with her husband instead of leading the mountain portion of the dig. Maybe the cold she'd been fighting had gotten worse, and she'd decided to sleep in.

Laurel swiped a trickle of sweat that persisted in rolling down her temple, despite the wide-brimmed canvas hat shielding her from the insistent sun. She tucked her exciting find into a sample bag, but before she could start to label it, her palm began to bleed again from under the bandage she'd put on it.

"Damn it," she muttered, trying to reposition the pad to cover it better, then ripped off a piece of duct tape to slap over the whole thing. So annoying that she'd stupidly jabbed herself while unearthing a sharp piece of what was likely part of a cup. She was just glad she hadn't further broken the artifact in the process. She started to label the ring bag again only to stop midword as her peripheral vision caught a movement nearby.

She glanced over to see a man walking up the steep, rocky mountain path that wound between dried brown scrub scattered with tufts of thriving green plants, as steady and sure-footed as the goats that sometimes trotted by with their neck bells ringing. As he grew closer, she blinked, then stared. The brilliant sunshine gleamed on his short black hair and sent shadows and light across his chiseled cheekbones and jaw, his straight nose and sculptured lips. His face was so startlingly beautiful, so classically Greek, she thought he might be a mirage. That it was the god Apollo himself walking up Mount Parnassus to visit the temple built to honor him.

She gave her head a little shake, wondering if the blistering heat was getting to her. She narrowed her eyes against the sunlight and looked again.

Not her imagination. And not Apollo, but most definitely a real man. Greek gods didn't normally wear khaki-colored dress pants and a short-sleeved, blue, button-down shirt that was open at the collar. A shirt that emphasized the obvious fitness of his torso and the deep tan of his skin. A steel wristwatch caught and reflected the sun in little white diamonds that danced on the craggy ground with each measured step he took.

The one word that came to mind was *wowza*. Who in the world was he? And why was he wearing such a surprising choice of clothing for hiking the mountain in ninety-five degrees Fahrenheit? Must be a local businessman, or possibly a reporter come to check out the dig. Or, with his knockout looks, a movie star planning his next film. She didn't normally watch many movies, but if that was the case she'd definitely find time to fit in a viewing or ten of him on the big screen.

Laurel snapped out of her fixation on the man and finished her notation on the ring bag. She stood and quickly tucked the bag inside her canvas apron, next to her trowel.

Tom and Melanie wouldn't be happy if she yakked to a reporter or anyone else before they even knew about her find.

He stopped to speak to one of the volunteers on the dig, who pointed at Laurel. The man's gaze turned to her, and even with twenty feet between them she could see his eyes were so dark they were nearly black, with a surprising intensity that seemed to stare right into her.

He resumed his trek toward her. He wasn't a tall man—probably an inch or two shy of six feet. But the broad muscularity of his physique, which she'd noticed wasn't unusual among Greek men, made him seem larger. Or was it the sheer power of his good looks and intelligent gaze that made him seem that way?

"Are you Laurel Evans?" he asked with only a slight accent to his otherwise American-sounding words.

"Yes. Can I help you?"

"I'm Dr. Andros Drakoulias." He reached out to grasp her hand in a firm handshake. His palm felt wide and warm, slightly rough and not at all sweaty as she knew hers was. She pulled her hand loose and swiped it down the side of her shorts, hoping he hadn't noticed the sweat or that just the simple touch made her feel a little breathless. "Your colleagues, the two Drs. Wagner, asked me to let you know what was going on."

"Going on?" She realized it was a rather stupid echo of his words, but there was something about the serious expression she now saw in his eyes that sent her pulse into an alarmed acceleration. "Why? Is something wrong?"

"They came to the clinic early this morning feeling feverish and ill. I've done some tests, and both have pneumonia."

"Pneumonia?" Laurel stared at him in shock. *Pneumonia?* How was that possible? "Melanie and Tom both had colds the past couple of days, but that seemed to be all it was."

"Unfortunately not. I have them on IV fluids and antibiotics, and I plan to keep them today and overnight at the clinic to see how they do."

Did this guy really know what he was talking about? Handsome didn't necessarily translate to smart. She studied him. Maybe it was wrong of her, but she couldn't help but wonder if the local town doctor had the knowledge and equipment to properly diagnose the problem. Should she take them to the closest large town instead, to be sure? "What makes you think it's pneumonia?"

A small smile touched his beautifully shaped lips. "Hippocrates could diagnose pneumonia by listening to a patient's chest, Ms. Evans. Ancient Greeks were at the forefront of medicine, after all. But believe it or not, even in our small-town clinic we have X-ray equipment and pulse oximetry to measure a patient's oxygen saturation."

Somehow, her face flushed hotter than it already was beneath the scorching noon sun. "I'm sorry. I didn't mean to be insulting." Maybe inserting a little light humor into the awkward moment she'd created was in order. "But I must say, despite the Greeks putting the Omphalos stone at Delphi to show it was the center of the world, many believe Egyptian physicians adopted an ethical code of medical care centuries before Hippocrates."

His smile broadened; he was seemingly amused instead of offended, thank heavens. "Don't say that out loud, Ms. Evans, or you may find yourself in a no-win argument with angry locals."

"Is there any other kind of argument with Greeks?"

"Probably not." The amusement in his eyes became a dangerously appealing twinkle. "I lived in the United States for fifteen years. I know Americans think everyone outside the US and Western Europe are somewhat backward and simple. If you like, I could go up to the temple and consult Apollo. Or perhaps pray to Asclepios for guidance?"

"Not necessary. I'm sure you're very experienced, Dr. Drakoulias. I just…" Her voice trailed off, because she didn't know what else to say and had a feeling she might stick her foot in her mouth all over again. She sent him a grateful smile, hoping that would make him look past her blunder. "Thank you for walking all the way up here to let me know. Right now, I need to stay at the site to supervise since Mel's not going to be here. But I'd like to come down this evening to see them. Where's your clinic?"

"In Kastorini, which is at the base of the mountain above the gulf waters. Just follow the old bell tower to the center of town—you can't miss us."

"What's the address?"

His straight teeth showed in a smile that gleamed white against his brown skin. An unexpected dimple appeared in one cheek, which added another attractive layer to the man who sure didn't need it. "There are no addresses in Kastorini, Ms. Evans. We're small enough that everyone finds their way around without."

No addresses? How did people get their mail and things? She wasn't about to ask, though, and make even more of a fool of herself. "Well, I'm sure I can then, too. Thanks."

"I do have a question for you." All the teasing humor left his face. "Were both of the Drs. Wagner working in one spot? Somewhere they might have been exposed to a fungus of some kind?"

"Not really. Melanie is in charge of this part of the dig, and Tom leads the dig in the adjacent cave discovered a few years after the initial excavation. Why?"

"Just that it's unusual for two healthy people to come down with pneumonia at nearly the same time. Which makes looking for an external cause something we need to think about. Has Melanie been in the caves recently?"

Laurel thought hard about what they'd excavated and where they'd dug, but couldn't come up with anything that might have made them sick. "I'm almost certain she hasn't been in the caves at all. At least, not since the first days of the dig two months ago. At team meetings, Tom shares the cave dig results weekly, and Melanie shares our results. It's more efficient that way."

"All right. We'll see how they're both doing tomorrow and decide then if it makes sense to look harder for some connection." He looked around at the extensive excavation. "I wasn't living here when Peter Manago tried building a house in this spot and they found the ruins. When was that—five or six years ago?"

Had it been that long? Five years since her family's shocking loss that had turned her world upside down? A loss that seemed like yesterday, and yet, in other ways, felt like forever ago.

"I think that's about right." She swallowed hard at the intense ache that stung her throat. "Have you been up here to check it out?"

"No, but I've been wanting to. Is it filled with treasures offered to Apollo and the oracle?" His eyes crinkled at the corners. "Everyone who grew up around here used to dig giant holes—or at least giant to us—that we were sure would expose a sphinx, or the Charioteer's horses, or something else that would make us rich."

"And were you one of them?"

"Oh, yes. Born and raised in Kastorini. Many a goat has likely fallen into one of my 'digs.' But after finding only rocks and more rocks and the occasional very exciting animal bone, I decided becoming a doctor might be a better way to make money."

She had to laugh. Money was definitely not the reason anyone dug in the dirt for a living. "No doubt about that."

"You must be finding something, though, or they wouldn't have been working at it for so long. What's here?" He looked around at the carefully plotted-out sections of earth. "Tell me about these squares you have marked off."

"Much of the time when you unearth a site that's several thousand years old, it's a bit like a layer cake. The oldest part of a settlement is at the bottom, with artifacts that reflect how the people lived then. Vessels used for cooking, style of art that's found, even the way a wall might be built, all can change a lot from the bottom of the cake to the top. But this site?" She loved sharing the excitement of this place with people who were interested. "The layers aren't there. There's no cemetery. No human remains, despite the number of buildings that housed probably a hundred people at a time. Which convinces us that it was temporary housing for pilgrims visiting Delphi."

"Interesting. How long, do you think?"

He stopped scanning the site to look at her with rapt attention in his beautiful eyes, and a dazzling smile that momentarily short-circuited her brain. What had she been talking about, exactly? "How long what?"

"How many centuries did the pilgrims come to stay here?"

"Oh." The man probably thought she was dense. "About five hundred years, we think. Amazing that people came here to consult the oracle and worship Apollo all that time."

"Did the small earthquake we had a couple weeks ago damage anything?"

That earthquake had scared everyone, but especially Laurel. When the earth had rumbled around them, her heart had about stopped as the vision of how she'd been told her parents had died had surged to the forefront of her mind. The quake had lasted only a few minutes, but her insides had shaken for hours.

"Some rocks and earth loosened and fell into the pits, but it wasn't too bad, thankfully."

"That's good." He seemed to be studying her and she wondered what her expression was, quickly giving him a smile to banish whatever might be there. "Do you have any photos of the things you've found?"

"We do. A number of tools and potsherds have been reassembled and I have pictures in a binder in that box. This section here," she said, showing him a large, cordoned-off rectangle, "is where several inscribed stones were found that are similar to the ones at the Temple of Apollo." And one of those stones was etched with the cryptic words that had convinced her mom and dad they'd find the priceless artifact Laurel was still looking for. That part had to be kept secret from most people, but she could show him the rest.

She pulled the reference binder from the supply box and flipped through it to show him a few of the best photos. They stood close together, the hair on his muscular forearm tickling her skin, his thick shoulder nudging hers, his head angled close enough to nearly skim his cheek against her temple. He smelled so wonderful, like aftershave and hunky man, that she found herself breathing him in. So enjoying his interested attention, she suddenly realized she'd gone on way too long.

"Sorry." She closed the book, feeling her face flush yet again, and not just from the blasting heat on the mountain. "I get a little overexcited sometimes."

"No. I'm fascinated." There was something about his low tone and the way he was looking at her with a kind of glint in the dark depths of his eyes that had her wondering if he meant something other than the dig. That thought, along with how close he still stood to her, kicked her heart into a faster rhythm and made her short of breath, which she knew was absurd. But surely there wasn't a woman alive who wouldn't swoon at least a little over Andros Drakoulias.

"My sisters tell me that when I talk about my work, I need to remember to look for eyes glazing over when I go on and on. Sorry."

"Had you been looking, you'd have seen my eyes were most attentive. And you should never apologize for talking about something you love."

The deep rumble of his voice, the warmth in it, seemed to slip inside her, and for a long moment they just looked at one another, standing only inches apart, before Laurel managed to snap out of whatever trance he'd sent her into. She sucked in a mind-clearing breath and turned to shove the binder back into its box.

"You've hurt yourself." His strong arm came around her side, brushing against her as he reached for her hand. His head dipped close to hers again as he turned her palm upward, his fingers gently tugging loose the tape and bandage to expose the darn gash that had started bleeding again.

"It's nothing." She swiped at the trickle of blood, trying to tug her hand from his, but he held it tight. "I cut it on a potsherd. I'll bandage it up better when I'm done for the day."

"When was your last tetanus shot?"

"Just before I came here, Dr. Drakoulias. Cuts and scrapes are one of the hazards of this job."

"I know. Last summer, I had to treat one of the workers on this dig for sepsis." His gaze pinned hers, his former warmth replaced by a stern, no-nonsense look. "When you come to see the Wagners, I'll clean and bandage it for you."

She opened her mouth to assure him she could take care of it just fine, but the words died on her tongue. The wide palm that held hers was firm yet gentle, and something about his authoritative expression told her any protest would fall on deaf ears. Part of her didn't want to protest, anyway. She realized, ridiculously, that it felt... nice to have someone want to take care of it for her. Probably because, for a long time, she'd been the nurse, cook, decision maker and overall helper for her sisters, without a soul to assist with all their challenges. Or, except for Tom and Mel, her own.

She reminded herself it wasn't as if there were anything personal about it, the man was just doing his job. "Not necessary. I have everything I need to clean and bandage it at my hotel."

"Necessary." His eyes still on hers, he slowly released her hand. "I'll see you at the clinic at, say, six o'clock?"

It was loud and clear she'd be in for an argument if she refused, and what sane woman would anyway? "Thank you. I'll be there."

The warmth of his palm lingered along with a little flutter of her heart as she watched him steadily stride back down the path, and she shook her head at herself. Mooning after the man was ridiculous, supersexy or not, since the dig was over in a matter of weeks and every second of her focus had to be on what she'd come here to accomplish.

She was already so late getting her career started. By the time her parents were her age, their accomplishments had been featured in numerous archaeological magazines. She could still hear them pointing out how they'd finished their PhDs in just four years, chiding their oldest about her schoolwork and GPA, about how important it was to be a role model to her sisters. Doubtless they would be disappointed in her if they were still alive. She dropped to her knees to get digging again.

The best way, the only way, she could begin to catch up, keep their memory alive, and make them proud, was by doing whatever she could to finish their work then finally get going on her own.

CHAPTER TWO

HOURS LATER LAUREL was finally able to shower off the film of dirt that clung to every bit of exposed skin, before studying the cut on her hand. It was less than an inch long, but deeper than she'd realized, which was probably why it kept opening up and bleeding. She washed it out with peroxide and knew that it wouldn't be a bad idea to have Andros Drakoulias make sure it was clean. Which of course had nothing to do with liking the feel of her hand in his.

The feeble hair dryer in the old, rambling Delphi hotel that the excavation team had rented rooms in for the summer blew about as much air as she would trying to cool a bowl of soup. The impact on the dampness of her long blond hair was practically nil, and she had to wonder why she'd decided to dry it anyway, when she usually just pulled it back.

She shook her head as she wrapped an elastic around her ponytail. Who was she kidding? She knew the reason, which was a certain megahunky Greek doctor her vain side wanted to look good for.

She threw on a sundress, swiped on a gloss of lipstick, and headed out of the door. Already perspiring again from the shimmering heat, she slipped inside the group's equally hot rented sedan. She nosed the car down the winding road out of Delphi, and, before she turned onto the highway, paused for a moment to take in the incredible view.

On every horizon, partly sheer cliffs scattered with pines met tumbles of boulders that looked as though they'd been broken apart then glued back together by some giant hand, or perhaps the gods and goddesses of Greek lore. The mountains cradled the valley below, filled with the distinctive silvery-gray leaves of an endless, undulating sea of olive trees that went on as far as she could see. Where the valley ended, the trees seemed to flow right into the Gulf of Corinth, the water such an incredible azure blue that, every time she saw it, she felt amazed all over again. And beyond that azure sea, another range of mountains met the sky that today was equally blue, but at times reflected an ethereal beauty when mistiness embraced the entire scene.

Just looking at it filled her with a reassuring sense of tranquility, the same way walking the ancient Delphi ruins did, hearing the voices of the past. Before she left, she'd take her camera on one last hike of this historic place that still felt so untamed. To remember it by.

With a last, lingering look, she turned onto the highway, her thoughts turning to Tom and Melanie. A bead of sweat slid down her spine as she wondered how they would be feeling when she saw them. Surely they'd have improved by now, since they'd been on antibiotics for hours.

For the first time all day, she let the niggle of worry she'd pushed aside grab hold and squeeze. After her parents had died, Mel and Tom had wrapped their arms around her as if she'd become their surrogate daughter. Advised her on grad school and now her PhD program. Helped set her up at digs close to home so she could still care for her sisters. Got her here as a paid assistant to work on her parents' project and her dissertation.

They were such special people. What if they were seriously ill?

No. Borrowing trouble was a sure way to have trouble take over, as her dad used to say. She'd had to be in charge at home whenever her parents were gone on digs, and full-time after they died. That had taught her a lot about leadership, and it was time to lead, not fret.

She had to get up to speed on what Tom's crew was supposed to be doing in the caves to make sure it happened. With so little time left on the dig schedule, not a single hour could be wasted by worrying. She knew Tom and Mel would agree, and that her parents would have too.

The sign for Kastorini was in both Greek and English, thank goodness. Laurel turned off the highway, concentrating on driving the steeply curving road that sported the occasional rock that had rolled down from the mountainside. And the term "hairpin curve"? Now she knew exactly what that meant.

If she hadn't already been sweating from the heat, this crazy trek would have done it. The road finally flattened and swooped toward a thick stone archway flanked by high, obviously ancient walls, and passing through it was like entering a different world. One minute she was driving with the mountain soaring on one side and dropping off on the other, the next she was surrounded by stone and stucco buildings sporting terracotta rooftops and draped with vines and magenta bougainvillea. Cheerful pots of flowers lined balconies and sat by inviting front doors. Farther down the narrow, cobbled street, men with small cups of coffee relaxed on patios in front of several tavernas, engaged in lively conversation as they watched her drive by.

The utter charm of the place made Laurel smile. And as Andros had promised, she easily spotted the ancient-looking clock tower and found the medical clinic with a few bona fide parking spaces right in front of it.

The building looked as old as the rest of Kastorini, and she wasn't sure what to expect when she went inside. A small, fairly modern-looking waiting room was currently empty, but within moments a young woman appeared.

"May I help you?" she asked.

The fact that, right away, the woman spoke English instead of Greek, proved Laurel's foreignness was more than obvious, though she'd accepted months ago that she didn't exactly blend in as a local.

"Hello. I'm Laurel Evans, working with the Wagners. I believe they're patients here? Dr. Drakoulias told me I could come see them."

"Ah, yes." Her pleasant smile faded to seriousness. "He is with a patient right now and wanted to talk to you before you see them. I am Christina, one of the nurses here. I will take you to Dr. Drakoulias's office."

Laurel followed the woman down the hallway. A side door opened, and she immediately recognized the deep rumble of Dr. Drakoulias's voice.

She couldn't follow many of his quickly spoken Greek words, but saw his hand was cupped beneath the elbow of a stooped-over elderly woman as they stepped from what looked like an examination room, obviously helping her stay steady as she walked. A small frown creased his brow just as it had when he'd been looking at Laurel's gash.

Whatever the woman said in return made him laugh, banishing the frown and making him look younger. His eyes twinkled as he shook his head, saying something else in a teasing tone, making her laugh in return. She lifted a gnarled hand to his cheek and gave it a pat, then a pinch that looked as if it had to hurt, but he didn't seem fazed.

Christina was chuckling too, as she took hold of the woman's other arm to walk with her back down the hall.

Laurel wanted to ask what the woman had said that was so amusing, and if she always pinched people like that, but didn't want to sound nosy. Dr. Drakoulias turned his attention to Laurel, and she felt the power of those eyes and that magnetic smile clear down to her toes. "Very punctual, I see. In my experience, the workers on the dig usually show up late. Or not at all."

"I admit it's easy to get distracted up there. But I had to learn fast how to keep track of time." Her own and everyone else's.

"So apparently you didn't find a gold statue today."

Her heart lurched hard in her chest and she stared at him, relaxing when she realized he was just kidding. "Not today, I'm afraid."

"Just so you know, I'd consider that a good reason to miss an appointment." He gave her a teasing smile that sent her attention to his beautiful mouth, which was not a good place for it to be. Thankfully, he reached for her hand and she followed his gaze to the new bandage. "Let's get this cleaned up."

"It's all right, really. I put peroxide on it and a clean bandage."

He grasped her elbow and walked to the sink, her injured hand still in his. "That's good, but I'd like to clean it again, nonetheless. Better to prevent an infection than have to treat one."

She couldn't argue with that, and again watched his fingers gently and carefully remove the bandage. He looked closely at her palm for a long moment before he spoke. "It's going to hurt a little, I'm sorry to say, but thoroughly washing this out is important. Are you ready?"

She nodded and braced herself as he turned on the faucet, holding the open cut directly underneath the cool stream. He was right, it definitely hurt, but no way was she going to be a baby about it. Biting her lip, she'd have sworn he about drained the town's entire water supply and was just about to yell, *Enough already!* when he finally turned it off.

He wrapped her hand with a towel and gently dried it. "You were very brave. I appreciate that you didn't scream in my ear like the last patient I did that to."

The eyes that met hers held a pleasing mix of humor, warmth and admiration in their dark depths. "I reserve screaming for activities that truly warrant it," she said. Then wanted to sink into the floor when his eyebrows lifted and something else mingled with the humor in his eyes. "Things like bungee-jumping, for example," she added hastily.

"I see. So you're a daredevil."

"Um, not really." Not about to admit she wouldn't bungee-jump unless her life depended on it, and definitely wouldn't admit the direction her thoughts had suddenly gone, she quickly changed the subject. "What is that stuff you're putting on there?"

"Just a topical antibiotic." With nowhere else to look, her gaze again got stuck on his face instead of his work on her hand. On his dark lashes, lowered over his eyes; his ridiculously sculpted cheekbones; his lips twisting a little as he wrapped white gauze over the cut. "This gauze bandage will keep it clean and dry, but I'd like to check it in a couple days."

"It'll be fine. Thank you." It suddenly struck her that she probably needed to pay him. "What do I owe you, Dr. Drakoulias?"

"First, I'd like you to call me Andros, since Dr. Drakoulias reminds me of my father and I don't want to feel old around a beautiful woman. Second, I'm the one who insisted on treating you, so it's on the house. I might get a bad reputation if I chase ambulances, then hand unsuspecting patients a bill."

She had to grin at the picture that conjured, and the smile in his eyes and on his lips grew in response. "So if anybody on the dig team gets hurt, I need to find a way to lure you to the site, then when your Hippocratic Oath kicks in, we'll get free medical care? Good to know."

"I'm pretty sure you'd have no trouble at all luring me there."

Did he mean, because he was interested in archaeology? Or something else altogether? After all, he'd called her "beautiful." She shoved aside the intriguing question, reminding herself she had work to focus on, and luring dreamy Dr. Drakoulias couldn't be on the agenda, even if he was willing to be lured.

Though the thought alone put a hitch in her breath and sent a little electric zing from the top of her head to her toes.

"Are we going to see Mel and Tom now? Where are they?"

His expression instantly became neutral and professional. "They're in the clinic hospital, which is attached to this building. But before you see them, I'd like to talk to you in my office."

"Why?"

"Because," he said, his lips tightening into a grim line, "they are both seriously ill."

CHAPTER THREE

ANDROS WAS ALL too aware of the woman following close behind him down the clinic corridor. She smelled good. Like sweet lemons or grapefruit strewn with flowers, and he had an urge to bury his nose in the softness of her neck and breathe her in.

Something about her had stopped him in his tracks the first second he'd seen her on the mountain. Her blonde hair was the color of sunshine, pulled back into a thick, untidy ponytail that had flowed from beneath a creased canvas hat that was definitely for function, not style. The blue eyes that had met his were sharp and intelligent, and there was an exotic look to her features that made him want to keep looking. Maybe not a classic kind of beauty, but there was something intangible and appealing about her. Her skin was practically luminous without any makeup at all. He hadn't thought much about it until this moment, but, compared to the carefully put-together women he used to date, he liked her natural look a lot.

Down, boy, he reminded himself. Now wasn't the time to forget he was trying to reform the man who'd liked women far too much in the past, made-up, natural or anywhere in between.

Andros opened the door to his office and gestured for Laurel to go inside, wishing there were a little more room to move around. Usually he didn't notice how his father's old wooden desk that Christina joked was the size of an aircraft carrier practically filled the small space. At that moment, however, he was intensely aware of the close quarters.

Standing or sitting within inches of Laurel wasn't the best idea, since he kept finding himself distracted by her scent and her smooth skin and soft-looking hair. There wasn't much he could do about any of those problems, though, and he wanted privacy for this conversation. The last thing he needed was for a local to come into the clinic and overhear that there might be a contagion nearby.

"Have a seat."

She sat and turned to him as he lowered himself into the chair next to her, trying not to bump his knees into hers. He pondered for a moment, wondering how much detail he should give her about the Wagners' condition. She had to be worried, but instead of bombarding him with questions like a lot of people would, she waited patiently. He looked into her serious blue eyes and decided she could handle the truth, and deserved to know.

"Unfortunately, the Wagners are no better. I'm frankly surprised and concerned about that, after having them on IV fluids and antibiotics all day. As I mentioned before, I'm keeping them here overnight for observation. With any luck, they'll improve, but we should have seen some improvement already."

"Doesn't pneumonia usually respond to antibiotics pretty fast?"

"Often, yes, especially in younger people and those with no underlying physical problems, like the Wagners. That's the good news. But sometimes it doesn't. The truth about this situation, though? The presentation of their pneumonia is unusual."

"How so?"

"According to what they told me, Tom got what he thought was a cold a couple days before Melanie did. This morning Tom's respiratory rate was about thirty breaths per minute, Mel's twenty. Which indicates to me that she may have gotten it from him, which generally doesn't happen with pneumonia. Both are showing symptoms of the pneumonia worsening." He paused, hoping she wouldn't get upset at what he had to warn her about next. "If that continues into the morning, I will recommend they be transported to a fully equipped hospital in a bigger city about an hour away. It has twenty-four-hour skilled care and equipment we don't have."

Her lush lips parted in surprise. "You really think that might be necessary? Can't you just give them a different kind of antibiotic or something?"

"It's not that simple. I'm hopeful they'll improve and we can manage it here. I'm just making you aware that's a possibility. I'd prefer you didn't mention it to them, though. No need to worry them unnecessarily."

"All right." She nodded. "Are they...are they well enough for me to talk to them? If I have to take over leadership of the dig, I need to ask some questions. Find out more about the cave dig, since we were supposed to have our team meeting for the week tomorrow."

The eyes that met his were full of worry and alarm, and he wanted to reassure her but couldn't. He hadn't seen pneumonia with quite this presentation before and figured she might as well talk to the Wagners now in case the situation slid south—which he feared very well might happen.

He stood, and she did too, biting her full lower lip as she looked up at him. Standing so close he could have tipped his head down to kiss her. The instant that thought came to mind, he looked into her eyes, the idea now so appealing, so damned near irresistible, he had to inhale a deep breath and quickly step back. "I'll take you to see them now. They're on oxygen but will be able to talk to you. I want you to wear a surgical mask."

"You think I could make them sicker?"

"No. I think they might make you sick."

"Make *me* sick?"

Her eyes widened, and he wanted to make sure she understood the possible risk, because he damned well didn't want her to end up in the hospital too. "I told you before that it's unusual they've both developed this. We just can't know if it's possibly contagious or not."

He turned and led the way down the hall, again very aware of her walking closely behind as her sweet, citrusy scent wafted around him. He grabbed surgical masks from the supply cupboard outside the hospital wing and handed her one before putting on his own.

The Wagners were the only patients in the six-bed wing, and he was thankful for that. Tom Wagner lay motionless, his eyes still closed as they came to stand between the two beds, but Melanie Wagner opened her eyes and reached out to Laurel. She held Melanie's hand between both of hers, and Andros realized too late he should have had her put gloves on. Or at least one on her good hand, and warned her not to touch the Wagners otherwise.

He mentally thrashed himself. Until they knew what they were dealing with here, every precaution had to be taken anytime someone came in contact with them.

"I'm so sorry to have to dump all the work on you, Laurel," Melanie said in a whisper. "Isn't this crazy?"

"Don't worry about a thing, Mel," Laurel said, her voice slightly muffled through the mask. "I'll handle everything until you're feeling better. Dr. Drakoulias says he hopes the antibiotics will kick in soon."

"You won't have any problems leading the team until we're better. You've impressed me since day one on this dig." Melanie gave Laurel a glimmer of a smile. "Find anything good today?"

"Mostly more potsherds. But the most exciting thing was a gold ring. I'm pretty sure it's seventh century BC, but you'll know that better than I. Can't wait for you to look at it."

"Me either. I—"

A coughing fit interrupted her speech, and when she finally stopped, her breathing was obviously more labored. Laurel turned to Andros, her eyes wide.

He glanced at the quietly beeping screen next to the bed and saw that Melanie's respiratory rate had increased a little more from the last time he'd checked, which was not a good sign.

"Let's keep this visit brief, Laurel," he said, leaning close to speak in her ear. "The more they talk, the harder they have to breathe. Did you say you need to speak to Tom? I'll wake him and you can ask him a couple quick questions before you go."

He didn't want her to feel as if he was rushing her out, but didn't like the look of either of his patients. He adjusted the oxygen flow to both of them before rousing Tom with enough difficulty that it added another layer of worry.

"How are you feeling, Tom?"

The man opened his eyes and stared up at him, his mouth open, obviously having trouble breathing. "Hard to get air."

"I know. I just gave you a little more oxygen, which will help." Damn. Might not be waiting until tomorrow to send them to the Elias Sophia hospital, if they both continued to struggle like this. Andros turned to Laurel, but, before he had to say another word, she obviously got his unspoken message, since she quickly turned to Tom.

"I'm going now, so you two can rest and get better. Real

quick, though, is there anything important I need to know about the cave dig that the volunteer crew can't tell me?"

"Just that we found some human bones. Exciting. Planned…" His chest heaved a few times before he continued. "Planned to share at the next meeting. I think they're older than the artifacts at the mountain site. Probably…Minoan, but…don't know…for sure yet."

"Okay. I'll talk to the crew and have them bring me up to speed. Don't worry about a thing." She patted his shoulder, and Andros stepped behind her to wrap his hands around her lower arms. She looked over her shoulder in surprise, but he couldn't risk her touching her eyes or pulling down her mask before she'd thoroughly washed her hands.

Her soft hair and enticing scent tickled his nose as he leaned forward to whisper in her ear. "I want you to wash your hands before you touch anything, especially any part of your body. Okay?"

She stared at him, then nodded slowly, saying a quick goodbye to both patients. Still holding on to the delicate wrist of her unbandaged hand, he led her across the room to the sink, squirted soap and stuck her hand under the faucet to wash it.

"I know how to wash my hands, you know."

"Except you're a bit handicapped right now. Can't wash the way you normally would, with one hand bandaged." As his fingers moved around and between hers, it struck him what an interesting contrast her hand was, like the woman herself. Slender, delicate, feminine fingers that were also hardworking and strong. "I want to make sure it's clean. The skin exposed on your other hand too, before I change the bandage."

"Change it? You just put it on."

"'Know Thyself' is one of the famous inscriptions at the temple." He kept washing, slowly now, enjoying too much the sensual feel of their hands soapily sliding together as he looked up at her, noticing the interesting flecks of green and gold in her questioning blue eyes. "My *yiayia* used to call me Kyrie Prosektikos, which means Mr. Careful. I believe in thinking things through and being appropriately cautious." Which had been true except for one notable aspect of his life he was determined to change. "So, yeah, I'm going to put on a new bandage."

"I'd say three bandages in an hour is careful, all right. If that doesn't sterilize it, nothing will."

He liked her smile. That she didn't roll her eyes or argue with him told him she trusted him, at least a little, to know what he was doing. "Glad to see you aren't doubting my doctoring skills anymore. Some of the tourists who come to this clinic never are convinced I know what I'm doing."

"What makes you think I'm convinced? Maybe I can just see you're hard-headed and bossy, and I don't have time to argue with you."

"Smart woman. You're right that I'd damned well get tough with you if I had to."

"Just remember I can get tough too. If I have to."

"Somehow, I don't doubt that for a second."

They stood there looking at one another, small smiles on their faces, before Andros realized he was just holding her hand in his, now, fingers entwined. He managed to refocus his attention on the job at hand instead of her captivating face and eyes, and very kissable lips.

Dried off and newly bandaged, Laurel paused as she was about to head out of the clinic door. "I'm worried, Andros."

He realized he liked the sound of his name on her tongue a lot better than the formal Dr. Drakoulias. When she looked up at him, her face filled with concern, he wished he could tell her she didn't need to be. But he was worried as well. "I know. I'm doing everything I can and will let you know how they are tomorrow. I'm planning to spend the night here to keep an eye on them. You have a cell-phone number I can call?"

"Reception is sketchy at the dig, but if you leave a message, I'll be able to get it when I'm back at the hotel." She scribbled her number on a piece of paper and pressed it into his palm, lingering there. "Promise to call me?"

"I promise." He folded his fingers over hers, squeezing gently to reassure her. It took effort to release her soft hand, to let her go. He stood there, motionless, to watch her walk to her car. Watch the gentle sway of her hips, the way her dress swung sensuously with each step of her drop-dead gorgeous legs. Watch the way her long silky ponytail caressed her back, until she'd gotten in her car and driven away.

He tucked the paper into his pocket and had a feeling he'd be tempted to call just to talk to her more about the dig. Just to hear her voice.

Which was foolish. The Wagners had told him the dig would be permanently over in just a few weeks and they'd be gone. She'd be gone.

Why did it have to be Laurel who was the first woman he'd felt this kind of interest in since he'd come home? The kind of interest that had his mind and body all stirred up. The kind of interest that made him want to take her to dinner, to wrap his arms around her, to touch her and kiss her and see where it led.

He squeezed the back of his suddenly tight neck and sighed. He had every intention of living the life of a model citizen—and a good father—putting behind him the wild reputation of his youth. Last thing he needed was attraction to a woman who would be leaving soon, tempting him to enjoy a quickie affair that would grease the town gossip machine all over again. Gossip he didn't want his daughter to have to hear about her dad.

He'd keep his distance. But he couldn't deny that the thought of spending even a short time with interesting and beautiful Laurel Evans sounded pretty irresistible.

"I know it's early, Dimitri." Andros paced up and down the hall of the clinic as he spoke to the infection specialist, barely noticing the dawn that rose over the mountain, filling the sky with pink and gold. "I wish I'd sent them last night. I wanted to give them time to possibly stabilize, but their respiratory rate's gone to thirty and forty breaths per minute. New chest films show dramatic worsening to progressive multilobar pneumonia."

"What's their oxygen saturation?" Dimitri asked.

"Both were hypoxic when they arrived. Now pulse ox says their sats have gone from ninety to eighty, even after giving them four liters of oxygen. This is acute respiratory failure, Di, and they may need intubation."

"Nikolaos will be here in an hour, and I'll send him right out."

Andros nearly slammed his hand to the wall. "We can't wait until the hospital's driver feels like rolling out of bed. Get him out here with portable oxygen now, or I'll bring them there. If they code on me, it'll be on your shoulders, since I don't have damned IV hookups in my car."

"All right, all right. He'll gripe like hell, but I'll have him there in an hour and fifteen."

"Good." He stopped his pacing to stare out of the window. "Get a blood test for fungal infection when they get there. I'm going to talk to the hotel management, and the archaeological crew they've worked with. See if I can figure out if there's some environmental cause."

"You think there might be?"

"Maybe. It's strange that they both fell ill days apart

with the same symptoms. So make sure Nikolaos and the EMTs use infection control precautions, just in case."

"Will do. Talk to you after they get here."

Andros shoved his phone into his pocket, called Christina to come in early and keep a close eye on the Wagners, then caught up on paperwork in his office. He tried not to constantly check his watch. After forty-five minutes that felt like hours, he decided to make sure the Wagners were ready to go the second Nikolaos got there. He took a quick right out of his office, practically knocking down Laurel Evans, who was standing just outside his door. How had he missed her presence, when he'd been so acutely aware of it yesterday?

"Whoa, sorry!" he said, grabbing her arms to steady her. "Didn't see you there. Hope I didn't bruise you."

"No bruises. Though I did wonder for a second if I was on a football field instead of in a medical clinic." Her hands rested on his biceps as though they belonged there, and he had to stop himself from tugging her closer. "Now I see your real MO. Forget chasing ambulances. You injure people, fix them up, then bill them."

He smiled. "Not my MO. But I did play football in college in the US. Glad to know I still have the moves." Though knocking her down wasn't the move he'd like to make on her. "What are you doing here?"

"I couldn't sleep. So I came to see how they're doing."

The pale smudges beneath her eyes didn't detract one bit from her pretty face, and he again nearly pulled her against him instead of letting her go. To comfort and reassure her, of course.

"Not good." He gave her arms a gentle, bolstering squeeze before dropping his hands. "I've called the Elias Sophia hospital, which is about an hour away. The ambulance is coming to get them now."

"Oh, no!" Her hands flew to cover her heart. "They're worse?"

"I'm afraid so." He didn't feel it was necessary to tell her exactly how much worse they were. With any luck, they'd soon be fine and she'd never have to know the seriousness of the situation. "Sometime today, I'd like to talk to some of your people who've worked in the caves."

"To see if there's something there that made them sick." It was a statement, not a question.

"Yes."

"I'll be heading up when I leave here. The crew should be there soon, and I need to talk to them anyway. If you have time, you can come with me."

"Once the Wagners leave for the hospital, I can go. Even though Melanie hasn't been up there recently, it's worth asking a few questions."

"If it's contagious, just being in the same hotel room might have exposed her to it, right?"

"Right." He'd considered the same thing. The woman was smart, no doubt about that. "I'm also going to check with the hotel management, see if any tourists were ill, or if any staff that live elsewhere have been out sick."

"Can I see Mel and Tom now?"

"I'd prefer you didn't." Andros managed to temper the vehement *hell, no* he'd nearly responded with. But her being exposed to them again wouldn't accomplish anything. "Talking is difficult for them right now. After they're settled in at the hospital, we can go see them there together."

She tipped her head sideways and seemed to study him. Was she wondering if he had some ulterior motive in wanting them to go together? Again, smart woman. He hadn't said it for that reason, but as soon as the words were out of his mouth, the small rush of anticipation he felt spelled out loud and clear that, even if they were just driving to see his patients, and despite his concern for them, he'd more than enjoy the time with her.

"All right. But—"

"Dr. Drakoulias!" Christina came hurrying out of the doors of the hospital wing. "The hospital transport is here."

"Finally." He turned to Laurel. "Stay here. I'll be back shortly."

With Christina's help, he, the EMT and Nikolaos got both patients loaded in a matter of minutes. About to shut the ambulance doors, the scent of sweet citrus reached his nose. He looked over his shoulder, and saw Laurel standing right behind him, waving to the Wagners as they lay inside on their gurneys.

"Don't worry about a thing," she said, the smile on her face obviously strained. "I'll come see you with updates."

He shut the ambulance doors, yanked down his mask, and barely stopped himself from raising his voice at the woman next to him. "What part of 'stay here' and 'possibly contagious' are you not understanding?"

"I was a good six feet from them. It seems to me you're overreacting a little, since you don't know if they're contagious or not."

"There's a difference between overreaction and caution."

"Maybe that's just something you tell yourself." She folded her arms and stared him down. "Are you going to be bossy like this when we go up to the caves?"

"I'm only bossy when I have good reason to be." In spite of his frustration with her, he nearly smiled at the mulish expression on her face. She was toughness all wrapped up in softness. "So the answer is yes. I'm staying outside the caves and you are too."

"I'm an archaeologist, Dr. Drakoulias. Detective work is part of what we do. The Wagners are my bosses and my friends, and I'm going to do whatever I can to help. The caves are part of the excavation I'm doing my dissertation on, and, with Mel and Tom sick, I'm in charge now. I have to learn exactly what they're doing there and maybe in the process spot something that could have made them ill. Since I'm pretty sure you don't own Mount Parnassus, I'm going into the caves."

"You say I'm bossy? How about I say you're stubborn?" He let out an exasperated breath. "If there's a fungal contagion, possibly connected to the caves, no one should go in who hasn't been there already. Hell, no one should go in there, period, until we have some answers. But if they have to, they need to wear masks. Which I'll provide. You, though, have to stay out for now."

"Are you afraid Apollo's python may be lurking in there too, ready to strangle me?" Her voice was silky sweet, at odds with the sparking blue flash in her eyes. "Don't worry, I'll bring my bow and arrows just in case."

Clearly, the woman had serious issues with being told what to do. "Listen, Laurel, you—"

"Daddy!"

He swung around in horror when he heard his daughter's little voice, and the sight of her standing just inside the door of the hospital wing with his sister and nephew, smiling her big bright smile, sent his heart pounding and adrenaline surging. His baby could not be in there when God knew what contagion might be in the very air. "Cassie. You can't be here right now."

"Why, Daddy?" Her eyes shone with excitement. "Is there really a python? I want to see!"

CHAPTER FOUR

LAUREL HAD BARELY blinked in shock at the little girl calling Andros "Daddy" when he'd strode to the child, snatched her up in his arms, hustled out the woman and little boy, too, and shoved the hospital doors closed behind them.

Heat surged into Laurel's face when she realized the man she'd been thinking of as dreamy Dr. Drakoulias, the man she'd been having some pretty exciting fantasies about all last night when she couldn't sleep, was apparently a married family man.

Why in the world had she just assumed he was single? Clearly, her instant attraction to him, along with wishful thinking, had blotted any other possibility from her mind.

Disgusted with herself, and, okay, disappointed too, she watched Andros crouch down next to the little girl. Surprisingly, he spoke to her in English. Why wouldn't the child speak Greek, instead?

"Cassie. There's no python. The pretty lady was just talking about the old story of god Apollo slaying the python dragon with arrows. Remember it?" The little girl nodded and Andros flicked her nose. "Know what, though? Remember when you didn't feel good with your tummy bug? There might be some germs in the clinic I don't want you to be around. I want you to go back with Petros and Thea Taryn, and I'll be home later."

Thea Taryn? Laurel didn't know a lot of Greek words, but she did know *thea* meant *aunt*. Which presumably meant the attractive, dark-haired woman was either Andros's sister or sister-in-law. Not that Laurel cared one way or the other, she thought with a twist of her lips. Married was married, and the thought of tromping over Mount Parnassus with him to talk to the crew together didn't seem nearly as appealing now.

Despite what she'd boldly stated, the truth was she didn't have a clue how to look for a fungus or whatever else could cause the kind of illness Mel and Tom had. She hadn't been in a lot of caves, but weren't most filled with all kinds of biological life she didn't know much about? Probably, she should simply focus on getting the excavation finished and hope no one else got sick. Getting it done was critical for a number of reasons, and Mel and Tom would doubtless want her to concentrate on that as well.

The cute little girl wrapped her arms around Andros's neck as he folded her close. Laurel's throat tightened as she watched the sweet moment, thinking of her own dad and all the times he'd held her exactly the same way. Thinking of how much he'd loved his four daughters, and how much they'd loved and admired him. Thinking how lucky the child was that Andros seemed to be a supportive and involved dad. One whose work enabled him to be with her all the time, and not away for months as her own parents had been.

She began to turn away at the same time Andros's head came up, and his eyes—dark and alive—met hers. He gestured to her to come over. She hesitated, then realized it was silly to feel embarrassed at her former hot fantasies. After all, he didn't know about them, thank heavens, and she was already over it. It wasn't as if she had time for any kind of relationship anyway, hot doc or not.

He stood. "Laurel Evans, this is my sister, Taryn Drakoulias, and her son, Petros."

That answered that question, she thought as they shook hands, though she should have seen the resemblance. Same dark hair, nearly black eyes and a slightly amused smile that implied maybe they both were privy to secrets no one else was privy to. His daughter had the same dark eyes, but her hair was a much lighter brown.

Laurel wondered if Taryn was divorced or had been a single mom, since she still used her maiden name. Or if she'd simply kept her name, but that seemed less likely, since Greece was still a very traditional country.

"This is my daughter, Cassandra." Andros smiled down at the girl, his eyes and face softened from the intense concern that had been on it just a moment ago. "Cassie, I'd like you to meet Laurel. She's an archaeologist, working on the dig up the mountain. You've learned a little about that, haven't you?"

"Yes! I have!" The child's eyes, so like her dad's, stared up at her. "Have you found lots of statues and gold treasures?"

If only. "Many things that are treasures to archaeologists, but not much gold, I'm afraid. Like father, like daughter, I see." Laurel smiled up at Andros then turned back to Cassie. "Do you dig holes trying to find ancient treasure, Cassie, like your dad said he used to do?"

"Oh, no." She shook her head, her chin-length hair sliding across her cheeks as she did. "Fairies are scared of big holes. I don't want to scare them. I want them to sleep under our plants so they're in the shade and live in the little houses they build in the ground under special rocks. They stay cool that way."

"I see." Laurel's smile grew, remembering how much

she'd loved pretend things as a little girl. Probably part of the reason she still loved classical myths today. "Have you seen the fairies?"

"Oh, yes." She nodded, very serious. "Sometimes they dance at night when there's a moon, and you can see them better. Sometimes they dance on my bed too, when they think I'm asleep."

Laurel looked at Andros again to see what he thought of his daughter's imagination. The lips she'd fantasized about were curved, and his eyes had attractively crinkled at the corners again.

No. Not attractively. Married, remember? Then again, he wasn't wearing a ring, so maybe he wasn't. That thought perked her up so much she nearly chuckled at how ridiculous she was being.

"We've made a fairy house out of stones, haven't we, Cassie? Have you seen any go in yet?" Taryn asked.

"No." Her little voice was filled with regret. "I think maybe I need to move the furniture around. Or put in something else. I don't think they like it the way it is."

Petros, who looked to be about five, chimed in, speaking Greek, but his mother stopped him with a hand on his shoulder. "English, please. It's good practice for you, and I don't think Ms. Evans speaks Greek." She turned to Laurel. "Do you?"

"Not much, I'm afraid. Trying, since I expect to spend a lot of time in various parts of the country on future digs, but it's not as easy as I'd hoped. I plan to study it more when the dig is over and I'm back at the university."

"Your work must be very interesting."

"It is. It also can be hot and dirty and takes a lot of patience, but the reward is worth it."

"Hot and dirty sounds like fun!" Petros exclaimed.

The adults' eyes all met, with Taryn looking slightly embarrassed and Andros quite amused at the sexual connotation of what were, really, innocent words. Laurel should have felt a little embarrassed too, since she was the first to use the unfortunate phrase, but instead found the fantasies she'd enjoyed last night popped front and center into her mind. *Dang it.*

"What were you going to say about the fairy house?" Taryn hastily asked her son.

"I told Cassie we should make toad or snake houses instead. There's no fairies around here."

"Oh, there definitely are, Petros," Laurel said. "I'm sure there are plenty nearby." As soon as the words were out of her mouth, she regretted them. How ridiculous to defend Cassie's belief in fairies, when the child had her aunt and parents to pretend with her, and it was just cousin dynamics anyway, which made it none of her business. Must be habit from the fun she'd had making up stories for her little sisters. From defending them, too, she supposed.

"You know about fairies?" Cassie stared at her, wide-eyed.

"Ancient stories of fairies and nymphs and all kinds of things are part of what I do." The child was adorable, and she found herself wishing she could play fairies with her right then. But it was high time to change the subject and get back to work. "Speaking of which, I've got to get going. The students and volunteers are probably already at the sites by now."

"I'll go with you." Andros turned to his sister and spoke in a low tone. "The dig leaders are pretty sick, and I'm going to ask the workers some questions about where they've all been. For now, don't go into the hospital wing until it's been sterilized. I'll let you know when I'm done seeing patients this afternoon. I'll pick Cassie up then."

Taryn looked surprised, but nodded without comment before turning to Laurel. "Nice to meet you. Perhaps before the dig is over, you can come for dinner and tell us about all you've found in our backyard."

"Thank you, I appreciate the invitation." Having dinner with the happy Drakoulias family would be interesting, and she had to admit she was curious to meet Andros's wife. If he had one. So long as she could keep from drooling when she stared at the man the lucky woman was married to. "Nice for you to have all of Mount Parnassus as your backyard."

"Yes, Miss Laurel! And you can see our fairy house," Cassie said. "And help me get the fairies to come."

"I'd like that, Cassie." The child's bright eyes and smile would melt anyone's heart. It made her think of her sisters with a sudden longing to hug them. She was surprised at how much she missed them, considering she'd practically danced with joy when the youngest had started college this year and Laurel could finally get to this dig.

The dig. She glanced at her watch, dismayed to realize how much time she'd lost this morning. Time she couldn't afford to lose.

She turned to Andros. "Are you able to leave right now?"

He nodded. "Let me grab—"

"Dr. Drakoulias." Christina stuck her head out of the door. "We have a patient with a possible broken arm."

His lips twisted as his eyes met Laurel's. "Guess I'm not. How about I find you at the other site when I can, then we'll head over to the caves?"

"Okay." A mix of both relief and disappointment battled inside her as she said her goodbyes and headed to her car. She didn't particularly want him looking over her shoulder as she took over what would hopefully be temporary leadership and talked to all the dig workers. But she'd like to have him with her to ask the cave-dig volunteers questions she wouldn't know to ask.

And of course it had nothing to do with wishing she could just look at him and talk to him all day long…

The temperature thankfully dropped a few degrees when the sun sank behind the mountain. Laurel kept carefully digging and cataloging, ignoring the stinging ache in her palm, even though she'd let most of the crew leave long ago. Shoveling dirt and rocks and working in this kind of heat wore everyone down by the end of the day, and she couldn't expect them to be as intensely committed as she was. This dig hadn't been their parents' baby, and they didn't know about what Laurel still hoped was here somewhere, just waiting to be found.

Between her time at the clinic and meeting with different crew members, she'd lost more than half the day, and if she had to work until nearly dark to make it up, she would. So disappointing that Andros apparently hadn't been able to get away. She'd asked the volunteers at the cave dig to stick around later than usual, but, as far as she knew, he hadn't shown. Every time she'd seen someone move into her vision, her silly heart had kicked a little, until she'd realized it wasn't him after all.

Time to go to the cave site to tell everyone they were through for the day. Hopefully it didn't matter that Andros hadn't been able to talk with any of them. Maybe Mel and Tom would be better after their hospital stay, and they could all quit worrying about why they'd gotten sick in the first place.

She stood and stretched her tired back, shoved her things into her backpack, and turned to walk the half mile to the cave site, realizing too late how dusk was closing in fast. With her head down, she concentrated on staying on the goat path, well-worn through the scrub, her mind moving from Mel and Tom, to how she could possibly pick up the pace of the excavation without them, then to Andros and how unfair it was that a man she was attracted to more than any she could think of in recent memory was likely a married man.

"You make a habit of working until it's so dark you can barely see?"

Startled, Laurel nearly tripped over her feet, heart pounding as she looked up to see Andros's unmistakable broad form moving toward her on the goat path.

She pressed her sore hand to her chest, huffing out a breath of relief and annoyance. "You make a habit of sneaking up on people to give them a heart attack?"

"Well, we did talk about my MO being injuring people, fixing them up, then billing them."

"Uh-huh. Too bad for you my heart is still in one piece."

"Good to hear. And I wasn't sneaking." He stopped in front of her. "Just hoping to find you on the way to the caves, since you've kept your poor workers imprisoned there, saying they couldn't leave until you said so."

"I didn't keep them imprisoned," she said indignantly. "I was hoping you'd show up to talk to them, since you thought it was important."

"I'm sorry. We ended up having one injury or illness after another, and I couldn't get away. Since they're still there, I'll go tell them they can leave now. I already spoke with two of them but wanted to find you before it got dark."

"I'll come with you." Being the team leader now meant she couldn't pass off her responsibilities to anyone else. Something she'd had to learn all over again every time she'd been frustrated, even a little resentful, at having to stay home to take care of her sisters. Her parents had made it clear that, as the oldest, that was her job, when all she'd wanted was to go along on their summer digs instead.

Finally, those responsibilities were behind her, and she

was here on this amazing mountain. Except her parents would never be with her too. Her new responsibility was to their memory and what they'd always expected her to achieve with her life.

"I was going to insist you do, so I'm glad I don't have to." He smiled, his teeth shining white through the dusk. "Don't want you breaking an ankle walking down this mountain to your car in the dark. I parked not too far from the caves, so I'll drive you and the crew back to it."

"Are you saying I'm clumsy? Or do you always worry like this about everyone?" She smiled back at him, feeling the same silly little glow she'd felt when they'd been together here before and he'd wanted to take care of her hand.

"Clumsy? You're as graceful as a dancer, Laurel Evans. Kyrie Prosektikos is just being cautious."

The little glow grew warmer at the sincerity in his voice. "Because you don't want to fix another broken bone today."

"That too." He reached for her bandaged hand, rubbed his thumb across her knuckles. "How's it feeling?"

A little shiver snaked up her arm at his touch, and she nearly closed her fingers around his until she remembered she shouldn't. "Fine, thanks." She tried to tug away from his grasp, but he didn't let go. If she confessed that her cut actually hurt like blazes, he'd probably march her back to the clinic and torture her again.

"Good. Watch your step, and hang on to me." He tucked her hand into the crook of his elbow and, resting his wide palm gently on top of it, turned to head toward the caves.

They walked in an oddly companionable silence. As she held his strong arm, the way he'd tugged her close to his body as they picked their way over the uneven ground felt oddly right. The intimacy of it, the evening sky beautiful with pinkly puffy clouds, filled her chest with a sense of calm pleasure, until she suddenly wondered if he knew she'd feel that way. If he was the kind of man who used his amazing good looks and charm to solicit affairs with women from the archaeological site, knowing they'd only be around for a while.

That unpleasant thought obliterated her sense of comfortable calm. "Tell me about your wife," she said.

It seemed there was a momentary hitch in his step, probably from guilt, and the chill that had filled her chest grew downright icy. "My wife?"

"Yes. Cassie's mother. Is she from Kastorini, too?"

"Cassie's mother was American. And we were never married."

This time, the hitch was in her own step. "Was?"

"Yes."

"I'm so sorry."

"Thank you, but she and I weren't…close. It's for Cassie you should feel sorry, since she barely remembers her. She passed away when Cassie was only two, and I got custody of her then."

He didn't offer more, and Laurel knew it would be rude to ask for details. The cold tightness in her chest turned to an ache for the little girl who would never know her mother. At the same time, it absurdly lightened a little at the thought that Andros Drakoulias was single and available. All the feelings of intimacy she'd felt just moments ago came surging back, making her hyperaware of how good it felt to be tucked against his warm, masculine body.

She mentally smacked herself. Maybe she couldn't shake this powerful attraction to him, but she wouldn't act on it. There was so much work to finish in so little time, and they were down two people to boot. Hadn't her mother always admonished her about never letting a boyfriend or crush get in the way of her focus on school or work? One hundred percent of her attention had to be on this dig and the important goal she still hoped to make happen.

Dusk had nearly given way to full darkness as they arrived at the entrance to the caves, and she released Andros's arm so no one would start any gossip, which at a dig could spread like poison ivy. Becka and Jason, two of the three volunteers, were packing up by the light of electric lanterns. "Where's John?" she asked.

"He's coming. Said he was working on unearthing another human bone and wanted to finish," Becka said.

"There's something I didn't ask before," Andros said. "Do each of you have your own section of the cave you work, or do you move around a lot?"

Becka swiped her hair from her eyes. "We keep to our own sections, mostly, unless Tom needs us to work somewhere else."

"Have you—?" Andros was interrupted by a violent coughing sound, echoing from inside the cave.

Oh, Lord, no. Laurel looked at Andros and saw his expression turn grim.

"Put these on. Now." He dug surgical masks from his pocket and quickly handed them out before putting one on himself. Another racking cough came from the cave just before John stumbled out, bending over and holding his chest for what seemed like minutes until it finally subsided, leaving him gasping.

Andros wrapped his arm around John's back, helping him stand upright. "You're burning up," Andros said, his voice slightly muffled through the mask. "How long have you been like this?"

"Had a cold the last couple days, like Tom. Got lots worse the past hour or so."

"Let's get you down to the clinic hospital and do some tests. My car's close by."

With John leaning heavily against him, Andros helped

him down the path. Laurel's throat tightened when she saw Andros had taken a second to put on surgical gloves as well.

She hoped and prayed this was something completely different than what Mel and Tom were experiencing. That it was just a cold, and he'd be feeling better in the morning. Not horribly sick and hooked up to oxygen the way Mel and Tom had been. That Becka and Jason would stay healthy. That they'd all be fine.

But what if John got worse? What if his symptoms were exactly the same? And if they were, where would that leave the dig?

CHAPTER FIVE

"So what do you think?" Andros asked Dimitri in a low voice as they stood in the doorway of John Jackson's hospital room at the Elias Sophia Hospital. "Same thing as the Wagners?"

"Presents the same, but that doesn't necessarily mean it is. We'll have to wait for the blood tests to come back, and we won't have Mr. Jackson's until a few days after the Wagners'."

Andros looked at the woman standing next to the patient's bed and couldn't help but be impressed at how calm she seemed through all the activity around them. How steady, despite the incessant beep of monitors, nurses slipping in and out of the room, and techs checking the patient's vitals. Far calmer and steadier than he might have expected her to be, considering the heightened intensity in the air.

Though lines creased her brow and the blue eyes visible over the surgical mask she wore held a deep concern, her composure didn't waver. She stood straight, talking to John about the dig.

Andros had already transferred the patient here this morning, just before Laurel had shown up at the clinic. When she'd asked for directions to drive here after the day's work at the dig, he'd instantly offered to bring her instead, wanting to see the Wagners and John, too. And if an hour's car ride enjoying her scent in his nose and conversation from her lush lips was part of his motivation, what was the harm in that?

When he'd first introduced her to Dimitri, she'd asked good questions, her responses intelligent and thoughtful. She hadn't overreacted or panicked, simply displaying clear leadership in taking over for the Wagners.

Andros's heart knocked in his chest when he saw her reach out to touch John's arm, relieved when he saw her hesitate and withdraw it. John said something Andros couldn't catch, and a smile touched her eyes as she answered him back then said goodbye. She turned toward the door, and her eyes met his, held.

"You have something going with the pretty lady?" Dimitri asked.

The surprising question had him breaking eye contact with Laurel to stare at his friend. "I just met her two days ago."

"Sometimes only takes two minutes."

And damned if that wasn't the truth. Or even two seconds, which was about how long it had taken for his interest to go from zero to sixty the first moment he'd laid eyes on her.

"And if you don't, you should," Di said in a lower voice, grinning and waggling his thick eyebrows like Groucho Marx. "I'll keep you posted on our patients." He headed down the hall as Laurel joined Andros at the doorway.

"John seems to be holding his own. Doesn't he?" Her questioning eyes seemed to be willing him to reassure her. "He doesn't seem to have as much trouble breathing as Mel and Tom did when I first saw them in your clinic hospital."

"Not at the moment. Hopefully he'll stay that way." He wrapped his fingers around her arm and drew her farther into the hall. "Di told you we just don't know if this is the same thing the Wagners have or not. An influenza or some other virus. Bacterial infection or fungal infection."

"When will you know?"

"Di asked to have John's test results expedited, but that will still take a couple days."

She nodded, that pucker of worry still on her face. "I'm so relieved, though, that Mel and Tom aren't any worse. Do you think they'll be released soon?"

"Hard to say. They're getting good care, so we'll keep our fingers crossed." He wanted to banish, for at least a little while, that deep concern clouding her eyes. There was nothing more to do here, and a glance at his watch showed it was already well past 7:00 p.m. "How about we have dinner here before we head back?" He'd thought of that, wanted that, from the moment they'd left Delphi to drive here. Time spent with her away from her work and his, away from Kastorini, away from the serious problems on both their minds.

"I probably should get back. Update the team and make sure they're okay."

"Why wouldn't they be okay?"

"Well, they…" Her voice trailed off and she gave a little rueful smile. "You're right, they're adults. I forget sometimes I don't have to play mom anymore."

"When did you have to?" Surely she didn't have children. Leaving them for the entire summer for the dig.

"Oh, for my sisters. It's a wonder my hair's not prematurely gray." The tone of her voice had lightened and she smiled. "The dig team has explored a few towns outside of Delphi on weekends, but not here. So dinner sounds lovely."

"Good." He let go of her arm, resisting the urge to hold her hand instead, and they headed to his car. "You in the mood for seafood, or Greek food, or both?"

"Anything. Everything. I didn't have much lunch, and I have to admit that, next to digging, eating's one of my favorite things to do."

"Yeah?" She'd obviously decided to let herself relax with him, to let go of her worries for a time, and he grinned at the sudden enthusiasm in her voice. "Something we have in common. I know just the place you'll like."

It was only about a ten-minute drive from the hospital to the waterfront, and, since it was early yet for locals to be eating dinner, he had no trouble finding a parking spot. "Sit tight," he said to Laurel as he got out of the car, going around to her side of the car to open her door.

"More of your worrying I'm clumsy?" she asked as he held out his hand to her. "Getting out of a car isn't quite as dangerous as walking down a rocky mountain in the dark."

"Being a gentleman pleases me. And because I can see you're a woman who cares about others, you won't mind indulging me, will you?"

"Ah, the charm of Greek men." She shook her head, but a smile tugged at the corners of her lips.

She placed her soft hand in his and stepped from the car. It felt so nice to hold it, just as it had when he'd washed her palm at the clinic, and he couldn't seem to make himself let go. A little surprised that she didn't release his either, he gave in to enjoying the simple connection. Stars began to wink in the darkening sky as they strolled down the brick promenade that went for a good quarter mile along the lapping gulf waters.

"I've been in Greece two months, and I'm still amazed at all the little restaurants that line the water in every town," she said, gazing at the lanterns and lights beneath huge umbrellas connected together, one after another. "So pretty. With comfy seats too, if you want, instead of a table. I wish there were more places like this in the States."

"I went to med school in New Jersey," he said. "I admit I never got used to the beach restaurants there. Always wanting you to move on your way right after you're done. In Greece, you're expected to eat and relax for the night."

"Somehow when you said you lived in the US, I was picturing LA or Montana."

Her eyes were filled with a teasing look, and he found himself drifting closer until his shoulder brushed hers. "LA or Montana? First, I'd say those two places don't have much in common, and second, I'd ask why."

"I'm not sure." She tilted her head at him, seeming to size him up, and he grew even more curious about what she was thinking. "Maybe because you seem sophisticated and at the same time rugged. Like a Greek cowboy."

Sophisticated but rugged sounded pretty good. As if she might find him attractive, and he certainly found her very attractive. "I'm more of a Greek goat boy than a cowboy, since it was my job to look after ours when I was a kid."

"Goat boy?" She laughed. "Sorry. Doesn't work at all for you."

"You might change your mind if I show up smelling like one of Cassie's goats sometime. She and Petros like to pretend they're horses and bring them into the 'stable.' Which is her name for our living room."

"Oh, my gosh, that's adorable."

"Not when your house smells like a barn."

Her laugh, the sparkle in her eyes, were sheer temptation. The kind of temptation that left Andros wondering if he could possibly resist. If he could keep his hands and lips to himself when all he wanted at that moment was to pull her close and kiss that smiling mouth.

He drew in a deep breath, glad they'd arrived at one

of his favorite restaurants, interrupting his dangerous thoughts. "Would you like to sit at a table, or have *mezedes* on these seats looking out over the water?"

"*Mezedes?*"

"You've been in Greece two months and don't know what *mezedes* are?" He teased her with mock astonishment. "Appetizer-sized plates for dinner, instead of one entrée. Eating various *meze* over a whole evening, preferably with ouzo to drink, is a Greek tradition."

"Ouzo? You're kidding. That stuff is awful!" He had to grin at the cute way she scrunched up her face. "Mel and Tom had us all try it at dinner in Delphi one night and I could barely swallow it."

"Don't worry. Ouzo's optional."

"Good, because the *meze* sounds wonderful. I like trying different things. And I want to enjoy seeing the water while I still can."

A reminder that she wouldn't be here for long. But when it came right down to it, what did it matter? He wasn't capable of futures or happy-ever-afters with a woman anyway. And they were far enough away that he didn't have to worry about the gossip Kastorini townsfolk used to love to share about him, back in the careless days of his youth. Which had extended into too many careless days with women in his adulthood, too.

They sat side by side in the cushioned wicker seat, and it took effort to concentrate on the menu instead of how close she was, how good she smelled, how pretty she looked. "So, no ouzo," he said. "What do you like to drink?"

"White wine, but don't let me stop you from drinking ouzo."

No way he'd be drinking ouzo. If he kissed her, he wasn't about to taste like the licorice liquor she hated.

Then reminded himself that kissing wouldn't be a good idea. "Have you ever tried retsina?"

"No. That's a Greek wine, isn't it?"

"Another thing that can be an acquired taste. Some people think it tastes like turpentine, or pinesap, but by the third glass, you'd like it."

"Third glass? Are you trying to get me drunk to take advantage of me?" He hadn't seen this mischievousness in her eyes before, and his heart beat a little faster as he thought of ways they could take advantage of one another and how much fun that would be. "How about I stick with sauvignon blanc?"

"I'm a gentleman, remember?" A gentleman who wanted to kiss her, wanted to know whether this attraction, this awareness, went both ways. Except he shouldn't want to know, because if she felt any of what he was feeling he'd find it even harder to keep their relationship strictly friendly and uncomplicated. "We'll get both, since you like to try new things."

"Far be it from me to not try a drink that tastes like pinesap."

Even as he grinned he wondered how her mouth would taste no matter what she'd been drinking, and yanked his gaze from her lips, handing her the menu. "What sounds good?"

She handed it back. "You've heard the phrase, 'it's all Greek to me'? Unfortunately, studying ancient languages doesn't help me read one word of that."

"Sorry. How about I order a few of my favorites, then we'll go from there? Grilled octopus, *keftedes*, which are fried meatballs I personally could eat a dozen of, peppers stuffed with feta, and olives from the valleys by Kastorini to start."

"Sounds wonderful, except maybe the octopus. Can't wrap my brain around eating those little suction cups."

She gave an exaggerated shudder that was almost as cute as her ouzo expression. "Maybe you haven't had them cooked properly. And I'm beginning to learn you're a little overdramatic at times, perhaps."

"Perhaps." Her lips curved. "I love that the olives are from that sea of trees. It's incredible how many there are."

"Over a million. And many are over a hundred years old."

"A hundred? That's a nanosecond in Greece."

"Says the archaeologist, not arborist."

They smiled at one another until the waiter showed up to take their order, then brought the wine. Andros let himself enjoy looking at her over his glass. Wished he could see her with that long, thick, silky hair of hers out of its restraint and spilling down her back. He nearly reached to grasp the ponytail in his palm, wanting to stroke the length of its softness with his hand, but stopped himself.

"Tell me about being mom to your sisters. How many do you have?" he asked, as much to keep from thinking about touching her as genuinely wanting to know more about her. Then instantly regretted the question, surprised to see the beautiful eyes that had been relaxed and smiling become instantly shadowed.

"Three younger. One just graduated college, one's a sophomore, and the youngest, Helen, is on a summer internship in Peru before she starts as a freshman in a few more weeks." She stayed quiet for a moment, and Andros was trying to figure out if he should start a different subject when she finally spoke. "My parents were the archaeologists who started this dig and were killed that first summer. That's how I came to take over the mom role. Did a pretty bad job of it half the time, but I tried."

"I'm so sorry. What happened?" His heart kicked at what a shocking loss that had to be. He put down his glass and rested his hand between her shoulder blades. "You must have barely been, what, twenty-two?"

She nodded. "I'd graduated college that May, and just a couple weeks later they came here to start working the dig. I was home watching my sisters. My parents were excavating a new pit and were inside it deciding how much deeper they could use machinery, when an earthquake hit. The rock walls collapsed on them."

"Dear God. I remember that earthquake's epicenter was right here on Mount Parnassus, and that some of the buildings in Delphi and Kastorini were pretty badly damaged. I can't believe your parents…" He trailed off, unable to imagine it. The shock of such a freak thing taking both of her parents at once.

"I know. It was…unbelievable. Devastating for us girls."

"That small earthquake a couple weeks ago must have scared the hell out of you. Brought it all back." She nodded, and Andros's chest squeezed at the pain on her face. "So you took over for your parents, taking care of your sisters."

"The court allowed me to become guardian. I'd watched them every summer anyway, when our parents were gone on digs. We managed. Survived. I'd planned to start grad school, but had to put it off for a few years. I hate that I'm so behind what my parents groomed me to accomplish by now. Far behind all that they'd accomplished by my age, but there wasn't another good option. It's…I knew it was what they would have expected, even though they would've been disappointed that school had to come second." The tears came then, squeezing his chest even tighter, and she quickly dabbed them before they could fall. "Sorry. Stupid to cry after all this time."

He couldn't figure out how much of her tears were from grief over her parents, or the pain of believing, somehow, that they would be disappointed with her. Surely she didn't really feel that way, considering how she'd stepped up and put her sisters first. At twenty-two, he'd been damned self-absorbed, for sure.

He took her chin in his fingers, turned her face so she was looking at him. "Never be sorry for being human and feeling pain, Laurel. Grief stays with us, sometimes for a long time. Until we learn what we have to from it to move on."

The way she forced a smile through her tears gripped his heart, and without thinking he lowered his head an inch and touched his lips to hers. Softly, gently, meaning to soothe. They were soft and pliant beneath his, and for a long moment the kiss was painfully, wonderfully, deliciously sweet.

They slowly pulled apart, separating just a few inches, staring at one another. Heat and desire rushed through his veins like a freight train just from his lips on hers. A heat and desire that had him wanting to go back for more, deeper and hotter. He fiercely reminded himself she was hurting, that he was supposed to be offering comfort. Not consumed with the need to lay her down on the cushioned seat and kiss her breathless.

Her eyes were wide, and inside that deep blue he thought he saw a flicker of what might be the same awareness, the same desire. Just as he began to ease away from her, she surprised the hell out of him, wrapping her palm behind his head, closing the gap between them and kissing him back. He found himself grasping her ponytail as he'd wanted to earlier, gently tugging her hair to tip her face to the perfect angle, letting him delve deeper. Her lips parted, drew him in as he learned the dizzying taste of Laurel Evans.

"Ahem. Your peppers and *keftedes*."

They both slowly broke apart, and Andros struggled

to remember they were in a public restaurant before he turned to the waiter. "Thanks."

The waiter responded with a grin and a little wink at Andros before he moved on to another seat farther down the promenade. He looked at Laurel, not surprised to see her cheeks were a deep pink. Hell, he had a feeling his might be too, and didn't know what to say. Maybe something along the lines of, *Sorry, I didn't mean to try to suck your tongue like you were the first* meze, *but you taste so good I couldn't help myself.*

He cleared his throat. "I—"

"You were wrong, you know," she interrupted in a soft voice.

"Wrong?"

"That I'd need three glasses of retsina before I'd think it tasted good. Just one taste from your mouth, and I know it's very, very delicious."

That surprised a short laugh out of him. "And I've come to have a new appreciation for the very appetizing flavor of sauvignon blanc." Her words, her smile, the heat in her eyes that reflected his own, nearly sent him back for another taste of her, but he somehow managed to keep his mouth to himself. He slid the plates of food closer to her. "Try the *keftedes* alone, and then with the *tziaziki*. Which, by the way, we either both have to eat, or neither of us."

"Why?"

"Because I don't want to smell like garlic if you don't. But if we both do? Nothing like a garlicky *tziaziki* kiss, I promise." And why had he brought up the subject of kissing when he was trying to behave?

He was glad to see every trace of sadness was gone, replaced by a slightly wicked smile that sent his blood pumping all over again. "Don't think it could beat the last one, but I'm more than willing to give it a try."

"I doubt it could beat the last one either. Guess we'll have to find out."

The memory of that kiss had the air practically humming as they looked at one another, and Andros knew he had to bring the conversation back to something less exciting to ratchet down his libido. Either that, or leave and steam up the windows of his car.

And that idea was so appealing, he nearly threw money on the table and grabbed her hand to get going on it.

"So," he said, stuffing half a meatball into his mouth to drown out the flavor of Laurel, "I assume you're going to shut down the cave dig for the moment."

"Shut it down?"

"Yes. With John sick now too, it's logical until we get some test results back."

"We only have a few weeks left of the dig as it is. And no one has any idea if they're sick because of something in the caves or not. For all we know it could be something a tourist brought to the hotel. Or even coincidence and not the same illness."

He was surprised as hell at her attitude and the suddenly mulish expression on her face, especially considering she'd seen how sick the three were and had seemed as worried as he was. "True. But it makes sense to wait until we get the test results. How could a few days matter?"

"Every hour matters. There'll be no more funding for this project. Which means whatever we have left to unearth has to be discovered soon, or it'll stay buried."

"Things will stay buried anyway. Unless a dig lasts indefinitely, I'd think you could never be sure what might still be there."

"True. And we have used satellite imaging and ground-penetrating radar and magnetometry to help us find what's still there. But those things are less reliable when it comes to the caves."

"So you're willing to risk someone else getting sick to give yourself a few extra days' digging." He couldn't help but feel frustrated, even angry about that, especially when an image of Laurel lying in a hospital bed, sick and nearly unable to breathe, disturbingly injected itself into his mind.

"I need to finish this dig for my parents." She frowned at him for a long moment before she finally spoke again. "But I'll compromise. I'll offer the team a choice about working on the mountain, and we'll stay out of the caves until the test results are back. Unless you can prove to me the pneumonia is definitely related to the dig, though, I'm not shutting it down."

CHAPTER SIX

"I CAN'T BELIEVE Kristin stayed at the hotel when we're already down three people." Becka sat back on her haunches and pushed her hair under her hat as she looked over at Laurel.

"It's fine, Becka." Laurel pulled a bag and pen from her apron to label the potsherd she'd dug up. "The reason I shared Dr. Drakoulias's concerns with the team was to give everyone the option to sit it out until the test results are back, if that's what they're most comfortable doing."

"But how could it have anything to do with the dig? We've been here two months with nobody getting sick."

"I agree. But until we have confirmation that it's not a fungal infection, I think everybody has the right to be extra cautious if they want, and we'll stay out of the caves for now."

"I don't get why he thinks there might be something in the caves. Mel hasn't been in there since June."

"It's possible she got something from Tom. But I figure it's more likely they got some random virus from some long-gone tourist while we had dinner in Delphi, or someone who stayed at the hotel. Though Dr. Drakoulias and I have both talked to management there, and as far as they know, nobody's been sick."

"So we should just keep at it, don't you think?"

"I'm planning to, but, again, I understand people being concerned. We all want this dig to end on a high note. Hopefully the three of them will be fine soon, and we'll find there's nothing to worry about." She prayed that was true, and that the high note was a certain big, knockout find she hadn't given up on.

"Well, I'm not worried about it. And I've gotta say, I'd rather be in the nice, cool cave than out here all day. I'd forgotten how beastly hot it is."

"Working in heat, cold and rain is part of the gig sometimes. And don't forget about the snakes up here. Gotta be tough to be a digger." Laurel smiled and tossed a water bottle to Becka. "We'll quit for the day in about an hour. Hydrate and take a little break."

Becka stood and swigged down some water. Laurel's smile grew at how much the girl reminded her of her sister Ariadne, and as she was wondering what her siblings were doing, Becka interrupted her thoughts with a chilling scream. Her heart knocked against her chest when Becka dropped the bottle and fell, writhing, onto the ground.

"What's wrong?" Laurel leaped to her feet and ran the few feet between them.

"Oh, God, my leg! What…?"

Laurel followed the girl's wide-eyed gaze, horrified to see that beneath the hand clutching at her calf, blood gushed down her leg, a shocking amount pooling around the dirt and stones she lay sprawled on.

"Becka. Let me see." Laurel's heart pounding now, she dropped to her knees and instantly saw what had happened. "I think your trowel cut you."

"I'm so stupid," the girl moaned. "You always said never to stick our trowel in our back pocket, but I did, didn't I? Did it cut through my shorts and fall out? Is it bad?"

"It's a pretty good gash." That was an understatement,

but the last thing Laurel needed was for the girl to faint or go into shock. "Let me get it wrapped up, then we'll have to get you down the mountain somehow."

Her mind frantically spun to first-aid classes she'd learned, and she prayed she remembered right. The injuries her sisters occasionally came home with had been pretty minor. Definitely nothing like this. Laurel had seen a few injuries on the digs she'd been able to go on close to home but hadn't been in charge. Why hadn't she paid more attention to how they'd stopped the bleeding?

Okay, she reminded herself grimly, freaking out and staring at it wasn't going to fix it. She ran to the supply box and dug through until she found gauze wraps on the bottom and the duct tape she'd used over her bandage. But when she kneeled next to Becka, the amount of blood pouring through the girl's fingers sent fear surging down her spine, and she knew she had to do something more than just wrap it.

"I'm going to try to hold it together and put pressure on it for a few minutes to slow the bleeding before I wrap it. Okay?"

Becka nodded. Just as Laurel began to lay a piece of gauze lengthwise on the cut, the girl let out a little moan, and Laurel looked up at her. Lord, she was staring at the blood, her face turning the ghastliest white. "Don't faint on me now." That was the last thing either of them needed, and Laurel quickly tried to move her into a sitting position.

"Sit up and put your head between your knees." It wasn't easy to press on the wound at the same time she pushed the girl's head down with the other. "Deep breaths. I'm going to press hard on your leg to stop the bleeding, so be prepared."

Becka thankfully followed directions. Every muscle tense, Laurel tried to gently bring the edges of the wound together, then pressed hard again. Becka cried out, biting her lip until Laurel was afraid it might start bleeding too. "I'm sorry. Hang in there. Once I get it wrapped up, I'll take you to Dr. Drakoulias."

As soon as the words were out of her mouth, her heart knocked again. What if the man wasn't in Kastorini, but back at the Sophia Elias hospital or somewhere else? Then she remembered she had his phone number. She'd call him as soon as she could get a cell signal.

The fear filling her chest eased a bit, and she took a deep breath. It would be okay. No matter where he was, she'd be able to ask for his help. How much that thought calmed her was a little shocking, considering she hadn't relied on anyone else for much help in a long time.

She just hoped he wasn't still annoyed with her the way he'd been last night. Then wondered why she'd let it bother her. Her job, her responsibility to her parents and the future they'd wanted for her were all wrapped up in this dig, and she couldn't care if anyone approved of how they finished things up or not.

"Can you press down on it the way I was while I wrap it? Try not to move the gauze I already have on there."

"Okay," Becka said in a strained voice, reaching down to do as Laurel asked. Finally she had it tightly wrapped, hoping to heck it wasn't so tight that it cut off the poor girl's circulation. She sat back on her heels and stared at the gauze, relieved that it wasn't turning red with more blood.

"Okay, let's go. I'll help you stand, then we'll grab Jason so he can help us."

With Becka's arm across Laurel's shoulders, they awkwardly moved down the path toward grid eight. She couldn't see Jason, and prayed he was down in the pit where he should be. By the time they got to it, Laurel already felt nerves and muscles pinching from trying to hold Becka's weight as she limped. "Jason! Are you here?"

"I'm here," a voice said.

Laurel nearly sagged in relief. "Becka's hurt. I need your help."

In an instant, Jason came running up the makeshift stone steps from the pit, a worried frown on his face. "What happened?"

"I stupidly put my trowel in my shorts pocket, and it cut through and dove into my leg," Becka said through clenched teeth.

"Rookie mistake." Jason gave Becka a little smile as he lifted his hand and stroked her cheek, the gesture tugging at Laurel's heart. She'd thought maybe the two college kids were becoming sweet on one another, but hadn't paid that much attention. "You okay?"

"I think so. Hurts like crazy, though, and I'll probably have some ugly scar."

"Scars from a dig are a badge of honor. Makes you all the more interesting."

"You think?" The girl rolled her eyes at him, finally looking less freaked out.

"Oh, yeah. Not that you needed to be more interesting."

"Okay, enough of the mushy stuff, you two," Laurel joked, glad to be feeling less freaked out too, after the first shock of it all. "Let's get her down the mountain to my car so I can take her to the clinic. It's pretty deep, and I'm sure she'll need stitches."

It was easier with Jason's help, or, really, with Laurel helping Jason, who took on most of Becka's weight. Laurel called Andros a few times, relieved when she finally got a signal and he answered.

"Is something wrong, Laurel?"

How had he known it was her? The man must have put her contact information in his phone. That thought shouldn't have affected her, since he probably did it for professional reasons, but she couldn't help feeling absurdly pleased about it. "Becka has a serious gash in her leg from a trowel. Are you at the clinic?"

"I'm here. Bring her right in."

Jason got Becka tucked into the car and hovered there as he fastened her seat belt. "I'd like to come with you, but I better get back to work. At this rate, we're not going to finish what we've started if I don't."

"I'll be coming back to the dig after we get her fixed up and settled in at the hotel. I'll let you know how she is," Laurel promised, partly to relieve his mind and partly to get going before there was some long, drawn-out goodbye. Becka's leg needed prompt attention. And he was right—they'd never get finished at this rate unless everyone who could still work did overtime.

Andros must have been watching for them, because as soon as she pulled up in front of the clinic, he strode out of the door and helped Becka inside, Laurel following.

"You can come along if you want, or you can stay in the waiting room," he said, speaking to Laurel over his shoulder.

"I'll come." If Becka was anything like Laurel's sisters, she'd want someone by her side. They might believe they were all grown-up, but inside they still needed someone to turn to for comfort.

Laurel's chest felt heavy when the memories unexpectedly bombarded her. She'd been Becka's age exactly when she'd fallen into the dark hole of grief her parents' deaths had left her and her sisters with. All those summers she'd been stuck home watching her sisters while her parents were working had seemed hard. Then she'd learned that had been nothing compared to what it felt like for that comforting support to be forever gone.

"After I take a look, I'll have to thoroughly wash it

out, okay?" Andros settled Becka by a low sink that was really more like an open shower, before his eyes met Laurel's. "Christina's not here right now. Want to help me get some supplies?"

"Of course."

She followed him into an exam room, and he pulled gauze, pads and a bottle of some liquid from a closet, handing them to her. "Were you with her when it happened?" he asked as he grabbed some sealed bags of what looked like syringes and suture kits and who knew what.

"Yes. It's a long, pretty deep gash. Not sure exactly how deep, but it bled a lot."

"What did you do for it?"

"Tried to bring the edges of the wound together, then pressed on it a while to stop the bleeding. Seemed to work well enough, then I bandaged it and brought her here."

"Sounds like maybe you should have forgotten about digging for a living and become a doctor."

Fascinated by that unexpected dimple that poked into one cheek as he paused to look at her, she nearly dropped the gauze and bottle and fumbled to hang on to them. "Since I feared I might pass out when I first saw all that blood, I think I chose the right career path."

"Think you'll faint if you watch me stitch it up?" he asked, a mischievous twinkle in his eyes. "If so, please stay in the waiting room. Last thing either of us needs is for you to keel over and crack open your beautiful head."

"I want to be there for Becka." She was aware of a deep feeling of relief that he obviously wasn't still irritated with her. Deeper than it should have been. And how ridiculous was it that him calling her head "beautiful" gave her a little glow inside as well? "Since I'm not responsible anymore for whether she lives or dies, I think I'll be okay."

He chuckled then instantly became all business when

they walked into Becka's room and Andros pulled a rolling stool up next to her. "Let's take a look."

Laurel watched him carefully peel off the layers of gauze and wouldn't admit for the world that she had to look away a couple times when she saw the long, raw slice in Becka's calf that again oozed a trickle of blood.

"Nice first-aid job, Ms. Evans," he said, glancing up at her with a smile in his dark eyes. "I'm impressed."

"Thanks. Hope I don't have to do it again."

His eyes crinkled at the corners as he held her gaze for a moment, and darned if her heart didn't skip a beat before he turned to Becka. "I'm going to put a lidocaine-epinephrine mix all around the skin, then inject it with some painkillers before I wash it out. This part's going to hurt, I'm sorry to say."

Laurel and Becka both watched him gently but efficiently smooth on a liquid with a cotton pad, all around the edges of the torn skin. When he was done, he looked up at Becka, his dark eyes sympathetic. "Going to inject the painkiller into the wound now, which isn't going to feel good either. But then it'll be nice and numb when I stitch it up. Okay?"

Becka nodded, then gave a little crying gasp before she bit her lip hard as she had on the mountain. Laurel reached for the girl's hand, not sure if she was comforting Becka or both of them, again thinking of her own sisters and how upset she'd be if they were in pain like this. She remembered many small boo-boos when they'd smothered her with grateful hugs and kisses after she'd patched them up, managing to smile at the sweet memories.

She had to turn away a couple times as he repeatedly stuck the needle down into the open wound. "Will you think less of me if I say I'm glad my parents were archaeologists and didn't groom me to be a doctor instead?"

Andros glanced up at her with a smile. "Nothing would

make me think less of you. And I have a feeling you'd be great at anything you put your mind to. Even medicine." He set aside the needle and vial, and attached a hose to the faucet.

"Thank God," Becka said fervently. "That was awful."

"I know. That's no fun, but you're doing great." He patted her knee. "Washing it out isn't a picnic either, so hang in there for me."

He hosed down the angry wound, washing it thoroughly as he'd done with Laurel's hand. She started to worry that poor Becka would bite right through her lip if she chomped on it any harder.

"When Dr. Drakoulias had to wash out the cut on my hand, I thought he might drain the entire Gulf of Corinth before he was done," she said, trying to distract the girl with a joke.

Becka managed a little laugh, thankfully. "Maybe then they wouldn't be able to catch any octopus to serve up at dinner, which Jason hounds me to eat every time. I can't get why he loves them. Doesn't he understand that those little suction cups weird me out?"

"Laurel thinks octopus suckers are a delicacy, don't you? Preferably washed down with ouzo." Andros's gaze lifted to hers for a brief moment, his dark eyes filled with that mischievous twinkle again as he winked.

"A delicacy if you're a whale or a Greek."

Andros grinned, and Becka laughed before the sound morphed into a pained yelp. "Sorry. Not much longer."

Laurel sent up a prayer of thanks that the washing out was finally over, except the stitching would probably be an ordeal for the poor girl, too. Andros leaned back to pat Becka's shoulder this time. "The worst is over. Thankfully, right? The stitching is going to take a while because I need to do it in several layers. But believe it or not, it won't hurt at all."

"Find that hard to believe," Becka grumbled.

"Can't blame you. And I find it hard to believe you cut yourself this deeply with a trowel—that takes a special talent." He smiled, and that adorable dimple poked into his cheek as he began to stitch.

"Yeah, I have special talents all right. Clumsy ones."

His amused eyes met Laurel's and she found her heart beating a little harder for no reason at all. "I need to repair this cut in the muscle first, to stop it from bleeding, with stitches that will dissolve. Then the subcutaneous layer of flesh, which will reduce tension on the wound and help keep it closed and healing. Then, lastly, smaller nylon stitches that will help it look better when it heals."

"Jason said having a dig scar is a badge of honor," Becka said. "But if you can keep it from looking Frankenstein-ish, that would be great."

"Even though Laurel has no faith in the local, backwater Greek doctor, I promise no Frankenstein."

"I didn't say…oh, never mind." The amused teasing in the dark depths of his eyes told her an embarrassed protest was exactly what he'd been hoping for, and she wasn't going to go there again.

Laurel tried to keep up a bit of light conversation with Becka to take the girl's mind off her leg. Even while she was talking about the dig and asking things like what all the team had done in Delphi last night while she was out with Andros, she found her mind mostly on him.

Watching how smoothly, efficiently and impressively he stitched Becka's wound, obviously having done it hundreds of times. Noticing, as she had when he'd worked on her own hand, how dark his lashes were, how his features really were reminiscent of a classical Greek statue, how beautifully shaped his lips were as he slightly pursed them in concentration. Remembering how they'd felt against hers, which made her feel tingly and breathless and…and…

Stupid. Above and beyond any attraction she felt for the man, and there was no point in denying she had plenty, this dig came first. And with three team members in the hospital and Becka now likely out of commission for who knew how long, it was getting scarily harder to imagine she could make happen what she wanted to accomplish before they ran out of time.

She inhaled, willing her heart rate to pretend it wasn't thrown all out of whack just from his nearness. Time to bring business back to the forefront, get Becka to the hotel and herself back on the mountain.

"Since I forgot I was supposed to lure you to the mountain so you'd feel obligated to give us free medical care, I'll need a bill from you," she said.

"I'll have the office manager get it to you. I know US universities have insurance for teams like yours. And my yacht payment is due."

She tried hard to be immune to the power of his smile, but failed miserably. "Then why…?" Her voice trailed off. She'd been about to ask why he hadn't given her a bill for her hand, then wasn't sure she wanted to hear the answer. If it was because of this attraction that simmered between them despite her wishing it didn't, she didn't want to know. Having it verbalized instead of just zinging in the air around them might make it even harder to resist.

"You have a yacht?" Becka looked wide-eyed at him as he finished slathering on the same antibiotic he'd put on Laurel's hand.

"Well, a yacht by my standards, but probably not by Aristotle Onassis's." His eyes were focused on wrapping Becka's leg with layers of gauze, a different gauze wrap and elastic bandage on top of it all. "It's a twenty-five-foot boat with a two-fifty-horsepower motor. Perfect to take you both octopus fishing on your day off."

Becka laughed, and Laurel wondered how in the world she was supposed to resist lusting after a Greek god who cared for his patients, seemed to be a good dad, had a delicious sense of humor and even more delicious mouth?

"Ready, Becka? Your leg feel okay?"

"I'm sure it'll hurt like crazy later, but right now it's nicely numb." She turned to Andros, who was scribbling on a pad. "Thanks a lot, Dr. Drakoulias."

"You're welcome. You'll need to get crutches to keep weight off it for a few days, and I have a couple prescriptions for you that you can fill either at the pharmacy next door, or in Delphi. Just—" The sound of his phone ringing interrupted him. He fished it from his pocket, and, glancing at it, frowned. "Excuse me a minute."

His serious expression sent a little jab of concern poking at Laurel's chest. She prayed it wasn't some bad news about the Wagners or John. That kick of concern heightened her awareness of him as she watched him stride from the room, his butt perfectly encased in his dress pants, his broad shoulders tugging the fabric of his shirt, his black hair catching the bright overhead light, making it gleam.

"Wow, Laurel," Becka said, turning to her with awe in her voice. "I didn't really see him very well at the caves when John was sick. He's, like, wow."

"Yeah. He is." Hadn't that pretty much been her first thought too? Even more so now that she knew how it felt to kiss him. Though she was going to stop thinking about that if it killed her.

"Anybody could tell he's attracted to you. If you don't go for that, you're crazy."

Oh, yeah, she wanted to go for "that." It might be crazy not to, but it would be just as crazy to get into a quickie relationship right now. Except every time she was around the man, her resolve to keep her distance seemed to disintegrate, and kissing him became the forefront thought in her head. Maybe Ate, the spirit of mischief, was lurking on this mountain, luring her into infatuation and recklessness.

The thought made her smile, thinking of how her sisters always rolled their eyes when she said things like that, as though mythical beings just might be real after all. "This dig is important to me, Becka." No one but the Wagners knew exactly how important. "I admit I'm tempted. Really tempted. But I just don't have time, and we'll be out of here in a few weeks."

"Yeah, I know. But still, you could—"

They both turned to the door as Andros walked back in, his expression seeming lighter, yet at the same time hard to read.

"That was Dr. Dimitri Galanos. He has interesting news."

Laurel stood and moved next to him, practically holding her breath. "What news?"

"First, John is unfortunately still on the ventilator, though they're taking good care of him. But the Wagners continue to improve, and their test results are back."

"And?"

"It's apparently some type of virus, though they're still not sure what." His eyes met Laurel's. "However, it's definitely not a fungal infection. So it appears they didn't get it from the caves."

CHAPTER SEVEN

"SO IF IT'S not a fungal infection, why do you still have that look on your face? I thought—" Taryn interrupted herself to tug her son's shirt as he stood on his chair. "Petros, sit down, please, and play your game. Lunch will be here soon."

"What look?" Andros rebooted the tablet his wriggling daughter held, pulled up a new game to occupy Petros, then gave his attention back to Taryn. "This is why we should've just cleaned your fridge out and eaten leftovers. Our children are monsters when we go out."

"Not monsters, Daddy! Fairies!"

"Uh-uh! I'm a monster, Uncle Andros!"

Both their protests and dark frowns were so indignant, he had to laugh. "Okay, an impatient ants-in-her-pants fairy, and a messy monster. Have another olive."

He handed both the kids olives. He watched his daughter pop it into her mouth, then fish the pit out with her small fingers, filled all over again with amazement that she belonged to him. His own flesh and blood in the adorable little package that was Cassandra Anne Drakoulias.

It hadn't been the way he'd expected to start a family someday. Making a baby with a woman he hardly remembered, and who hadn't felt a need to tell him about his own daughter. If Alison hadn't died, he might *never* have known. That tore at his heart and sent the guilt of how carelessly he'd lived his life even deeper into his bones.

But from the very first instant he'd met his child, he'd realized what an incredible blessing she was. God's way of helping him rethink how he lived his life when he hadn't even realized he needed to.

"Mom would be horrified if we ate leftovers after church. She'd hop the next plane from Scotland and be fixing her usual massive feast for us like she does every Sunday. And scold me for not spending the day cooking."

He chuckled, because it was true. "She'd be almost as horrified to see us in a restaurant. Good news is she will never know, and she'll be back to cook and fuss over us in no time. In fact, I'm dying for her *avgolemono* soup, which you refuse to fix for me."

"Fix it for yourself." His sister smirked, because she knew his cooking skills were practically nil. Something he should probably work on. "Anyway, tell me why you're still frowning and deep in thought about the pneumonia," she said, bringing back the original subject, as usual. Once his sister had something she wanted to talk about, she was going to finish no matter what. "It's not a fungal infection, so it's not from the archaeological dig, and not something the workers are going to spread around town. Right?"

"We may know what it isn't, but we don't know what it is. Maybe they were just in the wrong place at the wrong time and sat next to somebody who passed it on. But maybe it's something else."

"Like what?"

Exactly what was bothering him. "I don't know. Di doesn't know. But I have a strange gut feeling that this isn't over."

"I remember a lot of your gut feelings just being hunger pangs," his sister said.

"Which is why you should have let me eat your

pastitsio instead of coming all the way to Delphi for lunch." He grinned, willing his brain to stop thinking about the mystery. Time would tell whether he was right or wrong, and he hoped like hell he was wrong.

"Daddy, it's your pretty friend who knows lots about fairies!" Cassie said excitedly, pointing to the doorway.

He looked up and his heart gave a kick when he saw Laurel standing there with a few others from the dig, startlingly elegant in a long blue dress that skimmed her ankles and loosely hugged her curves. Elegant, and at the same time natural, with her beautiful hair in that thick ponytail she always wore it in, and little makeup on her exotic features.

Almost as though she felt his eyes on her, her gaze lifted to his and held, her lush lips parted in surprise until someone jabbed her arm and she turned to follow the host to their table. He had the urge to catch up with her, talk her into having lunch with them, but stopped himself. He knew a number of people in this place, and it wouldn't take much for elbows to nudge and knowing smiles and winks to be sent his way, starting gossip that no longer applied now that he had Cassie to think about.

"Can we ask her to eat with us, Daddy?"

Was his daughter a mind reader now? "Looks like she's eating with the dig crew, so let's not bother her."

"I won't bother her. I just want to ask a couple things."

Before he even realized what she was doing, Cassie slid from the chair and ran across the room to Laurel's table, with Petros following on her heels. "Cassie, you— ah, hell."

"Why 'ah, hell'?" His sister tipped her head at him with a quizzical look. "Seemed like she likes kids when I met her. She have the hots for you? Or is it mutual?"

"Why either one of those? Maybe we dislike each other."

"Yeah, right." His sister gave an indelicate snort. "I've never known a single girl to meet you and not be interested. And for the record, I've seen the way you look at her."

"I'm looking at her as someone connected to my patients. I'm building my reputation as an upstanding doctor and all-around good dad. Not looking for a woman."

"Uh-huh. Tell that to someone who doesn't know you that well. I'm well aware you have the occasional fling when you go out of town."

"I'm not a monk, but I only see a woman when I'm sure she just wants a fling too." He'd obviously have to try harder to keep his attraction to Laurel hidden. At least his sister couldn't see inside his brain as well, because she'd also learn that Laurel featured front and center in any number of fantasies at the moment. Then Taryn would laugh and shake her head and point out that there'd always been someone featured in his fantasies, and he'd have to point out—again—that was the old Andros, not the new, improved one.

"And of course I like to look at her," he continued. "She's a beautiful woman. But she's only here for a few weeks, and having some short thing with her wouldn't be worth the whole town gossiping about me and Cassie hearing it."

"So when are you going to give a relationship a chance to grow into something bigger than a fling?"

"You know as well as I do that I'm not capable of that kind of relationship."

"I don't believe that. Just because you used to go through women like Thea Stella goes through tissues, doesn't mean you can't have a long-term relationship. The lines to become Mrs. Andros Drakoulias started forming when you were about fifteen."

"I think you have to want one to have one."

"Maybe you just never met the right woman."

"Glad you have faith in me, but everyone in this town thinks different."

"People will always talk. I know I'm still on the subject list, having Petros without a wedding ring or a man who wanted to be involved in his life." His sister sighed. "So what if you were a bit of a playboy back in the day and gave the town some entertainment? That was a long time ago."

"Showing up in town with a two-year-old, shocking the hell out of everyone, wasn't all that long ago." After the phone call from Alison's brother, telling him about Cassie, the direction of his life had changed. Thankfully no one in Alison's family could take his little girl, or he might still not have her in his life. That second, he'd known becoming a more responsible man and moving to Kastorini with his daughter was his destiny, despite having to deal with the perennial tongue waggers. "One of these days, though, the past will be forgotten, if I behave myself."

"You never cared about the gossip before and you shouldn't now."

He glanced over at his daughter, talking animatedly to everyone at Laurel's table. "I have Cassie to think about."

"And I have Petros. We can flaunt our heathen ways together."

"We've always been experts at that." He had to grin. "How about we flaunt our newfound upstanding citizenship equally well?" The waiter brought their food, and Andros stood. "I'll get the kids."

He took one step and saw that Laurel was already headed their way, Cassie and Petros on either side of her, holding her hands.

"Lose something?" She smiled at Taryn before her eyes met his. Until he realized the moment went on a little too long and he quickly shifted his attention to Cassie.

"I did. My little fairy flitted away as soon as she saw you come in."

"And my monster followed," Taryn said.

"I asked Laurel if she'd come see our fairy house and tell us how we can get the fairies to move in."

A flood of instant pleasure filled Andros at the thought of her coming to Kastorini, spending time with him that afternoon at his home, while at the same time knowing it wasn't the best idea. "Miss Laurel probably has things she needs to do, Cassie."

"It's Sunday. Sunday is for playing," Cassie said, that cute frown on her face again. He had to smile, reaching out to smooth her brow with his fingers.

"True. But Miss Laurel may already have plans for how she wants to play today."

The second the words were out of his mouth, he knew exactly how he'd like to play with Laurel. His eyes met hers, and damned if his thoughts weren't reflected right back at him.

"At the risk of Cassie scolding me, I do have work to do today, since we're behind schedule," Laurel said, breaking the heated eye contact that somehow happened between them again. She looked down at his daughter. "But I'd enjoy stopping by for a short time to see your house and give a fairy-attracting consultation. It's the least I can do since your dad fixed up my hand for me."

"Speaking of which, I want to look at it again," Andros said.

"Thanks, but it's healing nicely."

"How did you get your boo-boo?" Cassie lifted up the hand she was holding, still wrapped in a bandage, and examined it with an interest that made Andros smile again. Who knew? Maybe his girl would become a doctor one day, carrying on the family tradition.

"I stabbed it with a potsherd. That's a piece of pottery

that's broken, and we try to find all the pieces so we can put it back together again."

"I'm glad my daddy fixed it for you. He's a good fixer."

"Yes, I've seen that he is." She looked at him again, and the warm admiration in her eyes had him wondering what she saw in his own. "Your food's going to get cold. You go ahead and eat and I'll come down at, what, two o'clock?"

"Park at the clinic, and I'll meet you there. We'll walk around town some and I'll fill you in on a little of its history on the way to our house."

"I'll be there." She patted both children on their heads and walked back to her table, her rear end gorgeously round and sexy in that clingy skirt of hers as she moved across the room.

Pretty oblivious to his lunch as he chewed, he became aware of Cassie jabbing her knife into the meat on her plate, and he quickly cut it for her as his sister softly laughed.

"What?" Though he damned well knew what. That it had been written all over his face, which he'd have to better control when Laurel came to town.

"Looking at her as someone connected to your patients?" Taryn's eyes gleamed with amusement. "Right. More like dessert."

"I want dessert, Mommy. Something really sweet," Petros said.

"Like uncle, like nephew." She chuckled, still looking at Andros with that sisterly smirk firmly in place. "Which means Kastorini's female population has much to fear in another ten years, Petros. Or much to look forward to, depending on your point of view."

Glad that Christina was on call for the clinic, Andros caught up on paperwork in his office. Not very efficiently, though, since he kept seeing Laurel's beautiful face and shapely body in that dress of hers that made him want to skim his hands along its fluid lines. Feel her curves beneath it. Kept interrupting his work and thoughts to walk to the clinic's big front window to see if she had arrived.

Since when did he act like a smitten schoolboy in the throes of his first crush? That first crush was so long ago he could barely recall it, probably because it had been followed by plenty of others before he'd left for school in the US. Even more after he'd arrived there, where the world, and the number of women in it, got a whole lot bigger than his hometown of seven thousand people.

So why had Laurel gotten so thoroughly under his skin, making him feel so oddly restless and itchy? Could it be because he'd spent the past two years showing he was a reformed man? Somehow, he didn't think so. There was some intangible thing about her that, for whatever reason, just called to him like some irresistible siren.

About to go back to his desk, or, more accurately, the desk he shared with his father, he spotted her dusty sedan on the road that rounded the steep curve beyond the bell tower.

And just like that, his chest felt light, his work and the mysterious virus forgotten, his restlessness replaced by focus. On her.

With a sudden pep in his step, he went outside, locking the clinic door behind him. The car nosed into one of the empty parking spaces, and the smile on Laurel's face seemed as carefree as he knew his own was.

He leaned in through the car's open window. "Are you Laurel Evans, fairy consultant?"

"I am." Her beautiful smile made his own widen. "And my fee for attracting fairies is very reasonable."

"What is your fee?"

"I'm still deciding."

The way she looked at him, her eyes a brilliant, sweet, hot blue, practically melted him where he stood, and he struggled against the urge to grab her up, sit in the driver's seat and pull her onto his lap to help her decide real quickly about that fee. Show he was ready and willing to pay up however she wanted him to.

Attracting fairies? Hell, if she attracted them as easily as she attracted him, his house would be overrun with the little things. He leaned closer to her in the hot car, a breath's distance away, her sweet, citrusy scent intensified by the heat of her body. "How long will it take to decide?"

"Hard to say, but I've learned to go with a gut feeling when I get one."

The breath rushed from his lungs and his heart bumped around in some off-kilter rhythm at her words. He knew exactly what he wanted, and from the way she was looking at him, she just might want the same thing. And how was he supposed to resist kissing her to find out? The question flitted into his mind, then promptly right out as, unable to think anymore, he closed the gap between them and kissed her.

Her mouth opened to his, moving, tasting, exploring in an excruciatingly slow dance that weakened his knees. Her kiss was sweet and hot and beyond irresistible. He cupped her cheek in his hand, stroking the fine bones there, the softness of her skin and wisps of hair adding another layer to the overwhelming sensual pleasure. He could feel her response, taste the small breathy gasps that touched his moist lips and sent him deepening the kiss until the loud, grumbling chug of a truck engine cut through his foggy brain.

He pulled his mouth from hers, barely aware of the truck disappearing with a cloud of black smoke puffing behind. Laurel's eyes were half-closed, her lips parted, their panting breaths sounding nearly as loud in the car as the truck had.

A jabbing against his ribs made him realize his torso was just about completely inside her car. He inhaled to catch his breath and clear his mind, thunking his head on the door frame as he extricated himself. A brain shake was probably something he badly needed.

"Ooh." She winced, scrunching up her face in that cute way she had. "That hurt?"

"No." Not nearly as much as stopping kissing her had. Which proved again that the woman was a siren, attracting him with her song and smile until he quit looking where he was headed, crashing on the rocks for all the world to see.

Hadn't he promised himself not to give the town any new gossip material? While getting it on with Laurel was about all he could think of at that moment, in a few weeks she'd be gone. If Cassie had to hear yakking about what a playboy her father still was, asking questions he didn't want to answer to a four-year-old, he'd hate himself for his weakness.

"Just leave your car here." He turned away from the question in her eyes, opening the car door and grasping her elbow with the hope anyone watching would just see it as a cordial gesture. "I'll be your Kastorini tour guide."

"Are you as good a tour guide as you are a doctor?"

"Not sure. You'll have to let me know if I'm good."

The heat and humor that sparked in her eyes made him think of that mind-blowing kiss, shortening his breath all over again. He wondered why he'd said it that way. Must be his subconscious thinking about the crazy chemistry between them.

Strolling the streets with her next to him felt strangely natural and right. Just as he'd felt after they'd been at the hospital in Vlychosia, reaching to hold her hand seemed a lot more normal than resisting it, which he managed only with extreme effort. The air around and between them held an odd tension, an intense awareness, that crackling spark he always felt around her. But at the same time he felt relaxed and comfortable as he told her about the various landmarks in town.

That relaxation diminished when he realized he could feel the curious stares fixed on them from houses they passed and from second-story windows of homes above the various shops. From the grinning men sitting at tables outside tavernas, drinking coffee or something stronger as they heatedly discussed whatever was the subject of the day, and enjoyed watching and talking about anyone who walked by while they were doing it.

He glanced at Laurel and could see she was aware of it too. "Living in a small town is a bit different from living in a big city. Didn't think I'd come back here because of it."

"But here you are." She looked up at him, one blond eyebrow quirked. "So why did you? Aside from the obvious charm of the place?"

She thought it was charming to be stared at? Or was she able to look beyond that to see the generations of history and how it connected all of them in a strong bond of community you couldn't find in a big city?

"Just decided it was time to come back. Take my place as town doctor beside my father." No need to tell her the whole story. How he'd never been sure he wanted that for a lot of reasons, including the embarrassment his parents felt from his actions, and his sister's too. But the sudden situation with Cassie had shown him he needed it.

"Your father is a doctor too? Why haven't I met him?"

"He and my mother have taken advantage of me being back. They're traveling around Great Britain at the moment. Were supposed to come back this week, but decided Ireland had to be added on to the itinerary."

"How long have you been back?"

"Two years. They've been to the States and Canada, on various European tours, and to Iceland since then, believe it or not."

"My parents also loved traveling," she said softly, her eyes instantly wistful and sad, as they had been last time she'd spoken of them. "Most of it for digs without us, but we did have a few great trips to national parks and Washington, DC, and other places they deemed too important for their girls to miss."

"Glad you have those memories with them." Now that he had Cassie, he couldn't imagine leaving her all summer every year, and wondered why Laurel's parents hadn't found a way to take their daughters with them. He let his arm slide around her shoulders to give her a brief, gentle hug. If he couldn't comfort someone in need, then to hell with those watching who might want to make something of it.

"I can see you give Cassie a lot of your time," she said, looking up at him with eyes that weren't quite so sad now. "That you're a good dad."

"I try to be." Wanted to be. And her words were a reminder, again, of why he shouldn't pursue the short but doubtless incredibly sweet time he knew he and Laurel could spend together before she left. "Thanks. Not sure that's always true, but I'm working on it." Working on it damned hard, if resisting the urge to touch her and kiss her counted. He shoved his hands in his pockets. "So here's the edge of town. The stone walls were built all the way down to the beach, complete with small angled cannon openings in the walls to defend against whoever wasn't in possession of the town and fortress at that moment."

"Is that a mosque? It doesn't look like a Greek church."

"It was. Built during Turkish rule. Later used as a school-house, then a taverna, and now it's owned by someone who lives in Athens and comes to stay here occasionally."

He drew her to the outer wall to look down, where its smooth stones ended at the beach far below and swimmers lounged on large, flat rocks tossed among the boulders and slapped by gentle waves. Farther down, colorful fishing boats bobbed at the long wooden dock. "Kastorini never had the same height advantage a lot of walled cities had during the Ottoman Empire, built way up at the top of a mountain, but we had other things going for us. Back in the day, citizens could see any approaching ships from far away on the gulf, and the mountain behind is so steep and prone to rock falls that it was pretty hard for invaders to sneak up on us."

"So your ancestors were likely a mix of Ottomans and Venetians, with a little Byzantine and Turkish spice thrown in with salt and pepper. You're like a finely flavored Greek stew."

"That's very poetic. Greek mutt's probably more accurate."

Her soft laughter, the sparkle in her eyes, filled him with pleasure, and, while he didn't wrap his arm around her again as he wanted to, he moved closer until their shoulders touched.

"This place is just beautiful," she said, gazing around at the curving, narrow streets, the old homes, the arches covered with masses of vivid flowers, her expression warm and admiring. She shifted her attention to the gulf waters and the misty mountains beyond. "It's no wonder you wanted to come back."

"There was a time when I didn't want to. Now that's hard for me to imagine."

"I'm just starting my journey as an archaeologist, ready to travel all over. But I'd be lying if I didn't say it's awfully appealing to think of getting to live here forever. Someday, when I'm ready, I think I'll look to settle in a place like this."

They stood there together for what felt like long, peaceful minutes, watching the brightly colored fishing boats and a large tour boat slice through the sapphire waters of the Gulf of Corinth. Her scent, sweetly mingling with the tumble of flowers nearby, wafted to his nose again. It reminded him of their kiss, how she'd smelled and tasted, and the memory of that sensory overload nearly had him turning to her to do it again.

He curled his fingers into his palms, trying to focus his attention on the boats below. Just as he was about to suggest they move on, she turned to him. "Must be incredible to have this kind of history be a part of who you are," she said. "Studying it, loving it and being drawn to it like I am isn't the same as being a part of it."

"I guess it is. Like anything, you take it for granted sometimes until you're reminded of it." He looked down at her, saw the sincerity in her eyes. Eyes a color close to the mesmerizing blue of the gulf. "You ready to go stir up some Greek fairies?"

"Ready. And I think you've already paid my fee in full, Dr. Tour Guide."

He wasn't going to ask if she meant the tour, or the kiss. And if it was the kiss, he'd be happy to go deep into debt. "Our place is down this street just a short way. Watch your step. These cobblestones will trip you up if you're not—"

"Andronikos!"

Ah, hell. He turned to see his aunt laboring up the street parallel to his. What was she doing in this part of town? "Good afternoon, Thea Stella."

"*Kalispera* to you as well." She folded her arms across her ample bosom and stared at Laurel. "Who's the girl and what's she doing here?"

Always polite, his *thea*. Not. At least she'd spoken Greek, so Laurel wouldn't understand the words. "This is Laurel Evans, from the archaeological dig near Delphi. Laurel, this is my aunt, Stella Chronis."

"Nice to meet you." Laurel extended her hand with a smile, but his aunt just stared suspiciously.

"Hmph. A very pretty one, as usual, Andronikos." His aunt turned dismissively from Laurel, and the rudeness of it nearly had him pointing it out to the woman. Probably best to grit his teeth, though, since Laurel might not have thought much of it, and any comment would just call even more attention to her actions. At least she continued to speak in English instead of completely excluding Laurel from the conversation. "My friend Soula's nephew wants to meet you to talk about medical school."

"I'd be happy to."

"Good. And while you're at it, tell him about your foolish mistakes and how to keep his pants on, Andronikos. Like you are finally doing now." Frowning, she glanced at Laurel. "I hope."

He'd thought he was too old to feel embarrassed about much anymore, but now knew that wasn't true. If only she'd kept speaking in Greek, after all.

Any chance Laurel might be oblivious to what his aunt was referring to? He glanced at her and saw a small smile on her face. Since Stella was as subtle as a sledgehammer, he knew she'd probably figure it out. With his aunt's brows still lowered into a near scowl, she grabbed his face and gave him a kiss on each cheek before trudging up the steep road without a backward glance.

"Andronikos? Is that your full name?" Laurel tilted her head at him as they resumed walking toward his house.

"Yes, after my grandfather. Quite a mouthful. My aunts and mother are the only ones who use it."

"I like it. Andros for warrior and Nike for victory. It suits you."

"You think?"

"I do think." Her beautiful lips curved wider. "So does your aunt feel a need to protect you from women on the hunt?"

So much for hoping she wasn't listening. "Or women from me, maybe. I had a bit of a reputation as a young man. Sorry she was rude to you, but don't take it personally. Stella enjoys being rude to everyone."

"And here I was feeling special."

He had to laugh at that, enjoying the teasing smile in her eyes, glad she wasn't hypersensitive, or thinking less of him after his aunt's remarks. "You are, believe me. I knew that the first day I met you, and you were so stubborn about me treating your hand."

"Stubbornness is a special trait?"

"Never knew I found it attractive until I met you. But combined with beauty, brains and your unique brand of humor? Oh, yeah."

The eyes that met his had a twinkle in them but seemed to be searching too. She didn't have to look hard to see he had a major jones for her, and he didn't know what the hell to do about it, since it appeared to be mutual. Maybe some intimate time together far away from Kastorini or Delphi would burn it out, since that was pretty much his MO anyway. Laurel was leaving soon, so she wouldn't want more than that either, and just thinking about all that made his pulse quicken. "So there's my house, on the right with the—"

"Daddy! Laurel!"

Just as it had every day for the past two years, his heart warmed at the sight of his daughter tearing up the road to meet them, hair and arms flying, leaving the front door wide open behind her. It warmed even more when she flung herself at him, as though it had been days instead of hours since they'd been together.

"*Koukla mou.*" He swung her into his arms, smiling at the excitement in her eyes, wondering how he'd gotten so incredibly lucky to have a daughter with such a sunny, happy nature. "What have you been up to since lunch?"

"Trouble with a capital T."

He heard Laurel laugh, and grinned. "Her usual answer. Gets it from her *papou*. I have a bad feeling that's going to be her answer for the next fifteen years, which strikes fear into her father's heart."

"Don't be scared, Daddy. I'm just kidding!" She wriggled from his arms and grabbed Laurel's hand. "Come on. I want to show you my fairy house."

"Cassie, let's be polite and offer Miss Laurel something to drink first. Didn't your Thea Taryn make lemonade this morning? Let's go inside and ask her for some."

"She's out back with Petros, kicking the football."

"I don't think I can wait that long to see the fairy house, Andros. Mind if we have some after?"

"It's here." Cassie tugged Laurel to the side of the house where a small strip of dirt contained various flowers his mother planted and tended for him.

"These flowers are so pretty!" Laurel turned to him. "Are you a gardener?"

"Can't tell a weed from a flower. When I bought the house, my mother couldn't stand the weedy scrub and planted them."

"My *yiayia* is good with flowers," Cassie said. "She lets me help her grow them."

"I don't know much about flowers, Cassie. Maybe you could teach me some things."

His daughter beamed at the suggestion, pointing at various blooms as she said some plant names. Andros had a feeling she might just be making them up as she went along, and his chest filled with warmth all over again as he looked from her to the woman sniffing blooms and asking questions, pretending she thought Cassie really was an expert.

Laurel's face was lit with a smile as bright as Cassie's, and he could see she'd been an amazing big sister. A sister who'd had to take on becoming their mother. How hard must that have been for her?

"It's good you have your fairy house tucked in among your *yiayia*'s flowers, Cassie. You probably know fairies love flowers. You know what else? They love olive wood too. I found this piece of wood that looks just like a little bed, don't you think?" Laurel pulled it from her purse and Cassie reached for it in awe. "I bet if we find something soft for a mattress, and put a flower petal or pretty leaf on it for a blanket, a fairy will love to come snuggle on it."

"Do you think fairies probably live in the olive groves, then?"

"I bet they do. I bet they're really close by, just waiting for a nice bed inside this nice house."

Seeing the two of them standing close together in front of his home, Cassie plucking flower petals, gave him a strange feeling. Just as he was trying to figure out exactly what it was, a cacophony of voices made him turn. Then stare.

What the hell? Two men were striding fast down the street, one carrying a microphone, the other following with a big camera on his shoulder. Numerous townsfolk were gathered around them, walking, talking and gesturing. Pointing right at him.

"Dr. Drakoulias? Doctor, we've been told there's a mysterious illness in Delphi, and patients came here to your clinic before they got so sick they had to be moved to the hospital in Vlychosia. Is it contagious? Are others in Delphi and here in Kastorini at risk?"

The guy shoved the microphone in his face, and he stepped back, not about to be railroaded into saying something that might trigger public hysteria. "We don't believe anyone is at risk. If you give me your contact information, I'll keep you informed as we know more."

The guy got annoyingly close, with the cameraman right behind him. "Does it have something to do with the archaeological dig? We talked to some of the people working there, and they said it might. And that the dig leader is here with you today." He shifted his attention behind Andros, craning to see around him. Anger swelled in his chest. He'd be damned if the man was going to harass Laurel and possibly scare Cassie.

"Again, I'll keep you informed."

The rude-as-hell jerk shoved past him and stuck the microphone in Laurel's alarmed face. Andros didn't even hear the questions the guy started bombarding her with, he just reacted with instinct. Stepped between them and went nearly nose to nose with him, ready to shove him away from her if he had to.

"Ms. Evans doesn't know any more than you do. Now get off my property." He turned to grasp Laurel's arm and Cassie's hand, hustling them both into the house and away from the media sharks he had a bad feeling had just begun their sniffing around for headline-grabbing blood in the water.

CHAPTER EIGHT

AFTER TALKING ABOUT the media mess with the dig crew for almost an hour, Laurel found herself tuning out the hub-bub of conversation as they sat on the back deck of their hotel, darkness shrouding the misty mountains beyond.

How they could still be rehashing the afternoon's ex-citement with the media showing up to talk to each one of them, she didn't know. Lord knew she was beyond tired of talking about it. The shock of them showing up in front of Andros's house had faded, but she couldn't get out of her head the surprising expression on Andros's face when he'd stepped between her and that reporter. His hard-eyed, angry look and aggressive posture had her wondering if he might actually punch the irritating guy, and she was thankful he'd simply cleared them out of there before she'd had to say much.

Part of her had wanted to tell him she could handle it, but the truth was she'd been all too glad he'd hustled her and Cassie away into his house. It hadn't occurred to her she might be asked about the sick crew members. Thanks heavens she had some time now to think of how she should answer.

The intrusion had ruined what had been an otherwise beautiful day. Spending time with adorable little Cassie had been even more fun than she'd expected, making her feel all warm and fuzzy inside. Helen had been twelve when their parents had died—about to start her teen years. Adorable in her own way, she'd been a little trying at times too. That might be true for Cassie as well, though she couldn't imagine the child being anything but cute as a button.

It struck her with surprise that Helen had been even younger than Cassie when their parents started spending entire summers, rather than just weeks, away. How had they been able to leave her that long? Later leaving all three under Laurel's insufficient care and guidance?

She didn't think she could do that if she ever had children of her own someday, no matter how much she loved her work. Then fiercely shook her head, feeling a bit like a traitor to judge her parents that way. Reminded herself of how they'd both explained they were showing their girls that family life had to be balanced with work life.

Reminded herself how important their work had been to both them and the archaeological world. Reminded herself it was just as important to her, which she'd nearly forgotten today as she enjoyed herself in Kastorini.

Would this sudden media circus create yet another distraction from the job they had to get done with fewer hands and little time? She'd reminded the crew they had to focus, and they'd all agreed. Still, she knew it was human nature to love being on camera and part of a medical mystery, despite worrying about Mel, Tom and John in the midst of it.

Restlessness overcame her, and she stood. "I'm going to my room to plan where everyone will be working tomorrow. Let's get an early start. Be at breakfast at seven a.m., please."

The nods and quick good-nights they sent her way were perfunctory as they kept up the steady yakking, and she shook her head, hoping it didn't continue tomorrow when they had to get digging instead.

In truth, she'd already planned out tomorrow's schedule and decided she needed some fresh air instead of a stuffy room. The street outside the hotel was so dark she could hardly see, and she paused, wondering what might calm this strange unease. Maybe just a long walk around the tiny town of Delphi, even a little mindless shopping she hadn't taken time to do much of, would be enough to help her refocus.

Every store owner competed for the summer tourists, staying open until midnight or later if a single customer was around. One or two shopkeepers stood in their doorways, enthusiastically promising her good prices if she'd just come in and look. Others were busy with customers who had likely earlier toured the ancient sites and the wonderful museum that held the incredibly massive statues, friezes and sphinx. And of course, the stunning bronze Charioteer. That famous Delphi antiquity just might be eclipsed if she could only locate the treasure her parents believed in.

The one they'd died trying to find.

Laurel gave her head another forceful shake and stepped into a jewelry store, wanting to rid herself of thoughts of death and tragedy, of failure and unfinished dreams. At the back of the store, she peered into one of the many open cases of jewelry. A silver necklace reminded her of the one she wore at that moment—the necklace her sisters had given her for her birthday a few years back.

She reached up to grasp it in her hand, glad to have something to think about that made her smile. The three of them had made a massive birthday cake for her, one that ended up flat on one side and such an ugly deep blue they'd all laughed themselves silly over it. But it had tasted good, and it had been a wonderful evening of sisterly togetherness. A lovely memory among so many special moments the four of them had had over the years. A lovely memory among some that were not quite so great. Memories of all the times she'd despaired over her lack of maturity and skill trying to raise them.

A pair of earrings caught her eye and she picked them up, wanting to look more closely at the silver swirls that curled around the stones, thinking they seemed similar to an ancient pattern on a bracelet they'd unearthed at the dig.

"Moonstones help protect you during your travels, I've heard," a deep voice said next to her ear. "Maybe you should get those earrings, since you'll be moving on soon."

She turned to see Andros behind her, but of course she'd known it was him. Even if she hadn't recognized his voice, every nerve in her body had, tingling and quivery and instantly alert to his nearness. Just as they had been earlier in Kastorini, when flirting with him had been so much fun, even as she'd told herself she shouldn't. When touching and kissing him had been at the forefront of her mind even as she'd been fascinated by the history of the place.

"What are you doing here?"

"Hoping to find you. Wondered if the media had harassed you anymore."

"Thankfully, no. And I don't need the moonstones quite yet."

"I thought maybe that had changed. That maybe you'd be closing down the dig sooner rather than later."

"Why would I?" She stared into his eyes, dark and serious, with a touch of something else. Puzzlement? Frustration? "I'm here until the funding ends and the university tells me I have to leave."

"Do you really want to have to deal with all the media

questions now? They might not have followed you here tonight, but I promise they'll be up on the mountain, hounding you."

"I can handle it. I'm not afraid of them. Speaking of which, while I appreciate the gesture, I didn't need you to rescue me today." Didn't need it, maybe, but hoped he didn't know how much she'd been glad of it.

"I know you didn't. Just didn't want him scaring Cassie."

The way his lips curved showed that was a lie, and that he probably knew she'd been lying too. She found herself smiling back. "Got to admit, he was pretty scary."

"I do have one question."

"That sounds ominous."

"Why? Why don't you just be done with it, so you don't have to worry about whether the illness has to do with the dig or worry about the damned reporters swarming around?" His hands moved to cup her face, tilting it up as he moved closer, practically torso to torso. "Surely after five years of excavating here, it can't matter much one way or the other if you close it down now or two weeks from now."

"We don't know what amazing artifact we still might find, just like we don't know anything about Mel and Tom and John and why they got sick. I…okay, I can't deny it worries me. But since we don't know if it had anything to do with the dig, I can't justify completely closing it."

He just kept staring at her, and, despite the unsettling, irksome conversation, Laurel found she couldn't move away from his touch. From the heat of his chest so close to hers. Couldn't stop her gaze from slipping from his eyes to the oh-so-sensual shape of his lips and back. What was it about this man that shook up her libido so completely?

"Until I met you, I'd always figured archaeologists

to be easygoing, steady academics who analyzed facts," he said.

"And the facts are…?"

"Three sick people with similar symptoms. Cause unknown."

"Those are pretty vague facts, if you could even call them that. I wouldn't have a chance at any kind of grant if I told them a dig site was kind of like another dig site, but I didn't really have any idea what might be found there or why."

His lips curved slightly again as he shook his head. "Who knew your head was as hard as the rocks you've unearthed?"

"Is that a compliment?"

The smile spread to his eyes, banishing the deep seriousness, and Laurel found herself relaxing and smiling too, in spite of everything. She didn't want to have to defend herself and her decisions and her goals to anyone, least of all this man she couldn't deny sent a zing with a capital Z through every part of her body whenever he was near.

Like now. Very, very near.

His lips touched her forehead, lingered, and, surprised at the deep pleasure she felt from just that simple touch, Laurel let her eyes drift closed until he dropped his hands and drew back. "If you won't listen to logic, at least let me buy you the earrings. Maybe they'll help you remember Delphi, and keep you safe on your travels into that damned cave."

"Not a good idea."

"Why? You afraid I'll expect a thank-you kiss?"

His expression was teasing and serious at the same time, and at his mention of a kiss Laurel's gaze dropped right to his mouth. She wasn't sure she should tell him about moonstone lore, but just as she decided that would be a bad idea the words came out in a near whisper. "Because for thousands of years, people have believed moonstones are a channel for passion and love from the giver to the receiver. A talisman for secret love. Carnal love. Can't risk igniting the power of a moonstone, can we?"

The scorching blaze that instantly filled his eyes weakened her knees, so it was a good thing his strong hands grasped the sides of her waist, pulling her flush against him. Everything about him seemed hot—that look in his eyes, the breath feathering across her lips, every inch of his body touching hers.

"I don't know. Can we? Seems like something's ignited even without the stones."

Whew, boy. Her body answered, *Oh, yes, we can, and right now, please*, while her brain tried not to short-circuit any more than it already was. She opened her mouth to say something—what, she wasn't sure—when she realized the shopkeeper had come to stand next to them.

"Welcome, welcome. May I assist you?" he said in a loud, robust voice. "Would you like a price for one or more of our fine pieces of jewelry?"

They both turned, and Andros dropped his hands from her. She should have welcomed the interruption to help her gather her wits, but really wanted to tell the guy to go away so they could get back to the steamy conversation that made her breathless. "No, thank you," she said. "I was just looking."

"Mister? Surely you wish to buy the beautiful miss something as beautiful as she is. At the best prices, you understand."

"We're still deciding if it's worth the risk. Thanks anyway," Andros said, his lips quirking as he looked at her, but that barely contained blaze that still smoldered in his eyes had her quivering all over again.

The man looked perplexed at Andros's answer, and

kept peppering them with questions and various offers as they made their way out of the store, shouting after them to be sure to return for 'the better price' than the original ones he'd been offering.

Andros's arm was around her back, her waist again cupped in his hand as they walked to the darkest end of the street. It curved around in a U-turn to the adjacent street full of more tavernas and shops, but Andros stopped next to a stone retaining wall, beneath tall, arching shrubs that grew from behind it.

He pulled her into his arms, flashing a smile that practically lit up the dark corner he'd finagled them to. "It's not helping, you know."

She had a pretty good idea what he was talking about, but said instead, "What's not helping?"

She could feel his hands splay open on her back, pressing her close, as his warm mouth touched her cheek, moved over to her ear, giving it a tiny lick. "Not having the moonstone. Don't need that to feel a powerful desire for you. To want to share some passion with you. I've been fighting it since the second I met you, but it's been a losing battle."

The low rumble of his voice, along with the little kisses he kept placing against her ear, her neck, her cheek, managed to narrow her entire universe down to those singular sensations. She let her hands slip up his wide chest, outlining his hard pectorals as she went, gratified to feel his muscles twitch and bunch beneath her touch.

She turned her face to give him access to her other cheek, because she liked the breathless feeling it gave her and wanted more of it. Apparently amused at that, he chuckled as he softly kissed every inch of sensitive skin on that side as well.

"I don't have time to…to get involved with you." Proud of herself that she'd managed to remember that, she tipped her head back as his tongue explored the hollow of her throat.

"I know. And I can't risk getting involved with you."

"Risk?" Risk? What did that mean?

"Never mind." His mouth moved in a shivery path up her throat until it was soft against her lips. "This isn't involvement, right? Just friendship."

That startled a little laugh out of her, and she felt his lips smile against hers. "Yes. Friendship with benefits."

And then he kissed her for real. Softly at first, then harder and deeper. Dizzy from the pleasure, she moved her hands up from his chest to cling to his shoulders. There were some firm, taut muscles right there, perfectly placed for her to hold on to so she could stay on her feet and not melt into a small hot puddle on the still-steamy blacktop.

One wide hand slid farther up her back to gently cup her nape, his warm fingers slipping into the hair against her scalp that had loosened a bit from her ponytail. She thought her heart might pound right out of her chest at the thrilling barrage of every sensation he'd managed to make her feel in a matter of minutes—hot, weak, strong and slightly delirious.

A sound of need came from one of them, a little moan from one moist mouth to the other, with an answering gasp in return. The kiss got a little wilder as he pressed her so close, she felt her body mold completely with his. In the foggy recesses of her brain, a bizarrely wild sound filled her ears, and for a moment she feared it had come from her. Then realized with relief that it hadn't, that, somehow, they were surrounded by a cacophony of cat meows.

Andros seemed unaffected, kissing her with a single-minded focus that weakened her knees all over again, until the crescendo of sound was so distracting, she was finally able to break the kiss to look around.

"What in the world is that?"

His eyes, glittering through the darkness, met hers with heat and humor. When he answered, the sound was breathless and amused. "Feral cats. They're everywhere in Greece. Haven't you noticed?"

"They've stared at us and walked around while we ate dinner on the outdoor patios here, but I guess I didn't realize. Thought they were pets of the owners." Still caught close in his arms, she turned to the tangle of shrubs next to them, astonished to see a nearly uncountable number of eyes staring at them luminously through the darkness. Big, small, up close and hiding deeper in the greenery; she couldn't imagine how many there must be.

"Greeks have a love of animals. And also can turn a blind eye to their needs sometimes as well, unfortunately. But many do feed the strays, when they can." He loosened his hold on her to dig something from his pocket, tossing it to the cats, then tossing more of it deeper into the thicket. The mad scramble that ensued made Laurel's heart hurt for the poor hungry creatures.

"Are they never neutered?"

"Just by a few of us. Our secret, though."

She looked up at him, so impressed at his caring. At his warmth, which he'd now shown her extended to all creatures, great and small. "Our secret. Though I didn't know you had surgical skills, too."

"I have many mad skills you don't know about." Their eyes met and held, and it was all there, swirling between them. The intimate smiles, the banked-down heat, the connection that made her feel as if she knew the man so much better than she possibly could after only days.

Had she ever felt such a strange, sensual connection

with any other man? As soon as the question came, she knew the answer.

Never.

"It's good that you help little creatures. Back at home, we—"

The harsh ring of his phone made them both jump. The instant he looked at its screen, a deep frown replaced every bit of the heat and humor that had been there before.

"Ah, hell." His gaze lasered in on hers for a moment before he took a few strides away to answer. "Di. What's the matter?"

The second she heard who it was, her gut clenched. The man wouldn't be calling on a Sunday night to catch up on the weather.

Her breath seemed to completely stop, and her hands went cold as she watched his expression get grimmer with each passing second. Finally he turned to her, and she found herself praying.

"Andros. Please don't tell me…Mel and Tom…" She gulped, not able to finish the sentence.

He reached for her hands and held them tight. "It's John. They're doing everything they can, but Di felt we should know. He's taken a turn for the worse."

CHAPTER NINE

"JOHN IS SICKER?"

The blue eyes staring up at him were wide and worried. Her hands had tightened on his so hard, her short nails dug into his skin. "The breathing machine is having trouble compensating for the pneumonia in his lungs, getting him enough oxygen. But they're giving him the best care they can." He'd known John's condition was becoming more precarious but hadn't seen any reason to alarm her more than necessary.

"What about Mel and Tom?"

"They're getting better every day." He stroked her back, hoping to soothe. "They're going to be fine, and hopefully John will come around too."

"Thank God." Her stiff posture seemed to relax just a little and she dropped her head to his chest, wrapping her arms loosely around his back. "I have to tell everyone he's worse. I have to give them a choice about whether they want to work at the site anymore. I still can't imagine they got sick from the dig, for all the reasons we've talked about. But who knows?"

"Wouldn't it end your stress to just shut it down, like I said before? Let your people go on home? You wouldn't have to worry about someone else getting ill or the media badgering you."

"I can't this second. Have to think. I don't expect you to understand."

No, he didn't understand, but now wasn't the time to get on at her about it. Not when she was feeling so upset and anxious. "I'll come talk to your crew with you. Explain his condition and answer any more questions they might have."

"Thank you. I'd...I'd appreciate that."

She slipped from his hold in what seemed like slow motion, as though it was a supreme effort. He was glad she didn't feel she had to shoulder the entire burden of talking to everyone about John's health.

They walked back to the hotel, silent but for the sounds of their feet on the pavement, the breeze rustling leaves in the trees, the mewls from hidden cats. The hotel seemed equally silent, and Laurel led him through a few cavernous rooms toward a door that led to a deck. Through the floor-to-ceiling windows, it was obvious even in the low light that the deck was empty.

"When I left awhile ago, they were all back here." She nudged open the door, and he followed her outside. The deck spanned the distance along the entire back of the hotel, but the only visible people were a couple in an embrace at the far end.

"Maybe they went to a bar. Or to bed, since I told them we'd be getting an early start."

"You want me to come back in the morning to talk with them then?"

"That's sweet of you, but no." She shook her head. "It's part of my job, though if he's any better in the morning, I'd really appreciate it if you tell me early."

"I admire that you're serious about your job and your responsibilities. Taking care of your sisters." He reached for her, stroked his hands up and down her soft arms. Soft, yet strong, just like her. "You step up to any task forced on you, no matter how difficult."

"Doesn't everybody?"

"No." Quite a few had doubted he could step up when he'd found out about Cassie. "You have a lot to be proud of, Laurel."

The eyes that lifted to his were somber. "Not enough. Not yet."

He wondered what she meant, but when he opened his mouth to ask, got sidetracked completely when she suddenly twined her arms around his neck, pressed her soft curves against him. Pressed her sweet mouth to his.

Her lips plied his, gentle yet insistent. A controlled kiss, but with a slight desperation to it he knew came from her fears for the Wagners, the stress of the dig, the worry of John's worsening illness. Of her parents' deaths just a mile from where they stood. He could sense all of it, feel all of it, as though their hearts and minds had melded together along with their lips, and he hurt for her. Wanted to erase some of that hurt as best he could.

He let his hands roam down her back, to the curve of her waist, found them sliding farther south to grasp the round, firm globes of her rear, pressing her against his hardness. He'd wanted to touch her like this, hold her like this, every time they'd been near to one another, every time they'd kissed. The feel of her was everything he'd known it would be, and it was all he could do to not let his hands explore more of her. Tug the straps of her dress down her arms to cup the small mounds beneath, learn their sweet shape. Help her forget anything but this moment.

Her fingers slid to the sides of his neck, into his hair, making him shiver, sending his pulse ratcheting even higher. He knew he had to get control of himself before he lowered her into one of the deck chairs and made love to her right there under the stars.

It took Herculean effort to pull his mouth from hers and suck in a deep breath. "Don't think either of us wants to be caught out here by your dig crew or, God forbid, somebody working at this hotel who lives in Kastorini. Or, best of all, media types back for another interview and photo op." And wasn't that a hell of an understatement?

"Then let's go to my room."

His heart jolted hard at her words at the same time every muscle in his body tightened, ready to grab her hand and head there at a dead run. "Laurel. I want you. Which I'm sure you know. But not when you're hurting. Not when you might regret it tomorrow."

"I won't regret it. Just tonight. Just this once." She cupped his face in her hands. "I can't let myself be distracted from what has to get done at the dig. But right this minute I don't want to think, I just want to feel. Not feel alone, but feel good. With you. Which, if I'm honest, I've wanted to do since we first met."

"Laurel." His hands tightened on her behind, which pressed her pelvis tighter against him. He nearly groaned. All he wanted was to make her feel good. But would he be taking advantage of a weak moment? The same way he'd often thoughtlessly done, not all that long ago?

"Andros." There was a flicker of slightly amused impatience in her eyes when she said his name in return. Her hands slipped to his chest as she took a half step back. "I'm not a wilting violet you need to look out for or worry about, if that's the problem. I'm strong, and I've been on my own a long time now. You have about five seconds to say, 'yes, that sounds great' or 'no, thanks.' So which is it?"

A surprised chuckle escaped him. The woman standing in front of him definitely wasn't a needy, weepy, sad soul. She was fire and light, toughness and softness, and he was the luckiest man alive that she wanted to be with him tonight.

"Yes, that sounds great."

Her response was to grasp his hand and tug him along behind her through the foyer, up three flights of stairs and into a tiny room. He shut the door behind him and leaned against it, wanting to give her one more chance to change her mind. One more moment to decide if this was really what she wanted tonight.

When she turned to him, the desire that shone in her eyes reflected his own. He took a deliberate step toward her, keeping it slow and easy, giving her just a little more time. A little more space.

"Something about the way you're moving toward me reminds me of a lion on the hunt," she said, taking an equally slow step as the gap between them closed from four feet to three.

"And something about the way you're moving makes me think of a siren. Sending me out of my mind. Making me crazy. Which has occurred to me more than once, by the way."

"Has it?" Another step brought her close enough to touch. Her fingers reached for his shirt buttons, began flicking them open one by one, and his heart thudded thickly in his chest in response. "I never thought of being a siren, until I met you. What if I confessed that, the moment I saw you on the mountain, you made me think of a warrior god? Maybe even Apollo himself."

His laugh morphed into a low moan as her hands slid across his skin to spread open his shirt, her fingertips caressing his nipples. "Oh, yeah?"

"Yeah."

"I don't think I have much in common with Apollo."

"Are you sure? I can think of several things."

If his self-discipline hadn't already disintegrated, it would have at the way she was looking at him, smiling at him, touching him. "Such as? I'm not musical, never shot an arrow in my life and can't claim to be a prophet."

His stomach muscles hardened, along with notable other parts of his body, when her hands tracked down his skin to unbutton his pants. "You're a healer, right? Not to mention you seem to create heat and light whenever I'm around you. And as for physical beauty, you—"

"Okay, enough of this torture." He swept her hands aside, lifting his fingers to the thin straps of her dress. "Part of me wants to let you keep going, so I won't have to wonder if I'm taking advantage of you. But that concern is dwarfed by wanting to give you what you asked for." He slipped the straps down her arms. "Which is to just feel."

"Believe me, touching your skin is a good way for me to just feel."

"I have a better way. And can't wait another second to see *your* physical beauty, which I've fantasized about for days." He reached behind her, unzipped her dress. Slid it down the length of her body until it pooled at her feet, and he could see her luminous skin. He smiled at the paleness of her belly compared to her tanned arms and legs. Swept his fingertips across her stomach and over her white bra, lingering at her hardened nipples. "I like your archaeologist's version of a farmer's tan."

She gave a breathless laugh. "No time to sunbathe at the pool. Sorry."

"I love it. It's just like you. A woman of contrasts, all light and dark." He kissed her throat, moved his tongue down her delicate collarbone. "Soft." He slowly moved down over her bra to take that tempting nipple into his mouth through the fabric. "And hard."

Her hands grasped his head again, holding him against her. He reveled in the little gasping sounds she made as he moved from one breast to the other, dropping to his knees to softly suck on her belly. The scent of her arousal surrounded him, so delicious he groaned as he pressed his mouth over the silky fabric covering her mound, moistening it even more.

"Come back...up here." Her voice was a little hoarse as she grasped his arms, tugging.

He wanted to stay exactly where he was for a while longer, but he was here to make her feel good. Do what pleased her, what made her happy. He stood and flicked off her bra, thumbed her panties down her legs at the same time she shoved his pants to his ankles. Kicking them off along with his shoes, he took her into his arms and kissed her, backing her toward the bed.

He broke the kiss to flick back the covers. When he looked at her, standing there gloriously naked, he realized there was one more thing he needed to see. He reached around to her ponytail, gently tugging at the elastic band there. "I want to see your hair down. I want to see it spread over you, feel it touching my skin."

A sensuous smile curved her lips and she reached behind to pull off the band, dragging her fingers through her hair as she brought it over her shoulders to cover her breasts, her pink nipples peeking out of the silken strands.

He touched its softness, stroking from her ears down over her breasts, and could barely speak at how beautiful she was. "I've wondered how you'd look. It's better than any of my fantasies. Just like etchings of beautiful sirens rendering men helpless with one glance."

"I hope you're not helpless." She reached for him, and he picked her up to lay her on the bed. Touched her and kissed her, wanting to give her the pleasure she deserved.

The little sounds she made nearly drove him wild, and he lay on top of her to feel all of her skin against all of his. Then suddenly froze in horror.

"I don't have a condom." *Damn it to hell.* "But I can still make you feel good."

"Well, I, um, I bought some recently. Just in case, you know?" She looked at him with an adorably embarrassed expression before leaning over to rummage in her purse, handing him one. A breath of relief whooshed from his lungs.

"Smart, beautiful, responsible and even resourceful. A woman a man can only dream of." He took care of the condom as fast as possible, because he couldn't wait another second to join with her, holding her close, slipping inside her moist heat with a groan.

They moved together, their eyes locked, and the universe narrowed to that one moment, skin to skin, breath to breath, soul to soul. Seeing her lying there, her beautiful hair billowing all across the pillow, his name on her lips, sent him over the edge. Watching her eyes, darkened with bliss, hearing and seeing her fall with him, was a moment he knew he wouldn't forget if he lived a thousand years.

Laurel stared at the pastel pink-and-blue sky, the morning sun still low over the mountains beyond their Delphi hotel. How was it possible to have so many different balls of emotions rolling all around in her stomach at the same time?

Last night, she and Andros had been lying bonelessly sated and content, skin to skin and heart to heart, when his phone had rung. A call that had obliterated every ounce of pleasure, delivering the shocking, unbelievable news that John had passed away.

Her throat and eyes filled with tears as that terrible tragedy, that horrible reality, took precedence over everything. When she'd called a late meeting to somehow tell everyone about his tragic death, the horror on their faces had been every bit as intense as her own.

Those other balls rolling around were from grief and fear. Worry and anxiety. John's death likely wasn't connected to the dig, but it was still a terrible, heavy loss. A loss that added to her determination to finish what she'd come here to do. Finish the work her parents had died for. And now John too.

She swallowed hard at the sickly churning in her stomach as she waited for the dig crew to show up again. She'd asked them to meet with her again after breakfast to give them options. A breakfast she hadn't joined them for, since she doubted she could get one bite of food down anyway.

John. Dead. How was it possible? She still couldn't wrap her brain around it.

And was that going to be Mel and Tom's fate as well? "No," she said out loud, fiercely. Willing it to be true. Praying for it. Andros had promised her they would be fine.

Somehow, the thought calmed her stomach and helped her breathe slightly easier.

"Laurel. Are Mel and Tom…still okay?"

She looked up to see Becka hobble into the room on her crutches, looking pale and upset. Worried. As they all did, now filing quietly behind her to lower themselves into the mismatched crowd of overstuffed chairs and sofas, their faded fabrics showing varying degrees of wear.

"Yes, they're okay. Apparently anyway. Dr. Galanos told me they'll likely be released soon, which would be wonderful. I…I need to talk to them, find out what their plans are." Did their plans include coming back to the dig? Or going home? Certainly, after what they'd been through, no one could blame them for doing exactly that.

As she was interim team leader, the painful job of contacting John's family had fallen to Laurel. Tears welled in her throat again as she remembered their stunned silence, then bewildered and disbelieving questions. Then a near hysteria of grief and pain that had cracked her heart in two.

Did it make her weak and pitiful that she'd been beyond relieved to finally be done with her deliverance of the shocking news, passing the phone to Andros to further explain and try to comfort? Probably, yes. But with her own memories of receiving the nightmare call about her parents forever burned into her heart and mind, it was all she could do to maintain her composure. To not begin sobbing with them, which would have just made it all the worse for John's family.

Laurel drew in a deep breath, swallowed again at the threatening tears. She looked at the dig team—her team—perched or sprawled on the chairs, and realized two were missing. "Where are Jason and Sarah?"

"Jason's coming in a minute," Becka said. "He's feeling a little sick to his stomach. Because, you know..."

Becka's voice faded away as a few team members looked down at the floor. Yes, they all knew. Jason had become good friends with John over the past months, even though the college boy had been seven years younger than John. Almost like a big brother to the young man, Laurel supposed, and her chest pressed in even tighter at the thought.

"Sarah didn't answer her phone when I called to ask if she was ready," one of the girls said. "Probably still in the shower or something. Or maybe she, you know, needed a little more time to compose herself."

Laurel understood. She wished she had more time, too.

"Well, let's go ahead and get started." Laurel braced herself to ask what she had to ask. Knew their answers might well mean working with a thin crew, and she'd simply have to put in even more hours on her own. In fact, she might prefer that. No matter how much she wanted to find the artifact, she couldn't feel good about possibly putting others at risk for it.

"This is a devastating thing for all of us," she said. "John was not only an enthusiastic, hardworking person, he knew a lot about archaeology after volunteering on so many digs the past few years. We'll miss him as a friend. And we'll miss him as a teammate."

All eyes on her, they sat silently, two of the girls sniffing back tears. Laurel dug her fingers into her palms, kept her eyes away from the anguish on the girls' faces, and forged on. "No one knows why John died. What he had, or where he got it, or even if it could possibly have been contagious. If it was the same thing as the Wagners or not. Dr. Galanos said the hospital is working to find out, but we just don't have those answers yet. So I must give you all the option of deciding whether or not you still want to be part of this dig."

"I do," Becka said instantly. "If it was contagious, we'd already have been exposed anyway, right? I feel fine, and it seems to me everyone else does too. What's the point of quitting now, when we're so close to the end? I mean, I found those cool coins just last week, and the day before Sarah found those amazing ivory feet, just like the ones in the Delphi museum! Think what else we still might find!"

Becka's impassioned plea lifted the weight in Laurel's chest ever so slightly and she managed a smile. "Thank you, Becka. Though you have to take a few more days off until your leg has had time to heal. I'm not asking you all to decide this minute. I'll be working on the mountain as soon as we're done here, and possibly in the cave as well. Those who want to join me are welcome, so long as you understand there may be a risk involved, and you're willing to take that risk. Any of you end up deciding you want to pack it in and schedule flights home, I completely understand and support your decisions."

Just by watching them, seeing who made eye contact with whom and what expressions they wore, made it fairly easy to figure out who wanted to go and who would stay. And who could blame them? No matter how few hands would be left, though, she had to keep believing there was still a chance to finish what she had come to do.

"Talk it over with one another. Feel free to take the day off, then sleep on it," she advised them. "You can let me know in the morning, and we'll go from there."

As she looked at the uncertain faces, her whole body felt a little numb, but jittery and anxious as well, and she knew the antidote was work. Give them time and space without them feeling as if she was hovering around to coerce them, or judge them. Last thing she'd want would be for someone to stay on from guilt. Shorthanded or not, everyone still working tomorrow needed to feel as passionate about the project as Becka did.

"I'm heading up, if anyone wants to go. If you decide to come later, you'll find me at the mountain excavation first."

She swung up her day pack, and Becka followed her to the stairwell. "Let me tell Jason you're ready to leave. I'll be right back."

Laurel's lips twisted a little that the only person still for sure on board was handicapped with a bandaged-up leg and couldn't work for days. She closed her eyes and lifted her face skyward. "Any way you two know where it is? Don't angels have special powers? I need your help, here."

"You talking to the ceiling, or yourself?"

She opened her eyes to see the dark chocolate gaze of the man she'd gotten to know, oh so intimately the night before. They were serious eyes, questioning. As he walked across the wide foyer, bronzed and strong and so gorgeous, the utter male beauty of him stole her breath.

That jittery nervousness in her stomach faded away to a feeling of warmth.

Which was dangerous. If this attraction had been a distraction she couldn't afford before, she could afford it even less now.

"Just talking to my parents," she said, keeping her voice light so he wouldn't read too much into it. "Hoping for some divine intervention."

Sympathy joined the other emotions in his eyes as he came to stand in front of her. His hands stroked her arms, slowly, softly, soothingly as they had last night. "Find any?"

"No luck so far. Guess I'm on my own."

"No. Not on your own." He pressed his lips to her forehead, and she found herself briefly closing her eyes, finding that simple touch also seemed to leach away some of her stress. "I'm here to help. Starting with talking to your crew if they have questions."

"Thank you." Their eyes met, and the reassuring touch of his hands on her arms made her wish it were that easy. That poor John hadn't died, that she wasn't beyond short-handed, that she wouldn't likely have to spend time away from the dig getting the Wagners settled back in Delphi or heading home, whichever they wanted. That anyone deciding to stay wouldn't be risking their health. That she wasn't facing imminent failure at what she'd wanted so much to accomplish. "They didn't say much. It might be good if you talked to them now. Maybe they'd feel more free to say or ask things with me out of the room."

"All right." He gave her arms a squeeze. "I don't have clinic appointments until nine. If—"

"Laurel! Laurel!"

They both turned to see Becka limping down the stairs, grabbing the handrail as she stumbled in her hasty decent. Panic was etched on her face, and an echo of it filled

Laurel too, making her stomach clench. What could possibly be wrong now?

Andros leapt up a few steps to grasp Becka's arm. "Steady now, before you fall."

"Oh, thank God you're here, Dr. Drakoulias!" The girl clutched at him. "It's Jason. He's really sick. I think—" She gulped down a little sob. "I think he has what the Wagners have. And…and John. Oh, God, what are we going to do?"

CHAPTER TEN

LAUREL SAT IN the dirt on the side of the baking mountain, bagging and labeling potsherds, barely paying attention as she did. Wondering why she was even bothering.

It was over. Finished. She wasn't going to prove her parents' theory. She wasn't going to get their names in archaeological journals one last time, and her own too, to jump-start her belated, fledgling career. Probably wouldn't even receive the grant she'd wanted so badly, enabling her to get going on a project of her own. One that would inch her toward accomplishing at least an iota of what her parents had accomplished by her age.

How could they have died for nothing? Why couldn't their last excavation have been worth more than potsherds and jewelry and artifacts that, while interesting, were similar to all those already unearthed in Delphi?

She'd wanted that for them. For herself, and for her sisters, giving them a small feeling of peace over her parents' passing. And now? Now she had to wonder if this work, their work, had been worth the very high cost.

Worth all the summers they'd had only a long-distance relationship with their girls. All the times Laurel had tried to play parent, while they had dug for history. Worth the hole left in their family that had started to form even before they'd died.

She swiped her dusty hands across her wet cheeks. John's family would be feeling the same emptiness, wondering why and for what, and her chest felt even heavier.

So often when digging, she could feel the spirits of the ancient people who'd lived there, hear them speaking, see them cooking in a vessel they'd unearthed, or wearing the jewelry they'd found. Sometimes it even felt as though the hand of fate was guiding her, showing her exactly where an artifact might be, drawing her there. But today the mountain was silent.

She pushed to her feet and looked into one of the wide, deep pits. The one that had been painstakingly re-excavated after her parents had been crushed by its walls. Her throat got so tight she could barely squeeze out the words. "So this is it, Mom, Dad. This is the best I could do, and I know it's not nearly enough. Not what you would have expected of me. I'm sorry."

She gathered up the few bags, walked the worn goat path to her car and cleaned up before driving to the hospital in Vlychosia. Andros had arranged for Jason to be transported there, and, no matter how much it hurt, she owed the living more than she owed the dead. Starting with Jason, to see how he was and see if there was anything she could do to help. Then talking with Mel and Tom to tell them the dig was over. To ask what she could do for them as well.

She peeked into Mel and Tom's hospital room, surprised they weren't there, and a jolt of alarm went through her, sending her quickly back out of the room. Had they gotten worse? Were they back in the ICU?

Heart pounding, she practically ran down the hall, trying to find someone she could ask. She spotted two men in doctors' coats about to round a corner, one with thick dark hair, a sculpted jaw and a muscular frame, and knew without a doubt who it was. "Andros!"

He stopped and turned, spoke to the man with him, then moved in her direction. She jogged toward him, breathless. "Where are Mel and Tom? They're not worse, are they?"

"No, no. They're fine." He cupped her face in his warm palm for a moment before sliding it down to her shoulder. "In fact, they're being released. I was going to drive them back to the hotel after all the paperwork's done."

She took a deep breath of relief. "What about Jason?"

"Not sure yet, but so far not worse. He's getting good nursing care, so let's hope for the best." He looked at his watch. "How about a cup of coffee? They won't be ready to go for maybe another hour."

She didn't know if coffee would lift her spirits or jangle her nerves even more. Regardless, being with Andros would be the one thing sure to help her feel at least marginally better.

The coffee shop was surprisingly large, but the tables were tiny, their knees bumping against one another's beneath it. He reached for her hand, and his warm strength felt so comforting, she twined her fingers within his.

"You talked to the dig crew, right?" he asked.

"Yes. I told them to make their travel plans to go home."

"Good." His brows were pinched together in a small frown as his thumb absently stroked up and down hers. "We want them to wait a few days before getting on a plane. Or being close to other people. Quarantined, basically. And I also want blood tests from everyone. If no one else gets sick, you can all go."

"You did blood tests for the Wagners and John. You know it wasn't a fungal infection."

"We're looking at other possibilities. With John dead and three others sick, the national infection-control folks are involved. We'll be doing a battery of tests this time, a viral serology panel, looking for emerging infections.

Something we maybe haven't seen before. Takes a long time to determine something that complicated, though, so I don't expect we'll know anything for a while yet."

His tone was as serious as his expression, and she realized it was a very good thing she'd shut down the dig. The pain she felt over not achieving her dream, her parents' dream, would be far worse if anyone else got sick. "It seems impossible that all this has something to do with the dig. But I know my parents wouldn't want anyone else to die trying to accomplish what they didn't have a chance to."

"Plenty's been achieved in the last five years of that dig, Laurel. Right? What more could there be to accomplish?"

She felt the supportive hold of his hand in hers, looked at the sincerity in his eyes, the caring, and nearly told him. But her lips closed and she shook her head. Even now, with the dig ending, she found she couldn't. Why, she wasn't sure, but it just seemed she should still keep the secret her parents had held close. "You never know. That's what makes you keep digging."

"I just realized I don't even know where you call home. I'd like to know, so when I think of you I can picture you there."

Home? Did she have such a thing anymore?

She'd been so consumed with everything that had happened, she hadn't even thought about leaving here in a few days. About not seeing him again. But the low, husky voice, the serious dark depths of his eyes, put that reality front and center. Added another layer of weight to her heart.

"Indiana. After my parents died, the only digs I worked on had to be close to where we lived, studying proto-historic Caborn-Welborn culture. But I recently sold the house, since my sisters don't need a place to roost any-more. And because I hope to head to Turkey soon, making that home for a while." If she could get the funding, which would be tough going, now. And why didn't that thought bother her as much as it had just last week? Must be the depressing reality of everything that had happened since.

"Protohistoric what?" His eyes crinkled at the cor-ners, and just looking at his beautiful features caught her breath. "That's all Greek to me."

Trust him to somehow make her smile, and he did too, just before he leaned across the tiny table and kissed her. Long and slow and sweet, and when he pulled back, the eyes that met hers weren't smiling anymore.

"If you think this thing might be contagious and that some of us might have it, you shouldn't be kissing me, you know." She was trying to lighten the moment, but her chest felt even heavier, knowing it just might be their last kiss anyway.

"Too late. But even if it wasn't, it's worth the risk."

Worth the risk? Her heart fluttered, and she thought of the moonstones, and their teasing about them. Wished maybe she'd gotten them after all, to remember him by.

As though she needed anything to help her with that.

"Andros."

They looked up to see Dr. Galanos standing there. "The Wagners are ready to go. I've arranged for them and the whole crew to stay in quarantine here. Getting it ready now, and it should be comfortable enough. Which of you is going to get the Wagners' things from Delphi and bring back the rest of the dig crew?"

"I am." Laurel stood and, with a tightness squeezing her chest, braced herself for goodbye. "Thanks for all you've done for us, Andros."

"Your car won't fit everybody. I'll help drive the crew back here."

"Thank you." Only a couple more hours before she didn't get to look at him anymore. Until they said good-bye one last time.

Their days in quarantine had seemed to drag on forever, and Laurel was glad it was finally over. Relieved that not a single team member had shown any symptoms at all. Beyond relieved that Jason had improved so much, they'd agreed to release him and let him go back to the States with them.

Andros had stopped in once, apparently meeting with Dr. Galanos. She and the Wagners had filled their time going through all the dig notes, writing summaries and outlines of the papers they'd publish, but it still hadn't been enough distraction for her to not hope it was Andros every time someone came in the room. For her to hope he'd stop in one more time to say goodbye.

But, really, why should he? It was a long drive from Kastorini, he'd likely been busy at the clinic, and it wasn't as though they were anything more than passing friends. Briefly lovers, though that fleeting moment was etched in her mind far more clearly than any other love affair she'd experienced.

She and the Wagners walked to the car to pack it up before they left for the airport to go home. It struck her that the word *home* felt hollow, just as it had when Andros had asked where she'd lived. What was there for her, other than her short-term teaching-assistant position? Finishing up the final pieces to her PhD?

Somehow, she had to get that grant for the dig she'd been so enthusiastic about just months ago. The dig she knew her parents would have been proud she'd pursued.

With any luck, she could find some success with that and push past this strangely restless emptiness in her chest.

"I feel like I've been in this hospital a month instead of nine days," Tom grumbled good-naturedly as he tossed their bags into the car.

"The best days of your life, considering we're still here on earth, thanks to the good care we got," Mel said.

"I know. And part of me feels odd, leaving. Like we should be going back to the dig to finish."

"Really?" Laurel stuffed her bag behind his and stared at him in surprise. "After the ordeal you've been through, I thought you'd run and never look back."

"They still don't know if it had any damn thing to do with the dig. If I felt strong enough, I'd go back right now, but I know I'm not up to it," Tom said, stopping in the midst of packing Mel's bag to give Laurel a long look that struck her as very odd.

"What? Why are you looking at me like that?"

"I just...I'm not sure I should tell you, but, ah, hell." He grabbed the back of his neck and sighed. "You know how sometimes we all get that feeling on a dig, like an invisible finger is pointing and you just have to follow it and look?"

Her heart sped up a little. "Yes. I know."

"I felt it in the cave. That last day. Real strong and compelling. Leading me toward the far left wall, just past a huge orange stalactite, about a hundred feet back. Farther in than we'd been excavating. I was going to dig some, but it got late and I wasn't feeling too good. I figured I'd be able to tackle it better the next morning."

"Which all could have been delirium, since that was the night you got really sick," Mel said. She wore a deep frown, shaking her head slightly at him.

"You think that's where it might be," Laurel said, barely able to breathe.

"I do. Mel doesn't want you to go in there, but honestly? I really think we were close. My gut just tells me it might be there."

She looked from Tom to Mel and back again, a surge of adrenaline roaring through her blood. Without one more second of thought, she yanked her bag back out of the car and could practically feel her parents pushing her on the way they so often had, even when she'd been frustrated by it. Wanting her to use these final two weeks to search a little longer.

She'd learned to listen to little voices in her head, whoever or whatever they might be. And these little voices? They might be the most important whispers she would ever hear.

"I'm going back." She leaned in to kiss Mel on the cheek, then Tom. "I'll keep you posted."

"Laurel." Mel reached for her. "I know your parents expected a lot from you. Were driven, and drove you too. And you always stepped up, no matter how hard it was. But they wouldn't want you to risk getting sick. Risk your life. Let it go. You have other digs in your future."

"But not a dig like this one. And like Tom said, you getting sick might have had nothing to do with the dig anyway. But I'll be careful. I'll wear gloves and a mask. It'll be okay."

"I know there's no point in arguing with you when you've made up your mind." The woman who'd stepped in to do quite a bit of mothering after Laurel's parents were gone gave her a fierce hug. "Promise you'll be careful. Promise you'll stay safe."

"I will. I'll see you back at the university in two weeks, and with any luck there'll be a treasure in my pocket."

"A little too big for your pocket," Tom said, hugging her and grinning. "If you find it, they'll build a whole new room for it in the Delphi museum, with your parents' names on the plaque. So many visitors will flock to see it, the Charioteer will be damn jealous."

"We'll drive you back," Mel said.

"No, I'll rent another car. Don't worry about me. Adventure is what I live for, remember?"

Funny how the day seemed blindingly brighter. Her chest filled with an excitement and energy she hadn't felt since before the Wagners got sick. And that excitement and energy sent her thoughts to Andros. Bombarded with memories of how he made her feel exactly that way too.

By the time she got the car rented and arrived back in Delphi, there was too little daylight left to head up the mountain to the dig. Being back in town made her thoughts turn to Andros again. Of strolling through the streets, feeding the cats, kissing him until she was breathless. Walking into the hotel filled her with memories of kissing him again on the back deck and of making love with him in her slightly lumpy little bed.

Not that she hadn't thought of him more times than she could count the past three days and nights in Vlychosia anyway.

Maybe after she checked in, she should call him. Just to let him know she was back. Then again, she knew he'd be unhappy with her going back to the dig, and even more unhappy that her first stop would be the caves, which she hadn't been in even once. And that he still believed might be the source of the mysterious pneumonia.

She didn't need the man's approval or permission or lectures. She'd been on her own for a long time, so why did she feel this need, this longing, really, to get in touch with him?

No. She shook her head and grabbed up her duffel. She'd been given one more chance to find the treasure. Tonight she'd look at the map of the caves, carefully drawn over the past three years, read through all Tom's notes, and make a plan. A plan that didn't include making love with Andros Drakoulias again.

"Hello, Spiros," she said to the desk clerk. "I'm back. Can I have the same room, or do you need to move me?"

The young man looked over his shoulder twice, then finally focused on her. The expression on his face could only be described as alarmed, and she wondered if the media coverage and the quarantine had spooked everyone.

"I am sorry, miss, but there are no rooms left."

"I'm absolutely fine, Spiros. The hospital gave us all a clean bill of health." She fished in her purse for the papers they'd given her, holding them out. "See?"

"I am sorry," he repeated. "But we did not know you were returning. We have rented every room for the next two weeks. I will call other hotels in Delphi for you, yes?"

"Thank you." She dropped her bag to the floor. Why hadn't she been smart enough to call as soon as she'd known she was coming back? Regardless, it didn't really matter. A place to stay was a place to stay, so long as she could easily get to the dig.

As the minutes ticked away and Spiros made one call after another, concern grew to alarm. She might not be able to understand a word he was saying, but the frown and worried look were plain. Finding a room wasn't happening.

"I am sorry, miss," he said yet again, looking remorseful. "It is high season, you understand. Every room is booked by tours and others. I am sorry."

"Thank you for trying. I appreciate it." So now what? She hauled her duffle over her shoulder again and went out the door and across the still-hot blacktop. There was only one solution she could think of. And how ridiculous that the solution sent happiness surging through her veins, sending her practically running to her car and jumping inside.

There was one person nearby who'd said he was there to help her any way he could. Was it her fault she needed a little more help from him now?

CHAPTER ELEVEN

"ONE MORE STORY, Daddy? Please?"

Andros slid the book from his daughter's hands, an easy accomplishment since her fingers had gone limp, her words slow and slurred. "Not tonight. If you sleep tight, I'm sure your little fairies will visit."

She smiled at the same time her eyes closed. He watched her roll to her side, pull her sheet up to her chest and fall straight to sleep. He tugged the sheet a little higher to tuck it beneath her little chin, wondering all over again how he could possibly be so blessed.

The stairs creaked as he made his way back to the living room, absently thinking he should see if he could find a way to quiet them. His handyman skills weren't up there with his doctoring skills, but surely he could figure something out.

Right now, though, there was something more important to figure out. He propped up his feet, put his laptop on his knees, and did another advanced internet search to look at various known pathogens, common and uncommon. Trying to read through it all, he found it hard to concentrate on the information. Damned difficult, in fact, because he just couldn't stop thinking of Laurel.

Di had told him the entire archaeological team had been cleared to leave quarantine, including Jason, thankfully. Probably they were all at the airport by now, maybe even already on a plane bound for the States. Leaving unanswered questions behind them, but he and Di and the virologists would eventually figure it out. Had to, because even though no one in Delphi, Kastorini or any other nearby town had come down with anything similar, they all wanted it to stay that way.

He closed his eyes and pictured Laurel's face. Her amazing blue eyes and pretty lips that sometimes smiled or cutely twisted when she was thinking. Lips that had kissed him until he couldn't think straight. He pictured her slim figure and how sexy her rear looked in anything she wore, even those loose, dirty work shorts of hers with pockets everywhere. But his favorite had been that silky long dress. No, not quite. His favorite was how she'd looked when her hair had been released from its ponytail, spilling across the pillow and her soft skin, tangling in his fingers as he made love with her.

Damn. Just thinking about her, all of her, made his breath feel a little short and his heart feel a little empty. How was it possible he could miss a woman so much, when he'd barely spent more than a few days with her?

He'd itched to go to Vlychosia to see her, to say good-bye one last time. Nearly had gotten in his car more than once, but stopped himself. Last thing he'd want to do would be to hurt Laurel, which he hadn't even realized he'd done to some of the women who'd briefly been in his life. He wasn't made for a real relationship anyway, and, even if he had been, what was the point of getting too attached to a woman focused on spending her life at digs around the world? Or for Cassie to? A little girl who had lost her mother far too soon just might be unconsciously looking for someone to take her place.

No, it was good Laurel had moved on, leaving no possibility of anyone getting hurt, or the storm of gossip he wanted to avoid.

He tried to refocus on the internet journal and the various viral beta groups, and was startled when his cell phone rang. He hoped it wasn't an emergency, but if he had to bundle up Cassie and take her the few houses down to his sister's, he suspected his little girl wouldn't lift an eyelid.

He dug his phone from his pocket. His heart jerked hard and his breath caught in his chest. Laurel. What could she be calling about?

"Dr. Drakoulias." He'd answered that way to keep his voice sounding calm and professional. Unemotional, so she wouldn't know how much he'd been thinking of her. Missing her.

"Is this the Dr. Drakoulias who told me he was here to help if I needed it? Unfortunately, I have a little problem."

"That would be me." Her voice sounded normal, with even that touch of humor he liked so much, so there must not be some terrible problem. He relaxed at the same time he felt instantly wired, alert, elated too, because hearing her on the other end of the line was like being given an unexpected gift. "What is this little problem?"

"Well, believe it or not, I'm in Delphi. But the hotel gave my room away, and there's not another room to be had in the entire town."

"You're in Delphi?"

"Yep, I am."

"And you need a place to stay." He couldn't imagine why she'd come back, but the way his heart had jerked in his chest when she'd first called was nothing to the gymnastics it was doing now.

"I'm afraid I do. There are a few hotels in Kastorini, aren't there?"

"One's full up for a wedding this weekend, which I know because a patient talked to me about it for half an hour today. The other two usually take on overflow from Delphi, so I bet they're booked too."

"That's what Spiros at my hotel told me." She sighed in his ear. "Is there any way I can hole up in the clinic or something, just for one night while I check out nearby towns tomorrow? Or maybe even briefly stay with Taryn?"

"My house has three bedrooms. No reason to call Taryn tonight, you can just stay here." The instant the words were out of his mouth, he pictured her here with him, sitting in his cozy living room, fascinating him with stories about the dig and about her life. Tousled and sleepy when he fixed her coffee in the morning. He wondered what she wore to bed, and a vision of something silky and skimpy came to mind, or, even better, her completely naked, glorious body. But even if she slept in an oversized T-shirt, she'd look sexy as hell.

That vision faded when he realized if anyone found out he had a woman staying in his house, the tongues would flap like crazy. And what were the odds no one would know? Pretty much zero out of a hundred. But he couldn't worry about that when Laurel needed someplace to lay her head. "Cassie's in bed, but she sleeps like a rock. Won't even blink if I put her in the car to come get you."

"Thank you." Her voice got softer, warmer. "But I rented another car. I'll be there in about twenty minutes, f that's okay."

"I'll be waiting." And each minute of it would seem ike two. At the moment, there was no way he'd get one hing out of the clinical information on his laptop, and he closed it, realizing the house could use some spiffing up. Cassie's toys lying all around didn't bother him, but probably making sure Laurel didn't turn an ankle stepping on one would be a good idea.

His arms were full of the last of it—multicolored plastic blocks he was trying to find the box to dump into—when there was a soft knock on the door. It opened a few inches, and beautiful blue eyes met his through the crack. "Hi. It's me. Didn't want to wake Cassie by ringing the doorbell."

"Nothing wakes that child up. Come on in."

The sight of all of her, not just those amazing eyes, caught his breath. She was wearing that dress he loved so much that embraced every curve, and her hair—God, her hair was down, out of her usual ponytail, falling in a shimmering golden waterfall over her shoulders. He stood there staring like a fool, an armload of plastic stuff preventing him from pulling her into his arms and kissing her until she was as breathless as he felt.

But maybe she didn't want that. Yes, they'd made love after the stress of learning about John's failing health, but that didn't mean she wanted to go there again. And he wanted her to feel comfortable in his house, not worried he might jump on her any moment like a flea on a kitten.

On the other hand, he might not be imagining the way she was looking at him. A way that said she might not mind him jumping on her at all.

Where was that damned box? "You don't happen to see a white box with pictures of blocks on it, do you?"

"Is this it?" She walked to the small door under the stairs where they stored Cassie's stuff. He'd already stuck a few things in there, and she bent over to open the door wider. He got so fixated on her shapely rear in that dress, he hardly noticed she was pulling the elusive box out from behind a huge stuffed lion.

"How come I put things in there twice and didn't see it?"

"I'm good at excavating, remember?" She held out the box, and he dumped the blocks inside. She turned and bent over again to shove the thing back behind the lion, and Andros gave up trying to keep his distance.

"You do realize you bending over in that sexy dress of yours is testing the limits of my gentlemanliness?"

"Is it?" She turned to him and took a step toward him, the amusement in her eyes mingling with the same heat he was trying to bank down. "Funny. Just looking at you in your T-shirt and jeans with your hair a little messy makes me want to test it even further."

To his shock and delight, she closed the gap between them, tunneled her hands into his hair and kissed him.

He wrapped his arms around her, lost in the taste of her, the intoxicating flavor he'd thought he'd never get to taste again. Her silky hair slid over his hands, his forearms, as he pressed her even closer, loving the feel of her every soft curve pressed against his body.

Still clutching his head, she broke the kiss and stared into his eyes. "I kept hoping you'd come back to the hospital one more time. To say goodbye."

"So you came to say goodbye?" He'd thought she'd already gone. So why did the thought of a goodbye now feel so bad?

"Not yet. Right now I'm saying hello."

"I like hellos better than goodbyes," he murmured against her lips before he kissed her again. The way she melted against him, gasping softly into his mouth as their tongues leisurely danced, made him think maybe she'd missed him too. That maybe she'd thought of him as much as he had her the past few days.

But she had a life in the States and a PhD to finish and papers to write. Grants to get and new digs to work on. Thinking of him or not, why had she come back?

"How long are you in town? And why?"

She drew back a few inches. "Well, I have some unfinished business. Don't know how long it might take, but—"

The shrill ring of his phone interrupted, and he nearly cursed it. He hated letting go of Laurel's warm body, but it would seem pretty odd to dance her over to the side table to answer the damn thing. "Dr. Drakoulias."

"Andros! It's Yanni. Dora's having the baby. Thinks it's coming soon."

"Do you think she's able to get to the clinic?"

"Yes. I think so."

"I'll meet you there." *Damn.* Timing being what it always was, Christina was in Athens for a few days. Not to mention that things just might have been leading somewhere very good with Laurel. "I'm sorry. Got to go deliver a baby that apparently is in a hurry to get here. Excuse me again."

He dialed the nurse midwife in Levadia who was on call for Christina. He huffed out an impatient breath when her husband said she'd gone to the grocery store. Didn't on call mean on call? "I need to hear from her as soon as possible."

"What's wrong?" Laurel asked. "You worried about the mother?"

"No. She's had a healthy pregnancy. But this is her fifth, and if she thinks it's coming soon, I believe her. Christina's not here, and the midwife on call isn't home. And it'll take her half an hour to get here anyway."

"Let me help. I mean, you just need an assistant, right? I don't need to be a nurse or anything?"

"Just need an assistant. Are you sure you're up for that?"

"Sounds like it would be an experience, and, hey, I'm always up for an adventure."

"Never thought of bringing a baby into the world as an adventure, but I guess it can be." He'd already seen the woman didn't back down from a challenge and had to smile. "It'll be faster if Taryn brings Petros here. I'll call her, then we can go."

"Looks like they're not here yet, which is good," Andros said as he pulled the car up to the clinic. "You can help me get stuff set up."

Nervous but excited too, Laurel followed Andros back to the hospital wing. She couldn't believe she was about to see a baby being born, maybe even be a part of bringing it into the world. Hadn't thought she'd ever want to, but, now that it was about to happen, she knew it would probably be an amazing experience.

Andros wheeled over a small cart from a corner with what looked like maybe a heating unit above it, and put a tiny little oxygen mask in the corner of the little crib, hooking it up to something. He pulled other strange things out from the supply cupboard, laid them on a thick metal table next to the hospital bed, then grabbed more items in his arms.

"I don't want to get in the way, but is there anything I can do?"

"I'm good right now, thanks." He tossed her a couple of plastic bags with what looked like blue paper inside. "Can you go see if Yanni and Dora are outside and bring them in here? Then put on that gown. Gloves too, after you come back, because I'll need you to handle the baby."

Handle the baby? What if she dropped it on its head or something? Nerves jabbed into her belly at the thought, though she should have realized she might have to take care of the newborn while he took care of the mother.

As soon as she got to the front door, a car zoomed up the street and swerved in front of the clinic, parking crooked. She rushed out of the door, hoping like heck the woman wasn't already spitting out the baby right there in the car, but if she had to catch the newborn, then, darn it, she would. A man leaped out and practically flew around to the passenger door, looking a little wild-eyed.

"Do you need help? Dr. Drakoulias is inside—do you want me to get him?"

"Ochi. I can bring her."

He swung the woman into his arms, and she wrapped her hands around his neck before burying her face in his chest. Her distressed cry was muffled, but Laurel's gut tightened, hearing her sound of pain. She ran to hold open the door and led the way to the clinic.

"Follow me."

Andros had already changed into scrubs and was busy putting towels next to the bed. He looked up and smiled. "Always in a hurry, Dora. Ever since we were in grade school."

The woman looked up and gave him a wavering smile back. She spoke in Greek so Laurel didn't know what she'd said in return, but apparently the woman still managed to have a sense of humor despite everything, as both men laughed.

Then just that fast, she apparently had another contraction, crying out as her face contorted. All humor was replaced by worry on her husband's face as he laid her on the bed, speaking to her soothingly. The sweetness and caring in his eyes tugged at Laurel's heart, and she wished she'd talked to her parents about what it had been like the times their own brood had been born. Made her wonder, for the first time, why they'd even had four children when their careers had been such a huge priority. Had their family been more important to them than she'd realized?

"I'm going to speak English, as Laurel doesn't speak Greek," Andros said, "so she understands what she needs to do to help. Okay?"

Both nodded, and he turned to Laurel. "Help me get

her clothes off and a gown on her, please." Despite the strangeness of the situation, it felt oddly normal to work together with him, and they quickly had Dora ready. Laurel was surprised it didn't also seem uncomfortable for the lower half of the woman to be completely naked, but maybe since it was obviously the last thing the woman was concerned about, it seemed like no big deal.

"This is an external probe, to monitor the baby's heartbeat." Andros attached a belt to her swollen belly, with some electronic gadget attached to it. "It's not as accurate as an internal probe we sometimes attach to a baby's head, but since your little one wants to come soon, I think this is good, okay?"

Both nodded again, obviously having complete faith in Andros, and Laurel looked at his face. Calm, but completely in command, and she knew she'd have the same exact confidence in him no matter what the situation.

"Are you all right? Do you want pain relief, Dora?"

"*Ochi.* No time. The baby...is coming."

He glanced at the monitor and his expression was neutral, but it seemed to Laurel it tensed a bit. "Baby's heart rate is dropping a little, Dora. Called bradycardia. Could be just from contractions, but we need to keep an eye on it."

"What do you mean?"

"If there's sustained fetal bradycardia, we'll need to get the baby out as fast as possible. Not to worry, though. And see? It's already recovering a bit."

Dora gave a sudden, extended cry, so agonized, Laurel winced for her. Yanni gripped her hand, looking nearly as distressed as his wife did. Laurel was so focused on the poor woman's pain she didn't notice Andros was leaning over the woman.

"You weren't kidding about it coming soon, Dora! Baby's on the way. The head is crowning. Time to push."

Laurel stared in amazement when she saw the top of the baby's head begin to emerge. She'd wondered if it might be gross or icky to see, but it wasn't at all. It was awe inspiring. Incredible.

"Oh, my gosh, it's right there!" She hadn't meant to exclaim that out loud and looked guiltily at Andros. He kept his attention on the baby and mother, but that surprise dimple poked into his cheek and she knew he was smiling.

"Yes. He or she will be here soon. Push again, Dora."

The woman grunted and groaned and pushed as her husband murmured encouragingly to her, but the baby didn't seem to move.

"Baby's heart rate is dropping again, Dora. We need to get the baby out. Laurel, I need you to put fundal pressure on top of the uterus."

"Fundal pressure?" Laurel's heart beat harder. She hoped she was up to whatever task this was he needed her to do.

"Basically, I need you to put your hands on the top of her belly and push hard. Put your weight into it."

"Um, okay." She positioned herself next to the woman and spread her hands on Dora's belly, feeling a little weird and a lot nervous. She pushed down, worried she might hurt her. "Like this?"

"Harder. As hard as you can."

Holy crap. "I'm afraid I'll hurt her."

"You won't. And we need to get the baby out."

Andros's intense expression sent her heart pumping even harder, and she gritted her teeth and put everything she could into pushing on the surprisingly hard expanse of poor Dora's belly. In the midst of the woman panting and pushing, and her husband speaking tensely in words that were probably supposed to be encouraging, Andros suddenly said, sharply, "Stop, Laurel. Stop pushing, Dora."

"What? Why?" Dora gasped.

"Baby's heartbeat is dropping again because the cord is around its neck. Give me a minute."

Almost as short of breath as the laboring mother, Laurel stared down at the baby's head, now out of its mother's body and being held gently in Andros's hands. Then her breath stopped completely and she felt a little woozy when she saw the baby was beyond blue, and the umbilical cord was wrapped several times around its neck.

She sucked in quick breaths to calm herself. Big help she'd be if she fainted in the middle of the birth. Andros slid his fingers carefully beneath the cord, gently loosening and unwrapping it, then finally slipping it completely off over the baby's head. "Okay, ready now. Let's have a last few good pushes, Dora. You're doing great. Can you help her, Laurel?"

Fear gave Laurel super energy, and she pushed hard on Dora's belly as the woman worked to deliver her child. After a few monumental pushes, the baby slipped from its mother's body into the waiting hands of Dr. Andros Drakoulias.

"Another girl!" Andros said, glancing up with a smile so big that that dimple of his showed again. "And she's as beautiful as her mother."

Dora sagged back, gasping and beaming, looking from the baby to her husband and back again. Yanni leaned forward to give her a lingering kiss, speaking soft words in her ear that Laurel couldn't understand, but at the same time she knew exactly what he must be saying.

Laurel felt about as wrung out as Dora, but wired too. She watched Andros rub the baby gently all over with a towel then put a bulb into her mouth to suction out fluids. The tiny thing seemed alarmingly blue, and the seconds seemed like minutes before the baby's head finally began to pink up, then her torso, as she cried out in lusty breaths.

The parents laughed and kissed, Andros grinned, and Laurel sagged, letting out a huge sigh of relief.

What an amazing experience. Scary and exhilarating and wonderful and unforgettable.

"You did a great job, Dora. Baby's had a bit of a rough time, so we need to get her warmed up and breathing well before I hand her over to mama." Andros's gaze met Laurel's. "Are you okay handling the baby, Laurel? She needs to be dried off with the towels to warm her up, wrapped with a dry one, then put under the heat lamp and given oxygen. I already have it turned on, so just position the mask over her mouth. I need to take care of Dora."

"Yes. Of course." She hurried over, not knowing exactly what to do, but whatever it was, she knew Andros would guide her through it if she messed up somehow.

He handed her the still slightly wet baby, and a moment of terror nearly stopped her heart. What if she dropped it?

"Don't worry. She's not glass." Andros gave her an encouraging smile. "Just dry her off like you would a little puppy after its bath, swaddle her up, then put her in the warmer." Andros grinned as though he'd read her mind, and she wondered what expression was on her face for him to see.

Heart thumping, she grabbed up a towel and carried the baby to the warmer. Softly, she began stroking the child with the towel, dumbstruck at the little brown eyes staring up at her as she did. As though the baby, just a few minutes old, was avidly studying her brand-new world.

"Dora, I'm going to give you some oxytocin to help your uterus clamp down and stop the bleeding. Okay?"

Laurel didn't look behind her, but knew the new mother wore the same expression on her face she'd had all along. Complete confidence that Andros would take care of everything.

She finished drying the baby, marveling at her mini fingers and feet, her tiny elbows and knees, then awkwardly swaddled her, sure any nurse would laugh at the pitiful job. The immeasurable good Andros accomplished every day struck her with awe. Yes, she loved her job. Following in her parents' footsteps. Uncovering history, learning from the past, was valuable to humankind's education. But this?

This put it in perspective. A dig wasn't life or death. It was about past lives and past deaths, but, when it came right down to it, helping others today and now was the most important thing anyone could do.

Helping her sisters become the people they'd become had been more important than getting her PhD done. More important than any dig, no matter how meaningful. She was glad to be free of the responsibility now, but postponing those things to raise and guide her sisters had been the biggest accomplishment of her life so far. How had she never appreciated that before?

The little baby staring at her from under the heat lamp raised her downy eyebrows, seeming to agree. Laurel smiled, stroking the infant's soft cheek, feeling a strangely serene, inner calm she couldn't remember feeling since before her parents died. For the first time, she realized that maybe having a baby of her own one day had its place on her list of life goals.

She'd head back to the mountain, into the caves, tomorrow. Hopefully she'd bring to a close her number-one goal. She'd leave no stone unturned to make it happen. But if she didn't?

She'd remember this sweet little baby's face, and be at peace with the outcome, knowing she'd given it everything she could.

CHAPTER TWELVE

"DID YOU REALLY help Daddy born a baby, Laurel?" Cassie asked as the three of them sat at the breakfast table, her usual excitement on her adorable face and sparkling in her brown eyes.

"I did. It was amazing. Your daddy's pretty amazing too." She looked at him over her coffee cup, struck all over again by his astonishing physical beauty, somehow magnified even more by the dark stubble on his chin and the faded T-shirt stretching across his thick chest and arms. And his inner beauty too, which she'd seen last night. Radiating competence and caring, reassuring the mother throughout even the scariest part of the birth.

"I know," Cassie said as she stuffed a piece of bread into her mouth. "How did I look when I was born, Daddy? Did I cry a lot?"

Andros stilled in midmotion, his gaze meeting Laurel's before he put his cup back down. "I wasn't there when you were born, remember, sweetie?"

Laurel's chest squeezed at his somber expression. Obviously, this was a painful subject for him, and she wondered when she'd finally find out about his relationship with Cassie's mother and how she'd died. A woman he'd said he wasn't close to. The knowledge that Cassie didn't have a mother made her heart ache for the child. But she was lucky to have a father who so obviously loved her, and an extended family too, in Taryn and Petros and her grandparents. Laurel knew from experience that could make even a terrible loss more bearable.

"Oh. I forgot." Cassie went back to eating, not seeming very bothered by the conversation, which eased the tightness in Laurel's chest. "When are we going fishing, Daddy?"

"As soon as you're done eating. I want to see that apricot go down the hatch." He picked it up and held it to her mouth and she lunged at it, nearly biting his fingers. "Ouch! Are you a wild dog this morning? I need all my fingers, you know."

Cassie giggled. "I'm a monster fairy. I have tiny teeth, but they're very sharp and hurty."

"Monster fairy? Sounds like a compromise with Petros."

His amused eyes met Laurel's, and they smiled together in an oddly intimate connection. How could sitting here at their breakfast table feel so normal, so right, when she didn't really know either of them all that well? How could it remind her of her own family, of breakfasts with her parents and her sisters that were the best memories of her life?

Moments she'd taken completely for granted until they were in the past. Until they could never happen again.

"You're not working today, Andros?" she asked, wondering how the only doctor in town had time to fish.

"Since Christina's gone a few days, I closed the clinic. Off work to play with Cassie, unless there's an emergency."

"Are you coming fishing with us, Laurel?"

"I can't. Unlike your dad, I don't have the day off." Filled with a sudden longing to join them, she fought it back. She hadn't been given this one last chance to find

the treasure just to twiddle away the little time she had.
Andros's brows quirked at her in a questioning look and
she braced herself. The man would not be happy about her
plans to go in the cave, but it wasn't his decision. Wasn't
his parents' dream she had one more shot at realizing. Her
chance to make them proud.

"With all the excitement, you never did tell me why
you came back. What is it you still need to do?"

She opened her mouth to tell him then closed it again.
Coward that she was, she didn't want to ruin this warm,
pleasant moment they were sharing. And didn't she deserve just a few hours of relaxation and fun on the boat
with them? Just for a little while before work took 100
percent of her time? The way it had for her parents?

"You know, work can wait a little while longer. Because, you might not believe this, but…" She leaned closer
to Cassie. "I've never been fishing. Will you teach me
how?"

"Yes! I will! Can I get my tackle box now, Daddy?
Please?"

"All right. I'll pack up the last of your fruit for a snack."

Laurel smiled as the child leaped from the chair and
ran off, her spindly little legs practically a blur. Maybe it
made her nosy, but she couldn't help being curious about
Cassie's mother and what Andros had said before. Now
might be the only chance she had to ask without the little
girl around.

"So. Maybe enjoying a little nakedness together doesn't
give me the right to ask," she began, wondering why she
felt suddenly nervous, like maybe she didn't want to know
the answer after all, "but Cassie is the sweetest little thing,
and I can't help but wonder about her mom. You said she
passed away?"

Andros stared down into his coffee cup, not responding, exactly the way he'd acted when she'd brought the

subject up on the mountain. That seemed like a long time ago now, but just as she was about to apologize for asking, for butting into something that wasn't her business, he looked up and fully met her gaze.

"Yes. As I said before, it's a sad thing for Cassie. But the rest of the story? It isn't one I'm particularly proud of."

Oh, Lord. Probably this really was something she didn't want to know and she wished she'd kept her mouth shut at the same time that she found herself desperately needing to hear it.

"I spent my youth going from one girlfriend to the next. Thought that was a good thing, what guys did, right? Now I wish my parents had yanked me aside and lectured me on respecting women, but they didn't. Don't know if they turned a blind eye or honestly weren't aware of it until after I left and they heard the gossip, but by the time I left Kastorini for school in the States, I had quite a reputation."

"You're a beautiful man, Andros, which I'm sure you know." Hadn't she about swooned the very first time she'd set eyes on him? "I bet it was a two-way street, with girls throwing themselves at you."

"Doesn't mean you have to take advantage of it. But I did. And when I saw the big, wide world of a college campus, then med school and residency? I felt like I'd moved from dinner to a full banquet."

"And you feel guilty about that." She could see it in his eyes. Guilt. And while a part of her felt uncomfortable, maybe even a little cheap at being just another woman who'd offered herself up at that banquet, she also believed he was no longer that young, careless man.

"Yes. I do." His eyes met hers again, intense and sincere. "Even before I found out about Cassie, I'd started to grow up. To see that women weren't something to be enjoyed at random, even if that seemed to be all they wanted, too. I took a step back to think about who I was and who

I wanted to be. Figured I just wasn't capable of a lasting relationship with a woman. Had never wanted one, but knew I needed to start being more careful about who I got involved with so no one got hurt. Then I got a phone call that brought that lesson home for good."

Laurel knew what that phone call must have been. Her heart twisted in a knot, and she covered his hand with hers and waited.

"Alison's brother—Alison was Cassie's mother—called me. Said she'd died in a car accident, and I was listed on Cassie's birth certificate as the father. Her parents were older and couldn't take care of a toddler, and the brother was single and traveled a lot. So they decided to contact me."

This time, his dark eyes were filled with pain. Remorse too, and her heart clutched even harder. "You didn't know."

"No. I didn't know. I wish she'd told me, though I hate to admit I barely remembered who she was. Maybe she didn't because she figured I'd be irresponsible."

"No, Andros, she had to know the caring man you are would have stepped up."

"Maybe, maybe not. When I first found out, there were plenty who knew me that doubted I would. And I wasn't sure I could blame them." He held her hand between both of his, his gaze not wavering from hers. "Maybe it happened later than it should have, but learning about Cassie brought me to that final step of realizing I was a man now, not a careless, self-absorbed boy. Which meant coming back to Kastorini to work with my father, as he'd always wanted me to. To raise Cassie here the way I'd been raised, to finally embrace the roots I'd been blessed to be given."

She tightened her hold on his hand, giving him a smile that she hoped showed she understood. That everyone had years they'd spent doing a whole lot of growing up, and it

vasn't always tidy or pretty. Hadn't she struggled to guide
ler sisters, often failing miserably because of her own
mmaturity? "Gotta admit, I find it hard to believe there
vas a time you weren't sure you wanted to come back. I
ove it here. Your place—your town—is truly special."
he had to bite back her next words, which had almost
een *and you're every bit as special, too.*

"It is. Special, and hard for me to believe." A small
mile played about his lips now, and she was glad to see it.
lappy he'd felt able to share all that with her, and happy
e saw she understood.

"By the way." He leaned in, a breath away. "Just so you
now, you're not just another fling to me. You're damned
pecial too."

Her heart knocked at the words she'd almost said to
im. She saw his smile, slightly crooked and more than
exy, just before his mouth touched hers. Her eyes drifted
losed to savor the sensation. Sweet and slow, tasting a
ittle like coffee and a lot like warmth and pleasure and
imple happiness. Just as she was sinking deep into all
f it, a banged-open door, followed by a voice so loud
t was hard to believe it came from a tiny little throat,
nterrupted.

"Got everything, Daddy and Laurel! Let's go feed the
ishies!"

aurel would never have believed that such a soft, comfy
ocoon of a bed would have left her tossing around with
ot nearly enough hours of sleep.

She'd sunk deep into its comfort, enjoying reliving the
eautiful day she'd spent on the water with Cassie and
Andros. Smiling as she remembered the tangled fish-
ng lines and the hook that had flown back to snag her
air when Cassie had yanked too hard at an invisible fish
he'd been sure was on the line. Seeing Andros's imme-

diate concern when he'd jumped up to carefully extricate it, the expanse of his wide chest in front of her face for a temptingly long time, making it nearly impossible to not breathe him in. To not wrap her arms around as much of him as she could and kiss him senseless.

Thank heavens Cassie had been chaperone, or she knew she couldn't possibly have resisted. And that realization knocked away all those pleasant feelings, leaving her frowning at the ceiling. Wondering about this deep contentment she felt here, and worried about it too. She had to be happy and content when she moved on from here, and each hour she stayed made her realize it might be a bigger adjustment than she'd expected to become a rolling stone, living in various places around the world as she built her career.

The only thing that had marred the day slightly were reporters showing up to sniff around. Apparently a few locals knew she'd returned and told them she was on Andros's boat. That situation had him looking beyond grim, which seemed a little unnecessary. Though she supposed having to answer questions and calm worried locals was a stress he didn't need.

She caught herself drifting back to the lovely memories of the day on the boat and opened her eyes again, annoyed with herself. She'd come back to Kastorini to find the statue, not play around with and lust after Andros Drakoulias. Really, she hadn't meant to come to Kastorini at all, and if she'd been able to get her room back wouldn't even have seen him again.

Except she had to face that this stern self-lecture was partly a lie. Consciously or unconsciously, she knew she'd have looked for a reason to come back here, even if that reason had been something lame and inane.

She flopped to her side, pinching her eyelids closed willing herself to sleep. Tomorrow had to be cave day

Not an easy day, either, since she hadn't worked in there at all and had only Tom's map and his "feeling" to help her find that statue. "And finding it means everything, remember?" she whispered fiercely to herself. "Everything."

Everything. Everything her parents had expected her to work toward. What her parents had died for. What was wrong with her that it seemed harder and harder to keep that at the forefront of her mind?

Her bleariness faded at breakfast, with Cassie's steady, cute chatter and two cups of coffee managing to help her feel upbeat again.

"A little more coffee, Laurel? Or more fruit?" Andros asked, holding up the pot.

"No, thank you, but it was delicious. If you'll excuse me, I have some things I need to get done today." She shoved herself from her chair and left the kitchen, feeling Andros's gaze on her back. What were the odds he wouldn't ask her what she was going to do, when she came down with her pack?

She didn't have to wonder long, as he stood just a few feet away from the bottom of the stairs. Her trot down the steps slowed, and she braced herself.

"You can't be serious. Are you nuts?"

Andros stared at her with disbelief and anger etched all too clearly on his face. He folded his arms across his chest and took a step closer, as though his size and maleness would somehow intimidate her.

"What do you mean?"

"I'm not stupid, Laurel. You're obviously planning to go into the caves."

She took a step toward him and stared him down. Well, up, actually, since she was now only inches away from him.

"I know you don't understand. I don't expect you to.

I'll wear a mask and gloves, just in case. But I need to look just a little longer."

"Look for what? More potsherds or a long-lost gold ring like countless others in Greek museums? Bones from thousands of years ago? I've talked to the Wagners about this dig, about the hundreds of items excavated. You've done plenty. Why can't you let it go? It's over."

"Not quite yet."

He turned to pace away a few steps, staring out of the window. His posture was stiff, and frustration practically radiated from him. Her throat tightened and her conscience tugged at her heart. The man wasn't worried about a contagion infecting Delphi or Kastorini or anywhere else.

He was upset because he was worried about her. She couldn't stand to let him think she was just an idiot. A stubborn fool. She owed him the whole truth.

"Andros," she said softly, walking toward him to place her hand on his back. He didn't turn, didn't respond, and she inched closer until her body nearly touched his. "This isn't about a few more potsherds. There's something important my parents believed would be found at this site. Something that will rock the archaeological world. Something I want to find for them, and for myself."

He turned to look down at her, that deep frown still between his dark brows. The worry still there too, but not the anger. "What? What could be so important?"

"There's a lengthy poem inscribed on one of the stones excavated near Delphi. A poem that talks about the Pythian games and the Charioteer and a golden Artemis, Apollo's sister. After studying the interesting metaphors in this poem, Mom and Dad became convinced the golden Artemis really existed in the form of a statue."

"They've been excavating for five years here with no statue showing up, Laurel."

"I know. But…" She wrapped her fingers around the warm skin of his arms. "The Wagners always suspected it might have been hidden in the caves, to protect it from looters after people no longer worshipped at Delphi. Tom thinks he felt where it is. So I'm going to look there a few more times."

"Felt where it is? What the hell does that mean?"

"Sounds ridiculous, I know. But surely you've had moments where you just had a gut feeling about something? A diagnosis, maybe, that comes to mind and seems right?"

He looked at her, not answering. After a long, tense moment, he finally shook his head and sighed. "You may be crazy, but even you know you can't go into a cave solo. I'll go with you."

"Andros, you don't have to—"

"Yeah, I do." He pulled her against him, and the lips that touched her forehead were gentle, not at all angry, and she was so relieved, she found herself leaning against him. Slid her hands up to his strong shoulders as his mouth lowered to hers in a kiss filled with frustration and sweetness and a slowly building heat that curled her toes and sent her fingers tangling with his thick, silky hair.

The heavy-lidded eyes staring at her were utterly coal black as he pulled back and ran his thumb across her lower lip. The sensual touch sent her breathing even more haywire, and she nearly drew his thumb into her mouth. Until she quickly reminded herself that heading to the cave was her priority for the day, not having delicious, sweaty sex with the hunkiest doctor alive.

"I really appreciate you…coming with me. I'm ready to go when you are."

His gaze lingered on hers a moment longer before he wordlessly turned and headed upstairs.

CHAPTER THIRTEEN

"I WAS EXPECTING it to be wetter in here. But most of the moisture's on the stalactites and stalagmites, not the ground at all," Laurel said as they moved through the cave, the light from their lanterns and helmet lamps swinging in wide arcs on the low ceiling, rocky walls, and floor.

"There is ground water in some caves on the mountain. Wouldn't that destroy artifacts?"

"Depends on the artifact." She pulled out Tom's map and looked at it again, trying to orient herself. "I thought working in here would be better than the hot mountainside, but it's a little creepy, don't you think?"

"The big bad adventure woman thinks it's a little creepy?"

The amusement in his voice was loud and clear even through the mask he wore, and she gave his arm a playful swat. "You're telling me you like it in here?"

"Interesting formations around. But I frankly can't see how the hell you think you'll find anything. A statue like you're talking about couldn't be buried in solid rock. If it was here, surely it would have been found by now."

She wouldn't admit she'd been thinking exactly the same thing. But Tom knew a lot more than she did, and he thought it was still possible. Who was she to doubt, when they'd been inside for barely half an hour?

"He said he got his feeling when he was about a hundred feet in, on the left-hand side. Behind some orange stalactite." She held up her lantern, peering for something orange, so focused she stumbled over a small, mounded stalagmite and might have fallen if Andros's strong hand hadn't shot out to grab her arm.

"Steady, adventure girl. We're not in a big hurry, here."

"Easy for you to say. You're not the one who has to head back to the university before the start of the new term." The words sent an unexpected jab right into her solar plexus at the thought of never being here again. On this amazing mountain, or in beautifully charming Kastorini.

Of never seeing Andros and little Cassie again.

But that was the nature of the life she wanted, wasn't it? That she'd trained for. Spend months of the year somewhere, meet new and interesting people, then move on. Maybe get to see them again the following year if a dig continued. But getting attached to one place for too long? Not a good idea for an archaeologist.

Remembering that wasn't going to be easy.

Andros hadn't said a word in response, and she wondered if he was thinking what she was. That he'd miss her. That he wished they'd had a little more time together to light up, then burn out, this…thing that had formed between them.

Definitely hadn't had enough time for either. And of all her regrets, she knew that was the biggest.

So aware of his warm hand still holding her arm, she moved farther into the cave, then stopped dead. "Look! A huge orange stalactite, over there!" She pointed, looking up at Andros, and his eyes met hers above the mask, strangely dark and intense at the same time they were touched with the humor she loved to see there.

"If we find it, can we keep the discovery to ourselves so I can put it in my living room?"

"Wouldn't suit your homey decor too well, I don't think. Let's look."

The sound of his chuckle vibrated practically in her ear as he squeezed in next to her behind the stalactite, his chest touching her back in the narrow space. Her heart thumped as she scanned the area. At first it looked as if it was nestled in by more expanse of solid rock that ended in a triangular corner, covered by a thin, shimmering layer of crystal. The excitement that had bubbled up in her chest when she'd first spotted the orange formation deflated a little as she moved in close to what she could now see was obviously a dead end.

"Looks like it stops right here," she said. "I wonder if Tom could have meant a different stalactite?"

"Maybe. Or his psychic feelings were really just indigestion." Andros wrapped his arm around her, splaying his gloved hand across her belly in a squeeze. A shiver slipped across her neck and down her spine as his deep voice murmured in her ear, "Gotta say, though, this cave is starting to grow on me. I like being smashed into close quarters with you. Except it's hard to nuzzle your ear with this damn mask on."

"You're the one who insisted on the masks." She turned her face and their noses and mouths touched through the paper, making them both laugh a little breathlessly.

"Kissing you this way is still better than kissing anybody else's lips." The eyes that stared into hers were hot and amused and held an absurd sincerity that had her pressing her mask-covered mouth to his again.

"You're ridiculous," she said, forcing herself to turn back to the crevice and remember why the heck they were in this cave to begin with.

He held his lantern up above her head. "Or maybe it wasn't indigestion after all," he said softly.

"What?"

"Look. There's an opening up here. Kind of jagged and narrow, but maybe big enough for a smallish person if you're careful. Dry too, and looks like it might expand to a bigger space once you're through."

Her gaze followed his and she jumped up and down, trying to see inside. She knew it was probably nothing but couldn't help feeling a ping of excitement anyway.

"I'll give you a boost." He put down his lantern and threaded his fingers together, palms up. "Step in my hands."

"Let me take my boot off first. Or better yet, I'll get on your shoulders and climb in so you don't have to lift my full weight."

"What, you think I'm a wimpy weakling?" He stopped her as she reached for her boot. "I'm wearing gloves, and you might get your sock all wet."

Wimpy weakling? She shook her head and grinned at the man who was about as far from that description as a human could possibly be. "Fine. But don't complain if you throw out your back."

She stepped into his palms and he lifted her so high, she was able to grab onto the edges and peer inside, the glow of her headlamp lighting the space. "It's big inside here, but kind of strange. Different from the cave we just came through."

"How do you mean?"

"There are chunks of stone and broken stalactites everywhere. And like you said, the crevice is real jagged instead of smooth like the cave walls."

"Aeons of moisture and minerals have glazed these walls. Since this crevice isn't like that, there's a reason.

Like maybe the earthquake a few weeks ago opened it when it had never been open before."

She looked down at him, his eyes vibrant and alive as they met hers. "Maybe you're right."

"Come back down. We'll grab the tools and open it up wider so we can both get inside."

Andros found a few sizable rocks to roll over beneath the crevice that they could stand on as they whacked at the edges of the opening. "Turn your head when you swing, so you don't end up with shards in your eyes. I hate removing stuff from people's corneas."

"And I'd hate it to be my cornea you had to remove stuff from." Looking at him balancing on that rock, a smile in his eyes as they stood close together in this corner working away, made her insides feel all gooey.

"Thanks for helping me. I really appreciate it."

"Like you left me a choice. I would've been a nervous wreck thinking of you getting lost in this cave. Not to mention I didn't want to have to spend my whole day off tomorrow hunting for you when you didn't show up for dinner."

"You don't fool me. I think you're enjoying this. It's an adventure, right?" She turned her head and closed her eyes as she gave another mighty swing at the crevice edge. Though mighty was probably an overstatement, since Andros had already bashed out a good six inches from top to bottom on his side.

"Okay, I admit it. It's intriguing." He leaned back and surveyed their work. "I think it's big enough. Come on, I'll help you up, then follow you in."

She stuck her foot in his hands again, and when she was halfway in he let go and cupped her derriere in his hands, shoving her far enough in that she was able to squirm the rest of the way and stand up. "Was that an excuse to fondle me?"

"Do I need an excuse?" He boosted himself in to stand in front of her, sliding his hand around her rear again and pulling her close.

She chuckled. "I guess not." She gave him another one of those paper-mask kisses, their eyes meeting over the top. "You realize I'm sorely tempted to pull down this stupid thing and kiss you for real."

"Me too. But we'll save that for a little later, hmm?" He grasped her hand as they picked their way over all the broken rock littering the ground. "This place definitely had a huge seismic shift just recently for there to be so much of this. I—holy Apollo, Laurel."

"What? What?" She looked all around, trying to aim her headlamp where he was looking.

"Something's back here, behind this tall half-broken wall. Gleaming, like metal."

Laurel didn't realize she'd stopped breathing, her heart pounding so hard it echoed in her head, until they stepped around the wall and every bit of air left her lungs in a gasp. "Oh, Andros."

Together, they stared silently at the stunning, life-sized gold statue of Artemis, gleaming as brightly as if it had just been polished by an ancient hand. She stood beautifully perfect beneath an arching ceiling, coins and jewels scattered around her feet in what had probably been homage to Apollo's sister.

Tears stung Laurel's eyes and throat, and a small sob burst from her mouth, muffled by the mask. She turned to Andros, and saw the same awe and amazement on his eyes she knew was in her own.

"You did it, Laurel. You didn't stop believing, didn't stop trying. This is...incredible."

"I'm not sure I didn't stop believing, but I wanted to believe, so much." She reached to touch it, reverently sliding her hand over the statue's intricately detailed gown, her ethereal face.

"Your parents would be so proud."

"They would. Yes, they would. Oh, my God, I can hardly soak it in."

She flung her arms around his neck and buried her face in his shoulder, letting the tears flow as his arms came around her. Tears of happiness and relief and joy, knowing her parents' work would be highlighted once more. Thinking how proud they'd be that she—with Andros's help—had actually found this spectacular treasure.

"Thank you, Andros," she whispered. "Thank you for helping me. For seeing the crevice. Hammering it open. For spotting…her. I…I don't think we'd be standing here in front of her if you hadn't."

His hands slowly stroked up and down her back. "Oh, you would have found her. That stubborn streak of yours would have kicked in, and who knows? Maybe that feeling Tom had would have come to guide you too."

She looked up, blinking at her tears. "I think maybe there's a part of you that believed in that feeling. That kind of guidance."

"Maybe." His eyes crinkled at the corners. "So now what, Ms. Evans? Who do you need to contact?"

"First, I—*Aahh!*"

They both ducked, startled by something swooping by their ears. Andros straightened and looked around, his brows lowered in a thoughtful frown. "I asked Tom if he'd seen bats in the cave, and he said no. But that was definitely a bat."

He released her and walked around, looking carefully at the various corners of the cave where he pointed his headlamp. "Bat guano. A lot of it." He looked upward, aiming the light around the ceiling that was much higher in this cave than the other one. "Bingo! Hundreds of bats curled up there sleeping. See them?"

"Okay, now I know for sure why I preferred working on the mountain instead of in here." She shuddered, creeped out by the creatures hanging shoulder to shoulder, as far along the cave ceiling as they could see. "Glad we found Artemis pretty fast."

"Bat guano, Laurel." He stared at her, a new excitement in his voice and gleaming in his eyes. "It can be a primary source of coronavirus infection if it's breathed into the lungs."

"Coronavirus? You mean like SARS and MERS?"

"Probably a mutated strain. Pneumonia is the most common clinical presentation of coronavirus, sometimes with nausea and diarrhea like Jason had. Renal failure and pericarditis. Sepsis, which we couldn't manage well for John. It all makes sense now!"

He grabbed her shoulders, practically dancing her around. "The reason no one got sick before the past couple weeks was because the bats were in this cave, not the one your crew was working in. Then the recent earthquake opened up that crevice, and the bats flew into the dig cave. Tom and Jason worked all day, breathing in the airborne dissemination of the virus."

"But what about Becka? She worked in the cave all day and didn't get sick. And Mel wasn't in here at all."

"Some people carry the virus, but never show symptoms, which could be the situation with Becka. And while coronavirus is primarily contracted through respiratory exposure to guano or animal secretions, like from camels carrying MERS, it can be contracted from very close person-to-person contact."

"So you've solved the mystery." Her excitement began to match his and she laughed as they did another little two-step around the cave. "Nobody in Kastorini or Delphi has to worry they'll get it. You're a genius!"

"We solved it together." He cupped the back of her head with his hand. "I never would have come in here if you hadn't."

"And Artemis might have stayed hidden forever." They looked at one another, and Laurel's heart swelled and squeezed at the same time. "Do you think she was hidden by the earthquake my parents died in? That maybe the only entrance got shut down to anything bigger than a bat?"

"More likely an earthquake from a thousand years ago, and if that's the case your parents would never have found it." He tipped his forehead against hers, speaking softly. "Maybe the gods felt bad about that, about the tragedy, and made another earthquake happen just for you in their memory."

"Yes. In their memory." She gave him a fierce hug, unable to identify all the powerful emotions swirling around inside her. They were grief and joy, sadness and amazement, and Andros was somehow wrapped up in every one of them.

"We have some work in front of us, Ms. Evans," he said, his voice that low rumble in her ear that always made her quiver inside. "I need to talk to Di and get the national infection control folks out here, take some samples. Have them check the blood work we have from your team to confirm it. And once it is, contact the media to calm the fears they stirred up before."

"And I have to call Tom and Mel and tell them we did it. They'll talk to the university while I contact the Greek Archaeological Society." She squeezed him tighter. "I can't wait to tell my sisters too."

"We should probably call the authorities to protect the statue. I doubt anyone would come in here, and it's hidden well, but, since it appears to be solid gold, I'm thinking there are one or two people who would like to get their hands on it."

"Except she probably weighs a zillion pounds."

"There's that." He chuckled. "I'll call Georgo, the police chief in Kastorini, and let him handle it however he thinks. He's an old friend and as honest as they come."

She slowly pulled herself from his arms. Holding his hand, she carefully stroked the statue one more time. "Thanks for showing yourself to us, beautiful. I know whoever created you as a gift to Apollo loved you, but it's time for the rest of the world to love you even more."

Andros gripped her hand and when she turned to him she was surprised to see his eyes were now deeply serious. "And I have a feeling the world will love her finder as well."

The rosy-gold sky was darkening around the mountains, the waters of the gulf a deeper blue from the low light, when Laurel and Andros finished what seemed like a never-ending number of calls and emails.

"Okay," Andros said, "I think we can finally relax and celebrate."

Laurel glanced up from her laptop, her heart skipping a beat as she looked at the man leaning against the kitchen doorjamb. He'd showered and changed, and his slightly damp black hair was curling a bit around his ears and at the nape of his neck. His snug jeans rode a little low on his hips, and a white polo shirt was startlingly bright against his bronzed skin.

She let herself soak in the sight of him, that uncomfortable swirl of emotions back in spades.

There was no denying she was crazy about this man. Smart, caring, and beyond beautiful inside and out. She adored his little girl and felt warmed and welcomed by this lovely town they lived in. Liked his sister too, and had a feeling she'd like his parents just as well.

But she would never know, because she had to leave. With Andros's help, she'd accomplished her goal, big time. Now could finish her PhD dissertation. Get the grant paperwork done and in, making sure the wheels were greased to get her dig in Turkey going when she got the grant money, which shouldn't be a question now. She'd assemble a team. Lots of qualified applicants would want to be a part of it after this monumental discovery. And there would be interviews galore—while she talked about her parents' conviction that they'd find the statue there, she'd take that opportunity to talk about her own upcoming dig, knowing her parents would feel satisfied and happy that she'd accomplished the dream they'd had for her.

All that should leave her feeling elated. But battling with that elation was the heavy reality that she'd be saying goodbye to this place. To Andros. She couldn't deny she wasn't ready to do that. Wasn't sure she'd ever be ready.

She managed a smile, determined to enjoy her last day or two with him. "We've earned a celebration for sure. What did you have in mind?"

His eyes took on a wicked glint, and his slow smile sent her heart rate zooming. How could a single look from a man make her feel like throwing him to the floor to have her way with him?

"Let's start with an aperitif. I got white wine for you, but of course I have retsina and ouzo as well."

"You know, believe it or not I do have a taste for retsina tonight. And maybe a little of that grilled octopus you say the restaurant down the street does so well."

"Yeah?" He took a few steps closer, and she set her laptop aside so she could stand and meet him halfway. "Sounds like you've become part Greek. Part of Kastorini."

"Maybe I have." Her eyes drifted closed as he pressed soft kisses on her temple, her cheek, the corner of her mouth. Her words echoed in her head, making her chest ache. *Maybe I have. Or maybe this place has become a part of me.*

"So, about you becoming part of Kastorini." The pads of his fingers slowly slipped across all the places he'd just kissed, ending up warmly cupping the side of her throat. His expression was surprisingly serious, at odds with his teasing voice. "You already know Greece is the epicenter of history just waiting for an archaeologist to find and share it?"

"Spoken like a true Greek, especially one born near the belly button of the entire earth," she said. "But a lot of other countries might argue with that perspective, Dr. Drakoulias. Not only in Europe, but China and South America and—"

He pressed his mouth to hers, effectively shutting her up. When he broke the kiss, his lips were curved, but his eyes still held that peculiar seriousness. Though she shouldn't think it was odd, since she found herself feeling very serious too.

"I know your passion is Greek archaeology," he said. She looked at him and nodded, though front and foremost in her mind at that moment was an entirely differently passion of hers. Passion for the man standing right in front of her. The man who stole her breath and had managed to steal a scarily large chunk of her heart as well. "But at the moment, there's a different subject on my mind."

"I might be able to guess what it is," she managed to say in a teasingly light voice.

"Probably not." His hands tightened on her. "I just wanted to say I wish we'd met in a different place in our lives. Before you had your exciting dig plans stretching out in front of you, and before I had Cassie to think about raising her here in Kastorini. But we didn't."

"No," she whispered. "We didn't."

"I'd ask you to come back and visit sometime when you're in Greece again, but I know that's not the best idea. Cassie already likes you a lot, and since she lost her mother I don't want her to become attached to someone who's not going to be around long. And, I...well, you know I'm not a guy with a very good track record. But want you to know that I'll really miss you."

"I'll miss you too." As she spoke she thought about what he'd said. And was filled with the bizarre thought that someday, when she worked in Greece again, she could visit Andros and see if, maybe, they might both be in a different place then. That Cassie might need another mother figure. And if they were, who knew? Maybe—

The door burst open, and they both swiveled toward it to see Taryn run in, frazzled and breathless. Andros let go of Laurel and strode to his sister. "What's wrong?"

"Have you seen the kids? They were playing in the backyard, but when I went to get them for dinner they were gone. I looked around but don't see them anywhere. And it's almost dark." She sucked in a breath. "They must be here, right?"

CHAPTER FOURTEEN

LAUREL FOUGHT DOWN her rising fear as the three of them searched for Cassie and Petros. It was nearly impossible for Laurel to keep up with Andros as he strode down streets and narrow alleyways, shining his flashlight into garden plots and patches of forest, calling the children's names in a voice loud enough to carry a long way through the inky night. Kastorini might be fairly small, but in the dark one house looked pretty much like another, so she tried to stick as close to him as she could. Last thing he needed was to worry about her being lost too.

"Let's check the schoolyard," Andros said in a controlled but obviously tense voice. "They both like to play there."

"But they've never tried to go alone, even during the day," Taryn said, sounding breathless and near tears. "I can't believe they'd go that far at night."

The terror in Taryn's voice clutched at Lauren's heart and brought back the frightening memory of her sister being missing, just a few months after her mom and dad had died. Helen had ridden her bike to a friend's house and hadn't come home for dinner. Laurel still remembered the icy panic she'd felt when she'd called and found Helen had left the friend's nearly an hour earlier.

She'd jumped into her car and driven up and down the

streets Helen would have ridden on, but she wasn't anywhere to be seen. Her chest had filled with an unbearable
fear as questions swirled in her head. Had Helen been ab-
ducted? Had she done something crazy in her grief over
their parents? How could she have gotten lost? Laurel remembered nearly weeping in relief when it had turned out
her sweet baby sister had just gotten a flat tire on her bike
and decided to take a shortcut when she walked it home.

It had been the first moment, one of many to come,
that Laurel had doubted she was capable of taking on the
care and guidance of her sisters full-time.

"We've looked close to home," Andros said. "We need
to think of where they like to go, what they might be
thinking."

A number of neighbors had joined the hunt, spread-
ing out through the town. "Cassie was excited telling me
about fishing with you and Laurel," Taryn said. "Surely
they wouldn't go to the boat."

Andros swung around to look at his sister, a low curse
on his breath. "Neither of them can really swim. Come
on."

They switched direction. Laurel thought they were
heading to the stone steps down to the water and could
hear the rising anxiety in both their voices. Could feel it
in her own heart. An olive branch snagged her hair, and
she had to stop to pull it loose. Then stared at the tree,
an overwhelming conviction smacking straight between
her eyes.

"The fairies!" she called out to Andros and Taryn as
she hurried to catch up. "You know Cassie and Petros
have been obsessed with fairies and monsters. Remember
when I told her they liked olive wood, and she asked if I
thought they lived in the olive groves? They both asked
me about it again and if monsters might live there too."

Andros stopped and stared at her, his eyes glittering

through the blackness of the night. He yanked out his phone and dialed. "Georgo, check to see if they might have gone to my boat on the water. We're going to the east olive groves." He hung up the call. "This way, Laurel." He grabbed her hand, and they backtracked up the steps and onto a dirt path. "You just might be right, and I hope to God you are."

After a five-minute near run to the grove, and another twenty minutes searching and calling, Laurel began to despair. She nearly blurted out the question she kept wondering, which was how long would it take to find them in the midst of thousands of trees? And how much time were they wasting if the kids weren't here?

But she managed to bite her lip, nearly drawing blood. Last thing Andros and Taryn needed was for her to pile on more doubt and fear with a stupid and obvious comment.

Andros came to such an abrupt stop, she nearly bumped into his back.

"What?" Taryn asked with wide eyes. "Do you—?"

He held up his hand. "Shh. I thought I heard them answer." He cupped his hands around his mouth, bellowing out to them, and Laurel's heart nearly stopped when she heard what might have been an answering cry.

"Petros!" Taryn nearly screamed her son's name and took off running through the trees, Andros moving in the same direction but veering more to the left. Laurel realized it made sense to spread out some and went in the other direction, trying to search for the kids with the flashlight, somehow watching where she was going at the same time.

Her entire heart felt lodged inside her throat as she called to them. Her ears strained to hear something, anything, and suddenly the small voices were in front of her. "Cassie! Petros!"

"Laurel!" The little girl sounded terrified.

"Oh, my God, Cassie, where are you?" She swung the flashlight through the trees, the light picking up eerie shadows she kept thinking were the children, and suddenly they were there. They rushed into the beam of light, both children grabbing her legs and crying.

"I thought I heard my mommy," Petros sobbed. "I thought I heard her and Uncle Andros."

"They're here. They're both here. You're fine. You're safe." She crouched down and hugged them against her, tears clogging her throat. She swallowed them down so she could let Andros and Taryn know she had them.

"Here! Over here!"

A dark shaped loomed out of the darkness. Andros. He swung both children into his arms, kissing their cheeks, then pressed his face against Cassie's hair. "You both scared us to death. Don't ever, ever leave the house without telling us. You hear me?"

Both nodded, and Cassie snaked her arms around his neck in what looked like a stranglehold. "I'm sorry, Daddy. Laurel told us there were fairies in the olive trees. But then it got dark and we didn't know how to get home."

The little sob in her voice stabbed straight into Laurel's heart and she took a step back, her hands clutching at her chest as Taryn ran up to hold Petros.

This was all her fault. Why hadn't she realized she shouldn't say something like that to a small child? She'd always known she hadn't truly been up to the task of raising her sisters. So how could she have just been thinking there might be a time she'd like to come back to Kastorini? To see if this something between her and Andros could blossom into something more? To mother this beautiful child?

"I have to leave," she said as she turned away, her heart feeling shredded from the anxiety of the past hour. From guilt and misery at her own inadequacy. She wasn't sure if she'd said it to herself or Andros or the fairies in the olive grove, but she now knew without a doubt she had to go.

Laurel rested her hand on the windowsill in Andros's living room, staring out at the night. Wishing she could see the charming homes with their terracotta roofs and tumble of vibrant flowers, the crooked little streets, the cats sitting grooming themselves by doors so colorful and intriguing they could have been from a story, making her want to walk through and read the next chapter.

But it was probably just as well the darkness shrouded it all. She'd be leaving in the morning, and the look and feel of this town was etched forever in her mind and heart anyway.

She heard the stairs creak but didn't turn. Sensed rather than heard Andros coming to stand behind her. His hands resting on her shoulders were warm and heavy. Adding to the weight she already felt there.

"She's sound asleep. I guess an adventure and scare like that takes it out of a little girl."

And big ones, too. "I'm willing to bet she and Petros stick close to home from now on." She turned, swallowing down the tears that formed in her throat again. "I'm so sorry I thoughtlessly talked about the fairies living in the olive groves. This was all my fault."

"Don't be ridiculous." His hands tightened on her shoulders. "You couldn't have known they'd get it in their heads to go there."

"I have three sisters. I watched them a lot when they were little. And after I took on their care full-time, I learned the hard way to be careful what I said. To think before I spoke when they talked about boyfriend crises and school dramas and plans to move to the Amazon jungle alone to study indigenous peoples."

"Laurel. Every parent does or says things they later wish they hadn't."

"I'm not a parent. Not anymore. And I can't be. I just finished that role, and I wasn't very good at it. I...I have a plan for my life, and I need to get started on that plan." A plan that, just hours earlier, she hadn't been 100 percent certain she wanted so very much anymore.

His gaze seemed to search her face for a long time before he finally nodded, tugging her closer to press the gentlest of kisses on each of her cheeks before fully pulling her into his arms and simply holding her. She wrapped her arms around his back and breathed him in, wanting to imprint his scent and the feel of his body on hers one last time.

She tilted her head up to look at him, touching his face, wanting to also imprint every beautiful feature of his face in her memories. Though she didn't really need to do that, as she'd committed it to memory weeks ago. It seemed perhaps he was doing the same, as he looked at her for long moments before he lowered his mouth to hers and kissed her.

Soft and sweet, the kiss was also filled with a melancholy, then with a growing heat until Andros pulled back and set her away from him. His chest lifted with a deep breath before he spoke. "You need me to do anything for you before you leave?"

There was only one thing that came to mind. "Yes." She stepped close again and wrapped her arms around his neck, but he grasped her forearms before she could kiss him.

"Laurel. We shouldn't. You mean more to me than a night of sex before you're out of my life forever. That's not who I am anymore, and it will just make saying goodbye even harder."

"Maybe it will. But you mean more to me too." She

stroked his cheek, cupped it in her hand. "I don't think it would be wrong for two people who care about one another to make love before they say goodbye, do you?"

"Maybe it wouldn't." He pressed his lips to her palm, lingered there. "Maybe the truth is I'm just trying to keep my heart intact here. But one thing I do know is that being with you one more time would be worth a few more bruises tomorrow."

The small smile he gave her added to the pain and pleasure swirling around her heart. "I agree." She tugged his head down to her and kissed him. Long and slow and with a building passion that weakened her knees.

He drew back. "Cassie almost never gets out of bed, but in case she has a nightmare or something we should go to my room. Come on."

He grasped her hand and led her to his bedroom. A comfortable-looking masculine space she'd peeked into but hadn't been inside. He shut and locked the door behind them. Holding her gaze, he gently tugged her hair loose from her ponytail. His fingers slowly stroked down the length of it, then he touched her forehead, her cheekbones, and chin with his fingertips as well. Much the same way she'd touched the Artemis statue, with a reverence on his face that made her ache. He finally reached for the buttons of her blouse, and with each one he flicked open, her breath grew shallower, her anticipation ratcheted higher.

"You are so beautiful, Laurel." He slipped the blouse from her shoulders, ran his fingertips across the lace of her bra until she shivered.

"As are you." She tunneled her hands beneath his shirt, loving the way his muscles tightened at her touch. Stroked her palms through the soft hair on his chest until impatience got the better of her and, with his help, she yanked it over his head and off. She wrapped her arms around him, pressed her lips to his warmth, and he seemed suddenly impatient as well, flicking off her bra and quickly undoing her pants, shoving them down and off, along with her panties, in one swift movement.

She wasn't sure how he managed to kiss her breathless, shuck his own pants and settle them onto the bed in a matter of moments, but it didn't matter. His lips caressed her throat, her collarbone, her breasts. His fingers moved over her skin and teased her everywhere, and she closed her eyes to soak in the delicious sensations one last time. And when the pressure built until it was nearly unbearable, he finally joined her. Twined his fingers with hers, palms pressed together, eyes meeting in a deep connection that went far beyond the physical one they were sharing.

"Laurel. Laurel." He whispered her name as he took her further, higher, and his name was on her lips when they fell.

CHAPTER FIFTEEN

LAUREL SAT IN the university's office for the archaeology school and stared at the letter in her hand, waiting to feel the jubilation that should have her jumping up and down. The letter announcing that her grant application had been approved, and the dig she'd planned in Turkey could begin as soon as she had the equipment scheduled, accommodations booked and a crew pulled together.

Her gaze slid to the sturdy cardboard envelope lying on her desk that held her doctorate diploma, and while she was proud of it, she didn't feel the elation she knew she should feel by having completed both those accomplishments in the past month.

And she knew why. Making love with Andros had felt so bittersweet, leaving her with even more memories of him that now filled her with more sadness than pleasure. He'd been right when he'd said it would just make it harder to say goodbye. *Had* made saying goodbye harder, or would have if she'd stayed long enough to say it.

Hours of tender kisses and lying quietly together, arms and legs entwined, had left her with too many emotions tangled up as well. And when she'd finally slipped away to the guest room so Cassie wouldn't wake up to them in bed together, she'd been unable to sleep. Thinking of leaving in a few hours, and saying goodbye to Kastorini. To everyone she'd become fond of. To Andros and Cassie, whom she'd become far more than fond of.

So she'd left, slipping out of the door and driving to the airport before dawn. Leaving a note had seemed like the best kind of closure, but now she realized it had been cowardly. She'd wanted to avoid the pain of those farewells, but the only thing that had accomplished was to leave her with a deep ache. Without a sense of closure after all.

She sighed and tried to pull her attention back to work. While she concentrated on making a long to-do list for the project in Turkey, Mel came into the office and leaned down to give her a hug.

"I heard about your grant, girl. Congratulations, you deserve it! Your parents would be so incredibly proud of all you've accomplished."

"I know. They would." And she was glad. Glad to know they'd be proud, in comparison to all the times they hadn't been so proud. All the times she hadn't quite lived up to the standards they'd set for her.

"And yet you don't seem very happy." Mel sat in the chair next to the desk and rested her elbow on it. "What's going on?"

"Nothing. I'm happy. Just tired, I guess. My moment of fame, being interviewed for magazines and on TV, has been pretty exhausting, I've got to say." She kept her voice light and joking, but knew Mel would probably see right through it.

"Mmm-hmm. More so than working ten solid hours digging rocks on a hot mountainside, which never seemed to exhaust you. So tell me the truth."

Laurel leaned back in the swivel chair, and just the thought of telling Mel made her feel like a traitor to her parents. To their dreams. "I achieved everything I wanted to this year. Got my doctorate, the grant money, and most incredibly, we found the statue. There's clearly something wrong with me that it doesn't feel like…enough."

"Maybe because it's not what you really wanted after all."

"Of course it is. I wanted to finish this dig for Mom and Dad, and I wanted to get going on the achievements they planned for me."

"What do you want for yourself?"

Laurel stared at her. "I already told you. Their work—"

"Exactly. *Their* work. Which doesn't have to be yours, Laurel. I know, as their oldest, they always expected—demanded—a lot of you. You took on the care of your sisters, which wasn't easy. Took on your grad studies, then took on the task of finishing the Delphi dig, with spectacular success. So why do you feel like that's not enough?"

She stared at Mel, gathering her thoughts. Asking herself that question. "Because it's not. For years, they talked about me heading up a dig as soon as I got my PhD. Planned to help make it happen so I'd get started in that role even younger than they were. I may be behind, but I still want to make it happen."

"For you, or for them, to fulfill their dream for you? Maybe it's time for you to ask yourself if what you thought you wanted is really just what *they* wanted." Mel reached to hold her hand. "Maybe focusing on all this has been your way of unconsciously dealing with the grief that's still inside you over your parents dying. A way to come to peace with that."

Stunned, Laurel met Mel's gaze. Was it possible she'd convinced herself she wanted to do the project in Turkey for that reason? Not because that was what called to her professionally?

"I…I don't know. But I do love archaeology. I love digging and finding and recording history. Really, I do."

"I know you do. Just think about the rest of it, will you?" Mel squeezed her hand. "By the way, Helen called me. Said she'd been trying to get hold of you and wanted me to tell you."

"Okay, thanks."

She stared at Mel as she left the room, still confused by their conversation, then dialed her sister. "Hey, sweetie, what's up?"

"Hi, Laurel! Guess what?"

She smiled at the enthusiasm in her bubbly little sister's voice. "What?"

"Professor Green said he wants me to come back to this dig next summer, after I'm finished with my first year of college! Do you really think it'll be a good thing to put on my grad-school applications?"

"Congrats! Yes, it definitely will. I'm proud of you for working hard and going for it." As soon as the words came out of her mouth, she wondered if she sounded exactly like her parents. Pushing instead of just encouraging. "But you may find other things you want to study after this coming year. Don't feel like you have to plan your whole future right this minute."

"Okay, I won't. Thanks for being the best big sister ever and for always giving me good advice."

Her heart squished at her sister's words. "I don't think I've always done that so well."

"Sure you have. I want to tell you how much I love you for that. How much all three of us do."

"I love you too." Laurel stared at the phone after they said their goodbyes. Realizing that all her sisters had said sweet things like this before, but she hadn't really heard them. Had she been too worried about how she was "failing" at being a parent to notice the things she might be doing right?

Maybe she'd been mistaken about a lot of things she'd been so sure of. And if she had been, maybe it was time to get it right.

"There's another picture of Laurel, Daddy!"

Cassie's stubby finger pointed at the photo in the magazine, but she hadn't needed to. Most readers probably focused on the pictures of the spectacular golden statue he'd been blessed enough to help find, but he saw only Laurel. Her intelligent blue eyes, her sweet, smiling lips, her beautiful face. Her hair—hair that he knew all too well felt silky soft within his fingers—spilling in golden waves over her shoulders.

"Yes. There are quite a few pictures of her in these magazines, aren't there?"

"Why?"

"Because the statue was an amazing find. There's nothing like it in the whole world, and Laurel's the one who kept looking for it."

"You helped her. You found it too. Why isn't your picture in here with hers?"

He wished there were photos of the two of them together, but it wasn't meant to be. Probably his penance for the years he'd dismissed the idea of a real relationship with a woman. Known he didn't have it in him.

But the way he'd missed Laurel the past month had him wondering if maybe he was capable of it, after all. That maybe he'd just needed to meet the right woman to feel that kind of commitment. Except she was traveling the world, and he had Cassie to raise here.

"She's the archaeologist. I just got lucky to be with her that day." And a few other magical days. More than lucky.

"Thea Taryn showed me your picture in the other magazine. The one about people getting sick. Laurel helped you figure that out, didn't she?"

"Yes. We made a good team." And as he said the words, the hollowness he'd felt since the moment he'd woken up and found her gone seemed to widen a little more.

"Why aren't you still, Daddy? A team with Laurel?"

He looked down into her wide eyes and his lips twisted a little, thinking what a simple question it was. One with a simple answer. "Her work takes her on adventures all over the world, Cassie. Our home is here in Kastorini, with Yiayia and Papou and Thea Taryn and Petros and everyone else."

"I like adventures, Daddy. And doctors can help people anywhere. Why can't we go on adventures with Laurel and come home to visit everybody sometimes?"

Her words were so matter-of-fact, the expression in her eyes telling him she thought he might be a little dense. And as he stared at her he wondered the same damn thing.

He'd brought Cassie to Kastorini because he'd thought that was where the newly mature doctor with a daughter needed to be. Taken his place beside his father, even though the man had practiced medicine for years without any problems finding a temporary replacement when he'd needed to.

He'd disliked being judged by the town, worried about disappointing his parents, couldn't let Cassie be exposed to gossip or become attached to a woman he might selfishly date for just a short time. But didn't part of growing into a responsible adult bring with it a responsibility to himself too?

"You may be onto something there, *koukla mou*. Maybe an adventure with Laurel is exactly what we need."

Laurel's hands were sweating on the steering wheel of her rental car as she drove up Mount Parnassus and parked. She got out and stared at the mountain, which hadn't changed since she'd left a month ago. Hadn't changed

aeons. Then turned to look at the incredible blue wa-
ers of the gulf that stretched to mountains on the other
de and to the sea of olive trees flowing down to meet it.

She'd loved this place the moment she'd arrived. Loved
even more after living in Kastorini for a few days.

Loved the man who'd been born here and was a part
f this place, and she hoped and prayed he wanted her to
e a part of it too.

He'd been silent for a moment when she'd called to tell
im she'd come back to Delphi on business. Didn't tell
im it was personal business, because it was too impor-
nt to talk about on the phone. Too critical to her future
appiness.

She walked up the goat path, stopping a few times
) lift her face to the brilliant sun. To the intense heat
te loved. When she finally got to the closed dig site,
te moved slowly to the pit that had collapsed during
te earthquake five years ago. The pit where her parents
ad died.

She knelt, picturing the horrific scene as she had so
any times before. But this time felt different. Their spir-
s were there with her on the mountain, and they were
niling at her, holding her, encouraging her. Not judg-
ig her, not disappointed in her. The occasional strife of
teir relationship that had lodged itself too long in her
rain faded away, leaving only the good memories of all
teir years together.

"I love you, Mom. Dad. Thank you for everything you
ave me, including my love of archaeology. And most es-
ecially my sisters."

She kissed her fingers and pressed them to the ground
or a moment. Then stood, and, when she turned, saw a
eautiful Greek man walking sure-footed and steady up
te goat path, looking exactly as he had the first time

she'd seen him. She smiled and her heart swelled at th
same time that nervous jitters quivered in her stomach.

She made her way back down the steep path to mee
him. "Hi." It wasn't a very original greeting, but all he
rehearsed words seemed to evaporate when she looke
into the dark eyes she'd missed so much.

"Hi." His lips curved just a little and he took anothe
step closer, until they nearly touched. "You called me t
help you find another statue up here?"

"No. I…I hope you'll help me find something else."

"What's that?"

"I lost my happy after I left here. I'm hoping you ca
help me find it again."

His dark eyes stared into hers as his hands cupped he
waist. "I'll do whatever I can to help you. But here's some
thing funny. I need your help with the same damn thing.

In a sudden movement, he tugged her flat against hi
and kissed her. She clung to him, the heat of his mout
and the sun burning down on them making her dizzy.

"I almost fell over when the phone rang and it wa
you," he said, "because I'd just pulled it from my pocke
to call you. Must have been that sixth sense you and Tor
believe in."

"Why were you going to call?"

"Because I realized I hadn't followed the wisdom c
the stone at Delphi that says 'Know thyself.' That I be
lieved I had, but was focused instead on who I thought
was, who I thought I needed to be. Not on who I could be.

"Me too," she whispered. "I—"

"I need you to know why I'd decided to call." H
pressed his fingers to her lips. "I wanted to tell the in
credible woman I'm crazy in love with that a four-yea
old girl is smarter than I am. That we don't have to sta
put in Kastorini. We can travel to be wherever you are
so you can do the work you love. I don't care where w

ive and neither does she. I just want to be with you, if
ou'll let me."

"Oh, Andros." She sniffed back stupid tears. "I came
o tell you I love Kastorini. I love Cassie, and most of all
love you. So much. I realized I wanted to be in Kastorini
vith you and Cassie, which could work if I concentrate
n digs in Greece instead of other places. And I realized
hat working around the world wouldn't make me happy
f you weren't with me."

He lifted one hand to cup her cheek, tunneling his fin-
ers into her hair. "Cassie told me we make a good team.
Maybe that means we do both. We live in Kastorini when
ou don't have to be on a dig outside Greece, and we live
vherever your work takes you when you do."

"That would…be good. Perfect, even." She reached up
o kiss him but he pulled back.

"There's one more important thing I need to ask." He
rasped her hands, and went down on one knee in the dirt,
vincing when his knee rolled onto a stone.

"Come back up." She tried to tug him, but it was like
ifting the statue of Artemis. Or Apollo. "You don't need
o do this."

"I want to do this." His eyes met hers. "Laurel Evans,
love you more than I knew it was possible to love a
voman. Will you marry me? Be my wife? My forever
eammate, wherever it takes us?"

The emotion in his voice had her choking back tears
gain. "Yes. I will. And, darn it, come up here so I can
iss you."

"One more minute." He reached into his pocket. "It's
ot a ring, yet, but maybe it will do until I can get one.
Iold out your wrist."

She looked down and gasped when she saw a bracelet
ircled with gleaming moonstones. "How did you find

time to run to the store to get this?" she asked as she held out her hand.

"I bought it after you left." His gaze was suddenly serious as he looked up from fastening it to her wrist. "I thought maybe if I held it close in my hand, it would keep you safe on your travels. Maybe even be that love talisman you talked about. Bring you back to me someday."

"Oh, Andros," she whispered, swallowing hard at another lump in her throat. "What did I say before about the charm of Greek men? How can I possibly resist the power of a moonstone? And of you."

"I hope you can't." He grinned as he rose, and that elusive dimple poked into his cheek. She laughed and sniffled and kissed it first, before she pressed mouth to his to seal the deal. "Thank you," he whispered against her lips. "I promise to do everything I can to make you happy."

"Being a team of three will definitely make me happy. With maybe a few more recruits when we're ready."

As he kissed her again, the warmth of him wrapped her with joy, and she didn't think it was her imagination that she just might be hearing the music of god Apollo from the mountaintop, playing in celebration.

* * * * *

LET'S TALK
Romance

For exclusive extracts, competitions
and special offers, find us online:

f facebook.com/millsandboon

⧇ @millsandboonuk

🐦 @millsandboon

Or get in touch on 0844 844 1351*

For all the latest titles coming soon, visit
millsandboon.co.uk/nextmonth

Want even more
ROMANCE?

Join our bookclub today!